THE
Man of Mystery;

OR,

UNDER THE ROYAL WARRANT.

EDWIN J. BRETT,
"BOYS OF ENGLAND" OFFICE, 173, FLEET STREET, AND ALL BOOKSELLERS.

"'I DEFY YOU OR YOUR MEN TO CROSS MY THRESHOLD!' CRIED RANDALL REDMOND."

THE MAN OF MYSTERY;

OR,

UNDER THE ROYAL WARRANT.

CHAPTER I.

CONTAINS THE NECESSARY EXPLANATIONS—THE FORCIBLE EJECTMENT BY SIR FERDINAND LOCKHART—HOW REDMOND AND HIS SON WERE MADE PRISONERS.

WHAT had been a really lovely day in the early part of June, 1610, had nearly drawn to a close, and the country was at rest.

Beautiful in the extreme looked the fields, on which a brilliant moon, high in a cloudless sky, shed a soft, enchanting, silvery light.

Scarcely a breath of wind was stirring.

There was no rustling of the leaves, no creaking of the branches.

The nightingale, pouring forth its gladness in its rich, thrilling tones, was heard to perfection.

There were not many people abroad to hear it, though.

The inhabitants of Whalley, generally speaking, were people who fully believed in the old proverb, "Early to bed and early to rise," though some of the villagers, if they chanced to be visited by relatives or friends, would, perhaps, go off on a moonlight trip through the forest.

But it was only the very boldest who ventured into the depths of the dark forest at night, for reasons which the reader will see in the course of this romance.

Pendle Forest was, beyond the shadow of a doubt, a place of mystery—mystery the most profound!

It was the home of the Black Witches, and the home also of one of the most extraordinary men the world ever saw —Bowolf, better known as the Forest Wizard.

It is to the place this man called his home that we conduct the reader on this particular night.

In about the centre of the forest stood a huge, complicated mass of stone, the remains, so it was said, of what, a century before, had been a monastery.

It was completely hidden from view by a mass of tangled brushwood.

It was surrounded by enormous oaks, the branches of which were closely woven into each other, and making a sort of network, formed a natural canopy, and afforded an effective screen from sunshine and rain.

Viewed by daylight, the spot was a lovely one—a beautiful fairy-like retreat.

At night, however, the aspect seemed to change, for any place more weird could not easily have been found.

Just before midnight, a man was making his way along what was evidently a secret passage leading from the main path, and which wound hither and thither in the most peculiar and bewildering fashion.

In height he was about four feet, but not in any way deformed, unless we take his enormous hands into consideration.

The name of this man was Fendyke —otherwise Hop-o'-the-Wind, a nickname given him on account of his extraordinary swiftness in running.

It was said by the maidens of Lancashire that Fendyke was the ugliest man the world ever produced; and certainly, as the reader will see, he was one of the most mysterious of men.

With almost incredible swiftness he made his way along the tortuous path.

Presently he reached the ruins, and plunging into their midst, he descended a long winding flight of steps.

Reaching a low wooden door, he pushed it open, and drawing aside a heavy curtain, which hung immediately behind it, he stood in a lofty vaulted chamber.

Crowds of curious-looking birds, beasts, and fishes were suspended from the ceiling.

Crossing this strange apartment, Fendyke reached another door, through which he quickly passed.

He now stood in a small, low-roofed chamber.

On a pallet in the corner of the room, lay the figure of a man.

This was the world-renowned Bowolf, the Forest Wizard, the man from whom everyone fled in terror.

He was, and for many years had been credited with possessing the power of the Prince of Darkness; and unquestionably, the seeming miracles he performed, fully entitled him to be classed as a man in league with the Evil One.

As Fendyke entered he slowly raised himself, got off the pallet, and stood erect.

In height he was about six feet. His figure was as straight as an arrow, his presence, though singular, was commanding.

He wore a loose black gown, which fastened at the throat with a diamond star; and his head was partially covered with a cowl, giving him a somewhat monkish appearance.

His beard was remarkably long and of snowy whiteness, but though this and the colour of the skin, showed the aged man, his black eyes still glowed with the vigour of youth.

"Well?" he queried.

"No, master," replied Fendyke, shaking his head, "it is not at all well."

"Give me the full particulars—but first, drink of that wine, else thy thirsty throat will not be sufficiently moistened to tell me of your adventures."

Fendyke obeyed his master with alacrity. Having taken a deep draught, he said—

"I went straight from here to the 'Black Bull,' and having got into the yard without being observed, I made my way to the little window at the back. It was slightly open, and I could therefore learn and see all that was going on. As you had said, the conversation of the villagers would be about the Redmonds.

"The sum due to Sir Ferdinand Lockhart is one hundred guineas. Unless this money is paid by to-morrow night at nine of the clock, Sir Ferdinand intends to turn them from their holding."

"The scoundrel!" muttered Bowolf.

"The villagers," continued Fendyke, "have been trying to make up the amount between them; but they cannot make up as many crowns."

"And Mistress Redmond?"

"Is on the point of death."

"Ah! And Sir Ferdinand knows this?"

"To be [sure he does. But nothing will stay his hand."

"All goes well, Fendyke. Randall Redmond *will take my place!*"

Fendyke, at these words gave utterance to a startled cry, and stepped back so suddenly that he nearly fell to the ground.

"This then," he whispered, "is the secret of your taking so much interest in the Redmonds?"

"It is. Randall Redmond will be your future master."

"I doubt it," said Fendyke, shaking his head.

"Why do you doubt it?"

"In common with everyone else, Randall Redmond hates you."

"What of that? I possess the power to make him do as I wish. That you well know. But listen to me, Fendyke. For years you have been my faithful and devoted friend—you have ever been true, and for that I vested you with powers not possessed by other men. But my time has come, and shortly we shall part for ever. The time given me was one hundred years, and in two more days my hundredth will come."

"Oh, master!" cried Fendyke, "is this not your own imagination?"

"No!" replied Bowolf, sternly and sharply, "it is not. Have you ever had reason to doubt what I say?"

"Never!"

" 'Tis well! You will find that what I now say will prove true. Mistress Redmond will never leave her house alive. Now, Fendyke, to-morrow night you, in a suitable disguise, will present yourself at Randall's house, and you will tell him to defy Sir Ferdinand Lockhart and shortly all will be well."

" But, master, what say you to discharging his debt ? "

" Fool! Would not that be crushing my own plans? The debt paid, would Randall listen to one word I had to say ? No! But penniless and homeless, cast into a dungeon, as he will be, for I well know his temper and the temper of his son, and violence will be offered to Sir Ferdinand and his men—it is then that he will listen to me. Now be seated, and I will tell you what will be done."

*　　*　　*　　*

At a distance of some four hundred yards from the forest was a place called Redmond Mount.

Upon its summit was a huge wooden building, the residence for many generations of the Redmonds.

Misfortune had overtaken the present occupier, Randall Redmond.

For years he and his son Rupert worked at their forge, and had received an allowance from a wealthy relation residing in London; but suddenly this relative mysteriously disappeared.

Some four years before the opening of our story, Sir Ferdinand Lockhart purchased the estate, which, among many others, included the house occupied by the Redmonds.

But after the purchase Sir Ferdinand went abroad for three years, the rent in the meantime never having been claimed.

On his return Sir Ferdinand conceived an intense hatred of the Redmonds.

The night following the one in which we introduce Bowolf to the notice of the reader was a sad one to the Redmonds.

In a small room on the ground floor of the house were four persons.

The first was Randall Redmond, a tall, powerful man of some fifty years; the second was the son Rupert, a handsome young man, and, like his father, in possession of great muscular power; the third was Doctor Smollet, and the fourth was Mistress Redmond, who lay white and motionless on the bed.

Deep silence reigned in that apartment.

Doctor Smollet gravely shook his head.

" I can hold out no hopes," he said ; " but it frequently happens that at the last moment consciousness returns."

" I almost hope she never more recovers consciousness ! " cried Master Randall, bitterly.

" Father ! " said Rupert, " why ? "

" My son, look at the hour ! Nine of the clock is advancing, and you may depend that, with the last stroke, Sir Ferdinand and his men will appear, and will force their way into the house."

"Never!" cried Rupert ; " never while I have the strength to bar their passage."

" Your words sound well, Rupert, for they show that you have inherited the courage of the Redmonds; but of what use would your and my strength be against the numbers that Sir Ferdinand will bring with him."

At this moment Doctor Smollet took the little lamp and advanced to the bed.

The rays from the lamp were thrown full upon the white figure lying there.

Mistress Redmond's face was now most distinctly seen, and all noticed that the expression which rested upon it was a most extraordinary one.

Redmond was about to make some remark, when Doctor Smollet raised his hand for silence.

" She will speak ! " he whispered.

After one or two spasmodic gasps, Mistress Redmond sighed softly, and then, in low, tremulous tones, which thrilled those within that apartment, she said—

" With the flight of time—what will they be ? What will they become ? Ever feared and dreaded, possessed of marvellous powers; the other—but, ah ! I see the figure of Sir Ferdinand Lockhart ! He bars the way. His hounds seize my son ; they hurl him to the ground ! They trample upon him— they——"

" Heavens above us ! " cried Rupert, " her mind wanders. Mother, mother ! your son, Rupert, is here. Speak, I implore you."

" Hark, Rupert ! " interrupted Master Redmond, laying his hand on his son's shoulder. " Hark ! the hour of nine is striking, and I hear the yelping of hounds, and the hum of voices."

" May heaven help you all," said the

doctor. "Had I the money, I would freely advance it to you."

"I understand you perfectly," replied Master Redmond, seizing the doctor's hand, "and advise you, for your life, to at once hasten away."

Doctor Smollet reluctantly quitted the house.

A strong party was now seen advancing, holding aloft flaming links.

And besides the men were a number of fierce bloodhounds, dangerous animals, though now they were held in leash by their keepers.

In the centre of the men, mounted on a powerful grey horse, was Sir Ferdinand Lockhart, a man rapidly becoming a terror to the poorer classes.

The very look of the dark, savage face, fierce eyes, and set lips, spoke most eloquently the fact that the owner was a tyrant.

His servants were not natives of Lancashire, or of the surrounding country.

They had come from Sir Ferdinand's estate in London.

But to return to the Redmonds.

"Rupert," said Master Redmond, as the doctor was heard to close the door, "our last moments at this house have come. Prepare yourself for the worst, my son."

"But what of my mother?"

"She is beyond the reach of his power, Rupert. She is dead," said Master Redmond, in a voice made hoarse with the intensity of his emotion.

"Dead!" gasped Rupert, once more approaching the bed and bending over.

"Reserve your feelings, Rupert, until another time. List! They are even now at the doors."

"Father, do you believe that Sir Ferdinand will order that my mother's body be taken from the bed where it now lies?"

"I do."

"By the heaven above us!" cried Rupert, in passionate tones, "I will defend my mother's body with my life. And you, father, what will you do?"

"Wait, my son," replied Master Redmond, grimly—"wait and see. Listen! they knock upon the door and shout. Let us descend."

"Unarmed?"

"Ay, unarmed. But, if necessary, we can readily arm ourselves. Weapons hang on the wall close to the door."

Sir Ferdinand's men were not *knocking* upon the door.

Thundering upon the door would be more accurate.

With the butt-end of a large riding whip, Sir Ferdinand was demanding admission; and he was assisted by two or three of his men, who used their weapons to some tune.

But this was not the only noise, for the whole party were shouting, and their shouts were echoed by the deep baying of the terrible-looking bloodhounds.

Suddenly the door opened, and Master Redmond and Rupert stood upon the threshold.

"The time has come, Randall Redmond," shouted Sir Ferdinand, with a fiendish chuckle. "Say, are you ready with the money due to me?"

"I am penniless," replied Master Redmond.

"Ha, ha!" laughed Sir Ferdinand. "I have found that the Redmonds were ever needy beggars——"

"It is false!" shouted Rupert.

"Peace, my son, for a moment," whispered Master Redmond.

"Let your son beware of his tongue," hissed Sir Ferdinand. "If he does not curb it, it may be necessary to get my bloodhounds to tear it from his mouth."

At these awful words, the whole troop of assistants rent the air with laughter.

A terrible look rested for a few minutes upon the face of Randall Redmond. His powerful hands were tightly clenched, and he seemed as if he would dash forward, and hurl the tyrant from his horse.

But he remembered the loved dead above—for her he would try to beg for a few hours' grace—a few short hours, during which the body might be lowered into its last home.

"Sir Ferdinand," he said, "you knew of the serious nature of my wife's illness?"

"By the Virgin's soul," laughed Sir Ferdinand, "it was but two hours back that I was informed that one of my hounds had died. If that did not disturb me, why should the knowledge that your wife is ill have any effect upon me?"

"Ill? Alas! she is dead."

"Then, if that is so, your greatest difficulty is removed. Randall Redmond," he cried, raising his voice so that all might hear it, "my will and pleasure is that you quit this, my house, at once. Hesitate but a moment, and you shall see what will follow."

"Monster—merciless tyrant!" cried Rupert, "would you cast forth my mother's dead body?"

"Monster, eh? Remember, Rupert Redmond, what I said about you curbing your tongue. Randall Redmond, your son has not been properly educated."

"If you mean I have not trained him to bow the knee, and cringe to such men as you, Sir Ferdinand Lockhart, then I plead guilty," replied Master Redmond, proudly; "but listen to me. I ask you to allow us to stay until my wife's body can be taken away, and let us take with us a few of the things of which she was so fond."

"Touch one article at your peril, Randall Redmond. They are *mine* since you are unable to pay the amount due to me. Now let there be no further waste of time. Again, I say depart."

"Villain, I do not intend to depart," replied Randall, "until I have got what I require."

"Seize the wretch!" thundered Sir Ferdinand. "Seize him and his son, and drag them forth. The dead body they shall have, but nothing else."

Several of the men, with drawn swords, moved forward.

But they quickly came to a standstill.

Rupert had reached down a couple of swords and daggers, and in the twinkling of an eye, his father and himself were armed.

"Ha!" cried Sir Ferdinand, "then it is evident that you intended to defy me?"

"Yes, I defy you, or your men, to cross my threshold."

Sir Ferdinand, for a few seconds, seemed speechless with rage.

He glanced at his men, and noticed that the foremost had shrunk back, not actually frightened, but overawed at the determined attitude of the powerful man and his scarcely less powerful son.

A ponderous blade Redmond held in his hand, and it was thoroughly well known that both he and his son could use a sword with fearful effect.

"Bring the dogs up!" cried Sir Ferdinand.

Far down in the valley his voice was heard, and to his astonishment, an answer came from afar; it was an answer in the shape of a deep groan of execration.

Looking back, Sir Ferdinand noticed what looked like a clump of trees, but it needed no second look to arrive at the conclusion that a crowd of villagers had collected, and were watching the progress of affairs.

"Ye groan, eh?" cried Sir Ferdinand, shaking his clenched fist in the direction of the crowd. "Wait! wait! and by the holy saints, you shall feel the weight of my vengeance. I will find out who led that groan. Among that crowd there is bound to be one open to accept a bribe. Now, one moment," he added to one of the men, who was about to unloose two of the bloodhounds he held, "another chance will I give him. Randall Redmond, quit my property."

He got no answer this time.

"Malediction!" he growled. "Let the two dogs go at them!"

An instant's pause, and the dogs, directed what to do by their keeper, plunged forward, uttering as they did so such savage howls that a strong man might well have quailed before them.

Randall Redmond did not quail, however, neither did Rupert.

What followed the rush of the dogs occupied but two seconds.

Two bright blades flashed in the torches' rays, two or three ear-piercing howls were heard, and the two bloodhounds lay upon the ground, their ponderous heads completely split in twain.

The effect of this upon Sir Ferdinand Lockhart was tremendous.

Anyone might have killed a couple of his servants, and the fact would have scarcely been noticed; but the slaying of two of his favourite bloodhounds made his blood broil with a desire for speedy vengeance.

"On them!" he shouted, drawing his sword. Pull them out—pull them out! Kill them if you can!"

Thus roused into action, several men

sprang forward, the foremost aiming a blow at Master Redmond with an axe.

Rupert caught the blow on the flat of his blade, and dealt the man such a fearful stroke that he was instantly stricken dead, and fell between the two hounds.

At the same moment, however, several more men sprang forward, and though Master Redmond struck down the first and second with lightning-like rapidity, he was soon overwhelmed by numbers, and forced into the passage.

The same occurred to Rupert, but before he could be overpowered he offered a most desperate resistance.

Is was not only a desperate but a deadly resistance, since no less than half-a-dozen of the tyrant's retainers were stricken down.

But they were overpowered by numbers.

The men, urged by Sir Ferdinand's loud voice, threw themselves bodily upon the courageous and unflinching pair, and thus Master Redmond and his son were prevented from using the deadly weapons they held in their hands.

Soon both were stretched upon the ground.

Each was firmly held by half-a-dozen men, who now awaited Sir Ferdinand's next orders.

Lockhart had watched and directed operations without leaving his saddle.

No doubt he considered it safer to remain where he was than attempt to enter the passage.

He did not give the expected orders for some few moments.

He fixed his cruel eyes upon the remaining bloodhounds, and seemed to be considering whether now was not the time to let them loose upon the pair.

They were defenceless now, and could offer but little resistance.

But Sir Ferdinand changed his mind.

He had thought of something better—probably something more cruel—for a savage grin was upon his face as he said—

'Get stout ropes, or take the leashes from the dogs, and tie the prisoners' hands firmly behind their backs. Then bring them forth."

Father and son were dragged to their feet, and the operation of securely binding them was very quickly accomplished.

"Have no fear, my son," said Master Redmond, as he was led forth, " our time will come."

"Keep thy tongue within thy teeth !" yelled Sir Ferdinand, as, raising his whip, he dealt Master Redmond a fearful slash across the face.

"I will make you fear me ere twenty-four hours are over your head," he continued, mockingly. "You and your son have slain two of my valued bloodhounds, but I have plenty more left. Anon you shall see how well they obey my orders, for they shall tear your son to pieces before your eyes."

To this atrocious threat Master Redmond would have replied.

But no opportunity was given him to do so, for he was dragged some distance away.

Rupert was now led forth.

Apparently he had received no injury in the fearful struggle which had taken place.

With head erect and with firm tread he came forth, and when against Sir Ferdinand, he directed a terrible look upon him.

Sir Ferdinand at once broke out into a loud, derisive laugh.

"Boy," he sneered, your fierce looks will not cause me to quail. Ho, ho ! Listen, vagrant upstart, you are in my power now. Right well do you know why I have longed for this moment. You, who have dared to pay court to my daughter beneath my own walls.

"By the holy saints ! a magnificent treat have I in store for Miriam. She shall see thee torn limb from limb by my bloodhounds. A most wholesome sight for so pretty and so loving a maiden," he sneered. "I will show her what short work I make of my enemies. What, would you dare reply to me ? Away with him. Place him beside his father."

Rupert would have replied, but he was allowed no time, for he was at once dragged brutally away.

Sir Ferdinand was now consulting with two or three of his principal men.

The consultation lasted for a few moments only.

Then he backed his horse close against the captives, saying—

"Now let the men this precious pair have murdered be brought out. When that is done let the house be fired. Judging from yonder crowd of villagers, not many persons within a few miles are asleep. They will see the flames, and will know that Sir Ferdinand has not only recovered his property, but has taken his revenge on the insolent varlets who have so insulted him. Proceed! Remove the men's bodies and fire the house!"

"But the body of Redmond's wife, Sir Ferdinand?" asked one of the men.

"What of it? The house will be her funeral pile; and, besides, the trouble and expense of burying her will be unnecessary."

"One moment," cried Master Redmond, passionately. "Spare my dead wife such a terrible outrage!"

"Pah!" replied Sir Ferdinand. "Not a moment will I pause, Randall Redmond. What I have ordered shall be carried into effect. Go!"

Several men went forward, and as they did so, so fearfully excited did father and son become, that they made frantic efforts to burst their bonds.

Such attempts, however, were fruitless, and so that the men should have less difficulty with them, they threw them to the ground, but they remained in a position to see all that was going forward.

Sir Ferdinand's men were observed moving the dead and injured back some distance from the house, and after this two men with links entered it.

There was then a pause of a few moments.

Presently the men came forth, and scarcely had they done so ere a bright light appeared in the basement, and rapidly increased in brilliancy.

Just as Sir Ferdinand was uttering a chuckle of satisfaction at the accomplishment of his dastardly design, several men cried out—

"Look, Sir Ferdinand!"

Sir Ferdinand turned and beheld what appeared to be a strange, weird-looking old woman advancing up the mount with extraordinary speed.

She seemed to fly over the ground.

"What is that?" asked Sir Ferdinand.

"'Tis a woman," replied a retainer; "and a mysterious-looking one."

"Perhaps she brings the money for these rascals," replied Sir Ferdinand.

Rapidly up the mount came the flying figure, and when close enough to be seen, the whole of the men cried—

"A witch! A witch! One of the witches from the forest!"

Sir Ferdinand's derisive laugh died away as if by magic, and a strange paleness spread over his features as he saw the figure flying towards the doomed house.

But, quickly recovering himself, he said—

"A witch, say you? What causes you to say so? Simply because the woman is attired in black apparel and wears a black hood over her face, eh? Well, if it is a witch, by the saints! there will be one witch the less in the forest, for see, she is going into the house, and will certainly be burnt alive."

Every eye was directed upon the burning building, and sure enough the figure disappeared within the house.

Three minutes had not passed, however, before the little old woman reappeared.

As she did so, a ringing shout rent the air, for the men saw that the little old woman carried in her arms the dead body of Mistress Redmond!

Eagerly did they watch the movements of this woman.

And what of father and son?

Could they believe their eyes? All seemed so strange.

"Help has arrived, Rupert, even at the last moment," whispered Master Redmond, his voice choked with emotion.

"You are correct," replied Rupert, who, however, did not take his eyes off the little black figure. "I wonder whether to that old woman belongs the strange voice I heard but a short time back?"

"A strange voice?"

"Yes. Did you not hear it?"

Master Redmond shook his head, and answered—

"No."

"I heard a voice," continued Rupert, "as though it came from a distance, and that voice said—'Rupert Redmond, help is at hand.'"

"There is some mystery in this, my son."

"Doubt me not, father. I swear I heard those words."

"But who could have uttered them to

you without being observed by these retainers?"

Rupert's response to this was drowned in another shout from the men.

Sir Ferdinand, since the mysterious woman had re-appeared, had sat upon his horse spell-bound as it were.

Was he to be baulked, after all, of the principal portion of his revenge?

It seemed so.

Who was this woman? Surely she could be no ordinary person?

She appeared gifted with the most extraordinary strength, since she carried the dead body of a woman considerably heavier than herself. And this with apparently the greatest ease.

She now seemed hesitating as to which path she should take.

Suddenly she started forward, the body placed partially over her shoulders, and came down the hill with the speed of a whirlwind.

The men were now completely terror-stricken, and with one accord they dashed to one side, thus making a clear passage.

Sir Ferdinand's horse had become highly restless, and pranced to such a degree, that Sir Ferdinand had the greatest difficulty in keeping him in hand.

The brutal baronet was himself more terrified than he would care to confess, but the idea of being baffled, and before the very eyes of his two captives, put a kind of desperate courage into his wavering heart.

As the mysterious woman (whom all now considered to be a witch) came past him, Sir Ferdinand snatched both his pistols from his holsters, and fired them one after the other at the flying figure, with no result, however.

On still went the woman—on towards the Black Forest.

Uttering a terrible cry of rage, Sir Ferdinand pulled his horse round, and plunged his spurs into its sides, but it would not move.

Its widely dilated nostrils, staring eyes and quivering flanks, showed how terrified the animal was.

With a tremendous cry, Sir Ferdinand leapt from its back, and drawing his blade, called on half-a-dozen of his men to follow him.

"See," he cried, "the mysterious being has stopped—no doubt to laugh at me—to laugh at all of us for cowardly fools. Follow, and we will capture the witch, alive or dead!"

So saying he took the lead, and after but a brief hesitation, several of his men followed at a run.

In a few minutes they were within two hundred yards of the strange woman, who had halted for a moment.

But she had no intention of remaining where she stood.

Turning swiftly, with a loud laugh she again went on with marvellous speed.

Nearly at the foot of the hill stood a mighty oak, the circumference of the trunk at the base being many feet; and the roots rising above the earth, and spreading in all directions, it was very desirable to steer clear of them if one wanted to retain a firm foothold.

But instead of avoiding, the mysterious creature made direct for the tree.

Getting close to it, she somewhat slackened her speed, and this allowed Sir Frederick and his men to get within seeing distance.

"Now we have her," exultingly cried Sir Ferdinand, "and witch or not, I will make short work of her."

The woman reached the tree, and at that instant, a startling clap like thunder rang out, a blinding flash lit up the scene for one second, the next complete darkness prevailed on all sides.

Sir Ferdinand and his men, horror-stricken, looked about for the woman.

She had disappeared, just as if the earth had opened and swallowed her up.

It was marvellous, for there was no secret passage or anything of the sort through which the woman could have so mysteriously disappeared.

And then, whence had come that thundering report?—whence that blinding flash of light?

"Men," exclaimed Sir Ferdinand, "I can penetrate the mystery! That woman had sold her soul to the Prince of Darkness, and he has claimed it. Fools! Why do ye stand there and stare at me like idiots? I doubt if either of you have the courage to enter yonder forest, so let us return; but, I warn you, say naught of what has occurred within the hearing of the prisoners. Let them remain in ignorance as to what has become of the body."

The party slowly returned, Sir Ferdinand being at their head.

Their crestfallen, scared appearance was instantly taken note of by the others, but before any questions could be asked, Sir Ferdinand cried—

"Silence! Beware of what I said!"

In the meantime, the house, which as we have already said, was a large one, and built almost entirely of wood, had been burning most furiously, the flames lighting up the country for miles around and causing the little crowd below in the valley to swell to a large one; and when it became known what was transpiring, many of the sturdier men were for arming themselves and making an attack on Sir Ferdinand and his men, but voices on all sides warned them of the vast power possessed by the villain Lockhart.

The tyrant watched the progress of the flames for some time, but at last he gave orders for the party to move.

In a short space the party were descending the hill on the opposite side, and proceeding in the direction of the sombre-looking Bourne Abbey, Sir Ferdinand's residence.

In the middle, side by side, with heads erect, walked father and son.

Sir Ferdinand Lockhart, mounted once more, led the way through the dark roads, thinking of the torture to be inflicted, in the secret dungeons upon his helpless prisoners!

CHAPTER II.

OF HOW RANDALL REDMOND AND RUPERT WERE CAST INTO LOATHSOME DUNGEONS —OF WHAT OCCURRED THEREIN, AND OF WHAT PASSED BETWEEN SIR FERDINAND AND MIRIAM.

THE Abbey was distant about half-a-mile from the mount, and its towering walls could be distinctly seen from most parts of the country.

It was now, and had been for many years past, Abbey in name only.

The original building was quite three hundred years old.

But from time to time portions of it had been pulled down and replaced, according to the fancy of the then owner.

A hundred years before we introduce the gloomy place to the notice of the reader, it had belonged to a wealthy upstart named Bourne, a man very much after the stamp of Sir Ferdinand—a cruel, calculating, heartless villain.

By him a number of the larger vaults below had been converted into dungeons, with what object the reader may guess.

Tradition had it that they had often been put to terrible use.

Otto Bourne held possession of it for nearly fifty years, and he at last came to a fearful end, for one night he was found in one of the dungeons, a huntsman's knife buried deep in his heart.

The mystery was never elucidated, though repeated attempts to unravel it were made.

Servants of Otto Bourne accused each other of the crime, with the result that awful encounters were constantly occurring.

The next-of-kin took possession, but he quietly disposed of the Abbey, and it changed hands two or three times before Sir Ferdinand took it.

Sir Ferdinand's wife had died some years previously; of his "daughter" we shall presently speak.

One of the retainers, when close to the Abbey, took a horn from his girdle and blew a loud blast upon it.

This was answered from another in a similar fashion, and then the great massive gates of the arched entrance were thrown back, and two or three linkbearers appeared.

The party halted, and Sir Ferdinand rode up to the gateway.

Addressing himself to a tall, gaunt-looking, elderly man, he said—

"What of Mistress Miriam, Hawkswell?"

"She has retired, Sir Ferdinand."

"Good. Now come hither, Hawkswell, and look——"

"Have you brought the *two?*" interrupted Hawkswell, in an eager whisper.

"Yes, that is what I was about to tell

you. I said that they would be prisoners, did I not?"

"You did, and your words generally come true."

"Now advance and look at the precious pair. They have done a vast amount of damage, Hawkswell. Two of my best bloodhounds have they slain, and many men are killed and injured."

"The villains!"

"So look to it, Hawkswell, that they are placed in the strongest dungeons you have, and let them be securely chained. Bear in mind that both are possessed of enormous strength."

"What of the wife?"

"She is dead."

"Ha! and her body?"

"Confusion take you! Think you I have not something better to do than reply to your questions? Wait and listen. Attend at once to the prisoners and silence the jabbering of the retainers. Moreover, pay no attention to what they say. I will give you particulars of all that has occurred anon."

Hawkswell, from whose girdle hung a heavy bunch of keys, pushed his way forward and issued directions as to the prisoners, who were then brought into the courtyard.

All having entered, the ponderous gates were reclosed, and Hawkswell, taking the lead, told the men to bring on the prisoners.

Sir Ferdinand placed himself before the principal entrance, so that the prisoners in passing should see him.

"Look your last on yon fair sky," he said, mockingly, "for I swear that neither of you shall go forth again, alive or dead!"

In defiance of the men, who frantically tried to push him onwards, Master Redmond paused, and turning towards Sir Ferdinand, he said—

"You appear to have forgotten this fact—that you are illegally detaining us. What authority have you for taking us prisoners?"

"What authority? My own! And I repeat that you shall never go hence, alive or dead!"

"Cruel, heartless tyrant! May heaven's vengeance speedily fall on you."

"Away with him!" cried Sir Ferdinand. "He shall have plenty of opportunity to talk by-and-by."

At the farther end of the courtyard to the right was a flight of stone steps, and down this went the party.

It was like walking into the very bowels of the earth, for the length of the flight of steps appeared to be interminable.

Hawkswell seemed to be a sharer in the intense hatred of his master towards Redmond and his son, for his remarks as he proceeded were as brutal as he could possibly make them.

The vaults were reached at last.

Many hundreds of times had the prisoners heard of them, but they had never before seen them.

They had also heard of the terrible stories told of the atrocious crimes which from time to time had been committed in them.

"Unless friends without interfere in our behalf," thought Rupert, "we shall never see daylight again. This is an awful doom!"

After traversing several vaults, none of which appeared to possess any ventilation save what they got from the doors, Hawkswell cried a halt.

"Here we are," chuckled the villain, selecting from his huge bunch of keys one which, judging from its rustiness, was not often in use. "Here we are. These are the dungeons you and your son will occupy, Master Redmond."

"It is a matter of but little moment to me or my son which dungeons your inhuman master orders us to be confined in. It is his hour of triumph now. But a day of retribution will come."

"Indeed!" sneered Hawkswell. "Well, it is my belief that if a day of retribution comes, neither you nor your son will be alive to see it."

With these words he inserted the key in the lock; but it had been so long in disuse, and was so fearfully hard to turn that a piece of iron had to be found and used as a lever to turn it round.

The door was open at last, and, as Hawkswell flung it back, such a vile odour emanated from the terrible dungeon, that almost every man present felt momentarily overpowered.

"Now," continued Hawkswell, taking one of the links, and preparing to enter the vaults, "the son will be placed in the opposite dungeon. Take him to it."

"My son," said Master Redmond, in

tones of the deepest emotion, "my heart tells me that this is the last we shall see of each other in this world."

"While there is life there is hope, father," replied Rupert. "After all, we may be rescued."

"Rescued!" thundered Hawkswell. "Rescued! Who, think you would be mad enough to attempt a rescue?"

"He is thinking of the villagers," said one of the men.

Hawkswell burst into a roar of derisive laughter.

"The villagers!" he said; "he might just as well imagine that an attempt at rescue might be made by an angel from heaven. For the courage of the villagers I would not give that, Rupert Redmond!"

And he snapped his fingers defiantly in Rupert's face.

"There are many stout hearts among the villagers," replied Rupert, "and a rescue would be attempted could a leader be found. If what has befallen us had happened to anyone else, a leader to attempt a rescue *would* have been found."

"Oh!" sneered Hawkswell. "And the name of this leader?"

"Rupert Redmond!" replied our hero stoutly. "And if you had shown yourself at the gates as quickly as you did when we were brought in, short work would I have made of you!"

"Beware, Rupert Redmond!" hissed Hawkswell, "remember that you are not only in the power of Sir Ferdinand Lockhart, you are in my power also. You will bitterly regret having uttered those words! But now, my men, take him to the dungeon door, whither in a moment I will join you!"

As he said this he strode into the vault.

The link he held threw a strange, weird glare around the place, the hoary walls of which were as damp as those of a vault beneath a moat.

But it was not the look of the dungeon which caused a startled cry to escape the lips of Master Redmond.

It was not the look of the vault which caused that cry to be echoed by the assembled men, who, with the exception of Hawkswell, had never before beheld it.

No! That cry was caused by a terrible object, which was in the very centre of the dungeon.

The vault was a low-roofed one; the roof, like all the others, being supported by short, massive stone columns.

In each of these columns were affixed mighty iron rings, from which depended chains more massive and ponderous than Master Redmond had ever forged.

Chained to the centre column was a grinning skeleton; but whether the remains were those of a male or female, none but one skilled in such matters would have been able to determine, for there was not a particle of clothing about the skeleton, which, in all its ghastliness, rested in a sitting position against the column.

A heavy iron band was about its waist, but how it had been placed there was a mystery, for there was no lock or other fastening connected with it.

The sight was a most awful one, and it was not to be wondered at that a cry of horror had been wrung even from the stout heart of Randall Redmond.

"Ha!" grinned Hawkswell, "that causes you to quake, eh? But see here," he added, as he waved the torch towards the stone floor, "see here. Look! here is a skull—here a thigh bone—here a dismembered hand—here a foot!"

And as he spoke he kicked the human remains disdainfully from him.

"Enough, enough!" said Master Redmond. "I see that, terrible as were the stories I have heard of this place, none of them does it justice. Heaven knows that I am no coward—that I am not superstitious—but I entreat of you, provide me with some other vault where I shall be free from contact with the remains of my fellow-creatures."

"Here is your dungeon, Master Redmond," replied Hawkswell, gleefully, "and here you shall remain until I receive further orders from Sir Ferdinand Lockhart. What his punishment of you and your precious son—Mistress Miriam's favourite, by all the blessed saints!—will be, I know not. He may torture you to death, or he may order that you be gradually starved. This latter order will be enforced until Sir Ferdinand makes known his exact wishes with respect to you. This skeleton will be your companion, and beside it you will be chained."

"Chained beside it! Villain, thou art indeed an inhuman monster."

Of this Hawkswell took no notice, except to again laugh gleefully.

By his orders, a heavy chain, with several iron bands, was brought in.

Each of these bands was provided with a lock, the key of which Hawkswell carried among the others.

One of the bands was soon found to fit, and it was placed round the prisoner's waist and re-locked; the chain was secured to a ring in the centre column, and Master Redmond's hands were un-fastened.

Thus was he placed side by side with the skeleton.

Could any punishment be greater than this ?

To the opposite end of the vault Hawkswell now walked.

Holding his torch aloft, he said—

"Behold this aperture. At certain times this will open and a small loaf, together with a jug of water, will be lowered. Here is the jug, which you will observe has a string attached to it, the other end being above. When you require water, you will fasten the string to the jug. As to the loaf, that will be thrown to you."

"Not one ounce shall ever pass my lips!" said Master Redmond, firmly.

"Ah!" chuckled Hawkswell, "the same thing has been said to me many a time, but I have always found that prisoners very quickly changed their minds. And now, my men, let us attend to the other captive. So, for the time, Master Redmond, adieu. If thy skeleton companion should become somewhat restless, and clutch your throat with his bony fingers, complain not to me. Forward men!"

Away went the men, Hawkswell being the last, and he was particular to see that the door was securely locked, and barred with a ponderous beam of oak.

Locked and barred on a prisoner about whose waist was a heavy iron band, secured by a massive chain to a stone column !

Rupert was within the vault Hawks-well had allotted him, and the men surrounding him were awaiting Hawks-well's orders.

The vault in which Rupert stood was a perfect counterpart of the one in which his father had been secured.

It smelt as foul, the walls were as slimy, and there did not appear to be the slightest ventilation.

Rupert, whose thoughts were naturally bent on the chances of escape, looked round the black walls.

There was no window—there was not the smallest aperture of any kind.

Casting his eyes about the stone flooring, he saw with a shudder several human bones, but there was no skeleton chained to a column.

When Hawkswell entered, Rupert, stifling the feelings of horror which crowded his breast, was standing erect and firm, a fact which so exasperated Hawkswell that, thrusting his face close to Rupert's, he hissed through his clenched teeth—

"So you look like that at me, eh? Ha! ere long your proud spirit will be broken! You will yet grovel and cringe and beg for mercy—mercy that will be denied you! Beggarly upstart —*you* who have dared to make love to the betrothed of a highly-bred gentle-man! *You*, the son of a poverty-stricken hound! You——"

What else he would have said never left his lips, for Rupert, worked up to a state bordering on madness by being thus taunted by this horrible specimen of humanity, giving utterance to a sharp passionate cry, suddenly stepped back, stooped for an instant, and then, exert-ing all his strength, burst the bonds which bound his hands behind his back.

His action had been unexpected and instantaneous.

There was no time for Hawkswell to step back; there was no time for the men to hurl themselves on Rupert, and, by the exercise of their united strength, overpower him.

As swiftly as a flash of lightning, Rupert sprang forward, and, with his clenched fist, dealt Hawkswell such a mighty blow, that he was at once felled to the ground.

Such had been the force used, that the man was rendered insensible, and the torrent of blood which flowed from his face, showed where he had received that crushing blow.

But, as might be expected, the instant

after the blow was delivered, Rupert was once more secured.

Pinioned back and front, he was borne to the ground, and held there by a dozen men.

A savage crew were these men, and more than one felt inclined to plunge his weapon into Rupert's heart.

They only refrained from so doing, because they were well aware of the fact that their action would meet with the disapproval of Sir Ferdinand.

One picked up the pitcher with which this vault, like the others, was provided, and, without waiting to see in what condition the contents were, dashed them into Hawkswell's face.

The result was that Sir Ferdinand's chief man was saturated with water, which, for foulness of smell, and slimy, inky blackness, could hardly have been equalled—certainly not excelled.

Apparently it had no effect.

Not a single movement did Hawkswell make.

It was then decided to inform Sir Ferdinand of what had transpired, and a man named Morgan, as brutal a ruffian as Hawkswell, went off to Lockhart.

He found him in an ante-room adjoining the banqueting hall.

Seated before a table, well laden with the choicest of meats and wines, Sir Ferdinand was enjoying himself, and at the same time, thinking as to what he would do with his prisoners.

No sooner did Morgan make his appearance, than he leapt to his feet.

"Ha!" he cried, "I see by your face that something has occurred. Quick! What is it? Neither has escaped?"

"No," was the reply.

Sir Ferdinand breathed a sigh of relief.

"What is it, then?" he asked.

"Sir Ferdinand, as we were all warned, that Rupert Redmond is a demon. When within the vault, he suddenly burst the thick bonds which fastened his hands, sprang upon Hawkswell, and dealt him such a terrific blow, that it stretched him insensible and bleeding on the ground."

"By the holy saints!" replied Sir Ferdinand, raising aloft his clenched fist, "no human being was ever tortured as I will torture him. But Hawkswell has now recovered?"

"No; that he has not. I came to you, Sir Ferdinand, thinking that when I told you what had taken place, you would at once repair to the vaults."

"Ay, that will I," replied Sir Ferdinand, seizing his sword, and buckling it about him. "Ascend and call Mistress Miriam's maid; but no," he added, as a savage smile rested for an instant upon his face. "No; I have thought of something better. Return to the vault, and take this flagon of wine. It is powerful, and a draught may restore Hawkswell to consciousness. Say that I shall be below in a short time."

Morgan bowed, took the wine, and departed, returning to the vaults by the way he had come, though he halted long enough in one of the corridors to drink more than half of what the bottle contained.

Sir Ferdinand, having re-arranged his attire, took a lamp, passed through the central hall, and ascending the first and second flights of stairs, reached a broad landing, containing four doors, each of which was artistically draped with crimson and gold curtains.

Before the first he stopped for a moment, as if uncertain how to act, but suddenly he seized the handle and turned it.

He found the door locked, and his annoyance was evident from the muttered imprecation which left his lips.

Raising his hand he knocked softly.

He was at once answered.

A low, sweet voice asked—

"Is that you, Margaret?"

"No," said Sir Ferdinand, "it is *I*."

"*You*, Sir Ferdinand? In heaven's name, what want you?"

"I want a word with you, Miriam. Hasten, therefore, and open the door."

To Sir Ferdinand's astonishment, the door was at once unlocked, thrown open, and Miriam Lockhart appeared.

Fully attired she was, and it was quite evident that her couch had been untouched.

Miriam was a most beautiful girl of eighteen—tall, slender, and with a wealth of magnificent dark brown hair.

Dark brown was the colour of her eyes, and they were large and lustrous.

The Lancashire maidens generally were the most beautiful girls in the kingdom, but when Miriam came to

"'YOU HAVE EVER LOOKED UPON ME AS YOUR ENEMY!' CRIED THE FOREST WIZARD."

He has been attended

She tried hard enough to be firm, but it was a failure.

The last time she and Rupert had been together was beneath the wide-spreading trees in the wild, but lovely forest.

Their arms had been wound tenderly about each other's waists, and they had thought that only the bright moon and stars were looking upon them; but Sir Ferdinand had shown that *he* had been present.

She had risked much in leaving the Abbey to keep the appointments she, from time to time had made with handsome Rupert Redmond; her maid, Margaret, had assisted her, and had watched and listened to ascertain whether Sir Ferdinand was suspicious —and all had been fruitless.

"Oh! how noble, how handsome he looked when I last saw him," thought poor Miriam, as she followed Sir Ferdinand into the gloomy depths of this old Abbey. "Alas! how changed he must now be. There must have been fighting —yes, I am sure of it! Oh! pray heaven my brave Rupert has met with no mishap. And his father — that noble-hearted man — and his dying mother. Sincerely do I pity all of them."

The vaults were quickly reached.

Morgan met them, expressing not the least surprise to see Miriam, and conducted them to the terrible dungeon where stood Rupert.

Again he had been bound, and this time in such a way that it was out of all question that he could break away.

A fierce, determined expression rested upon his face, as he turned it towards the doorway.

But that expression instantly vanished as his eyes rested upon the beauteous Miriam.

A cry of astonishment rose to his lips.

Miriam saw — from more than one deep cut upon his face, from his disordered hair and dress—that Rupert had been roughly handled, and she directed a glance full of love upon him.

"Miriam, look at this villain!" shouted Sir Ferdinand, "and tell me what he now looks like. Ah, I see that you still sympathise with him. Behold! see what he has done to Hawkswell."

Hawkswell, who had been attended to by the men, had recovered consciousness, though such had been the force of the blow that he still felt somewhat dazed, rose, and showed a fearful cut over the left eye.

The sight was a terrible one; but it did not have a repulsive effect on Sir Ferdinand. It put him in a greater rage than ever.

"Base, low-born hound!" he roared; "you shall feel the weight of my vengeance! Hawkswell, you shall be amply avenged! Now Miriam, listen to the sentence I pronounce upon him."

"Sentence!" replied Miriam. "You dare not sentence him!"

"You will see it carried out. This is the sentence: he is to have two days within this vault, and not a crust is to pass his lips. He will remain securely bound. On the third night, still bound, he will be thrown into the centre of the vault, and the bloodhounds let loose upon him!"

A wild shriek left Miriam's lips.

But Rupert still stood erect, the expression upon his face unchanged.

Apparently he was unmoved at this most terrible sentence.

"You dare not carry out such a terrible sentence!" cried Miriam, passionately. "You *dare* not, I say!"

"And why not?"

"Because you would be fearful of exposure and the fate to follow."

"Who is to betray me? My men are all sworn to preserve the strictest silence as to what takes place here."

"I would expose you," answered Miriam. "I would be the one to lay the information."

"Indeed. Then forewarned is forearmed. We will take care that you do not get the opportunity of lodging an information. Hawkswell, into your safe custody I place this girl. See that she is well guarded until the night arrives for her to be a witness to the punishment of this upstart."

"I will see that she is safe enough. You do not intend that she takes her meals with you, Sir Ferdinand?"

"No. Margaret will take her what she requires."

Rupert was now chained to one of the columns, and the door was closed upon him.

Two of the men, carrying links, led the way up the stairs, Miriam being close behind them.

But Sir Ferdinand was not at her side, nor was he immediately behind her.

A number of his men brought up the rear, and Sir Ferdinand was the last of all.

"Poor Miriam!" thought Rupert, "what will her devotion to me cost her? Will the wretch have that sentence carried out? And she be present. Horrible! And not the slightest hope can I entertain that anyone will interfere on behalf of my poor father or myself!"

Wait, Rupert Redmond!

Wait and see what wondrous things will occur within the Abbey in which you are now confined!

CHAPTER III.

IS FULL OF ASTOUNDING AND MOST MYSTERIOUS OCCURRENCES—AND TREATS OF THE MANNER IN WHICH RUPERT ESCAPES FROM THE ABBEY.

TWENTY-FOUR hours passed away.

Neither of the unfortunate prisoners could tell how long they had been within their respective dungeons.

The twenty-four hours had seemed to them like several days.

It was not far off the hour of midnight, and without the Abbey all was wrapped in darkness and silence.

On the battlements Hawkswell and several of the men were watching.

For hours and hours a storm had been threatening.

Suddenly a low muttering in the far distance gave the warning that the tempest was approaching. The low muttering was presently followed by a fearfully vivid flash of forked lightning, which came dangerously near the Abbey.

The thunder which instantly followed it was so loud and fierce that the very foundations of the building seemed to be shaken.

"Come," said Hawkswell, "let us get within, or one or two of us may never live to see the storm over."

In a few moments the tempest increased to such an extent that even the men doing duty in the vaults fled from their positions, and rushed to the servants' hall.

The dazzling flashes of lightning, the peals of thunder, which sounded like the repeated discharges of artillery, became truly alarming, so much so that even Sir Ferdinand became terrified.

The prisoners saw not the lightning, but they heard the thunder, and felt the effects of it, for so terrific were the peals that even the dungeons were shaken from end to end.

The chain which fastened Randall Redmond allowed him sufficient room to sit down on the stone flags, but little enough had he availed himself of the opportunity.

The awful darkness, his close contact with the horrid skeleton, the foul smell pervading the place, had had but little or no effect upon his nerves.

He was troubled, it is true, but it was respecting his son and the removal of his wife's body by the mysterious old woman.

Most intently did Master Randall listen to the raging of the terrific storm.

Suddenly—in the midst of a tremendous peal of thunder—a loud "crack!" rang out, and instantly the dungeon became illuminated with a light of dazzling brightness.

Startled beyond the power of description—for he thought a flash of lightning had cut its way through some portion of the solid cells—Master Redmond turned.

But even as he turned the bright light vanished, and once again darkness the most profound reigned in his dungeon.

Then a portion of the wall on the left fell back, and once more a light appeared.

But it was not a bright light this time.

It was that of a small silver lamp, carried in the hand of a man, who now stepped forth, and whose appearance filled Randall Redmond with wonder.

The man who came from that aperture was Bowolf, the forest wizard.

Being clad from head to foot in black, only his fine face and long, white beard could be seen.

Under his left arm he carried a ponderous black volume.

Slowly he came from the aperture with silent steps.

Having passed through, the solid block of masonry, which thus strangely had rolled back, resumed its position.

"Randall Redmond," said Bowolf, "you do not seem inclined to ask by what extraordinary means I am able to present myself before you."

"No," replied Randall, hoarsely; "I know you are able to do many wondrous things. Well enough do I know that you are in league with the Evil One. Else if you were not, solid walls would not fall back at your bidding, nor would you have been able to do many things I know you have done."

"You express no surprise at seeing me?"

"Why should I? But this I will now ask: Why have you thus appeared before me?"

"Randall Redmond, you are aware that I have always taken an interest in you and your family?"

"An interest! Ay, so I have been told. And what sort of interest? You have tried to weave about me that terrible web by which the soul is lost for all eternity."

"Speak not rashly. You have ever looked upon me as your enemy."

"Have not I every reason to hate and detest you? Your name—the name of the terrible fiends in your power—the forest o'er which you rule, and everything else connected with you?"

"Randall Redmond, you know well enough that had I thought proper, I could have left you alone in your difficulty. Now let me recall to your remembrance what you considered to be a strange thing. Throw back your mind twenty-two years. You were just married, when thieves broke into your house, and stole all you were possessed of. Was not that so?"

"You speak the truth," replied Randall, starting.

"Weil," continued Bowolf, "one night a messenger roused you from your bed.

You yourself answered the door; the messenger placed in your hands a packet, and disappeared.

"You opened that packet, and found that it contained gold pieces, amounting to treble what you had lost."

"You are right. Then you knew this messenger?"

"That messenger was Fendyke."

Randall started in astonishment.

"Impossible!" he said. "What you have been speaking of occurred twenty-two years ago. If Fendyke and the messenger were one and the same, Fendyke would now be an old man."

The Forest Wizard smiled grimly.

"Fendyke was the man," he said, "who, by my instructions, placed that packet in your hands. And Fendyke is the same man who, last night, rendered you a still greater service."

"Rendered me a service last night? What service? I have not set eyes on the mysterious man for some time."

"The service rendered you by Fendyke last night," continued Bowolf, "was this: When the body of your faithful wife was in danger of being consumed by fire, Fendyke dashed into the doomed house, took your wife in his arms, sped away with her, and disappeared."

The excitement of Master Redmond, as Bowolf said this, was intense.

"The one who rescued her," he gasped, "was clad in woman's attire."

"Most true. Fendyke was so disguised."

"And my wife's body?" cried Randall.

"Is safe within the forest, where no one can touch it."

"I cannot thank you," said Randall, "for I know that you must have some fiendish idea in your head."

"Stay, stay!" interrupted Bowolf, "and listen to what I say. Redmond, I am vested with more powers than you dream of. At my bidding, even the iron band, which fastens you to this column, drops at your side."

Sure enough this was so, for the words had barely left his lips before the iron band, with a loud clank, dropped against the stone column.

But Randall moved not.

"You still express no astonishment," said Bowolf, surveying the captive's tall, powerful frame with admiration.

"No," replied Randall. "Were you

to say to these mighty columns of stone, 'Move back,' I should expect to see them obey the order."

"Redmond, you believe that I possess the power to deliver you and your son from the ruffian who owns this abbey?"

"I do believe you possess that power. But I would not ask you to use it on my behalf."

"Listen again to me, Redmond. You know not what occurred in the vault wherein your son is confined. You know not that last night Sir Ferdinand, in the presence of the beautiful girl who loves your son, pronounced sentence upon Rupert."

"Sentence!" cried Randall, fiercely, "sentence! He dare not carry any sentence, as he calls it, into effect. He threatens only."

"As yet you know him not. You can rely upon it that the sentence he pronounced will be carried into effect—unless your son should escape."

"And what was the sentence?"

"That he should be torn limb from limb by bloodhounds."

"'Tis not the first time he has sworn that his bloodhounds should worry my son to death," groaned Randall.

"And he is your only child," said Bowolf, in solemn tones.

"Yes, my only child."

"The son you promised your wife, as she lay on her death-bed, to protect and defend, even at the cost of your life."

"And willingly would I purchase his life at the cost of my own," answered Randall, drawing his figure erect. "I repeat, Bowolf, at the cost of my own life, but not at that of any other."

"Redmond, in a few hours my time on this earth will expire. One hundred years were given me—for a certain reason—and the expiration of the hundred years is close at hand. It was agreed that at the expiration of one hundred years, I should appoint a successor to hold the key of the many mysteries with which I am surrounded. I have watched for twenty years and more, and at last I have found one to succeed me."

"Ah!—his name."

"*Randall Redmond!*"

"No, no!" gasped Redmond. "Away! tempt me not. Rather would I go forth into the world an outcast."

"Redmond, if you take my place, you will be possessed of the power to make every man, woman and child love and bless you."

"Ah, that this were so," replied Randall, fervently.

"I swear that what I say is correct," said Bowolf. "Think of your son, Randall Redmond; think of the terrible death to which he is doomed unless he can escape from his dungeon. Think that this terrible death will occur in another twenty-four hours; and then think that, if you choose to make a compact with me, both you and he will be free."

"And for whom do *you* make the compact?" asked Randall, with a shudder.

"You shall learn all within a few hours, if you will sign this book."

As he spoke he opened the black volume, and held the lamp over a page of peculiar mystic-looking writing.

"Why show me what I cannot read?" asked Randall.

"Nay, I do but show you where to place your name. Take the volume in your hands."

Mechanically, Master Redmond held out his hands, but even as he grasped the heavy volume, there rang out a clap of thunder of so fearful a character, that the very flooring shook violently, caused him to start, and to drop the volume from his hands.

"I can stay but little longer, Randall Redmond," said the wizard, "and the offer I make you can never be repeated. Sign this book, and you and your son will be free. You will take the place I, for years and years, have occupied. From a humble cottager you will become a man of wealth—a man vested with marvellous powers. Refuse, and you know the result."

"I will sign," cried Randall. "Give me the pen and ink. Yes, my son shall be saved. At any cost—even at the cost of my own soul he shall be saved."

As he spoke another fearful clap of thunder shook the masonry, and for the space of a few seconds it seemed as if the whole Abbey would topple over.

Bowolf opened his cloak and took out a dagger.

"Take this," he said; "your own blood must be the ink with which to sign this book. Here is the pen—now, quickly!"

Randall shuddered violently.

But the next instant he caused the blood to flow from his arm, and with it wrote his name in the black volume.

"Good!" said the wizard, in tones of great satisfaction. "And now to effect your son's release. But you must bear in mind, your son must not know what has become of you."

"What! What mean you?"

"You are to bid him adieu. Not a human being must know what has become of you. From now the name of Randall Redmond disappears, and you will be known as THE MAN OF MYSTERY!"

A bitter groan left Randall's lips as these words were uttered by this mysterious man.

Never to own his own son again—the son he loved far better than his own life!

"I shall *see* him?" he asked.

"Yes. But your appearance and your voice will be changed—your own son will not know you—nor will anyone else, with the exception of one—Fendyke. Do you repent of having signed the book?"

"No," answered Randall, in low tones. "But I would not have my son know at what a price his release has been effected."

"Come, no further time must be lost. Behold!" cried the wizard, raising his hand.

Back, without the slightest sound, rolled the large block of masonry.

Randall stepped quickly forward, but as he reached the aperture, a flash of lightning, of dazzling brilliancy, illuminated the whole of the dark place.

It was followed by a deafening peal of thunder.

"Fear not," said Bowolf. "No harm can now befall you. For the third time the lightning has struck the Abbey."

"Which way do I go?"

"Follow me," replied the wizard, darting through the aperture.

Randall followed him, and the stone again resumed its position.

The lamp carried by the Forest Wizard shed quite sufficient light around the place to enable Randall to see where he was going.

He found himself at the foot of a long and exceedingly narrow flight of stone steps—steps but little used, judging from the fact that each was partially covered with moss and lichen.

This was evidently a secret staircase, which most likely was unknown to anyone save the wizard.

Without uttering a word, Randall followed Bowolf to the top of the stairs.

There the wizard paused, and struck a portion of the masonry three times.

A block of it rolled aside, and Randall saw that they were in the open air.

Torrents of rain were descending; the sky was black as ink, and the repeated vivid flashes of lightning, and discharges of thunder, showed that the fearful storm had by no means come to a conclusion.

"I thought you would have taken me to the dungeon in which my son is confined," said Randall.

"Nay; that may not be. Here you will await him. Take this sword—gird it at your side; it may be of service to you. I go now—remain where you are, against this projecting stone. You will see me no more until you see me in yonder forest. But you will see Fendyke. He has his instructions. No doubt they will be the last given him by me."

So saying, the wizard disappeared the way he had come, and Randall was alone.

Most bitter were his reflections! What had he done to purchase his son's liberty?

At present he could hardly realise the enormity of the sacrifice he had made.

But it was too late to recede from the compact.

With his life's blood he had signed—what?

Ah! he had yet to learn.

*   *   *   *

Rupert's patience was not by any means so great as his father's.

Only once had he thrown himself down on the damp stone flooring, and that was when he had completely exhausted himself by repeated and frantic attempts to burst the bonds which bound him.

If he had done so—what then?

He could not have removed the chain.

His own, and the combined strength of a dozen men, could not have snapped those ponderous links.

The startling peals of thunder suited his mood.

Suddenly a most peculiar noise fell upon his ears.

It sounded close behind him.

The curious noise was repeated twice.

He had not long to wait, for presently a mass of stone suddenly but noiselessly moved back, and the tall, dark figure of the Forest Wizard appeared.

Could he believe his eyes? Did he really behold this mysterious man?

"You know me, Rupert Redmond?" asked the wizard.

"Know you?" replied Rupert, huskily, and not for an instant taking his eyes off his mysterious visitant. "Too well; though, thank heaven, I have never had any dealings with you. But, in the name of all that is wonderful, how is it you have thus contrived to appear before me? Do walls move back at your bidding?"

"Many of them."

"Are you familiar with secrets which perhaps are not known to the owner of this place?"

"Seek not to penetrate mysteries of which I hold the key, Rupert Redmond. Rather seek to know the reason I am here."

"When I think of your dark history as I have learned it—when I think of the fiends in human form by whom you are surrounded, I do not require much time to think and decide what you are, Bowolf. But I have no fear of you."

"I am glad of it. But there is no time to waste. Learn, Master Redmond, that I am here to release you."

"Release me? To taunt me, you mean."

"I taunt no man! I repeat that I am here to release you; and you will be released in the same way as your father."

"My father!" cried Rupert, excitedly; "you tell me that he is rescued? trifle not with me."

"I am not in the habit of telling falsehoods, Rupert Redmond," returned Bowolf, in severe tones. "Your father is at liberty, and at this moment is awaiting you."

"You, then, have rescued him?"

"I have. Follow me, and you shall see him in a short time, and say adieu to him."

"Adieu?" replied Rupert in astonishment.

"Yes; it is necessary that, in order to escape Sir Ferdinand's persecutions, he goes abroad for a time."

"Does he agree to that?"

"He does."

"Then, if that is so, I can give no objection."

The wizard took a knife from his girdle, and cut Rupert's bonds.

Next, he touched the ponderous chain in a peculiar fashion, with the result that it fell, as Randall Redmond's had fallen.

So utterly astounded was Rupert that he scarcely knew what to do or say.

"Now, Rupert, ere you go hence, you shall see and speak with the maiden on whom you have bestowed your affections. Could I grant you a greater favour than this?"

"No, no!" exclaimed Rupert, clasping his hands fervently. "That, indeed, would be an inestimable favour; but," he suddenly added, "detection would be certain, and Miriam would suffer."

"If you carefully follow the one who will lead you to Miriam's chamber, little fear will there be of detection. For some time longer the storm will rage, and Sir Ferdinand will not go forth until it has subsided."

"And the one to conduct me?"

"Is here!"

As he replied, Bowolf stepped aside, and the figure of Fendyke was disclosed.

He was now clad entirely in a costume of tight-fitting black.

A short cloak was thrown about his shoulders, while beneath his arm he carried a broad belt, sword, dagger, and a pair of elaborately mounted pistols.

Rupert, on many occasions had seen this strange man.

Many a time when our hero had been in the forest at night, Fendyke had dashed past him, sometimes on horseback, but more often on foot.

He had always regarded him, as indeed did everyone else, as an imp of the Evil One.

No sooner was Fendyke disclosed than the lamp the wizard carried in his hand flickered and went out.

"I will light it," said Fendyke; "but it will only be necessary to keep it alight while you, Rupert Redmond, buckle these useful articles about you. On the sword and dagger I carry, you may safely rely. They are of pure Damascus steel, and they are presented to you with the hope that you will never part with them. On the pisto you may also rely. Depend upon it they will never miss fire."

While speaking, Fendyke had kindled a light and relit the lamp.

The instant the gloomy dungeon was again illuminated, Rupert saw that the wizard had vanished.

Fendyke noticed his astonishment, and said, with a smile—

"The presence of Bowolf is no longer necessary. On me you can rely. Let me assist you—soh! Now, are you ready?"

"Yes. But, in case we are attacked, how would you defend yourself? You are not armed."

"I carry no arms, it is true," replied Fendyke, grimly; "but, if we are attacked, you will see that I am well able to defend myself."

Rupert was now perfectly ready.

About his waist, in place of that cruel band of iron, was a broad, powerful belt, having on each side a steel loop.

In each of these loops a pistol was thrust, while on his right side hung the dagger, and on his left, the sword.

Rupert naturally imagined that Fendyke, like Bowolf, was intimately acquainted with the secret passages and staircases of the Abbey, and he, of course, thought that he would conduct him through the aperture whence Bowolf had come.

But he did nothing of the sort.

He blew the lamp out, took Rupert by the wrist, and drew him towards the door.

Then Rupert heard a faint sound as of a key being cautiously placed in a lock.

Another moment, and the dungeon door slowly moved back.

"Now," whispered Fendyke, "take the hem of my cloak, and you will then be sure of your footing."

Locking the door of the dungeon, Fendyke went on.

Through many long passages and vaults went the pair, in the most profound darkness.

Not once did Fendyke halt.

Rupert's thoughts were now fixed upon Miriam, whom he knew to be a prisoner in her own apartments.

To those apartments we will precede him.

We have already seen the floor Miriam occupied, and we know there were four doors upon it.

The four apartments were occupied only by Miriam and her maid, Margaret, a pretty fair-haired girl.

Margaret had one room, which she used as a bed and sitting-room, the three others being used by Miriam as bed, dressing, and sitting-rooms, respectively.

Not one of the rooms was calculated to make a young girl feel particularly happy at the best of times, so gloomily were they furnished.

The furniture was almost all of ponderous black oak, which sombre material was not at all relieved by the heavy dark hangings on the walls.

Miriam was seated beside the table in the centre of the sitting-room, while opposite her sat Margaret.

The former's tearful face—her whole attitude, in fact—betokened despair, and while Margaret attempted to cheer her, her own face showed how terribly anxious she was.

"Margaret," said Miriam, after a somewhat long pause, "pray look without and see if the storm shows any sign of abating."

Margaret rose, and going to the little window, pulled aside the curtain.

At the instant she drew back the curtain a fearful flash of lightning darted across the window and rent in twain a mighty oak tree which stood within a hundred yards.

The shriek which left Margaret's lips, and the crashing of the oak as it toppled to the ground, caused Miriam to utter a startled exclamation.

Hastily rising, she dashed to the window.

"What—what is it?" she cried; "lightning?"

"Yes, it was a fearful flash; but that—that was not all. Mistress, go to the window—look!"

Hastily Miriam drew aside the curtain and looked out upon the balcony.

She saw nothing but inky blackness—nothing did she hear but the hissing of the rain, which fell in perfect torrents.

"I see nothing, Margaret," she said, turning from the window. "What has alarmed you?"

"Mistress," whispered Margaret, "I saw a most horrible *human face!*"

"Impossible!" replied Miriam, with difficulty repressing the cry of alarm that rose to her lips. "You must be mistaken. No one could possibly reach the balcony from below."

"I swear that I saw a fearful human face! The face of an old man with a long white beard, and whose head was shrouded in a black hood. The face of the mysterious Forest Wizard!"

Startled and alarmed as Miriam undoubtedly was, she nevertheless shook her head.

"You must be mistaken, Margaret," she said. "Let us be seated once more. Oh, that this dreadful storm would cease."

"It is indeed a dreadful storm. Ah, Mistress, would that we were both miles away. Had we been, I think I should have been tempted to pray that the Abbey and all the merciless fiends within it would fall a prey to the lightning."

"Margaret, your mention of the name of this wondrous man, Bowolf—whom I have often met—has awakened strange fancies."

"Met!" said Margaret wildly. "Where?"

"In the forest."

"At night?"

"Yes, at night."

"Holy Mary protect us! Then it is indeed most strange that you are alive at this moment."

"Not at all. Bowolf never offered to interfere with me. Why should he?"

"They say that even pure and innocent maidens on whom he sets his eyes he makes, sooner or later, his victims."

"Idle talk, Margaret. The idle fancies of the very old and the very young."

"He has never spoken to you?"

"Never. But I was about to say that your mentioning his name made me remember the fact that Bowolf for years has had the reputation of being the most skilful compounder of deadly poisons ever known."

Once more did Margaret clasp her hands.

"Poisons!" she gasped. "Mistress Miriam, what has caused you to think of poisons?"

"What if we could possess ourselves of some deadly drug, Margaret, and poison the bloodhounds?"

"I understand now. But, alas! suppose we did? Suppose I were successful in poisoning their food, and every bloodhound died? Rely upon it Sir Ferdinand would have more ere many hours had passed. Poor Master Rupert!—oh, what a horrible death will be thine!"

"Hold, Margaret, hold. Let us still hope that a rescue may be attempted."

"An attempt at rescue might have been successfully made while the prisoners were on the road here—but of what use would it be now? Alas! I fear me that Rupert Redmond and his father too are doomed to certain destruction. There is no hope."

"Oh, Rupert!" cried Miriam, starting up and pacing the room with impatient steps. "Oh, my love! You in whom I had centred all my hopes of future happiness, what must be your agony at this moment! Rupert—my Rupert! if but for one short moment I could clasp you to my heart I should be happy."

"You can. Rupert is here," cried a voice.

The curtains beside the window moved back as the window flew open, and Rupert with outstretched arms, rushed from the balcony into the room.

One stifled cry only did Miriam utter.

The next moment she rushed forward, and was folded to Rupert's breast.

The first few joyous moments over, Miriam said—

"Rupert, by what extraordinary means have you been enabled to get here?"

"Look!" replied Rupert, as leading Miriam to the window he drew aside the curtain and showed the end of a silk rope.

"You have descended from the roof."

"Exactly."

"Oh, heaven! one false movement and you might have been dashed to atoms. But tell me quickly how did you escape from that terrible dungeon? Surely you must have friends within the Abbey, for I see that now you are completely armed."

"Nay, dear Miriam, my friends came from without the Abbey. The name of one is Bowolf——"

"Ha!" interrupted Margaret, excitedly, "then I was not mistaken."

"Continue, dear Rupert," said Miriam, no less excited than her maid.

"The name of the other is Fendyke."

"The wizard's servant. And what has caused Bowolf to behave thus kindly to you?"

"I know not, dear Miriam," answered Rupert; "but I believe it is out of regard for my father. No doubt he is one of the many who sympathise with us, and on this occasion, as you observe, he has used the great power he possesses to free me and my poor father also."

"I will not ask by what marvellous means—I will not think of what terrible power he has used to accomplish this," faltered Miriam; "it is enough for me to know that you are out of that awful dungeon. But do not deceive yourself, my beloved Rupert. You are not yet free. Nay, you will not be free until this gloomy Abbey, the scene of many terrible tragedies, lies a long distance behind you. And I tremble when I think of the fearful way in which Sir Ferdinand will vent his rage upon me —ay, and upon poor Margaret.

"But tarry no longer here, Rupert. Go, go, I entreat of you. Away! Hide yourself in the forest. There, in the centre, Sir Ferdinand will not dare to go."

"Your advice comes too late," thundered the voice of Sir Ferdinand outside the door. "The escape is discovered, the quarry is here, and, by the holy saints, we shall have him, alive or dead!"

A wild, agonising shriek of despair was uttered by Miriam and Margaret.

No sooner had Sir Ferdinand spoken than it became evident to those within the apartment that he was not alone, for now came a thundering upon the door, accompanied by shouts of "Open, open at once!" and the loud clash of steel.

"Rupert," groaned Miriam, pointing wildly to the window, "go—fly at once. Though, alas! I fear it is too late."

"Give me the axe!" thundered Sir Ferdinand, raining a volley of heavy blows upon the door. "Miriam," he shouted, "as you value your life open this door. Girl, are you aware that you are dealing with Rupert Redmond, who for his freedom has sold his soul to the Evil One? Open, I say."

"No, no," replied Miriam; "I will not! I cannot until he has gone. My life may pay the forfeit, but I will willingly sacrifice it if he is saved!"

"Misguided girl—your life shall be forfeited if he escapes!"

Rupert had not gone.

No; erect in the centre of the room he stood, his fine figure displayed to the fullest advantage.

"Miriam," he said, "fly with me! The man, Fendyke, is above on the roof. With his help all will be well. You need apprehend no danger. Come, dear Miriam—come."

"No, Rupert, no—it may not be. Margaret has ever been my devoted friend. I cannot leave her."

"Oh, yes, yes!" pleaded Margaret. "Go, dear mistress—go! You may escape to the forest, and anon to London, where an interview with the king may be obtained. On my shoulders let all the blame fall. Rather one life be sacrificed than two!"

During the foregoing conversation, the thundering on the door, and Sir Ferdinand's furious threats had continued with increased violence.

But these were not the only sounds which fell upon Rupert's ear.

From without came Fendyke's warning voice.

"Beware, beware!" it said, "lest all my help be unavailing. "Come, and I will save you; delay and you are lost!"

"Rupert!" cried Miriam, frantically. "Oh, I beg of you—fly! Another moment and you are lost!"

Sir Ferdinand, who was wielding an enormous battle-axe, had smashed one of the panels of the door to atoms.

No sooner was the aperture made than two or three of the men discharged their pistols.

The ringing report of the shots had barely ceased, when two other thundering reports rang out, and a shriek of mortal agony was uttered on the other side of the door.

Those two shots had been fired by Rupert, and one of them had proved successful, for one of the men, a big, burly ruffian, who stood close beside Sir Ferdinand, fell, pierced to the heart.

Not the remotest idea had Sir Ferdinand or his men that Rupert was armed.

But the discovery was no sooner made than the men turned from the door.

But it was only momentary.

Sir Ferdinand's threats had the effect of urging the men to renewed efforts.

"What!" roared Lockhart, "would you not seek to avenge a slain comrade?

"What, Hawkswell! what, Morgan! do you quail at the thoughts of encountering this beggarly boy?"

"Nay," growled Hawkswell, "I should fear him not, could I but get to close quarters."

Again the ponderous axe went to work, and at every stroke huge pieces of wood were sent flying in every direction."

At last, just as Rupert was imprinting a last kiss on Miriam's white lips, the door was smashed open.

The first to enter was a man of the name of Kepworth, an individual who was both butcher to the establishment and man-at-arms when necessary.

He was a tall, muscular fellow, and thinking probably to elevate himself in the eyes of Sir Ferdinand, he rushed towards Rupert with up-raised sword.

"Surrender!" he shouted; "surrender!"

"Not for you," replied Rupert, adroitly parrying the violent thrust made at him, and attacking him with such fury that the man was compelled to back towards his companions.

He reached them, but in a dying state, for Rupert dealt him such a fearful blow on the head that it was impossible he could survive it.

Sir Ferdinand was now worked up to a state of ungovernable rage.

He would have struck Miriam had not Margaret dragged her mistress out of harm's way.

Wildly waving his sword, Sir Ferdinand dashed to the open window, through which Rupert had passed.

Just as he reached it another terrific flash of lightning darted across the black sky, illuminating the Abbey and the country for miles around.

The balcony was plainly visible, but not Rupert.

Apparently he had vanished.

Chancing to look up, Sir Ferdinand saw the end of a rope.

"Here, my men," he shouted. "Behold the way the boy is escaping—over the roof; and unless I am much mistaken, he has someone to assist him."

"Maybe his father has also escaped to the roof," suggested Hawkswell, for Sir Ferdinand had not overheard either Miriam or Rupert say anything respecting Master Redmond.

"Nay, I'll not believe that," replied Sir Ferdinand. "But lead the way, Hawkswell—lead the way to the belfry. From the door there we can easily reach the roof, and before he can escape, unless the Evil One himself is aiding him."

"Which is more than likely," muttered Morgan. "It already appears as if the Prince of Darkness has had a good hand in this extraordinary business."

Dashing through the apartment, Hawkswell, who carried a murderous-looking knife, led the way up to the belfry, a somewhat small wooden structure, suspended from the roof of which was the alarm bell.

"Now forward," cried Sir Ferdinand, "and a hundred crowns to the man who captures him."

This stimulated the now flagging energies of the men, and forward they rushed.

But not a soul was to be seen.

"This way," said Hawkswell, pointing to a tall stack of chimneys. "If he reaches the ground from the roof, it will be there he will make the attempt—look! I see a rope tied round the stack."

"Away, then," almost shrieked Sir Ferdinand, who, however, remembering the unexpected and fatal discharge of Rupert's weapons below, did not venture to approach the stack himself.

Hawkswell, Morgan, and several of the men were quickly beside the chimneys.

Here the roof was slightly sloping, the rain had rendered it slippery and dangerous, and so they had to be careful lest, suddenly missing their foothold, they should be hurled to the ground far below.

Two or three of the men behind carried links, but though they waved them about in every direction, no one was to be seen.

Sir Ferdinand was about to issue instructions to some of his men to search every portion of the roof, when two figures dashed from behind the stack, and instantly the men found themselves engaged in a combat with the escaped prisoners, Master Redmond and his son.

Sir Ferdinand's astonishment was intense. So confounded was he to see that the father also, by some extraordinary means, had contrived to extricate himself from the horrible dungeon below—a dungeon from which no previous prisoners had ever been known to escape, that he stood as if petrified for some few moments.

In the meantime a desperate and determined fight was in progress.

Already—though but a few moments only had elapsed—three men had fallen.

Several shots had been fired at close quarters.

Sir Ferdinand crept up as far as he dared, and resting his pistol on a projecting stone, took deliberate aim at Randall Redmond, he being nearest to him, and fired.

But Randall fell not.

Sir Ferdinand, with feverish haste, plucked forth his other pistol, and was about to take aim again, when suddenly a black figure rose before him out of the darkness.

Ere he could express any astonishment, his pistol was snatched from his hand, and with the butt-end, he received a terrific blow in the face.

With a terrified cry, he darted back with such impetuosity that, had not one of his men stayed him, he must have fallen headlong from the roof.

Recovering himself after a few seconds, and seeing that the mysterious black figure stood within twenty paces of him, calmly leaning against a chimney, he shouted to some of his men to attack him.

Half-a-dozen rushed to the spot, but they had scarcely reached it when Fendyke—for he it was—started back a pace or two, and hurled something before the men.

It exploded with the report of a cannon.

A flash of intense brilliancy lit up the figures of the men; the next moment four of them dropped dead.

Instantly a panic seized the remaining men, and in defiance of Sir Ferdinand's commands, they turned and fled.

"Now," said Fendyke, "is the time. Let us hasten, or Sir Ferdinand will rally his men below."

"Adieu, my son, adieu!" cried Master Redmond, sheathing his blade, and clasping Rupert to his heart. "I must leave you for a time. Seek your mother. She is within the forest. Fendyke will appoint a time for you to meet him, so that he can conduct you to the spot. Once more adieu. Look to the future, Rupert, and hope that we may meet again."

Another moment, and Master Redmond had descended the rope, and was speeding away in the direction of the forest.

"Descend first," said Fendyke to Rupert. "Canst thou not hear the shouts and cries below? See the glare of the torches! Hark! Sir Ferdinand is urging on his men."

Down the rope went Rupert, as quickly as it was possible; and the ground being reached, Fendyke followed him, with such lightning-like rapidity, that it seemed as if he scarcely touched the rope.

Already Sir Ferdinand and his men were in the courtyard; and the din caused by their voices, the clash of arms, and the repeated crashes of thunder were fearful.

"This way," whispered Fendyke, seizing Rupert by the arm—"this way."

He drew him towards the outer wall, and a small door being reached, the pair dashed through.

But not unobserved.

Not only Sir Ferdinand, but also several of his men saw them, and with all speed they made for the spot.

Through the door they rushed in a body, those who carried firearms discharging them without looking to see where they aimed.

But no sooner was the door passed than a shout of astonishment was uttered by all.

The two persons they expected to encounter were mounted on a magnificent black horse, Rupert having the reins, and Fendyke being behind him.

Away dashed the animal, followed by a volley of shots from the men.

But apparently it was not struck. At any rate it continued its course, and soon the Abbey lay a long distance behind the fugitives.

Away, away tore the horse, its speed being tremendous.

Seemingly the double weight upon its back did not affect it in the slightest degree.

The Blackburn and Chatburn cross-roads being reached, Fendyke cried a halt, and the instant Rupert drew rein, he jumped to the ground.

Rupert was about to do likewise, when Fendyke checked him.

"Remain where you are," he said, "for the animal is yours."

"Mine!" exclaimed Rupert. "Since I have no home, and possess no accommodation for the horse, of what use is he to me? And who has made me a present of him? Bowolf?"

Fendyke bowed, saying—

"Yes, Bowolf made you the present, and he also made you a present of this."

So saying, be took a purse from his pocket, and handed it to Rupert, who, however did not offer to take it.

"What does the wizard expect in return?" he asked.

"Nothing!" was the reply. "But I beg of you accept his presents. Both will be of service to you. As you but just now said, you have no home. That money will procure you a temporary one."

"Well, I accept his presents, but I shall still believe that he will expect some return."

Thereupon Rupert took the purse, a heavy one, and placed it in his pocket.

"To-morrow night," said Fendyke, "you will meet me within the forest. You know the riven oak in the Thorn Path beside the Hollow?"

"I know it well," replied Rupert with a shudder, "but I have always carefully avoided it, for 'tis haunted."

Of this Fendyke took no notice.

"Be there at midnight to-morrow," he said; "and be careful you are not observed by any of Sir Ferdinand's men, for he is bound to have spies about. You will no doubt find me awaiting you, but if by any chance I should not be there, you will await me. Let nothing drive you from the spot, for you will bear in mind that if you depart your mother must be placed in her grave without your having a last look at her."

"Fear not, mysterious man," said Rupert, "I will be there."

"Until then, adieu."

The next moment Fendyke had vanished.

Lost in wonder—not unmixed with dread—Rupert remained where he was, for some few moments, alternately peering to the right and the left.

As Fendyke did not reappear, he set off for Blackburn, determined to seek quarters where he would be free from observation until the morrow.

CHAPTER IV.

OF THE WONDROUS SCENE IN THE FOREST, AND OF HOW SIR FERDINAND ONCE MORE ATTEMPTS RUPERT'S RECAPTURE.

BEFORE describing what took place in the forest, it is necessary that we should have a little more to say with respect to Sir Ferdinand.

It also becomes necessary to introduce to the notice of the reader a young man who will be a most conspicuous figure in the course of this romance, and his mother.

Catharine Melburn had just turned forty, but she might very easily have passed for at least ten years younger, for she was almost as beautiful and as graceful as she had been when, in her teens, she had been hailed as the most beautiful woman in London.

While still a London beauty she married Richard Melburn, one of Queen Elizabeth's trusted secretaries.

By her marriage she had one child, a son Richard.

Two years after the birth of the child, Master Melburn died, and left the whole of his property to the wife for life, after which it was to go to the son; and, in the event of his death, to a distant relative.

Mistress Melburn and her son, now twenty years of age, resided at Melburn Manor, a magnificent palatial residence, distant about half-a-mile from the Abbey.

Some twelve months previous to the

opening of our romance, Sir Ferdinand and Mistress Melburn met.

The meeting led to invitations on both sides, and in the result the two arrived at an understanding, approved by the son.

The " compact " was to this effect—

On a certain day, to be decided on, two marriages were to be consummated.

One was between Sir Ferdinand and the beautiful Mistress Melburn, the other between Richard Melburn and the lovely Miriam.

Rupert thus had a rival in Richard.

A bitter rival too.

It was about mid-day when the porter at Melburn Manor espied Sir Ferdinand riding towards the house.

He at once admitted him into the grounds, and noticed that Lockhart's face was as pale as death, that his eyes appeared restless, and that he trembled either with apprehension of something about to happen, or with suppressed rage.

" Is Master Richard within ? " asked Sir Ferdinand.

" He is," was the reply, " but I fancy he is just about to go out."

" Have you heard aught of what occurred at the Abbey last night ? "

" No, Sir Ferdinand."

" Then it is useless for me to question you."

So saying, he spurred on his horse and quickly reached the door.

Richard had observed his approach, and he went to the door to meet him.

He was astonished at the alteration wrought in Sir Ferdinand's appearance in the course of a few hours.

" In the name of all that's wonderful," he cried, " what has occurred ? "

" The prisoners have escaped."

" Escaped ! " shouted Richard, starting back. " Did you not have them placed in the dungeons ? "

" Yes," replied Sir Ferdinand moodily, as he dismounted.

" Then how did they escape ? "

" Come within and I will tell you all. Ha ! here is your mother. You look pale, Catharine. The storm, no doubt alarmed you."

" It terrified me in no small degree," replied the lady; " but if I am pale, what of yourself ? You are as white as death."

" No wonder, either," said Richard; for that upstart chainmaker and his son have escaped."

" Indeed," replied Catharine calmly.

" Indeed, you say," cried Richard. " I should have thought you would have been overcome with astonishment."

" Why ? I am not acquainted with the places in which they were confined, neither am I yet aware whether they had any assistance in effecting their escape ! "

By this time the sitting-room had been reached.

" Yes," said Sir Ferdinand, " they certainly did have assistance—that of Bowolf, the Wizard of the Forest."

It was now Richard's turn to become pale.

" You saw him ? " he asked, in low tones.

" Nay, but I saw one who turns out to have been no other than Fendyke, and where Fendyke is, you may be sure Bowolf is also. It is said that he possesses the power to make himself invisible to mortal eyes."

Sir Ferdinand now gave a full account of how Rupert was discovered in Miriam's room, of the fight on the roof, and of the escape, to all of which Richard listened with wrapt attention.

" Have you come to me to ask what I think you had better do under the circumstances ? " he asked, when Lockhart had concluded.

" Nay, I have come to ask your assistance in an attempt to re-capture Rupert Redmond."

" You know where he is, then ? "

" I do not; but there can be no doubt he is not far off. At midnight he will be within the forest. You know Black Braddell ? "

" Right well; and he knows *me*," replied Richard, with a fiendish grin.

" He was at the cross-roads when Rupert Redmond and Fendyke rode up, and he overheard what passed between them.

" Mistress Redmond, who, it appears, was taken into the forest by the hag who rescued the body at the risk of her own life—is lying, ready for interment. It is quite evident that Bowolf is at the bottom of it all. Now I propose that we surprise the burial party and capture Rupert."

"Or slay him," suggested Richard.

"Precisely. Until that youth is dead," said Sir Ferdinand, "there is but little hope that Miriam will give you her hand."

"Willingly, you mean?"

"Exactly. If we are compelled to employ it, force shall certainly be used."

"I think we have already delayed too long," said Richard. "What if we now fix a day."

"I am quite agreeable," replied Sir Ferdinand, stealing a glance at Mistress Catharine.

"Mother," said Richard abruptly, "I wish you to name the day."

Mistress Melburn looked up sharply.

She was about to give some angry reply, but the fierce look upon Richard's face effectually checked her.

"I am not particular," she said. "Say one week from now."

"One week from now be it," cried Sir Ferdinand, joyfully. "One week from now, Richard, the beautiful Miriam will be yours, and so will her enormous fortune."

"And on that day," said Mistress Melburn, "you will give us Miriam's history? You will tell us whose child she really is?"

This was quite an unexpected question.

Sir Ferdinand scowled darkly as he replied—

"That secret must for the present remain mine."

"It is of but little moment to me, so that her money is mine," observed Richard. "And then my mother's money becomes yours, Sir Ferdinand—at least, as long as she lives. This important matter has now been arranged to our satisfaction—my satisfaction, especially, for to make that girl my wife, to have her in my *power*," he hissed through his clenched teeth, "I would sell my very soul.

"There is no love on Miriam's side for me. She detests and hates me. I have had it from her own lips, and, therefore, there can be no doubt about the matter. But let us return to the escaped prisoners, Sir Ferdinand."

"You will help me, Richard, to re-capture them?" queried Lockhart, anxiously.

"Help! Help is hardly what it will be called. I will assume the *command*, Sir Ferdinand. Leave it to me to be in the thick of any fight."

"There will be no fight whatever, if we cautiously make our advances alone."

"Good! Yet it will be as well if we have a goodly number of men in the background, for this Bowolf may be close handy. I can muster a score of men in whom I can place implicit confidence."

"You had better pick for your score men who will not fly in terror from the first tree they see swaying its branches in the moonlight."

"My men are no believers in the idle nonsense of the village. Are you, Sir Ferdinand?"

"Nay," was the reply, but it was only a half-hearted one; but Sir Ferdinand added quickly, "Are you?"

"Yes, and no. By that I mean I can believe what I have seen. That, however, is not much."

"Though what you say you saw was sufficient to prostrate you for many hours," said Mistress Melburn.

"What was it?" asked Sir Ferdinand eagerly.

"I don't care about relating the story, but this is what occurred: A month ago I was on a visit to Beckford Castle, the residence of Master Montgomery. I intended to stay a week, but my host being called to London on the second day of my visit, I returned home. At midnight I started, but Master Montgomery's excellent wine had proved far too strong, for, in defiance of me, my horse would persist in going the wrong way.

"I must have fallen off to sleep in the saddle, for presently the horse stopped, and I looked about me in a dazed kind of way.

"For some time I could make out nothing except that I was in the forest. The most profound darkness reigned. I looked before me, and dimly saw a pool of water with a riven tree in the centre.

"As I looked a low sweet voice asked, 'Is it you, Richard Melburn?'

"I glanced around, but not a soul could I see.

"I replied, 'Richard Melburn it is. Who art thou?'

"THE GAILY-ATTIRED YOUTH INVITED RUPERT TO SEAT HIMSELF."

"But the voice answered not. Suddenly a brilliant light burst over the black water, and I beheld at least a score of the most horrible beings a man ever dreamt of."

"Men or women?" queried Sir Ferdinand, whose attitude showed how deeply interested he was in this extraordinary recital.

"I have been unable to decide whether they were men or women."

"Could you not tell by their voices?"

"Nay. But let me continue. These horrible wretches were joined by others. One after another the black forms rose out of the darkness and rushed into the light, which continued to shine brilliantly and steadily over the water.

"Suddenly the whole of them joined hands, and then became as motionless as statues.

"Again I heard the sweet voice. Then the riven tree in the centre of the pool seemed to open, and a tall beautiful young girl appeared.

"Spellbound I continued to watch the movements of this young girl, who carried what looked like a rod in her hand.

She waved it around her thrice, and then pointing the rod towards me, she said—

"'Ruin to Richard Melburn.'

"No sooner had the words left her lips than the assembled creatures simultaneously gave utterance to one piercing cry of 'Richard Melburn, thou art doomed!'

"Then away they went round and round the pool with the velocity of a whirlwind; and as they went they chaunted these lines—

"'Shunned be Melburn, tyrant, hound!
Shunned by all for miles around—
May peace by thee be *never* found!
Oppressor of the lowly hind,
Fate's strongest fetters thee shall bind,
And ruin seize thy kith and kind!'

"I waited not until their mad dance had concluded, but putting spurs to my horse, I made my way out of the forest as quickly as I could. And now, Sir Ferdinand, what think you of the story? It was to me an awful sight."

"If Sir Ferdinand possesses the common sense I have always credited him with," said Mistress Melburn, "he will think what I think of the story."

"And that is?" asked Sir Ferdinand.

"That Richard was intoxicated when he left Master Montgomery's house, that he fell asleep in the saddle, that the horse wandered into the forest, that Richard, while asleep, dreamt the story he has just told. He woke up to find that the horse had stopped in the forest and the darkness; the silence and gloom filled his heart with terrror, and he turned and fled."

"No!" thundered Richard. "It is false. I was wide awake."

"I don't know what to think of it," said Sir Ferdinand. "It is almost too marvellous for belief."

"Well, well," said Richard, "I have no doubt the time will come when you will be able to judge whether the story I have told is true or merely the account of a dream. Some such scene may be enacted this very night."

"Nay," answered Sir Ferdinand, "I don't think these witches, if such they were, would make their appearance in the face of a body of armed men. But now let us adjourn to your apartments, and make the necessary arrangements for the capture of Rupert Redmond."

*　　*　　*　　*

It wanted some little time to the hour of midnight when Rupert reached the forest.

A beautiful moon lit up the country for miles around.

Singularly enough, however, before Rupert had been on the road a few minutes the moon disappeared, and the sky became overcast with masses of clouds of inky blackness.

In fact the heavens once more seemed ready to hurl forth another storm of equal violence to the last.

In consequence of the intense darkness, Rupert had to use the utmost caution, not only in traversing the roads, but also to guard himself against a surprise.

The whole way from Blackburn to the forest he kept one hand on the reins and the other on the butt of a doubly-charged pistol in his holster.

Not a soul did he meet until he came to the cross-roads.

He had no sooner reached this spot than a man suddenly sprang before him.

Instantly Rupert snatched the pistol

from its holster, and presented it at the fellow's head.

"Hold, hold !" cried the man in piteous tones, as he raised his hands and fell upon his knees ; "hold, good sir, I pray you !"

"Ha !" said Rupert, returning the pistol to its holster, "so 'tis you, Black Braddell, eh ? How came you to be here ?"

"I was but passing," replied the man, rising and approaching our hero, "on my road to Blackburn, Master Rupert. I had not the slightest idea it was you. Hearing the tramp of a horse's hoofs, I thought maybe a rich stranger was passing—perhaps a person seeking information as to the neighbourhood, and who would pay for such."

"In other words," replied Rupert, "you thought a person from whom you might beg a crown was approaching. Well, Braddell, I have a crown to spare, and here it is."

Black Braddell was most profuse in his thanks.

This man was the beggar of the neighbourhood.

For years and years he had prowled about the country.

It was whispered that, had he thought proper, he could have told many a dark story respecting the proceedings of Sir Ferdinand and Richard Melburn.

There were not a few who believed that Black Braddell was by no means the indigent fellow he represented himself to be, but that in some mysterious corner he had stored a huge pile of money.

But always in tatters and rags, his appearance excited universal sympathy.

But for all his rags, and his apparent harmlessness, Black Braddell was a knave of the blackest dye.

He would always play the eavesdropper for whoever paid best.

This was the man who had been present at the cross-roads when Fendyke and Rupert had parted on the previous night, and he had sold the information to Sir Ferdinand.

"You have not asked how I managed to escape from the clutches of the monster yonder," said Rupert, pointing in the direction of the Abbey.

"Eh ?" cried Braddell in startled tones. "Escaped ? I heard not that

you were in Sir Ferdinand's clutches. But a little while back I learned that your house had been accidentally burned down."

"Whoever told you that, told you false !" said Rupert, sternly. "You could not have been in the village last night."

"Nay, I was miles away."

"Well, you will soon hear the true story. I cannot now stay to tell you aught of what occurred. But tell me—did you see anyone as you came along the road ?"

"No one."

"Good ! And now let me caution you. Say not a word to a soul that you chanced to meet me."

"Fear not. But what of your father, Master Rupert ?"

"I know not where he is."

So saying, he resumed his journey.

Black Braddell moved slowly on in the direction of Blackburn, but Rupert was no sooner out of sight than he turned, and went off at a run across the fields towards the Abbey.

The forest reached, Rupert selected a path well known to him.

After encountering many difficulties, he was at last compelled to dismount, for the branches overhead became so dense that it was dangerous to proceed farther mounted.

After a short search he found a spot where his horse might remain out of sight until he should again require him, and then he made his way to the place appointed by Fendyke.

Here, as everywhere else, almost total darkness prevailed.

The threatened storm had not yet burst forth, not the faintest breeze stirring the trees.

Of the spot where he now stood most of those who knew it had a profound dread, for it was generally believed that the place was haunted.

Often strange noises had been heard by the passers-by, and many fearful sights had there been witnessed.

Despite Rupert's great courage, a feeling of horror crept over him as he stood beside the hollow and thought of the many awful tales he had heard.

He fixed his eyes upon the black water, and it seemed to him that the centre, where stood the riven tree, became illuminated with a faint bluish light.

"It must be the hour of midnight," thought Rupert, impatiently. "I hope that this strange being will keep to the time he appointed. I feel that I shall not be able to stay here long."

Ten minutes more passed, but Fendyke appeared not.

Suddenly Rupert heard a rustling sound not far from where he stood.

"'Tis he!" he muttered, turning in the direction of the sound.

But no one appeared.

"Strange," thought Rupert. "I could have sworn that I heard a sound as of a man pushing his way through the tangled brushwood. Ha! there 'tis again; and, heaven! I hear sounds on all sides of me."

Just as suddenly as they began they ceased.

But only for a few seconds.

The sound Rupert heard in the first instance was repeated, but it seemed nearer.

Determined to ascertain what it was, our hero pushed aside the branches.

Scarcely had he done so when there was a sudden rush, and his arms were pinioned to his sides.

At the same moment the flash of a lantern revealed the fact that the point of a sword was within an inch or two of his breast.

The light also enabled him to see by whom the blade was held—Richard Melburn.

"Stir a step, Rupert Redmond," shouted Richard, and I drive this sword into your heart."

"Ay," said a voice, which Rupert had no difficulty in recognising as Sir Ferdinand's, "you have plenty of opportunity now, Richard. Spare him for the present, or slay him on the spot, as ye think best."

Rupert was so completely thunderstricken, that for a few moments he could neither speak nor make any resistance; but he quickly found his tongue.

"Cowards," he cried, "thus to attack a single man. Unhand me, or you will repent it! Richard Melburn, this appears to be your work. Beware, I shall not forget it, villain!"

"I will take care that while you live you don't forget it. 'Tis useless your struggling, Rupert Redmond, you are surrounded by our men."

But, notwithstanding this warning, Rupert continued to struggle: and, by a stupendous effort, he freed himself from the grasp of the men behind him, and leaping lightly aside, his blade flashed in the rays of the lantern.

"Don't let him escape!" roared Richard. "Seize him, my men!"

The two who had pinioned Rupert's arms to his sides dashed towards him.

The first was instantly cut down by a fearful blow delivered full upon his head.

The second, falling back, missed his footing, and fell headlong into the black pool.

"Come forward, Richard Melburn," cried Rupert. "Come forward, if you have any courage, and let the sword's point decide whether Miriam shall be yours or mine."

"Impudent varlet!" thundered Sir Ferdinand, furiously. "Dare you mention her name in the hearing of her chosen husband!"

"Her chosen husband!" replied Rupert, scornfully. "He is not her chosen husband, and never could be. But it is well known that Richard Melburn is an arrant coward, and would not risk a hand-to-hand encounter with me or anyone else able to wield a sword."

"It is false!" replied Richard. "I would not avoid an encounter with you, but I should not be fool enough to engage with you here. The Evil One with whom you are in league——"

"Idle childish fancy," interrupted Rupert. "Our escape from the Abbey has placed this in your head. But beware! I see that you and your men are creeping gradually towards me; and I will sacrifice my life rather than allow myself to again fall into the power of the brutal tyrant, Sir Ferdinand Lockhart."

"Brutal tyrant!" hissed Sir Ferdinand. "Remember that I promise to force those words down your throat. Beggarly boy that you are, when again I have you in my power, I will order your instant destruction."

As he spoke, one of the men, who had crept more forward than the others, unobserved by Rupert, as he supposed, made a sudden plunge at him.

Rupert stepped quickly back, levelled his pistol, and shot the man dead, his death cry ringing with terrible distinctness in the ears of his companions.

While yet the weapon quivered in Rupert's hand—while yet the smoke shut out the dim outlines before him, our hero felt a hand upon his arm.

A voice, which he instantly recognised as Fendyke's, whispered—

"Turn, Rupert, and follow me quickly, and you will escape. But if they follow—well, you will see what will happen."

Rupert did not hesitate.

Away he went beside Fendyke, still keeping his sword firmly clutched in his hand, and ready to defend himself as long as strength should be vouchsafed him wherewith to wield his trusty blade.

In the meantime the shot, and the cry of mortal agony which accompanied it, filled the hearts of the two leaders with apprehension.

The one shot had sounded to them like several.

But it was the echoes only they heard.

Recovering themselves after a moment's pause, Sir Ferdinand shouted—

"Light the links, my men! Light the links. I believe he has escaped!"

"Ay, light the links," shouted Richard. "Keep your swords well in hand, and after him, all of you! By heaven we will have him or burn down the forest!"

These words had scarcely passed his lips when the threatened storm burst forth.

A fearful flash of forked lightning was followed by a rattling volley of thunder, which seemed to shake the very ground whereon they stood.

Both Sir Ferdinand and Richard turned slightly pale, and the former said—

"You forget, Richard, that you are in the midst of the forest of mystery. I should not be surprised if what you uttered called forth the spirit of this fearful storm."

"Bah! onward, Sir Ferdinand. Ha! they have him in sight. Ho! there, hold the links higher!"

"Can you see him now, Hawkswell?" asked Sir Ferdinand, as he caught sight of the figure of his leader, who was now ascending a somewhat steep hill—a hill covered with trees and tangled brushwood.

"Yes," answered Hawkswell, "but it is somewhat difficult to follow in their footsteps. There are two of them now."

"Fire, then—fire, I say, and bring them down!"

At once a score of shots rang out, but they proved fruitless, for on Hawkswell plunging a little forward, he saw that the two figures in front were still pursuing their way.

Suddenly they plunged into such a denseness of brushwood that they were shut out from sight.

"Where are they now?" queried Sir Ferdinand, excitedly. "Who is the other man? Is it his father, think you?"

"No, of that I am certain. The man—for I suppose it is a man—is very short."

"Fendyke?"

"Yes."

"Hark ye, Hawkswell. Cast all your superstitious fears to the winds, and make a dash forward, and seize them. What part of the forest are we in now?"

"They have led us a roundabout way, I am thinking," said Hawkswell, looking anxiously about him; "unless I am much mistaken, the hollow is just over the hill."

"But we have just left it."

"Yes, but they have led us all round."

"Look!" cried Richard, pointing his sword towards the top of the hill, "look at those figures—one—two—why, by all the saints, there are *three* now! Ha!"

His exclamation was caused by a vivid flash of lightning, which, darting from the heavens in a zigzag fashion, almost touched the top of the hill.

Three figures were most distinctly seen—three black figures, standing abreast, their cloaks thrown over their shoulders, and naked blades in their hands.

"What is to be done?" whispered Sir Ferdinand. "I propose that we advance up the hill."

"Yes," replied Richard, "I agree with you, Sir Ferdinand, that we must assume the lead. Wait but a moment."

Richard gave Hawkswell instructions to tell the men to see that, before they advanced, their pistols were loaded.

But the order was no sooner given than it was found that the ammunition contained in the pouches carried by the

"THE MEN WITH A WILD CRY RUSHED UPON THE THREE."

men was rendered useless by the rain, which now fell in perfect torrents.

Sir Ferdinand and Richard in despair took the lead, and the order to advance was given.

The rain had not only saturated the ammunition pouches and the clothes of the men, but it had extinguished many of the links.

Thus the whole party were in semi-darkness, though every few seconds the place was brilliantly illuminated by the lightning.

In the meantime the three figures on the top of the hill had remained as erect and as motionless as statues.

So motionless indeed that, but for the fact that their cloaks, flying before the breeze which had now sprung up, showed them to be human beings, one might have been inclined to take them for trees.

While they stood there the lightning played about them in all directions, and frequently the electric fluid plunged into the earth at their feet.

The advance was made, the men going up the hill at a fair pace, and gaining confidence every moment, owing to the offers of rewards from Sir Ferdinand and Richard, and from the fact that neither of the three above fired upon them, by which they concluded that their ammunition, like their own, had been rendered useless by the rain.

In a sort of irregular half-circle (for the tangled brushwood prevented them from properly forming) the men advanced, Sir Ferdinand being on the one side, and Richard on the other.

Presently they approached far enough to make out that the centre man was Rupert; the faces of the two others could not be seen, owing to the fact that that of one, a tall and evidently powerful man, was concealed by a cowl, while the other was masked.

Still this latter individual both Sir Ferdinand and Richard had no doubt was Fendyke.

For one instant, when the parties were within a few paces of each other, a pause occurred.

Then the men, with a wild cry rushed upon the three.

What followed was the work of a few seconds.

There was a ringing report of firearms and a clash of steel—a clash heard even above the muttering of the thunder—and then it was seen that three men lay dead upon the ground.

Rupert and his companions seemed possessed of the rapidity of the lightning itself.

Hawkswell, who was nearest to the tall individual wearing the cowl, and whose figure was entirely concealed by a flowing black gown, made an attack upon him with sword and the knife it was his habit to carry.

But all of a sudden he darted back among his companions, loudly declaring that the sword of the cowled stranger had sent forth flashes like lightning, as it struck his own weapon, and his arm was powerless.

His companions paused not an instant to ask themselves whether such an extraordinary circumstance could be true, but, turning, they fled like the wind down the hill, and Sir Ferdinand and Richard followed them.

Rounding the corner, they saw that what Hawkswell had said was correct. The Hollow was before them.

The men could not proceed round this at any great speed.

They made their way round it cautiously, some going on the one side, and some on the other.

Suddenly they were startled by a wild, unearthly cry.

So loud, so awful was the sound, that the men with one accord paused.

Their blood seemed suddenly frozen in their veins.

The cry was repeated, and it was instantly followed by a peal of laughter, or what sounded like laughter.

This in turn was followed by a series of fearful cries.

Here and there a shout of despair was heard, the shout being answered to the right and the left with astounding rapidity.

"On, on!" yelled Richard and Sir Ferdinand, both of them now shaking with fear. "On, on!"

But the men would *not* proceed farther.

In a dazed kind of fashion they looked about them, wondering what these awful cries could mean.

Another moment and their attention became fixed upon the black water, which up to now they had been enabled to see only by aid of their links and the lightning.

It was no wonder that their attention became fixed upon this mysterious piece of water; it was no wonder that, as they gazed spell-bound upon it, their swords fell from their hands, and that they themselves seemed as if about to drop to the ground.

The blackness had left the water, and a faint light, in the form of a circle, had spread over it, the riven tree being in the centre.

Bluish at first, the light changed colour repeatedly, increasing in power every moment; but eventually a light of ghastly whiteness was shed over the water.

The feelings of the astounded men could be ascertained by a single glance at their pale faces and their staring eyes.

Sir Ferdinand was far more terrified than he cared to show.

Richard's recital of that morning, concerning the spirits of the forest, at once recurred to him.

The young man had been right, then! This story was no drunken dream, as Mistress Melburn imagined, for here was at least, a repetition of what he had seen on that fearful night.

Sir Ferdinand Lockhart was not a courageous man, but he would rather have opposed a dozen armed men than be compelled to face anything which could only be regarded as supernatural.

He looked at Richard, whose face was ashy pale.

But presently the youthful villain, somewhat recovering his presence of mind, shouted once more to the men to get clear of the forest.

The sound of his voice broke the spell which seemed to have bound the men, and they made a movement to fly.

Before they could move a pace, however, a tremendous screech broke upon their ears, and a couple of large white owls hovered for an instant, first about Sir Ferdinand, then about Richard, and finally they settled at the very top of the riven tree, where they remained close together, their great glittering eyes fixed upon the circle of light.

Then on all sides arose wild, unearthly shrieks, howls and cries of despair.

So appaling and so unearthly were these cries, that one might have fancied that all the fiends from Hades had been let loose, and had gathered about this awful spot.

But now the owners of the strange voices were no longer invisible.

At a signal, brilliant white lights appeared on all sides, as if by magic.

Out of the darkness came figures of men and of women, figures of terrific aspect—awful figures, the first glance at which was enough to freeze the marrow in one's bones.

Uttering strange, unearthly cries, these weird occupants of this most mysterious forest issued forth, now slowly, now fast, and went towards the pool, thus surrounding Sir Ferdinand, Richard, and the men, who now felt their hearts sink with horror.

Each hideous old man, and each hideous old woman—for there was not a young one to be seen—carried a long staff in his or her hand, and at another signal they commenced a low, monotonous chaunt.

It was an incantation of forest spirits.

Presently a green light appeared beside the riven tree, and almost at the same instant a portion of the tree seemed to open.

So far Sir Ferdinand had seen that Richard's recital had been only too true.

But here it stopped.

A person issued from the aperture; but it was not a *lovely* woman.

On the contrary, she was a most hideous old hag.

She was clad in what appeared to be a black robe, fastened at the waist with a belt, on which was a number of mystic characters.

Her head, covered with long hair, was surmounted with a high-crowned hat, and she carried in her left hand a staff.

Her face could be plainly seen in consequence of the strange light upon the water, and the mystic lights burning on every side. Though these lights were seen burning steadily enough, no human hand held them.

The eyes of this old woman blazed with terrific fury; indeed, the entire expression upon her hideous face showed that she was labouring under powerful emotion, and the fierce expression was heightened by her grey locks, which fell in wild disorder about her bare neck and high shoulders.

This old woman was Mother Frampton, the chief of the Black Witches of Pendle Forest, and it was believed that she was the mother of Fendyke.

The appearance of Mother Frampton was the signal for silence—a deep silence.

It was a terrible scene of mystery.

"Sir Ferdinand Lockhart," said the old witch, in harsh, grating tones, "you shall not leave Pendle Hollow until you have learned that, of all men, you are the most hated. Black-hearted tyrant that you are—cowardly monster—your cup of bitterness is filled, and you shall now learn what it is to partake of it. Sir Ferdinand Lockhart, you are doomed!"

"Doomed, doomed!" was echoed on all sides by the spirits of the forest.

So overwhelmed was Sir Ferdinand, that he felt compelled to clutch a tree to prevent himself from falling.

Ere the echoes of the fearful cry of "doomed" had died away, smothered as they were by the angry mutterings of the thunder, another voice, loud and terrible, broke upon the ear.

Every word could be heard, and this is what it said—

"Thy heart's desire to us is known,—
Reflected in the pool is shown
        Thy wish!"

Instantly Sir Ferdinand's and Richard's eyes were directed upon the pool.

What they beheld was enough to call forth a cry of alarm.

Reflected in the pool was the figure of a handsome lady, clasping to her breast an infant.

As Sir Ferdinand looked, the lady raised her face, and he recognised the features of Mistress Melburn.

The reflection remained there but an instant, however.

When it had vanished, the voice continued—

"Doomed be thy child before its birth.
'Twill live a month—then mother earth
        Will claim it for its own.
            Doomed, Sir Ferdinand."

Again the word "doomed" rang out on all sides—it appeared to be uttered with all the power the dreadful beings could muster.

Sir Ferdinand felt ready to sink into the ground.

The desire of his life—the wish for a son and heir—to be thus brought before him was so astounding, that he could scarcely believe that he had actually seen Mistress Melburn reflected in that dreaded pool.

The old witch, Mother Frampton, again spoke—

"Hand-in-hand, Sir Ferdinand Lockhart and Richard Melburn—hand-in-hand for villainy. But ye shall be foiled. Your plots and plans shall fail. Know, Sir Ferdinand, that Richard Melburn will never marry Miriam Lockhart, who is the daughter of——"

The old hag was here interrupted by a loud, terrified cry from Sir Ferdinand.

Suddenly starting forward, he said—

"Hold, hold, I conjure you. If you hold the secret of her birth, I charge you reveal it not—reveal it not."

The old witch seemed to reflect for a moment.

Presently she said—

"Be it so. The name shall not now be uttered. But, in order that it may be proved that we do possess the great secret, you will remain, Sir Ferdinand, while Richard Melburn proceeds with the men."

Here Richard found his tongue.

"No! I will not stir without Sir Ferdinand," he said, fiercely.

"Thou art already doomed, false knave!" said Mother Frampton. "Depart! Hesitate not, as you value your miserable life!"

"Go, Richard," whispered Sir Ferdinand—"go! I will join you anon."

"And reveal to me the secret?"

"What secret?"

"The secret of Miriam's birth. For now that this hideous old hag has mentioned it, I long to be made acquainted with the particulars."

"Nay, I must refuse to furnish you with any particulars relative to the secret of Miriam's birth. If you continue to press me, then all must be at an end between you and Miriam."

"No, no," answered Richard, hastily. "Since you so refuse, I will not again ask."

"Richard, above all things bribe your men to silence as to what has here occurred, and tell your mother nothing."

"I will do as you say," replied Richard. Turning, he called to his men, who were only too glad to follow him.

As Richard hastily departed, his ears were assailed by jeers, hoots and cries of a fearful description.

And the cries ceased not until the edge of the forest was reached, nor did the strange lights disappear, for they danced hither and thither on all sides of him, like Will-o'-the-Wisps.

Sir Ferdinand remained near the pool, the light upon which, as well as those surrounding him, disappeared as soon as Richard and the men withdrew.

But the horrible beings remained grim and silent, looking at him.

The storm had now ceased, and out of a clear sky shone a brilliant moon, which penetrating the dense natural canopy overhead, was reflected in the mystic pool, and brought out with striking distinctness the figures of the men and women surrounding it.

The old witch, Mother Frampton, had disappeared for a moment, but she quickly reappeared, for, to Sir Ferdinand's alarm, her voice was heard close beside him.

"Follow me, Sir Ferdinand," she said.

"Whither, mysterious being?"

"You will see anon. Follow me, and without looking behind. No one will offer to injure you—at least, not on this occasion."

Instantly Sir Ferdinand placed his hand to his side.

His sword was gone; his dagger alone remained.

Mother Frampton hobbled on, the horrible troop remaining where they were, much to Sir Ferdinand's relief.

Mother Frampton led him up and down the most intricate paths—paths it would be impossible for him to attempt to discover again; and Sir Ferdinand, with fear, kept close to her.

But as he went, his fears began to vanish, and he proceeded to form plans in his mind for the capture of the horrid beings who made the woods their home.

But what had Rupert Redmond to do with these witches of the forest?

He had received positive proof that Rupert and his father must be associates of this uncanny crew.

Then he began to wonder what had become of Rupert, Fendyke, and the tall, cowled stranger.

He was not long to remain in ignorance.

In the meantime, Fendyke, as soon as the men fled down the hill, said—

"Sheathe your sword, Rupert Redmond, you will no longer require it. Sir Ferdinand and Richard will be in good hands for some time. Ho, ho! Sheathe your blade, I say, and accompany me."

"Gracious powers!" cried Rupert, suddenly, "where is the man who joined us, and who fought so splendidly?"

"Gone about his business, no doubt," grinned Fendyke, who had removed the mask from his really repulsive face; "but I advise you to ask no questions. Walk by my side, Rupert Redmond. That is well. Now listen to what I tell you. Your mother is about to be interred in a manner befitting a lady. But you will have to swear to silence as to what you see and hear. You agree to this?"

"I do."

"Good! But let me warn you that the breaking of your oath means death, no matter where you may be."

"I am not in the habit of breaking any oath I may take," replied Rupert.

Fendyke now set off. Passing through places where it seemed it was absolutely impossible for mortal to tread, he at length came to an abrupt halt.

"Here, Rupert Redmond," he said, "I must bid you adieu. When and where I may again speak to you I cannot say. You may shortly see me again, but speak we shall not."

Rupert looked about him, but it was here so dark that it was impossible to tell what was on either side of him.

He felt dazed and bewildered.

"Mark well what I say," he said, in stern tones. "If I find myself in any difficulty, I shall blame *you*."

"Suspicious, mistrustful youth!" replied Fendyke, in bitter tones. "Is this your gratitude for what I have done for you? If wrong was intended you, think you that you would have escaped from the Abbey?"

"Pardon me," said Rupert, "my words were somewhat hasty. But I am still thinking that this mysterious master of yours, Bowolf, will expect of me some return for what he has done."

"Dismiss all such thoughts from your mind. Bowolf, the Wizard, is *dead!*"

"Dead!" exclaimed Rupert, with a violent start.

"Yes; but I can tell you no more. Remain here a few moments, and presently you will be on the spot where the body of your mother lies."

So saying, Fendyke disappeared.

Almost at the same moment, Rupert beheld a light advancing.

Another moment, and the tall figure of a man, clothed from head to foot in black, stood before him.

"Rupert Redmond?" he asked, in deep tones,

"The same," replied Rupert.

"Follow me."

Half-a-dozen paces he went forward; then he paused and held the lantern in such a position that Rupert could see what was before him.

His astonishment was great when he beheld what looked like the entrance to a well.

There was a flight of steps within it.

"Enter and descend," said the man.

"But," replied Rupert, "how am I to proceed in the darkness?"

"Descend," again said the mysterious stranger.

Without further hesitation, Rupert entered the dark, well-like aperture, and commenced the descent.

Occasionally he looked back, and he saw the light above shining brightly, though he failed to see the hand which held it.

But all of a sudden a loud noise was heard above.

It sounded to Rupert like a heavy flap being shut.

He looked up and saw that the light had vanished.

He was now in total darkness, and for a moment he paused.

He felt that he was in the midst of the home of all that was supernatural and unearthly.

He had reached the bottom of the steps, and was in a subterranean passage; but whither did it lead? and how was he to proceed?

He soon knew. A deep hollow voice, which seemed to proceed from a long distance, said—

"Advance, Rupert Redmond. There is nought to fear."

Rupert set his teeth firmly together, and went forward.

He felt the ground soft beneath his feet, as if he were walking on earth overgrown with moss.

The distance traversed was great.

Frequently he stretched his hands on either side of him, but he felt nothing but a wall.

Presently he saw a dim light ahead.

As he advanced it increased in brilliancy, and he quickly made out two figures holding links aloft.

Both were of the same height as the one who had conducted Rupert to the entrance of the subterranean passage, and both were clad from head to foot in black, neither ornaments nor arms being visible.

He was about to speak to them, but they placed their fingers to their lips, and pointed ahead.

Still further on went Rupert, and he at length reached a tall oaken door.

It flew open, and what he now beheld was astounding.

He found himself on the threshold of a small chapel, the decorations within which, though tarnished and faded, must at one time have been splendid.

But Rupert's eyes were not fixed for more than a few seconds upon the chapel itself.

His gaze became riveted upon the occupants.

Ranged all round the chapel were at least a score of men, clad in black.

Beside the altar, which was illuminated by half-a-dozen tapers, stood four more of these mysterious-looking persons as erect and as silent as statues.

But this was not what caused Rupert to utter an exclamation of astonishment.

Standing in front of the altar was the parson of Whalley parish church, and by his side stood the sexton.

On a raised dais near them was a black oak coffin.

"Come forward, Rupert Redmond," said the parson, "and fear nothing. You wonder why I am here. I will tell you. I was asked to officiate at the burial of a lady. I consented, and my sexton did the same.

"We were taken to the edge of the forest, blindfolded, and placed on horseback. We at last found ourselves being carried down a flight of steps, and finally our bandages were taken off, and I found myself in this chapel.

"I then learned that the body to be buried was that of your mother, Rupert. Of the weird and utterly mysterious circumstances connected with this burial we must ever preserve a strict silence. For before this altar have we been sworn to secrecy."

"All this is quite as mysterious to me as it is to you," replied Rupert.

The lid of the coffin was taken off by the sexton, and our hero beheld the body of his mother.

She was clad in the costliest raiment, and the look upon her face was so calm and peaceful that Rupert was compelled to give way to the emotion which filled his heart, and, falling on his knees he burst into tears.

Hark ! What was that ?

Was it a sob he heard close beside him ? Or was it but the echo of his own ?

The parson directed a swift inquiring glance towards the huge column beside Rupert, and against which a tall man—far taller than any of the others—was standing.

The clergyman thought he saw this man craning his neck forward, as if trying to get a glimpse of the body.

Presently Rupert rose, the sexton screwed down the lid, the parson read the service for the dead, and the coffin was carried by half-a-dozen of the mysterious men, and placed beneath a huge stone on the right of the chapel.

All was quickly finished, and then a bag of money was handed to the parson, and he with the sexton was hastily conducted to the chapel.

Rupert was about to follow when a deep voice said—

"Hold, Rupert Redmond. Retire beyond the last column on the left, and watch. But, be warned—utter no sound as you value your life !"

Rupert obeyed, and stood behind the last column in such a position that he could not be seen by anyone unless they came close to him.

He had no sooner taken up his position, than every taper within the chapel was extinguished.

But suddenly, from where the altar stood, a light appeared—a white light of dazzling brilliancy.

It flooded the whole of the centre of the chapel.

Rupert could see from end to end of the nave, and so plainly that he could almost read the inscriptions on some of the stones, beneath which lay the bodies of many a man, whose life had been a deep and impenetrable mystery.

The white light seemed to travel up and down the nave, as if in search of something, but finally it stopped and concentrated all its power upon one particular spot.

Rupert saw that the stone whereon the light rested was much newer than any of the rest; and that the letters upon it had not been cut many years.

The right and left of the chapel were wrapped in semi-darkness, the mysterious men ranged about it looking like statues draped in black.

The entire appearance of the chapel was indeed weird and ghastly in the extreme.

A pair of folding-doors on the right were presently opened, and through them came several women.

It needed no second glance to see that they were the Black Witches, and that the leader was Mother Frampton.

Rupert could not make out their number, in consequence of the semi-darkness in which they stood ; but presently a couple of links were lit, and these threw a weird, strange light over the wondrous scene.

But our hero was not now looking upon the horrible faces of the witches.

His startled gaze was directed upon the figure of a man in their centre.

It was Sir Ferdinand Lockhart.

His arms were bound behind his back, his hat was gone, and so also was his cloak.

His face was ashy pale, his hair was flying about his head in a state of the wildest disorder, his eyes were staring, and full of terror.

He looked like a man being brought from his prison cell and conducted to the block.

In a few moments he stood at the bottom of the chapel.

A deep, solemn silence now filled this strange place.

"Look up, thou man of blood !" cried a deep voice. "Look up, Sir Ferdinand Lockhart !"

The speaker could not be seen. Not one of the black-robed men moved.

Sir Ferdinand slightly raised his head.

The voice continued—

"Do you know, Sir Ferdinand, why you are brought here?"

"No," replied Lockhart.

Encouraged somewhat by the sound of his own voice, which, however, was low and harsh, he continued—

"I have no knowledge how it is that I am subjected to this outrage. But the time will come when I——"

He paused abruptly, for he saw that a score of fierce-looking eyes were directed upon him.

Remembering that his life hung upon a thread, he did not continue.

But the mysterious voice did.

"Sir Ferdinand Lockhart," it said, "gaze at the spot whereon shines that light."

"Well?" queried the trembling villain.

"What think you is beneath that stone?"

"I know not; neither do I care."

"Can you see that an inscription is cut upon the stone?"

"I can."

"It shall be read. Listen!—

"'TO THE MEMORY
OF
WALTER DUBOIS,
Who was murdered on the night of the 14th of October, of the year 1594.'"

As these words were uttered, a tremendous cry left Sir Ferdinand's lips— a cry that rang again and again through the chapel.

The mention of the name Walter Dubois, had had such an effect upon him, that the Black Witches had difficulty in causing him to retain his feet.

All this was a mystery to Rupert; but some of the mystery was to be quickly solved.

The voice, in deep, solemn tones, continued—

"Sir Ferdinand Lockhart, *you are the murderer of Walter Dubois!*"

"No, no," shrieked Sir Ferdinand; "I am not! I did him no harm! I was his best, his most loved friend! What horrid conspiracy is this? Who is it that seeks to impose upon me? And for what purpose——"

"Silence!" interrupted the voice, in thundering tones—"silence! Your hypocrisy will avail you nought here. Sir Ferdinand Lockhart, listen while the story of Walter Dubois and his *loved* friend is told."

At this moment a low voice, which seemed to proceed from someone exactly behind Rupert, whispered—

"Mark well what is said, Rupert Redmond."

Like lightning did Rupert turn, but he saw no one near him.

However, he determined to listen.

"For some years before that fatal month in the year 1594," continued the voice, "you and Walter Dubois were apparently on terms of the highest friendship. Walter Dubois was a man of vast wealth and great worth. You had taken a fancy to his beautiful wife, and you determined to make her yours. But your wicked passion betrayed itself.

"Walter Dubois' wife told her husband all, for woman was never more faithful and true than she. The day of reckoning came. Walter followed you to Whalley, where, as you said, you had business with the then owner of the Abbey, and he confronted you on the borders of Pendle Forest.

"Honourable man that he was, he offered you the choice of weapons. You chose swords, and you both went into nearly the centre of the forest.

"It was a beautiful moonlight night, and no one being present to interrupt you, you had ample opportunity to bring the duel to a termination.

"But you, coward that you ever were —took advantage of this man. Even while he was drawing his sword, you dashed upon him, and plunged your dagger deep into his heart."

The speaker paused, as if to see whether Sir Ferdinand would answer.

But he breathed not a sentence.

His appearance now was fearful.

He was utterly astounded with the revelations being made.

The voice continued—

"At the moment that the heartrending cry of the dying man rang out, as he fell on the green sward and at your feet, the moon seemed as if she had suddenly altered her course, for her rays penetrated the canopy of green exactly overhead, and shone full upon Walter

Dubois, and upon his murderer, who, with the blood-dripping dagger clasped in his hand, seemed listening for the faintest sound.

"Suddenly a couple of white owls darted in front of you, and hooting dismally, settled themselves near the body.

"After deliberation you decided what to do.

"You made your way out of the forest, and you returned in four hours, carrying a black bag, which contained a pickaxe and spade.

"With these you set to work, first, however, compelling the owls to fly. You dug a hole at the foot of a gigantic oak, and in that you placed the body of your victim.

"After some little time, during which active search was made for Walter Dubois, and in which *you* were the principal, it was generally supposed that he had met with his death at the hands of robbers, and that he had probably been buried as a man unknown.

"By one person at least were you suspected, and that was by the wife. She scorned your offers; she declared she hated you. You persecuted her, you rendered her life a burden to her. What was the result? She was poisoned, and her little child, Miriam, you took away from her home!"

Rupert contrived to check the great cry which rose to his lips as these last words were uttered.

For a few moments a mist seemed to float before his eyes.

The voice continued—

"The will was examined, and it proved that Miriam was entitled to an immense fortune, the whole of the deeds and documents of which were contained in an iron box, placed in a certain room in Dubois' house. *When that will was made, Walter Dubois had considered you his greatest friend.* It left you the guardian of Miriam (in the event of aught happening to her mother), and sole custodian of her wealth. How have you treated this poor orphan? How treated the daughter of the man you murdered?"

"It is a black, infamous lie!" gasped Sir Ferdinand. A conspiracy is being formed against me. I am innocent of slaying Walter Dubois."

"Say you so? Then for a few moments the dead shall return to life!"

As these words were spoken, three tremendous knocks were heard.

They seemed as if they had been delivered with a mighty hand beneath the very floor of the chapel.

Before Rupert could fully recover from his astonishment, the stone whereon the mystic light had shone quivered slightly.

Then slowly it raised itself, and finally stood on end.

No human hand was seen to touch it

"Come forth, Walter Dubois," said the mysterious voice, in low, gentle tones. "Come forth, I command you, and thus prove the truth of what has been said."

Instantly a dense bluish vapour began to rise from the black aperture, and amid it was observed a human form.

With increasing brilliancy the white light shone out, and it seemed to have the effect of dispelling the vapours to some extent, for, in a few seconds, the face and form of the human figure were perfectly distinct.

The face was that of a remarkably handsome young man—the figure well-proportioned and graceful.

That face and figure were recognised by Sir Ferdinand, for giving utterance to an ear-piercing shriek of terror, he fell prostrate to the ground.

As he fell, the figure vanished, the stone noiselessly resumed its place, the white light disappeared, and only the dull glare of the links now illumined the chapel.

Rupert was about to start out from the position he had occupied, when he felt his arm seized.

"Wait no longer, or there may be danger," said a voice. "Come with me."

Rupert would have asked to learn the sequel to these extraordinary proceedings, but the hand upon his arm tightened, and the voice repeated—

"Come, and quickly."

A door immediately behind him opened, and he was led through it.

A link was burning in a bracket, and by its rays, Rupert saw that his conductor was one of the mysterious men in black.

This individual took down the link,

and then told Rupert to follow him as rapidly as he could.

But our hero was so overwhelmed with all that he had passed through—he felt so stupefied with the horrors he had beheld in that mysterious chapel, that he had the greatest difficulty in keeping up with his conductor.

Several times did he ask the man to explain but a little of what he had seen.

But he got no answer whatever.

Another door was presently passed through, and Rupert soon made out that he was once again in the subterranean passage.

The end was quickly reached, and here the link was extinguished.

Another moment or two, and Rupert was in the depths of the forest.

"Still follow me," said the man, "and I will lead you to the spot where you have left your horse."

Within the space of five minutes, Rupert was mounted on the broad back of his beautiful steed.

"Continue to follow me," said the man, "and I will lead you out of the forest by a path known to but few. Therefore you will be unobserved. Nay, offer no objection. And now listen to what I am commissioned to say."

"By whom were you commissioned?"

"By the MAN OF MYSTERY."

"Bowolf?"

"You have been told that Bowolf is dead. Such is the case. He is dead and buried."

"Then another occupies his place?"

"Exactly."

"And his name?"

"MORNA."

"I will try not to forget the name."

"You may try as hard as you will, but you could *never forget* the name. Again I say listen. Avoid Whalley, avoid every human habitation, and make your way direct to London. When there you will open this letter. That is all I have to say. Now, follow me, Rupert Redmond, and speak not."

CHAPTER V.

IN WHAT MYSTERIOUS MANNER A MESSAGE WAS CONVEYED TO RUPERT—OF THE CONTENTS OF THE DOCUMENT—AND OF WHAT HAPPENED AT THE "BELLE SAUVAGE."

THE journey from Whalley to London was a long one, and, moreover, in consequence of the state of the roads, it was a difficult one.

Rupert thought that he never should cover the first ten miles.

On the evening of the second day, having taken many rests on the road, he reached London.

And he had no sooner reached the City, than he repaired to a hostelry, for the purpose of examining the letter, the contents of which he was, as will very readily be supposed, most anxious to ascertain.

The first words which met his eyes were—

"To be destroyed as soon as read."

These words were on the outside.

On opening the letter a single sheet of paper, of a parchment-like texture, and another smaller sheet, were revealed.

On opening the latter, he was astonished to find that it was an order on a Lombard Street goldsmith for a large sum of money—sufficient, in fact to meet his wants for a long time to come.

The letter was to this effect—

"Rupert Redmond, this is written by one who takes the greatest interest in your welfare. Be guarded and cautious as to your conduct, and, above all things, always heed the contents of any document you see in this handwriting. Troublous times are, I fear, before you. But, in the greatest of difficulties— in the greatest of dangers—forget not that you are the son of Randall Redmond— forget not that you are the son of the man who, though poor, was the soul of honour. Remember that he and your dear, dead mother loved you from the bottom of their hearts. Fight your way through the world, Rupert, bravely, always remembering that the *living* is continually thinking of you—that the eyes of the *dead* look down upon you from heaven. And forget not this—that your two greatest enemies are Sir Ferdinand Lockhart and Richard Melburn.

"MORNA."

"Morna!" gasped Rupert, suddenly starting from his chair, "Morna! The Man of Mystery! Chief of all the mysterious men and women I saw. Away!" he cried, hurling the documents from him, "away! lest I contract some foul disease that—but no, no! What am I saying? Truly he must be a dreadful man—a man in possession of the powers of the Prince of Darkness; but, nevertheless, he must take a vast interest in me. And," he added, his voice trembling with deep emotion, "how highly he speaks of my poor father and my dead mother! My hapless father! Chased from the country, compelled to fly to escape the persecutions of this monster in human form—this murderer. Alas! I may never see him again!"

Little did Rupert dream that the man who had signed himself Morna *was his own father!*

For it is not necessary that the veil of mystery should continue to be wrapped about this personage; the reader will be better able to understand what is to follow if he is in possession of the fact that Morna is Randall Redmond, or perhaps we had better say, *was* Randall Redmond.

Rupert picked up the letter, and on again reading it, found that a postscript was added.

It was—

"Repair to 'The Belle Sauvage' on Ludgate Hill. There remain until another message is sent you."

After a few moments' reflection, Rupert decided to do exactly as he was directed, so, setting out he made his way to Ludgate Hill, and put up at the "Belle Sauvage," where he remained until the evening of the sixth day, without anything of importance occurring.

The "Belle Sauvage," in the days of which we write, was one of the largest hostelries in the City of London, and the name of Belle Sauvage Yard still remains on Ludgate Hill.

It was full of quaint old rooms with oak wainscottings, in some cases stone floors, and in all cases vaulted ceilings.

The room which Rupert occupied was on the third floor of the house, and could be approached in many ways, including the balcony without, which communicated with the other balconies by stairs.

During his stay here, Rupert had many things to think about, but the principal was how to communicate with the king, for he had resolved to lay before his majesty Sir Ferdinand's persecution, not only of himself and his father, but of Miriam.

He was well aware of the fact, however, that the king, who had the assurance to allow himself to be called not only the King of England, but the Solomon of the world, was not easily got at, but still, he thought, a slice of luck might throw one of his majesty's favourites in his way, and thus the difficulty might be removed.

Lost in thought Rupert sat; nor did he notice that it was almost quite dark until one of the servants appeared with the lamp.

"What is the noise I hear below?" asked Rupert.

"That, your worship," replied the girl, "is a new arrival. A great fuss is being made because it is one of the court lacqueys."

"A court lacquey! Is that a novelty here?"

"Why, yes, indeed, your worship. A court lacquey is considered a person of considerable importance in the City, especially by tradesmen."

"Ah! I understand."

"Perhaps your worship would like to join the party below. You are very dull here; and I am sure that *you* would be considered a person of some importance by those downstairs."

"How so?"

"Why because, your worship, all of them are old and ugly—at least, they are not very good-looking."

Rupert, despite his grave thoughts, could not repress a smile.

Certainly he had been dull, remarkably dull, ever since he had been at the inn.

"I will join the party below," said Rupert, "and very glad indeed shall I be to pass a pleasant hour."

"THE TERRIBLE SWORD WAS BROUGHT INTO PLAY WITH TELLING EFFECT."

In a few moments he descended, and was warmly welcomed both by the jovial host, Jack Runciman, and his red-cheeked, buxom wife.

By the host he was conducted to the principal room, a huge, lofty apartment on the ground floor of the house, and which was illuminated by a monstrous oil lamp suspended from the centre of the vaulted roof.

The roof contained at least a couple of score of persons, all men, and, judging by their costumes, each very well-to-do in the world.

The person on whom Rupert's eyes became fixed was seated on a barrel in the centre of the room.

His costume was exceedingly rich, and Rupert could at once see that he certainly was a "lacquey of some importance."

In age he was about twenty—certainly not more—in stature short.

That he was a person of jovial disposition was also evident, for his little blue eyes twinkled with merriment, while his voice, though somewhat "squeaky," had the tone of a merry schoolboy.

About this individual were congregated the whole of the persons in the room, and eagerly were they listening to what the lacquey was saying.

A moment's attention told Rupert that he was telling them about the arrangements the king was making for the capture of the witches with which England was infested, and in the matter of which, as Rupert quickly learned, everyone was deeply interested.

He quickly caught sight of Rupert, and he was evidently struck with his appearance, for at once rising, he said—

"No doubt you, young sir, take a great interest in these matters?"

"I can't say I do," replied Rupert, "for, at present, I know nothing about them."

"What! Know nothing of them? By the Virgin's soul! never in all my life was I so astonished. Well, your reply, young sir, has made me so thirsty that I must call for another tankard."

"Do so," replied Rupert, at once taking a fancy to the youth, "and I will pay for whatever you choose to drink."

This offer gladdened the heart of the gaily-attired youth, and seizing upon a chair, he placed it beside the barrel, and invited Rupert to seat himself by his side.

Rupert soon discovered that this youth was valet to the young Duke of Buckingham.

King James had two idols: the first was his son—that ill-fated son—Charles, and the second was the duke, his dear beloved "Steenie," who, he thought, could do no harm, and for whom nothing the world produced was too good.

Rupert took the first opportunity of checking the course of the court lacquey's narrative by ingeniously insinuating that he was hungry, and perhaps the youth was hungry too.

"Hungry!" exclaimed the youth, "hungry is hardly the word. I am famished!"

"In that case," said Rupert, "I propose that we eat. I am just about to order supper. Will you join me?"

"Agreed!" exclaimed the youth, darting from the barrel with remarkable agility. "I am with you heart and soul. Where shall we partake of the little collation? Here?"

"No. Perhaps you will join me in my room above."

"With the greatest pleasure in life. You then, sir, are staying here?"

"I am—and you?"

"I am a visitor until to-morrow morning only, and I will ask the host to allot me a room adjoining yours."

The supper was quickly served, which Rupert considered would be relished by his companion.

The wine was not forgotten, for Rupert knew its value as a loosener of the tongue.

"Why," exclaimed Rupert, on the conclusion of the supper, "we have been together all this time, and yet we know not each other's names."

"Ah, most true! And yet it never struck me. Why, my name is Stephen Varley, valet to His Grace the Duke of Buckingham. And yours?"

"Rupert Redmond."

"Of London?"

"No, of Whalley."

"Whalley!" cried Stephen, "Whalley! Why that is a name I have heard a score of times within the past few days. Is not Pendle Forest thereabouts?"

"Yes. Do you know it?"

"I? Thank heaven, no!" replied Stephen; "and from what I've heard of it I have not the least desire to make myself acquainted with it. Why, Master Redmond, not long ago you said you knew nothing of witches, and yet your home is in the very heart of them."

"Pardon me, you are entirely mistaken."

"Or someone tells most atrocious lies," said Stephen. "Why, I assure you, Master Rupert, that the whole court is ringing with most extraordinary news. It is to the effect that witches, and other strange persons, with which, it seems, the forest swarms, have lately committed the most atrocious outrages. But in a day or two we shall be made acquainted with full and proper particulars, for Sir Ferdinand Lockhart, one of the gentlemen on whom these witches have been practising their black arts, is coming to London."

Here, indeed, was unexpected but most important news.

Sir Ferdinand coming to London, and yet no message had been received by our hero.

"Surely," thought Rupert, "if the Man of Mystery takes so great an interest in me, he would have let me know that Sir Ferdinand was coming to London."

"Depend upon it, Master Redmond," continued Stephen, "the king will make arrangements which will not suit these accursed witches. I heard that he intends to have every one of them brought to the stake and burned alive. I hope I may be lucky enough to see a few of them so treated. And so you know nothing of the witches of Pendle Forest, eh? The worst—the very *worst*—because the most powerful in England. No doubt you lived too far away, and you were fortunate; for to be bewitched certainly means death.

"But, hist! What is that? St. Paul's striking the hour of midnight! I must be bestirring myself, for in a few minutes, no doubt, his grace will arrive."

"His grace! You did not say that you expected anyone."

"Did I not? Then it was an omission which I will at once rectify. His grace the Duke of Buckingham is going to stay here until the morning. Strange place for a high and mighty personage to stay, eh? But, you see, his grace has been transacting business with some of the goldsmiths. I expect he will bring with him a number of jewels, some or all of which he is about to present to a lady on whom he has been pleased to bestow a portion of his affections. No doubt I shall see you in the morning. Until then, adieu! Remember, I thank you most sincerely for your kind entertainment, and if I can be of any service to you, command me."

As Stephen rose, a loud clattering of horses' hoofs, and the rumbling of heavy wheels, told that a traveller had arrived.

Even before the wheels could stop, the host was upstairs.

"Come, young sir," he said, "here is the duke. I trust you have not been indulging too deeply."

And he surveyed Stephen with a most anxious air.

Stephen certainly had consumed almost all the wine which had been supplied, but nevertheless he was perfectly steady and collected, and very calmly he descended the stairs to receive his great master, the duke.

The ostlers, carrying flaming links aloft, stood beside the doors, and Rupert, looking from the window, saw his grace leave the coach.

He noticed that the duke carried a small bag in his hand, and he concluded that the bag contained the jewels of which Stephen had spoken.

The duke at once repaired to his rooms, which were on the second floor, and under Rupert, and in half-an-hour the closing of a door on Rupert's landing told him that Stephen had retired.

About the same time the closing of the doors below, and the shooting of bolts, showed that the house was being closed.

But though the most profound silence reigned, Rupert felt not the slightest inclination to sleep.

The startling intelligence, which he had so unexpectedly received, had effectually dispelled all desire for sleep.

For some time he paced the room in a state of the greatest agitation.

But remembering who was below him he ceased his pacing, and seated himself in the ponderous arm-chair.

How long he sat there he knew not, but it was certain that he dozed off.

He awoke with a start to find that the lamp had gone out, and that the room was in total darkness.

A strange feeling was upon him, what, he could not tell.

"I could have sworn that I heard something move," he thought, as he looked cautiously round the apartment.

Rising, he went to the door and tried it.

It was as he had left it, locked and bolted.

Again he resumed his seat, but barely had he done so, when a long piece of oak wainscoting, close against where he sat, shot upward with the rapidity of lightning.

Instantly Rupert was on his feet, and as his blade leapt from its scabbard, he said—

"Who goes there? Speak, or on your head be the consequences!"

"Hish! hish!" was the whispered reply; "let not your voice be heard, lest the person below be alarmed, and the household be roused."

"Who are you?" gasped Rupert, astounded at the calm and deliberate fashion in which these words had been uttered.

"No matter who I am," was the reply. "I am here by command."

"By command! Whose command?"

"The Man of Mystery!"

"Ha! And you bring—what?"

"A letter. But procure a light, for I have to warn you."

Rupert, after some difficulty, relit the lamp, and his eyes at once sought his visitant.

He beheld a tall, thin, though muscular-looking man, clad in suit of tight-fitting black, and wearing a mask which entirely concealed his features.

Apparently he carried no arms, except a long, sharp-pointed Spanish dagger.

"I will not ask you to unmask so that I may see your face," said Rupert, "lest I be refused."

"Which you unquestionably would be," answered the man.

"You are from Whalley?" asked Rupert.

"Nay; my quarters are in London. But I have received this letter from a person who came direct from Whalley, and whom, no doubt you have seen."

"Fendyke?"

"The same. My business with you was simply to leave this letter in your hands, but an accident placed me in a position to convey you a timely warning."

"Indeed! What is it?"

"As I entered——"

"How did you enter?" asked Rupert, eagerly, as he fixed his eyes on the black aperture beside the fire-place, for the panel had not closed of itself.

"No matter *how* I entered, Master Redmond," was the reply. "I would willingly tell you how, and acquaint you with the many mysteries of this house—mysteries with which the host and every man who has ever owned this house, know not of—but I dare not. Yet stay! One secret I will show you, but that will be solely for your own protection. Now you must first read the letter, and I will then tell you of my discovery."

Rupert tore open the letter, which, in appearance, was the exact counterpart of the first, and read these words—

"Sir Ferdinand Lockhart, Richard Melburn, Mistress Melburn and Miriam are about to go to London. Sir Ferdinand is making the journey ostensibly to consult with the king; but it is believed that the journey is made in order to carry out the compact made between Sir Ferdinand and the Melburns. It is supposed that Sir Ferdinand is about to marry Mistress Melburn, and Richard will marry Miriam. The party will set off to-morrow morning.

"MORNA."

"Never!" cried Rupert, crushing the letter in his hand. "He shall never marry Miriam! I will rescue her from their clutches at all hazards. Great heavens! this warning has, I fear, come too late."

"Not by any means," was the calm reply. "This letter left Whalley this morning. The party will set out to-morrow morning, and as they will have to take a coach, you have plenty of time to decide what should be done. But now for what I was about to say, for I have no time to spare. In entering this house I passed through the vaults at the back. Reaching a cellar, the flap of which looked into the yard, I heard voices. Listening for a moment, I was soon convinced that the persons talking were not connected with the house.

"From what they said it appears evident to me that their intention is to rob someone within this hostelry. I thought it might be you they intended to rob."

"Nay," replied Rupert, "they can have no designs upon me. I have never made a boast that I am in possession of any money. Neither, indeed, am I, for though I hold a draft on a Lombard Street banker for a large amount, it is of no value but to the owner."

"Well, it struck me that you had some suspicion that all was not right."

"How so?"

"Because, instead of finding you in bed, as I expected, I find you fully dressed."

"I was too restless and uneasy to go to bed," replied Rupert, "and I am now glad that I did not do so."

"The news I have given you does not render you uneasy?"

"By no means."

"I am certain you will find before long that London swarms with robbers —ay, and assassins—men who think nothing of sacrificing a human life for a few paltry guineas. But mark this, Rupert Redmond."

And the mysterious visitor led Rupert across the room, to where stood a tall sideboard and cupboard combined.

"No doubt you have used this since you have been here?" asked the stranger.

"I have," replied Rupert, who thought it quite possible that the man would suddenly disappear through the cupboard before his eyes. "A few of my articles are within it."

"Pray open it."

Rupert did so.

"You see nothing?"

"See nothing?" repeated Rupert, fixing his eyes intently upon the interior of the cupboard. "No, I do not see anything particular."

"Place your hand at the bottom, and on the right."

Rupert did so.

"Now what do you feel?" asked the man.

"I feel an iron rod."

"Good. Now if anything happens while you stay here and occupy this room, you will enter this cupboard— which you can easily do by removing the first shelf—and if you pull the rod upward, the flooring whereon you stand will descend."

"Marvellous! But whither will it descend?"

"Into a closet on the next floor, and which is fixed in a bedroom. I tell you this secret so that you can escape from any danger which threatens you in this apartment."

"I sincerely thank you, and trust that during my stay here, which will be until day dawns only, nothing will happen which will cause me to avail myself of the secret you have taken the trouble to explain."

"And now, Rupert Redmond, adieu."

"Adieu, and thanks for your service."

Turning swiftly, the man advanced to the aperture, through which he instantly disappeared, and the panel resumed its former appearance.

Rupert examined it from top to bottom, but no trace could he discover of a secret spring.

"'Tis now too late to retire," he thought, "even if I felt disposed to go to bed, which I do not. Nay, I will snatch what sleep I can in this chair."

It was, however, a long time ere sleep visited his eyes, but at last he dropped off.

He was awakened by a loud crash, as of the shattering of glass.

At once starting up, he saw that the lamp had burned very low, so that the room was in a state of semi-darkness.

"In the name of heaven what could that have been?" thought Rupert. "Surely I could not have been dreaming? It could hardly be——"

He was interrupted by a loud cry, as of a person in pain, and there was heard a voice shouting for help.

At the same moment there was a violent knocking on his door, and Stephen's voice was heard shouting in terrified tones—

"Master Redmond! Master Redmond! for heaven's sake come and help! My master is attacked by robbers!"

Again arose loud shouts, and then high above them Rupert distinctly heard the clash of steel, as if a furious and determined fight was being waged below.

At once Rupert remembered the warning, and the fact that his strange visitor had said that he heard the voices speaking of jewels, and Stephen's information as to his master's errand at once occurred to him.

He turned, as if to rush to the door and admit Stephen, but instead of doing so, he shouted to him to descend the stairs.

Dashing to the cupboard, he pulled the shelf out, and hurling it and its contents to the floor, jumped into the cupboard, and pulled the rod as he had been directed.

The cupboard at once commenced to descend, and in the most rapid and noiseless fashion.

In the meantime the cries and the clashing of steel below had continued; but as the extraordinarily - contrived cupboard abruptly stopped, a far wilder cry rang out.

It was a cry of " murder! " uttered in tones which left no doubt in Rupert's mind that the person who gave utterance to it was in imminent danger of his life.

Where the door which led to the bedroom was Rupert, of course, had not the remotest idea ; but making a plunge immediately before him, the woodwork yielded, and the next instant he found himself in the bedroom occupied by his grace, the Duke of Buckingham.

A most extraordinary scene was presented to his astonished eyes.

The two rooms—the best in the house —communicated one with the other by a pair of folding doors.

These were thrown wide open, and between them, only partially attired, the front of his shirt saturated with blood, which fast trickled from a wound he had received, stood a tall, handsome young man.

It was the Duke of Buckingham.

Armed only with a sword, which, however, was now broken at the point, he was valiantly defending himself from the attacks made upon him by several men.

The wide-open window showed plainly enough that the balcony had been utilised as a means of ingress by these ruffians.

Rupert's rapid glance told him that the duke had defended himself to some

purpose, for two men lay on the floor, one dead, the other writhing in agony.

Four horrible wretches, whose appearance at once told Rupert that they were some of the lowest ruffians London could boast, were attacking his grace with terrific fury.

Had not help been at hand, it is certain that the duke's life and property would have been forfeited, for he was now so weak from loss of blood, that more than once he reeled as if about to fall.

All we have described was taken in almost at a glance by Rupert.

Not an instant did he pause.

Drawing his sword he rushed forward, and placed himself before the duke, who, astonished at his sudden appearance, at once fell back.

The men were no less astonished.

They had neither heard nor seen him make his appearance in the bedchamber.

For the space of a few moments the men paused ; then with a cry of rage they attacked Rupert, and with such fury that he was compelled to fall back several paces.

They were powerful men, but their knowledge of the sword was the knowledge of the bloodthirsty assassin.

The tallest and evidently the most powerful of the four, with a savage oath plunged forward, and raised his long rusty blade to strike.

His sword descended, but the blow was easily warded off, and the next instant down came Rupert's blade fair on his head.

The effect was fatal to the ruffian.

The man, giving utterance to a fearful scream of agony, dropped lifeless at the feet of his companions.

All this had taken but one-tenth part of the time it takes us to write it, and, in the meantime, the whole household had been aroused by the shouts of the duke, the cries of Stephen, the ringing of the steel, and the loud tramping of the ruffians' boots on the floor ; and as the crowd of visitors and servants increased, the terrified host summoned up sufficient courage to thunder upon the door with a monstrous stick.

But the duke did not attempt to open the door.

Weakened, as we have said, by loss of blood, and the tremendous exertions he had made, he stood in a leaning attitude against the bed, watching, as if fascinated, the rapid passing of Rupert's weapon.

There appeared to be something extraordinary about this blade.

It was the one which had been presented to Rupert, together with the pistols, by Fendyke.

A magnificent weapon it was, certainly, but it was not the excellence of its workmanship that caused the men to utter astonishing cries.

What was it, then?

It was this—that the blade, wielded with such marvellous rapidity and such deadly effect by Rupert, seemed possessed of the power of emitting flashes of fire.

Rupert had wielded this weapon with effect before, but until this moment he had not noticed that the sword appeared to be possessed with power distinct and different to that of any blade he had previously handled.

The fall of the tallest and, it seemed, the principal man of the four, had the effect of causing the others to pause.

But it was not a long pause.

Exasperated beyond measure at being so completely foiled, the three made a dash upon Rupert.

Again the terrible sword was raised and brought into play with telling effect.

The three men seemed to be absolutely dazzled by the extraordinary rapidity of Rupert's passes, so much so that the centre one, losing all command of himself and stepping a pace or two in advance of his companions, met a sudden death, for, as swiftly as the lightning's flash, Rupert's blade passed completely through his heart.

All thoughts as to the jewels vanished from the heads of the others.

Uttering cries of terror and alarm, they fled back to the window.

But one never reached it, for Rupert, drawing one of his pistols, fired.

The aim was true.

The ball took effect in the shoulder of one of the men, and giving utterance to a piteous howl, he fell backward to the floor.

Just as the shot was fired the duke recovered himself sufficiently to be able to open the strong oaken door.

Directly the door was opened the people swarmed in.

Plenty of light was now directed upon the scene, for several of the servants carried lamps and tapers, which, however, were held by fingers which trembled like the leaves of an aspen.

Stephen was the first to rush in.

His face was deathly pale, and he was in such a state of excitement that great drops of perspiration were rolling down his plump cheeks.

No sooner did his rolling eyes rest upon his master than, clasping his hands, he fell upon his knees, and gave expression to the intense joy which filled his bosom, by exclaiming in loud, fervent tones—

"Thank heaven! thank heaven! my master is safe!"

"Your grace," cried the host, holding his arms extended, so that the excited guests and servants should not crush too far forward, "I pray you, shall I send at once for a doctor?"

"Nay, I thank you. I shall not require his services."

"But, your grace, you are most greviously wounded. You are smothered in blood."

"That is true. I have received a good cut or two, master host, but nothing more. Stephen, procure bathing materials and a skin bandage; and, master host, let one of your servants procure me some brandy."

"To be sure. Oh, your grace, I would have lost half the money it has been my fortune to make that this had not occurred. We can never hope that your grace will again patronise our establishment."

"Do not fear, master host, I shall patronise it. You cannot help what has occurred. Every hostelry is liable to the attacks of these ruffians. But we are forgetting this young gentleman," he added, quickly turning to Rupert. "Your name, brave sir?"

"Rupert Redmond, your grace, at your service."

"Redmond—Rupert Redmond," mused the duke. "It seems as if I had heard that name before. I may remember presently."

Aloud he said, as he held forth his hand and, taking Rupert's, most warmly pressed it—

"For the inestimable service you have rendered, Rupert Redmond, I thank you."

His voice, charged as it was with emotion the most intense, left no doubt in the minds of everyone present as to his sincerity.

"If," continued the duke, "I can at any future time be of service to you, command me, and you shall see that my gratitude will be shown in anything you may require—that is, anything that it is in my power to do. By the soul of the blessed Virgin!" he cried with a burst of admiration, "your sword is a weapon to be kept from at a safe distance! Never did I behold a sword wielded with such marvellous rapidity and dexterity. You are indeed master of the weapon, Rupert Redmond. But we will talk together in a moment. Host, yonder man, who has been the recipient of a bullet, is not, as you observe, dead. I pray you, therefore, let your servants attend to his wound, give him some sort of stimulant, and then let him be given into custody. A rope and a short shrift shall be his portion."

"And well will he deserve it, your grace," replied the host, advancing to the man.

He had not lost consciousness, and had heard all that had taken place.

He had recognised the fact that the individual they had attempted to rob was a person of high importance, and he knew, therefore, that the threat of a rope was no idle one.

The servants soon got him to his feet, and conducted him towards the door.

There the duke called a halt.

Taking a lamp from one of the servants, he held it immediately before the man's face.

"Your name, scoundrel?" he asked.

"John Eccles."

"You and your companions came here to get possession of a certain case containing jewels?"

"I'll not deny it," replied the man, hoarsely. "And anything else we could lay our hands on."

"How did you get to know about the jewels?"

Stephen winced, not with fear, but with apprehension, for he wondered whether he had inadvertently mentioned the matter to anyone other than Rupert.

"Why should I tell you how we got to know?" growled the ruffian.

"Because I command you to tell me," replied the duke.

"Tell you or not, I suppose I may expect the rope?"

"Better answer," said the host, "and perhaps the duke may show you leniency."

"Yonder man," said the ruffian, pointing to the one Rupert had first sent to his account; "yonder man saw a coach roll up to the goldsmith's in Lombard Street. At the time he was disguised; he entered, and overheard the fact as to the delivery of the jewels. But he told us the gentleman was *servant* to a nobleman, instead of, as I see now, the person being the nobleman himself. Well, we have had a good try for them, and they were worth trying for, and," he added, directing a fierce, savage look upon Rupert, "had it not been for *him*, we should have had them."

"Not *all* of you," replied the duke, grimly, as he pointed to the men he had slain. "Well, my man, fortune went against you this time. Take him away, for the *look* of the villain turns my blood cold."

Stephen by this time had approached Rupert, but he was so overawed by his attitude and the blood-dripping sword he still held, that he did not offer to speak.

"Stephen," continued the duke, "superintend the removal of these men."

This was soon concluded, the men being unceremoniously bundled down the stairs and placed in a disused cellar.

The duke's head was then bathed, the hostess having this honour; for so she and all the servants considered it. And his wounds having been carefully bound, the window was securely fastened by the host.

"Pardon me, your grace," he said, "but may I be allowed to ask this valiant young gentleman a question?"

"To be sure."

"Master Redmond," said the host, "will you be kind enough to inform me how you managed to get within these apartments? I am curious to know, because, until his grace opened it, the door was locked."

"Ha! to be sure," said the duke, "the matter had slipped my memory. Pray give us this information, Master Redmond."

Rupert never expected this question. What was he to do?

Should he reveal the secret?

A few seconds' consideration only, and he concluded that he ought to do nothing of the kind.

Since he had been in the bedchamber he had looked around very carefully.

But he himself failed to see the place where he had entered.

The walls to the right and left were apparently firm and solid.

The secret portion through which he had entered had noiselessly closed of itself, and he had no more idea than those present as to where that portion was.

"It may seem strange to you," replied Rupert, "but I must decline to answer your question."

The host was thunderstruck at the reply, and he showed it, too.

"Am I to consider, sir," he said, "that you are a person in league with the Evil One himself?—that you are a person capable of going through stone or brick walls, or what?"

"Can you really not answer, Master Redmond?" queried the duke, who was much astonished at Rupert's reply.

"I would rather not; in fact I am *incapable* of answering."

"Passing strange," said the host. "Well, young sir," he added, in severe tones, "though I certainly admire your bravery—though I certainly must admit, as the noble duke himself does, that, but for your opportune arrival, his grace must have been murdered, I nevertheless cannot again let apartments to a person who is such a mystery."

"Retire host," cried the duke; "perhaps the young man will presently change his mind, and give you the particulars you seek."

"I trust it may be so," said the host; "and let me add, Master Redmond, that if a—but no—I mean no insult. But I would crave permission to say that I would willingly pay down the sum of a hundred guineas to learn how Master Redmond flashed from his room into this. Heaven's blessing on us all! The years and years I have lived here, your grace, and never before was I so utterly astounded as I am at this moment. I do hope Master Redmond will, as you hint, feel inclined to change *his* mind and thus ease *mine*."

"My endeavours shall be used to so persuade him," replied the duke, closing the door on the host.

The duke, without seeking Stephen's aid, now quickly attired himself, and well did he look in his handsome costume.

"My sword, as you see," he said, "is broken. But, nevertheless, I will place it in its scabbard, for it rendered me excellent service. That fellow's head must have been remarkably hard, for my blade snapped on his skull for all the world as if it had been dashed on to a blacksmith's anvil. Master Redmond, will you permit me to look at your blade?"

"With pleasure, your grace," replied Rupert, at once unsheathing it and handing it to the duke.

The crimson stains he had partially wiped off with his kerchief, but *only* partially, when he had sheathed it.

But *now* it was as *bright* as if it had but just left the hands of the finisher.

Its brightness was dazzling.

Rupert was astonished, and so was the duke, who attentively examined the blade.

"A very valuable weapon," he said. "What is the value of this, think you— this stone at the hilt?"

Rupert had noticed the stone, but he had not considered it of much importance.

"I am quite unable to inform you, your grace," he said.

"It is a ruby," continued the duke, "and an extraordinarily large one; and here I see are some letters."

He was right!

And these letters Rupert had entirely overlooked!

His surprise was now intense, and his features betrayed his astonishment plainly enough.

"The letters are of a mystic character," continued the duke—"letters one would expect to see in some ancient tome. Though I know something of Latin, which these words resemble, I do not think I could--no, it would be impossible for me to attempt to decipher them. Perhaps *you* can interpret them?"

"I am not by any means the scholar that your grace must be," replied Rupert; "and I must confess to you that, until you pointed them out, I had not noticed the letters, which are most curiously formed."

"No doubt the weapon was presented to you by a very dear friend?"

"Nay, your grace, the sword was presented to me by—by one who takes a great interest in me. At the same time was presented to me this pair of pistols."

And he handed them to the duke, who, just beneath the lock-guards, observed characters similar to those on the sword.

"I advise you to take every care of them," he said, "for there is something remarkable about these weapons. I am not superstitious, but I am fully persuaded that there is something entirely out of the common connected with them. But now let us be seated. You will drink with me?"

Rupert required nothing; but thinking he might offend the duke if he refused, he said he would do as his grace wished.

"Now," continued the duke, "I have, I fancy, remembered why your name particularly struck me. The name of Redmond was mentioned to the king yesterday in connection with some terrible proceedings at Pendle Forest, which, it appears, is the home of all that is dark and mysterious, and also the home of a host of wretches, called the Black Witches. Over all these, as I understand, reigns a man of mystery, who styles himself Morna, the meaning of which name I, at this moment, forget. But you, of course, have no connection with the Redmonds mentioned to the king, so tell me what you know——"

"Your grace," interrupted Rupert, "I am the one whose name was mentioned!"

The duke started from the table as if he had been shot.

"Who then," he cried, "have I been talking to? Great powers! *you* the Redmond mentioned in the dispatch to the king?"

"One moment, your grace. From whom did the dispatch come?"

"Of the matter I know little; but I remember that the dispatch came from Sir Ferdinand Lockhart, who is about to clear the whole of Pendle Forest of these fiends in human form; but it strikes me that the king will find a better man than Sir Ferdinand Lockhart for the business."

"Your grace, may I be allowed to ask you to resume your seat, and to listen to the story which I would tell you?"

"You have rendered me a great service and I cannot refuse what you ask," answered the duke, resuming his seat.

Rupert told his story steadily, evenly, and with great feeling.

But, as might be supposed, he made no mention of the many mysteries with which he had been made acquainted.

The king's favourite listened intently to the story he told.

He was greatly interested.

On its conclusion he said—

"From what you say, Master Redmond, this Sir Ferdinand and Richard Melburn must be a pair of scoundrels!"

"They are, indeed, your grace!" cried Rupert; "and the story I have told you, before heaven I swear it is true."

"I believe you. Soh! Sir Ferdinand will play a double game, eh? And so, indeed, will his confederate, Richard Melburn."

"Your grace," said Rupert, "you said you would do me a service if it lay in your power."

"Ay, so I did, and so I will. What is it?"

"Advise me."

"Well, that is a reasonable request. I *will* advise you, my young friend, for in the future I *will* be your friend, but you must promise me most faithfully that the fact of my advising you shall be kept a profound secret."

"I promise that solemnly."

"Be seated then, and, here, another glass will not hurt you. Now, here is success to the plan I shall disclose to you!

"Listen! You have received positive proof that this poor girl will be forced into a marriage with the brutal Richard Melburn. Good! Of course they are about to come to London and go to the mansion of Walter Dubois —I know it well—feeling certain that they will not there be interrupted; for they do not know you are in London.

Now, to effect an entrance into this mansion would probably be a difficult matter. I would not advise you to attempt it. What I advise is this—that you intercept the party on the road."

Rupert started.

It was a bold proposition, and how was it to be done?

"Your grace," he said, "I would make the attempt if I had one I could depend on to assist me."

"To be sure. I am coming to that. If you agree to make the attempt, I will send you one on whom you can rely—one who will flinch at no danger, nay, one who glories in running any great risk."

"I should be happy, indeed, to make the acquaintance of such a person," replied Rupert; "and since I can have one to assist me, one on whom I can rely, the attempt shall be made."

"If you show the same determination and courage which you have shown here, Rupert Redmond," said the duke, warmly, "the attempt is bound to be successful. You and the person I shall send you will find out the darkest point of the road along which they will travel, and you will make a sudden and determined dash on the coach. Taken by surprise, and thrown into a state of terror, you can manage to place the poor girl behind you on your horse. Have you a horse?"

"I have; and a more powerful or fleeter animal was never shod."

"Good! When you have your sweetheart behind you, away you go at your topmost speed. And now, respecting your desire to see the king. Well, I will do what I can for you. Rely upon that, for I owe my life to you."

"I am afraid, your grace, that should Sir Ferdinand Lockhart get the king to listen to him before I can, he will damage my reputation beyond all redemption."

"If your attempt on the coach prove successful," smiled the duke, "I fancy that all Sir Ferdinand's thoughts as to his interview with the king will be knocked out of his head. Now I shall be taking my departure as soon as it is daylight, and within an hour afterwards, the person I have spoken of shall visit you. And now before we part, let me ask you—do you intend to reveal the secret of the way you so suddenly appeared here?"

"Your grace, I must decline to do so, for did I reveal the secret, I should be revealing what is not mine, and violating a solemn promise."

"Well, well, though I certainly should like to know, I will not press you. You must do the best you can with the host."

At daylight the duke's coach rolled up to the hostelry, and his grace entered.

Despite the endeavours of the host to keep the particulars of the terrible tragedy which had occurred a profound secret, one of the servants had spread the news, and the duke found the coach surrounded by a mob of people, who greeted him with deafening cheers as the lumbering vehicle rolled off down the yard.

It was past eleven of the clock when Rupert, looking from his window, saw a horseman ride up to the door.

In a few moments a knock came upon the door of his apartment.

Opening it, he admitted a tall, powerful and active young man, of about his own age, attired as a well-to-do citizen.

"I came from the duke," said the visitor, producing a note and handing it to Rupert.

"You are very welcome," replied Rupert, "for I was beginning to fancy that, after all, the duke's many engagements might be the means of causing him to forget his promise."

"On further acquaintance with his grace," was the smiling reply, "you will find that he forgets nothing—at least, nothing of importance."

Rupert opened the note and read these words, which had evidently been hurriedly written—

"The bearer's name is Reuben Renard. His advice is frequently acceptable. Remember that I await the result of your journey with interest."

"Master Renard," said Rupert, holding forth his hand, "most happy am I to find a companion. I was fancying that the duke would send me some old soldier. I am indeed happy to find my companion a young man of about my own age."

Reuben Renard warmly clasped Rupert's hand.

"I trust," he said, that our acquaintance will not end on the termination of our first adventure, which, I sincerely hope, may prove entirely successful. And now, as the distance to be reached by nightfall is very great, I propose that we partake of some refreshment, and at once set off."

"Agreed! And now, Master Renard, it strikes me that you have some sort of resemblance to the duke, himself."

"Truly. I am distantly related to him—in fact, I am a relative with no expectations. Ha, ha! I am, as the duke is pleased to call me, a youngster of Fortune, and I hope you are the same—not that I would have everyone like myself—a dependant on the purses of others, but because, if you are the same as myself, there is all the more reason why our acquaintanceship should prove a firm and a lasting one. So now let us call the host, and order what we require."

The bell was rung, and the host himself answered it.

His face did not wear a pleased expression by any means.

He directed a keen, significant glance upon Rupert, who, however, took no notice of it.

He was determined not to reveal the secret.

The order for the required refreshment having been given, the host said—

"A word with you, if you please, Master Redmond."

Rupert accompanied him outside the door.

"The most diligent search has been made in the room occupied by the Duke of Buckingham," said the host, "but all attempts to discover any secret passage have been fruitless. Now will you, before you go, be pleased to tell me how you managed to get from this apartment to that below in such a mysterious fashion; for, as you are, like myself, only flesh and blood, it is impossible that you can have dropped through the ceiling."

"Again, I must refuse you the information you seek," answered Rupert; "but I swear most solemnly that the secret shall never by me be used to your disadvantage."

The host was highly discomfited, as his face plainly testified.

"You look an honest young man," he said, "and that you are a courageous one there can be no question; but still I cannot understand you. I shall never rest until the mystery has been penetrated."

Rupert and Reuben set out on the journey soon after taking their repast.

Reuben's horse was a powerful animal; it was, indeed, one of the best from the duke's own stables.

Both, therefore, were splendidly mounted, and both were well armed, and they looked fit for any fight or adventure.

CHAPTER VI.

SHOWS HOW RUPERT AND REUBEN ATTACK THE COACH—OF THE RESISTANCE—AND OF THE RESULT.

THE actual object of Sir Ferdinand's visit to London was certainly to see the marriage carried out between Richard and Miriam, though, at the same time, he was most anxious that his own marriage should take place in *case* Mistress Melburn should think fit to change her mind. And he determined that the ceremony, or ceremonies, should take place at the mansion of Walter Dubois — Chelsea Priory—with which great, beautiful, though in many respects, mysterious residence, we shall presently deal.

On the night previous to the departure, Sir Ferdinand and Richard held a long consultation.

"We had better now arrange all details," said Sir Ferdinand. "We have already decided that your mother, Miriam, and her maid, Margaret, shall travel in the coach."

"Yes; they must go in the coach," replied Richard, "and you must ride on one side, and I on the other; for if we do not, it is likely that Miriam will shriek for assistance. What I have been thinking is this : Would it not be the better plan to gag her ? "

"Miriam," replied Sir Ferdinand, with a grin, " is nearly yours. Do as you like with her ; but I do not think that the gag will be necessary. I will warn her maid."

"There is only one coach at present here," said Richard—"a lumbering old thing. However, we must make the most of it. I will place in it six of the most powerful horses I have. And now, have you discovered Rupert Redmond ? "

" Nay, not one sentence have we heard of him. He has disappeared as if one of the witches had snapped him up, and whisked him clean off the earth. As to Miriam's constant raving——"

"Sir Ferdinand," interrupted Richard, savagely, " when Miriam is mine, I will avenge myself on her. She shall suffer for the insults she has heaped upon me through that hound, Rupert Redmond. I will break the proud heart of the beauty ! I will crush her as I would crush a worm ! "

"Or as you would crush Rupert Redmond could you get hold of him," said Sir Ferdinand ; " but there is one thing, Richard, though we have no suspicion as to what has become of Rupert, we know that his father is beyond the power of offering us any obstruction. We have received the most positive assurance that he has gone abroad."

" Yes, I think that is certain ; but the son remains. However, we have nothing to fear from him. It is, however, just as well to be on our guard, Sir Ferdinand, so I propose that we take with us four of our most trusted men—two of yours and two of mine. I propose that they ride at a distance from the coach— say a hundred yards. Thus, if anything unexpected happens, such as an attack by highwaymen, we can instantly summon them to our assistance."

" It shall be done ; but I cannot spare Hawkswell. He must remain in charge of the Abbey."

"You have men in your service who can handle a sword, or a pistol far better than Hawkswell," said Richard. "Select whom you please, while I will do the same. The marriage concluded— Miriam's vast wealth mine—I will set about finding Rupert Redmond. I

would willingly give up one-half of what will be mine if I knew where I could set my men upon him at this moment."

Before they separated the men were selected, as were the horses.

When they set out, six powerful horses were harnessed to the coach, and these were controlled by three men acting as postilions.

Behind them, at a distance of a hundred yards or so, rode four more men, each well mounted, and armed to the teeth.

Miriam was conveyed from the Abbey in a sedan-chair.

Whither she was about to be taken she had not the remotest idea, neither had her maid, though she repeatedly tried to obtain some inkling as to the destination of her mistress and herself.

When Miriam and her maid were handed into the coach, they knew that the journey was to be a long one.

Sir Ferdinand and Richard, each thoroughly well armed, and mounted on two of the best horses that could be got, were the last to ride up.

Between them came Mistress Melburn, who was magnificently attired.

The whole of the proceedings had taken place in the courtyard of the manor, and in semi-darkness.

Many times had poor Miriam essayed to speak ; but on each occasion she had been checked by a gruff voice, saying—

" Preserve silence ! "

Miriam was amazed when the door of the coach was pulled open, and Mistress Melburn was handed in.

She looked hard into the beautiful face as if to read what was passing in her mind.

But nothing could be read there.

Miriam wondered whether this woman was as much her enemy as Sir Ferdinand, and as her son Richard.

Apparently Mistress Melburn divined her thoughts, for she said—

" Why weep ? Why not accept your fate calmly ? "

" Will you tell me whither we are bound ? " asked Miriam.

" To be sure," was the instant reply. " Has not Sir Ferdinand told you. We are about to go to your beautiful mansion at Chelsea. You do not remember it, of course. No, you must have been too young. It is a fine place they say. And I have no doubt we shall all be very happy there."

"What is the object of the journey?"

"Can you not guess?"

"I fancy I can, madam. I am about to be forced into a marriage with your son."

"I trust force will not be necessary; for by the time London is reached, you will have arrived at the conclusion that submission will be the best thing you can do."

"Never, madam! Never! I hate your cruel son! I have the same loathing for him as I have for a venomous reptile!"

"Oh! you *have*, eh?" hissed a voice, close beside her; "you *have*, eh? My turn will soon come, then beware!"

Uttering a slight scream, Miriam turned to see Richard's face staring in at the window.

Never did human face wear an expression of more savage ferocity and hatred than Richard's at this moment.

"Wait," he said, "wait until you wear on one of the fingers of that lily-white hand a band of gold, which proclaims you to be a wife. You shall then know what it is to insult me in the way you have! "By Hades! you shall suffer for it! Not one hour's happiness shall you know."

"Richard, Richard," cried Mistress Melburn, "how dare you utter such words?"

"Silence!" growled the villain.

"Richard," whispered Sir Ferdinand, "let us delay no further. I am impatient to proceed, for there is no telling where the spies of that accursed Morna might be. That imp of the Evil One, Fendyke, may not be far off. Now, my men, light the coach lamps, extinguish the torch, mount, and away!"

All were ready in less than five minutes, and the gates being thrown open, the coach proceeded.

Slowly at first it went, but the high-road being reached, and Richard having issued the command, away it went at a tremendous pace.

Four horses was the number usually attached to the vehicle, but, as we have seen, on this occasion it had six.

Sir Ferdinand was in terror until Whalley was left far behind, for he was apprehensive of the mysterious beings of the forest.

He was well aware of the power they wielded, and he had not for one moment forgotten his terrible experiences of the night in the forest and the chapel.

Little did he dream that Rupert Redmond was the possessor of that terrible secret — that secret he had thought so securely locked within his own black heart.

It is not necessary for us to give particulars of that journey—or at least the greater part of the journey—for nothing worthy of mention occurred.

Miriam had uttered no cries for assistance.

Her attitude was that of a person who had abandoned herself to utter despair.

Through the night the journey was continued, but when daylight dawned, a halt of several hours was made.

This, however, was quite contrary to Richard's wishes, for he would have continued the journey until it was concluded.

But the horses were tired out.

As soon as nightfall came the road was again taken, and, the horses being fresh, their speed promised to be as great as ever.

The host of the hostelry at which they had stayed most strongly advised Sir Ferdinand and Richard to stay for at least an hour or two longer.

"A storm has been brewing for a long time past, your worships," he said, "and it will not be long ere it bursts forth; and, from what I see of it, it will be a terrible one."

"We are used to storms," replied Richard, haughtily; "and even if one were now to commence, go we must."

"Remember, your worships, that you may be caught in the storm on Brickley Heath. Then what would you do? There is no place within miles at which you could seek shelter."

"If the storm breaks forth before we can cross the common," replied Richard, "we shall use our spurs unsparingly; and, besides, master host, there *is* a house within two miles of Brickley Heath. *You have forgotten the Round House.*"

The host stared.

"I know myself better than to mention that place to any of my customers," he said. "I should not like to think that any of them were acquainted with the notorious Morecombe, the poisoner."

"Were I you," snarled Richard, "I should put a bridle on my tongue. Take my advice, and don't call the owner of the Round House a poisoner, or you may live to rue it. Remember, Morecombe is an herbalist."

The host shook his head.

"Say what you like, my masters, you won't shake *my* opinion," he said.

The party had not proceeded much further than a mile before, from out the black, heavy sky, burst a dazzling flash of lightning.

It was followed by such an appalling clap of thunder, that the very ground seemed to shake. The spirited animals attached to the coach, as well as those ridden by Sir Ferdinand and Richard, plunged fearfully, and for some few moments it seemed as if they would become unmanageable.

But the repeated application of the spur and riding whips brought them somewhat to their senses.

The storm had burst, and it came on with a vengeance; the flashes of lightning and the peals of thunder were truly awful.

"Hold!" cried Richard, suddenly. "Where are we? Here everything is as black as ink, and the lightning does not enable me to see whether we are in the right path or not."

"We are on the edge of Brickley Common," replied the foremost postilion.

"But are we before the principal road?"

"I can't say, your honour; for I can't see a couple of feet before me."

"Let us proceed and risk it," said Sir Ferdinand, looking around him as if he feared that some mysterious personage would suddenly spring up beside him; the rain is beginning to fall, and if we don't proceed we shall be nearly drowned."

"But," answered Richard, "if we go on ahead without first ascertaining whether we are actually in the right path, we may suddenly find ourselves in the midst of some deep pool, from which it would be impossible to extricate ourselves. However, since there is no help

for it, why on we go. Now, my men, urge on the horses. By the saints, the storm increases every instant! I trust you are not frightened, Mistress Miriam?" he sneered, as he placed his face against the window.

No answer was returned.

She still sat in the same attitude of utter despair.

Mistress Melburn, however, was very greatly alarmed; so much so, that she had buried her face deeply in the cushions.

On again went the coach, and Richard having ascertained that the four men behind were proceeding all right, joined Sir Ferdinand.

At last it was evident that the wrong path had been taken.

Presently they reached a huge clump of trees, which, being divided in the centre, admitted the passage of a coach, and the horses were plunging through, when suddenly a bright flash lit up the darkness a little way ahead, and a sharp crack rang out.

There was no mistake about this.

It was no lightning this time; it was the flash and report of a pistol.

And the shot had been effective, for one of the leading horses stumbled and fell, pitching his rider.

The unlucky postilion's head came in contact with the trunk of a huge oak with stunning force.

"Highwaymen!" thundered Richard. "Look! I see two horsemen ahead! Ho! What ho! forward!" he roared to the men behind, who, in obedience to orders, had stopped every time the coach had come to a standstill. "What ho! Bring a link here!"

Sir Ferdinand had snatched his pistols from his holsters, and had fired them in the direction from which the shot had proceeded, but the only reply they elicited was a mocking laugh.

The hand which had fired the pistol was Rupert's.

He had been able to discover that this was the coach they wanted, for he had heard Richard's loud voice some distance off.

Well enough did he know that to cry "Hold!" would be useless.

No sooner had Sir Ferdinand discharged his two pistols, than both Rupert and Reuben rode forward.

"A CRY OF JOY ESCAPED RUPERT AS HE SAW LYING AT HIS FEET, HIS PISTOLS, SWORD, AND A BELT."

The darkness was here far greater than on the open common, owing to the huge trees which surrounded the spot, and the only light was from the two sickly oil lamps burning on either side of the coach, and the reflection of the flashes of lightning.

So when Rupert and Reuben rode forward, their features were not discernible.

Just as Rupert reached the coach door a flash of lightning of more than usual brilliancy made his features distinctly visible to those within the vehicle.

The first to recognise his face was Miriam.

Giving utterance to a piercing scream —a scream of heartfelt joy, she started up.

"Rupert! Rupert!" she cried in loud, passionate tones, "save me! oh, save me!"

"I am here for that purpose, Miriam," replied Rupert, "and I *will* save you— I——"

His voice was lost in a tremendous cry, uttered by Richard and echoed by his men, and to Rupert's and Reuben's astonishment they beheld no less than six men dashing upon them.

They had not bargained for this.

Not the slightest idea had they that Sir Ferdinand had four well-mounted, well-armed men in reserve.

The lightning, as the coach crossed the heath, revealed Sir Ferdinand and Richard only.

Sir Ferdinand heard Miriam's cry, and he communicated to Richard that they were stopped by Rupert Redmond.

The effect was electrical.

If Richard had been enraged by being stopped by men he thought were highwaymen, what was his rage now that he knew who had stopped them?

With a wild shout he himself led the advance, and the whole six of them flung themselves upon Rupert and Reuben.

In less time than it takes to write, two saddles were emptied.

Rupert shot one man dead, and one was stricken down by Reuben's bullets.

But there was no time to re-load, for Richard, Sir Ferdinand, and the men left, did not hesitate to fire, and a desperate sword fight was quickly in progress.

Once again was Rupert's marvellous sword wielded with deadly effect; for, of the two men left, one, missing his guard, fell backward on his horse, his head nearly cloven from his shoulders.

So desperate and determined was the fight on both sides that each man had risen in his stirrups, the better to fight. And amid the clashing of the steel and the roll of the thunder, were heard the piteous cries of Miriam and her maid.

But Mistress Melburn uttered no cry.

She had left the coach, and utterly forgetting that she was risking her life by so doing, was standing beside the door.

There cannot be the least doubt but that the battle would have terminated in favour of Rupert and his courageous companion had it not been for the two postilions, whose presence had been entirely forgotten by both sides.

Both of these men were tall brawny fellows, and had been watching their opportunity.

That opportunity presently occurred.

Both, when they set out, had been armed with daggers; but on the journey one of them had lost his weapon.

But he soon found an article which, as it proved, would be more effective than a dagger.

This portion of the heath, being the most densely wooded, was covered with pieces of timber, large and small, which had been torn from the huge trees during the recent storms.

Upon one of these pieces the unarmed postilion seized, and holding it in both hands, crept towards the combatants, his companion, the naked dagger ready in his hand, being beside him.

Miriam saw their intention, and she leaped from the coach and rushed madly to the spot.

"Rupert! Rupert!" she cried, "beware! Turn your horse— ah!"

She was too late, or rather, it was too late for Rupert to pay heed to her warning.

The huge, heavy piece of wood was raised on high, and brought down with fearful effect on our hero.

It was indeed a cruel, cowardly blow, but it received the hearty approval of Richard Melburn, by whom it was witnessed.

Reuben wheeled his horse round, and

raising his blade, aimed a furious blow at the coward.

But at the same moment the postilion, with the dagger, "hamstrung" his horse, the immediate effect of which was to bring horse and rider with a crash to the ground.

At the same instant Richard and Sir Ferdinand flung themselves from their saddles.

Rushing forward Richard seized Miriam by the shoulders, and violently shaking her, said—

"Ah! you thought to escape, eh? But you are mistaken. Back—back to the coach, or, by heaven, I will not be answerable for what I may do to you."

And Richard brutally dragged her back to the coach.

His face was livid with rage.

"Why couldn't *you* have prevented her from leaving the coach?" he yelled in his mother's ear.

Whether Mistress Melburn heard him or not we cannot say.

Certain it is that the savage voice of her son did not cause her to shift from the position she had taken up, one inch.

From the look upon her beautiful face—a face now as white and set as marble — and the staring look in her eyes, she might have been taken for a statue.

Richard paid no heed to her.

Thrusting Miriam into the coach he banged the door to, then observing that Margaret was close by, he seized her in the same unceremonious fashion as he had seized her mistress.

"Unhand me, brute!" she cried. "Unhand me, coward!"

"Go to *her!*" yelled Richard, pointing to Miriam, who had sunk upon her knees within the coach. "Go to *her.* Another time I will deal with you."

In the meantime the postilions, by directions of Sir Ferdinand had seized upon Reuben, and tied his arms firmly behind his back.

Just as this task was accomplished, Richard came up.

He found Sir Ferdinand, coach-lamp in hand, bending over the prostrate figure of Rupert.

"Is he dead?" he asked.

"Nay, not quite dead," was Sir Ferdinand's reply; "but I don't fancy there's *much* life left in him. By all the fiends, the blow delivered upon his head by Merlin, was enough to have felled an ox."

"Merlin!" shouted Richard. "Merlin, come hither, knave!"

The postilion who had dealt Rupert the cowardly blow came forward.

"Merlin," said Richard, "remember that I shall not forget your courage (!) and as soon as ever we return to Whalley a hundred golden pieces shall be yours."

"Better divide the sum with his companion," said Sir Ferdinand, "for he hamstrung the horse on which this wretch (pointing to Reuben) was mounted."

"No; there will be no occasion to *divide*," sneered Richard, "as you can as well afford to give the man a hundred pieces as I can afford to give this man the sum I named."

"Be it so. He shall have them. And now let us decide what is to be done with these two. How it rains! And the lightning is as bad as ever."

"I will tell you what is best to be done," replied Richard. "I would have something to say to this impudent pauper, and I will torture him."

"If you do not slay him where he now is," said Sir Ferdinand, "depend upon it you will have trouble with him in the future. Why should you preserve his life?"

"I will tell you," whispered Richard. I would question him respecting the mysterious occurrences at the abbey. I would wring from him the truth respecting a great deal of what has occurred at the forest. And, no doubt, you would like to penetrate the mystery——"

"Hold! hold!" gasped Sir Ferdinand, "I entreat of you speak not of the forest nor of its terrible occupants. When we lay all the particulars before the king, his majesty will speedily think of a plan to entrap the whole."

"Including the Man of Mystery?"

"Ay, including the fiend who calls himself Morna."

"And the man who is known as Fendyke?"

"Yes, Fendyke will be captured also."

"Do not be too sure of that. I fancy it will be pretty difficult to capture a man who possesses the power of disappearing through the earth at a moment's notice."

"A thing *you* have never seen him do."

"Have I not? I am not so sure of that. But I am certain of this—we have here the wretch I hate with all my soul. And he shall be preserved until I have the time to question and torture him."

"Where is he to be imprisoned?"

"He shall be conveyed to the Round House across the heath."

"Ha! you think of placing him under the care of Morecombe?"

"Exactly," chuckled Richard, a fiendish grin spreading over his face.

"Well, but to whom will you give the task of conveying him to the Round House?"

"Listen! The coach will not again be interrupted. So I propose that you take it under your charge. I require one man only. You can manage very well with the two postilions."

"What of the dead?"

"I will see that they are buried. And," he whispered, "I will question this youth, who was fighting with Redmond."

"Good; sound him well. Promise him any reward you think proper."

Up to this point the storm had continued with unabated fury, but now it lulled, and was fast rolling away.

"To horse, my men," cried Sir Ferdinand to the postilions; "to horse, and let us resume our journey. Yet stay; arm yourselves with the pistols and swords of these dead men. Thus, if we *are* again attacked, we shall be well prepared to defend ourselves."

The postilions, having armed themselves with the weapons of the fallen men, remounted.

The word was then given, and the coach resumed its journey.

Richard watched it until the dull glare of the lamps had vanished in the distance, and then turning to his man, said—

"Is your pistol loaded?"

"Yes, your worship," was the reply.

"Then stand here in front of this scoundrel, and if he attempts to move fire! I am going to get assistance from the Round House."

"But in case this Rupert Redmond happens to get up?"

"He will do nothing of the sort; for the simple reason that he is too much injured to rise without assistance."

For the first time Reuben spoke.

"Beware what you do, villains," he said, "or you may live to repent it."

"Silence!" shouted Richard, dealing him a tremendous blow on the shoulder with one of his pistols. "Silence!"

"Your action proves what sort of a ruffian you are," replied Reuben, scornfully.

"Ay, that may be. And *your* action proves you to be a highwayman, and, consequently, a person entitled to be put to death without ceremony."

"What do you propose to do with us? If it is your intention to put us in prison for the attempt on the coach, then let it be done quickly. My friend is in such a state that he requires instant medical attention."

"*Does* he?" sneered Richard. "Then he will not get it. But what I have to say to you shall be said elsewhere. Mornson," he said to the man, "attend to what I have said. And remember this—answer no questions."

So saying Richard galloped off.

Straight across the heath he went, and he did not draw rein until he had reached his destination.

The "Round House," so called on account of its being of circular shape, was a very ancient stone structure.

At one period of its existence it had been used as a small chapel and residence by a number of monks.

Closed for many generations, the property was sold to the Duke of Essex, who, after having it on his hands for many years, disposed of it to a man named Morecombe, who, for many years, had in London carried on an extensive practice as an apothecary, &c.

Richard rode up to the arched doorway, and, with the butt of his pistol, knocked gently at first, and then, receiving no answer, thundered upon it with all his might.

A little wicket, fixed in the door, was presently opened, and a voice asked—

"Well, thou noisy fool, and what do you want?"

"I want to see your master, and at once."

"Oh, oh! Why it's Master Melburn, isn't it?"

"It is; and knowing that, why do you not instantly open the door?" cried Richard, springing from his saddle.

"All in good time, my fine fellow; all in good time. Rome wasn't built in a day, and, moreover, you forget that my limbs are not so active as yours."

Another minute and the door was thrown open by an elderly, gaunt-looking man, who carried a smoking lamp in his hand.

"Master Morecombe is engaged in making a most important experiment," he said, "and it is very doubtful whether he will see you."

"Master Morecombe will be only too glad to welcome one of his best patrons," answered Richard, "so let there be no further delay. I am here on a matter of the greatest importance."

The man tottered off up the long narrow passage, and disappeared up a flight of stone steps.

Reappearing in a few moments, he told Richard to ascend.

As the villain reached the first landing a door in front of him opened, and Morecombe appeared.

He was a man of middle height, somewhat bowed though, and with hair and beard of great length, and as black as ink.

His countenance spoke volumes. Anyone at the first glance could see that the man was a villain of the blackest dye.

"Welcome—welcome, Richard Melburn," he said, in tones which, however, expressed anything but pleasure. "I suppose you have stopped here out of the storm?"

"You suppose wrongly. Besides, the storm is now fast passing away. Morecombe, I have no time to waste in reciting a long story of some remarkable events which have just happened on the heath. I will therefore give you a summary."

Richard's "summary" was one part truth and three parts falsehood.

No name did he give until he had concluded his recital, when he said, in reply to Morecombe's question—

"The name of the leader of this attack is Rupert Redmond."

No sooner was the name pronounced than Morecombe, giving utterance to a startled cry, exclaimed—

"The son of Randall Redmond?"

"Exactly. So *you* are acquainted with that upstart family, eh? As a friend or as an enemy?"

An expression of demoniacal rage instantly settled upon Morecombe's face as this question was asked in a sneering, derisive manner.

"Randall Redmond," he replied, hoarsely, "is not my friend. He has no greater enemy than myself. He stole from me the girl whom I had sworn to make my wife."

"You, of course, mean Rupert's mother."

"I do."

"Well," chuckled Richard, "this certainly is news to me. I always understood that you were no lover of women?"

"Neither am I. But I loved the woman I refer to years and years ago. Hard enough have I tried to ruin Randall Redmond. Soon after his marriage even, I had all his money stolen; but, by some mysterious means he very quickly got more—far more than was taken."

"Trouble no further about Randall Redmond," said Richard, "for, in order to escape the vengeance of Sir Ferdinand Lockhart, he has fled abroad."

"I can, however, revenge myself upon the son."

"Not so. You will, however, have the satisfaction of seeing *me* take my revenge upon him. Listen, Morecombe. You have told me that below in the vaults of this old dwelling, there are instruments of torture."

"Ay, so there are. Scores and scores of them."

"We will use a few of them on Rupert Redmond," chuckled Richard, rubbing his hands gleefully together. "And if his companion refuses to answer the questions I shall put to him, the torture shall be applied to him as well."

"Precisely. And old Macrone (this was the man who had admitted Richard) shall assist us. He passes much of his leisure in the cleaning and preserving of the instruments below, in which he takes a strange interest. But you want assistance, you say. Will my two men and old Macrone be sufficient?"

"Amply sufficient. Summon them at once. Have you a sedan-chair?"

"No. But do you mean to say that you would give Rupert Redmond this comfort? Pshaw! Let the men fling him across the saddle. He can be safely brought here in that fashion. Has he lost much blood?"

"I am unable to say."

"Humph! It may be more serious than you expect, and perhaps you will be baulked of your revenge. However, as soon as I see him I shall be able to tell in what condition he is."

Morecombe called his confidential assistant, Macrone, and gave him his instructions.

In a few minutes, Macrone and two other men, armed with pickaxe and shovels, set out with Richard, and they quickly reached the scene of action.

"Well," Richard asked the man, "has the wretch recovered consciousness?"

"He has not, your honour," was the reply.

"Good. And this one? Has he been asking you any questions?"

"He has never opened his lips."

"Very good. We shall make him open them directly, I'll warrant. Macrone."

"Here, your worship."

"Take this man, and throw him across one of the saddles."

"Ha, ha!" chuckled Macrone, who, as his master had hinted, was a very fiend for torture. He thoroughly enjoyed it in any form.

Rupert was seized upon, and in the roughest fashion possible, thrown across the saddle of one of the horses.

The dull thud told only too plainly what his treatment had been.

A deep groan left Reuben's lips.

Oh, if he had his arms free, he would soon get possession of a weapon of some kind, and exact a bitter vengeance.

The men set to work, and quickly dug a large hole in the thoroughly soddened earth.

Into this the bodies of the dead were thrown, and the earth shovelled in and trodden down.

Then Richard arranged the party, and the journey to the Round House was commenced.

The building being reached, Rupert was pulled from the horse, carried upstairs, and placed in Morecombe's chamber—his experimenting chamber— and afterwards Reuben, well guarded, was brought up.

"Look at this ruffianly hound!"

cried Richard, "and see whether you can recognise him."

Morecombe placed a pair of spectacles on his snub nose, fixed his little twinkling, cunning eyes upon Reuben's face, and closely scrutinised his features.

"Nay," he said, "I fail to recognise him; but judging from his dress, he is a person of no consequence."

"That is quite certain," answered Richard, derisively; "for if he were a person of the least importance, he would not be with Rupert Redmond."

Morecombe now examined Rupert.

That examination was a remarkably brief one.

"He has not lost a quarter of an ounce of blood," he said; "and that is the reason that he has remained unconscious for such a length of time. I will bring him to his senses in a few moments."

He was as good as his word.

From a shelf he selected one of a large number of small bottles.

Then he took from a case a lancet.

With the latter he quickly opened a vein in Rupert's arm, and one or two drops of the liquid contained in the bottle, he poured into his ear.

The result was not long waited for.

In a few seconds Rupert moved.

Then a series of sharp convulsive movements passed through his frame.

He sighed deeply, opened his eyes, looked about him in a dazed kind of way, and then softly uttered the name of Miriam.

That name, uttered, as it was, in tones of tender endearment, instantly aroused all the savage fury within Richard's breast.

He darted forward, and, with a howl like that of a wild beast, he dealt Rupert such a blow on the face with his open hand, that he rolled from the low table on which he had been placed to the floor.

"Brutal hound!" cried Reuben. "Would my hands were free, by all the saints I would have thy life! Cowardly wretch that you are, to strike one who is unable to raise his hand to defend himself."

"Beware!" hissed Richard, clapping his hand on his sword hilt. "Beware! I warn thee but that another word is required, and I will drive this blade deep into thy heart!"

"Ay, ay," sneered Reuben; "I've no doubt whatever about the matter. It is evident that you are brute enough for anything."

"Better keep your hands off Rupert Redmond," said Morecombe; "at least, for the present. Let him have time to collect himself. Not that I have any sympathy for him," he added, with a fiendish grin. "Ah, if his father knew that he was in the house of Morecombe! By Satan——"

"Whom you serve," interrupted Richard, with a chuckle.

"Ay, whom I have the honour to serve. Whose agents have instructed me in all the black arts practised by mankind, and who gave me a knowledge of drugs possessed by no other man."

"Except the Man of Mystery—Morna, as he is called—the mysterious individual who suddenly took up the mantle dropped by Bowolf, whom the Evil One claimed when his allotted time had expired."

"Bah! I am better informed than you, Richard Melburn—far, far better informed; and I know that Bowolf *died by his own hand!*"

Richard shook his head.

"You do not believe it?" continued Morecombe.

"No; I do not."

"Such is the case, then. Bowolf, for eighty years, endeavoured to find out a certain thing. He swore that he would continue in search of the secret if he should live to be a hundred years. In the course of his researches, it was revealed to him that he *was* to *live* one hundred years; but if, at the expiration of that time he had not discovered the secret, he was to die by his own hand, previously however, bequeathing all the property in his possession, together with all his secrets and mysteries, to another. That he has done, and the inheritor is Morna."

"And who is Morna?"

"That secret it has hitherto been impossible for me to penetrate; but I do not despair of eventually unravelling the mystery."

"Well, now let Rupert Redmond be removed—and bear in mind, Morecombe, that you are responsible to me for his safe custody."

"Trouble not yourself about his safe custody," replied Morecombe, with a grim smile. "Whoever gets within this old building, goes not hence without my consent. Macrone."

"Here, here, close handy," replied Macrone.

"Take this youth *below*. You know where?"

"I *fancy* so," replied Macrone, who thereupon calling in his men, had Rupert carried out of the apartment.

Up to this moment he had not recovered full possession of his senses.

He was still in a dazed condition, as was evidenced by the fact that, though he could see Reuben, no expression of recognition overspread his ashy, pale face.

"Now, then," said Richard, as he turned to Reuben, and folded his arms across his breast, "a word or two with you."

"I want no word with such as you," replied Reuben, haughtily.

"But," snarled Richard, "we have the power to detain you a close prisoner. If I did right, I should slay you for your insolence; but I will overlook it on conditions."

To this Reuben made no reply.

"You do not ask on what conditions," said Richard.

"No," was the reply.

"Well, listen. If you will answer the questions I shall put to you, I will let you go, and give you a handsome reward for your trouble. Now, your answer."

"It is this: untie my hands," replied Reuben, in firm tones, "give me a sword, and stand before me if you dare!"

"Insolent braggart!" cried Richard.

"I am not," replied Reuben, quietly. "If you will but loosen my arms, I will show you that I am not bragging."

"Since he will not comply with your request," said Morecombe, "he had better be placed below. A few hours in the vault Macrone will place him in will bring him to his senses."

"Very likely," replied Richard; "but since I cannot wait the few hours, he will be confined there three or four days. But again, sirrah, and for the *last* time," he thundered, stamping his foot with rage, "will you answer the questions I would put to you?"

"I will not."

"Then below with him!"

"Shall Macrone apply the torture?"

"Yes, he shall with a vengeance, when I return. Away with him, I say!"

Once again Macrone and his men were called, and Reuben was marched off between them.

"Now listen to it, Morecombe," said Richard. "Though our party have suffered much in this attack on the heath, I am glad it has taken place, because we know for certain where Rupert Redmond is; and we know that it is impossible he can now interfere with the marriage.

"Don't forget, that no matter what may happen—no matter by whom you may be summoned—you must not leave this house. I look to you for the safety of both the prisoners."

Morecombe burst into a wild laugh.

Rubbing his hands gleefully together, he said—

"I tell you again that it is *impossible* that anyone placed in either of the vaults can escape. Will you descend and examine the dungeons?"

"Not now. I repeat that I must set out."

"Be careful how you go, for you have now only one man with you."

"That is true; but I do not fear any further attack."

"Your man is mounted," said Macrone, who reappeared at this moment, "and is waiting with your horse."

Richard at once descended the stairs, followed by Morecombe, who accompanied him to the gate, where another short consultation took place between them.

Richard then rode off, his man following at a respectful distance.

CHAPTER VII.

OF WHAT REMARKABLE EVENTS OCCURRED WITHIN THE ROUND HOUSE—AND OF THE STARTLING AND TERRIBLE APPEARANCE OF THE MAN OF MYSTERY.

THE reader is familiar with two or three of the horrible dungeons within the Abbey.

But the vaults of the Round House were more loathsome, more strongly built, and in every way superior as places of confinement, to those owned by Sir Ferdinand Lockhart.

The chains affixed to the walls, and the rings fastened in the stone flooring, were of tremendous thickness, and powerful enough to have confined a Hercules.

Morecombe and Macrone, who was entirely in the former's confidence, had, from time to time, made thorough examinations of the place.

They had even gone so far as to dig up the flooring of one of the vaults in the hope of finding treasure.

Nothing of the sort did they discover.

But they found heaps of human bones, remnants of clothing, arms and armour.

Also they had found secret passages of most artful construction — passages leading to subterraneans of enormous length.

But though they were under the impression that the Round House contained no secrets, which were not known to them, they were mistaken, as the reader will presently see.

On the day following the attack on the coach, Rupert was visited by Morecombe, who was accompanied by Macrone and the two men.

Our hero felt stronger, but his head pained him dreadfully.

A good deal of what had passed between Morecombe and Richard he had overheard, and when alone he pondered deeply over it.

He soon remembered the name of Morecombe.

He recollected that his father had hinted that he was one of the most dangerous men anyone could deal with, and that he had an account with him, which, one day, perhaps, would be settled with death to one, or both.

Was this Morecombe the same man? Could he be the poisoner his father had mentioned?

At last he slept soundly for several hours.

He was awakened by the rattle of a key, and the falling of chains.

Rising with difficulty, for his waist

was encircled by an iron band of enormous thickness, to which was fastened a ponderous chain, he stood erect, and awaited the coming of his visitors.

Morecombe was the first to enter.

He was followed by Macrone, who carried a link, and the two assistants—wretches who had taken an active part in many a fiendish scheme.

"Soh !" Morecombe said, " you have recovered ? You are now in full possession of your senses, eh ? "

"I am," answered Rupert.

"Very well. Then you are in a fit condition to understand what I say. A stranger I am to you, to be sure ; but no stranger to your father. Are you aware of that fact ? "

"I know nothing of you, villain," said Rupert.

"Better *rouse* his recollection," growled Macrone.

"Whatever you may do would be of no aid whatever to my recollection," answered Rupert, "which, despite the brutal treatment I have received is perfectly clear."

"But all your thoughts are fixed upon the lovely Miriam, eh? I don't wonder at it. The Redmonds were ever in want. And it is not to be wondered at that one of their number wishes to fill his pockets by espousing the daughter—I mean Miriam Lockhart."

"It is false, villain ! " replied Rupert. "It was many a long day, after I first made Miriam's acquaintance, before I learned that she was an heiress."

"Ah, ah," sneered Morecombe; "tell that tale to Sir Ferdinand Lockhart or to Richard Melburn, and see whether they will feel inclined to believe such a statement. But now answer my questions.

"When you were captured, your sword was taken from you and placed in its sheath. The pistols also have been taken from their holsters, and the weapons have been examined by me. Each is marked with letters forming words of a mystic character. I have *tried*, but have failed to interpret their meaning. I, therefore, request you to do so."

"I am unable to satisfy you."

"How did the weapons get into your possession ? "

"I refuse to say."

"Pause and reflect," warned Morecombe.

"I require no time for reflection. I will not satisfy your curiosity."

"Those weapons were given you by a person skilled in mystery, someone familiar with secrets I would give half of the time I have to live to know. Tell me the name of this person."

"I will not."

"Beware. Close against this vault is a chamber filled with instruments of torture. I have but to give the word, and you would be dragged into it, and made to undergo the most excruciating agony."

"No agony would cause me to reveal a secret I have no right to divulge."

"I am determined that you *shall* answer me. Obstinate fool! Would you risk your life for the preservation of what you call a secret ? "

"I would."

"Dolt ! you will soon alter your tale. Hence with him, Macrone."

Macrone produced a small key, and unlocked the chain at the part where it was attached to the wall.

At the same time, Morecombe called to the men to have their pistols in readiness.

This they did, each man having a loaded pistol in each hand.

Rupert was escorted to an opposite chamber, the vaulted ceiling of which was crossed by ponderous oaken beams, which were fitted with huge iron hooks, rings, chains and ropes.

The walls were hung with implements of torture—instruments of most hideous and fantastic shapes.

"What shall first be used ? " whispered Macrone, his eyes glistening with fiendish joy.

"None will be used at present," replied Morecombe.

"None. Then why is he brought here ? "

"I wish to threaten him—to frighten him."

"Ah, you will have some difficulty in frightening him. And I wanted to show you the action of two or three instruments, the uses of which I have but lately learned," said Macrone, in disappointed tones.

"Be not impatient. I will give him six hours, and then if he still refuses to answer my questions, you shall use whatever tortures you think proper on him."

Aloud he said—

"Look around these walls."

"I am looking," replied Rupert.

"What do you see?"

"Instruments of torture; many of them similar to those hanging on the walls of the Abbey which owns the inhuman brute, Sir Ferdinand Lockhart, as its master."

"Sir Ferdinand Lockhart may have many instruments of torture in his possession," said Macrone; "but not any capable of producing such intense agony as those in my charge."

"Rupert Redmond," said Morecombe, "I will give you six hours for reflection. If, at the expiration of that time you still refuse to answer me, then I shall give my man full license to treat you as he thinks proper—perhaps torture you to death."

"I fear not," answered Rupert, scornfully. "You will find that no torture will cause me to answer you."

"We shall see. Back with him!"

"Mayhap his friend can answer your questions," suggested Macrone.

An eager, anxious look at once settled upon Rupert's face.

His anxiety was not as to whether Reuben would answer Morecombe's questions, but to learn how his comrade fared.

Morecombe noticed that look, and quickly interpreting it, he said—

"Ah, you would like to be informed respecting your haughty comrade, eh? Well, you shall learn all if, at the expiration of six hours, you answer my questions."

"And, in the meantime, shall the sword and pistols remain in my charge?" queried Macrone.

"No," answered Morecombe, sharply; "not for one instant shall that flashing blade and wondrous stone go out of my keeping."

Rupert was hurried back to the vault, and again locked to the wall.

Morecombe then quitted the dungeon, Macrone locking, bolting, and barring the door.

Several times on the way to the chamber used as an experimenting room Macrone spoke to Morecombe.

But he received no reply.

Morecombe seemed lost in profound reflection.

But when he reached his chamber, he said—

"My resolution is formed, and once again I must summon to my aid my master's agent."

"No, no," gasped Macrone. "I beg you will not do so. Besides, what do you need of him?"

"Information. I feel certain that this obstinate fool will not answer my questions, thus I should not be able to learn the meaning of these mystic characters, which it seems to me must have come from Pendle Forest. The one whom I am able to summon will give me the information I seek."

"How know you that?"

"Idiot! Is he not able to do anything?"

"But look at his price."

"That is my business, and not yours. Away to your quarters, and come not until you shall hear my summons."

Macrone hurried away with all speed, while Morecombe, throwing himself into a huge chair, the legs of which were the thigh bones of a human being, the two supports at the back being mounted with grinning human skulls, he once more gave way to reflection.

The mystic characters upon Rupert's weapons were agitating him in no small degree.

That he had seen those characters before he felt certain.

But the question was—*where?*

Suddenly leaping to his feet, Morecombe pulled open one of his drawers in the table and brought out the weapons.

Very closely did he examine the stone in the hilt of the sword, and carefully did he scrutinise the mystic letters, carefully weighing and pondering over each of them.

Then he drew the weapon from its sheath.

Instantly two flashes of dazzling brightness seemed to leave the blade.

So blinding in their intense brilliancy, and so swift were they, that Morecombe let the blade fall from his hands.

At the same moment a stifled cry of wonder left his lips, and he continued to look upon the glittering weapon like one fascinated.

After some moments of wonderment

and deep thought he picked up the sword.

But he did so very cautiously, as if afraid that the flashes would be repeated.

But they were not, and, with all speed, he returned it to its sheath, and replaced that and the pistols in the drawer, which he carefully locked, and placed the keys within the folds of his mantle.

Morecombe now lit a taper, extinguished the lamp, and then making sure that the door of the chamber was securely fastened, opened a cabinet and took out a number of human skulls.

Advancing to the centre of the chamber, he placed them in a circle, chanting the while in low, monotonous tones some strange incantation.

Then he placed within the circle of skulls a large ring of iron, and into this he threw a lighted piece of tow.

Into this again he threw the contents of several phials, as well as several handfuls of herbs.

The result of this extraordinary composition was, that flames of various colours and of dazzling brightness arose until they licked the vaulted ceiling.

The chamber was completely filled with such a blinding, suffocating smoke, that it seemed almost impossible that a human being could remain in it and live.

"The flames are straight," chuckled Morecombe, as he gleefully rubbed his hands together, "and that means that he whom I wish to see will appear at my call."

Gathering up his mantle, and seizing upon a long glass rod, he proceeded to go round and round the circle, stirring the fire as he went, and uttering a long incantation.

Pausing at last, he said in loud tones—

> "By the bones of the dead,
> By the flood and the fall,
> Haste hither, dread demon—
> Haste to me at my call!
> I call thee, dread demon,
> For I know thou art near;
> Again I command thee,
> Dread demon—APPEAR!"

The last word was shrieked out rather than spoken; and it was hardly uttered before a curious hissing noise was heard, the flames divided in the centre, and a tall, dark, red figure suddenly appeared before the Wizard Morecombe.

"What seek you?" asked this mysterious person. "Who am I to place in your power?"

"On this occasion no one," replied Morecombe. "I seek information."

"It shall be yours. But the same price must be paid as if you wished me to place in your power a man, woman, or child."

"I agree to it."

Morecombe rapidly told the story of Rupert's capture, and he then spoke of the weapons.

"Here," he said, "I will read the letters upon them."

And he spelled them out.

His astonishment was great when, instead of receiving an interpretation of them, the dark, red figure replied—

"I am powerless in the matter. Though I know right well what they mean, I dare not tell you."

"And why? In the name of your dread master—why?"

"Because the owner of these weapons is a Christian," replied the mysterious visitant. "And had you considered the matter as it should have been considered, you would not have summoned me."

"I implore you tell me the meaning of these letters," cried Morecombe, as he fell on his knees.

"I repeat," was the reply, "that I am powerless to do so. Many times have you summoned me, and I have always obeyed you. This is the only time I have failed to do your bidding; and I repeat once more, that I am powerless to do as you ask. Hark! I am summoned away. Farewell!"

Instantly he disappeared amid a volume of flame.

The moment he had vanished, the flames died out, and the chamber once again was illuminated by a solitary taper.

On his knees, in an attitude of despair, Morecombe remained for some considerable time.

"I will not abandon the hope of finding out the meaning," he muttered at last. "Every volume I possess will I search. And that failing, I will force it out of Rupert Redmond by torture. Yes; and he shall not only feel the torture, but he shall stand and witness the agony of his friend."

* * * *

In total darkness, in the silence of the grave, was Rupert buried.

So also was Reuben; and, though close against each other, it was impossible for them to hear each other's voices, for the walls were of solid stone.

How long after Morecombe and Macrone had taken their departure Rupert had been in the vault he had no means of telling; but he guessed it must have been three or four hours, if not more.

He had been thinking of Miriam—thinking of what was in store for her.

"They may torture me," he said, bitterly; "but what torture is in store for thee, my love? What torture could be greater than forcing thee to marry one you hate with all your soul?"

"Oh, this fearful suspense!" he cried, suddenly rising. "Can there be a more terrible torture than to remain here, chained like a wild beast, in a loathsome dungeon, in total darkness, and in silence —a silence which will soon drive me mad?

"Ah! what was that? A footstep? Has the time for torture come, and, perhaps, death also? Hark! *Was* that a sound? Or was it but imagination? Ha, there it is again! By heaven, it is near me! It is around me! How strange all seems!"

It seemed as if a person were using a rasp, and then it sounded like the distant pattering of feet.

Suddenly a blaze of light shot down from the vaulted roof—a light of wondrous brilliancy—which bore a striking resemblance to the mystic light our hero had beheld in the chapel in Pendle Forest.

Giving utterance to a cry, Rupert, forgetting the ponderous iron band and chain which fastened him to the wall, sprang forward.

Instantly the chain became unfastened, and fell with a loud clank to the ground.

Rupert, in astonishment, placed his hands on his waist.

The band had gone!

It had fallen to the ground with the chain.

"Fendyke! Fendyke!" cried Rupert, in low, trembling tones, "speak, I implore you! Fendyke, is it you?"

"No," replied a deep voice above. "Fendyke is miles away. Look on the ground at thy feet, Rupert Redmond."

Rupert looked. A cry of joy escaped him as he saw, lying at his feet, his pistols, his sword, and a belt.

When he again raised his eyes the strange light had vanished.

"Am I awake?" thought Rupert, now standing erect, and passing his hand across his eyes in a dazed kind of way.

"Yes; this is no dream. Here are the weapons—here in my hands. I clutch them firmly. I feel the coldness of the steel. No, this is no dream. My precious sword and my pistols are within my grasp. By the heaven above me look to thyself, Morecombe! for I will cleave my way through you and your villainous men, and rescue Reuben or die within these walls! Never shall it be said that Rupert Redmond left his friend to die without making an effort to save him. And now for action!

"Here is a strong belt—ah! the one I was wearing," he continued, as he felt for and picked it up. "Heaven! with what strange mysteries am I surrounded! Whose voice was that? I cannot think; my brain is in a whirl. But, thank heaven," he continued, in rapid, excited tones, while, at the same time, he buckled on the belt and thrust the pistols into their places; "I am free— free, so far as the chain and the accursed ring are concerned. Some attempt is being made to rescue me, for this is somewhat like the mysterious occurrences at the Abbey. But the voice—the voice. Whose was it? Could it be that of the Man of Mystery, he that takes so strange an interest in me?"

By this time Rupert had buckled on his sword, and loosened it in its scabbard.

"Something else may occur," he thought, as he impatiently began to pace the stone floor. "A portion of the wall, or even one of the columns may open."

But nothing of the sort did occur.

Once again all was as silent as the grave.

Rupert's impatience increased every moment.

He wondered whether Reuben had been so strangely visited.

Then again he wondered whether it was known to the Man of Mystery.

"Yes," he reflected, "that must be so, since he got to know that I was here. It is marvellous how these mysterious beings get hold of the information they do. Apparently neither bars nor bolts, nor stone walls obstruct them."

Presently he paused in his impatient pacing.

Though he had not heard footsteps advancing, he heard the key placed in the lock, and the bars being removed.

"The time has come," he muttered through his clenched teeth. "Heaven knows I am against the shedding of human blood; but it must be shed now, for I am determined to escape, and quite as determined that Reuben shall be free."

As he spoke, he drew his blade from its sheath.

It was Macrone who was unfastening the door; but Morecombe was beside him, and the rear was brought up by the two men, both of whom, as before, had a loaded pistol in each hand.

"The time he has been in here," said Morecombe, "has, no doubt, caused him to change his mind; and even now your pleasure may be spoiled."

"Not so," chuckled Macrone; "he is an obstinate fool, and you will find that he has not changed his mind. Though," he added, with a fiendish grin, "he may change it after one or two of my instruments have been applied to his limbs."

"No doubt," scowled Morecombe. "Now you two," he added to the men, as he placed one on each side of the door, "stand there and watch his movements narrowly. Now, Macrone, have you— but wait! I have thought of something. I will bring the sword down here, and promise to set him free, and present him with the weapon if he will tell me the meaning of the mystic characters."

Macrone did not think this was a good idea by any means. He wished to try the instruments of torture on the two prisoners.

He longed to see the captives' joints start from their sockets, and to hear them shriek and pray for the mercy which would not be shown them.

But he knew that he had better not tell Morecombe that he did not consider it a good idea.

"Don't throw the door open until I return," were Morecombe's last words.

And yet Macrone felt sorely tempted to open the door and taunt the prisoner.

Morecombe was absent but a few moments.

Then was heard a rapid pattering of feet, wild startled cries, and presently the poisoner dashed in between the three, looking more like a madman than anything else.

Certainly his starting eyes, his distorted face, and trembling hands would have led anyone to believe that he had taken leave of his senses.

It was some few moments before he could speak. At last he burst out—

"Marvellous! I said that these weapons were possessed of some strange power. They have vanished."

The men looked askance at the speaker.

"Vanished?" repeated Macrone. "How can that be? Did you not place them in your chamber?"

"I did."

"And under lock and key?"

"Yes, in a drawer. And I found the drawer as I had left it—locked; but the weapons were gone. Quick, quick!" he thundered. "Open the door, for I am under the impression that we shall find the prisoner gone."

"Fear not," replied Macrone, shaking his head. "We shall find him there."

So saying, he flung the door open.

Morecombe raised the link he carried high over his head.

But as he did so, Macrone and the men gave utterance to a fearful cry of terror.

There was a swift rush, what appeared to be flashes of lightning danced before their eyes, and the next instant one of the men lay upon the ground, his head cleft in twain by the dreadful blade Rupert wielded.

The other man, failing to pass Morecombe and Macrone, who were struggling desperately together to reach the stairs, he levelled his pistols at Rupert and fired.

Both weapons exploded with tremendous noise; but Rupert was not harmed.

The man never again pulled a trigger, for, in another moment, he lay dying across the body of his companion.

So sudden and unexpected had been Rupert's terrible onslaught, that neither Morecombe nor Macrone gave an instant's thought to defending themselves, though each was armed with a dagger.

Escape was the only thing they thought of.

Morecombe, by the exertion of all his strength, managed to reach the stairs first.

Macrone was about to follow him, when Rupert dashed upon him, and drew him backward with such force that he fell with a crash on the flags.

Rupert snatched a pistol from his belt and fired at Morecombe's retreating figure.

But it was too late.

Morecombe had turned the corner, and was thus out of the line of fire.

But the shot was so close to him that he heard it flatten itself against the wall.

Rupert and Macrone were now in darkness, owing to the fact that Morecombe had taken the link with him.

But Rupert could feel Macrone with his foot.

"Rise, scoundrel," he hissed. "Rise, or I will drive this blade through thy wretched body!"

Macrone gave utterance to a succession of dismal groans.

"I am smothered in blood," he gasped. "All my strength has left me."

"Rise, I say! Quickly! I will have no delay, so that that monster in human form may have no time to arrange of his plans. Rise!"

And stooping, he seized Macrone, and pulled him to his feet.

"I see the twinkling of a light in yonder torture chamber," said Rupert. "A lamp or link burns within it. Go and bring it to me. Hasten, or you die."

The light—a lamp—was burning within the torture chamber, and it had been placed there by Macrone.

The wretch soon fetched it, though it was with the utmost difficulty that his trembling hand could hold it.

"Now," said Rupert, "proceed to the vault occupied by my friend, and release him."

"I have not the keys," faltered Macrone.

"Nay, replied Rupert, "but they are on the flags yonder, where you dropped them."

"I dare not open the door," said Macrone. "Morecombe would slay me if he knew I released the prisoner."

"I will slay you where now you stand!" cried Rupert, "if you do not instantly pick up those keys and do as I tell you."

Macrone hesitated but an instant.

The pistol barrel was within a couple of inches of his head—the finger upon the trigger.

He picked up the keys and shuffled off to the vault in which Reuben had been placed.

Removing the bars and chains he inserted the key in the lock, and opened the door.

Then he raised the lamp on high.

"Reuben," cried Rupert.

He paused, thunder-stricken.

No welcome voice was heard in reply, and the light showed that the vault was empty.

"You are deceiving me, villain!" cried Rupert, turning fiercely to Macrone; "you have taken me to the wrong vault."

"Nay," was the reply. "This was the vault in which he was placed. Yonder is the iron ring and the chain which secured him."

"Then what has become of him?"

Macrone slowly shook his head.

"Look you," said Rupert, placing his hand upon his throat, and the pistol barrel against his forehead; you are in the secret. You well know what has become of him. Tell me where he has been taken, or you forfeit your life."

"There is a secret passage leading from the vault," replied Macrone, in surly tones, "and, no doubt, Morecombe, after he rushed upstairs, made use of that passage, and conveyed the prisoner to another dungeon. By this time the life of your friend has, no doubt, been forfeited in retaliation for what *you* have done."

"By heaven, if my friend has been slain, I will slay you and Morecombe, and I will not leave this neighbourhood until I have levelled every stone of this accursed house with the ground. A secret passage, you said. Proceed to it."

Macrone entered the vault, and walking to the wall exactly opposite the door showed a large oval-shaped piece of stone.

"This is the entrance," he said; "but as you see, it is closed, and can only be opened from the other side."

"I will ascend the stairs," said Rupert, snatching the lamp and the keys from Macrone's hands, "and you will remain *here* a prisoner."

"Oh, no, no!" gasped Macrone; throwing himself upon his knees. "Mercy—mercy! don't leave me here. If Morecombe should be killed I shall starve to death."

"And a fitter punishment for such a wretch as you could not well be found," answered Rupert; "but kneel not to me. Not one spark of mercy will I show you. If aught happens to Morecombe, here you certainly will remain, for I will hurl these keys where they shall never be found again."

A yell of terror left Macrone's lips.

He started up and rushed towards the door, but Rupert, seizing him, hurled him backward with fearful force; and before he could rise he closed, locked, and barred the door.

Then, a pistol in one hand, and the lamp in the other, he ascended the stairs.

No doors obstructed his progress.

He passed two or three of enormous thickness, but neither of these had Morecombe stopped to fasten.

He had not forgotten them in his mad flight, however; but he knew that if he had fastened them, he would be cutting off Macrone's escape.

On went Rupert, but cautiously; for the way was entirely unknown to him, and every step he took he risked his life, for Morecombe might be secreted in some spot whence he could take aim at him with deadly effect.

Presently he reached the end of a short corridor.

He was about to turn the corner when a loud voice, the voice of Morecombe, shouted—

"Hold! Another step and you die!"

Rupert paused.

The voice was close to him; but where?

He soon found out, for Morecombe continued—

"Beware, Rupert Redmond! Your friend is in my power, and if you attempt further violence, I will slay him. Behold!"

As he spoke a pair of heavy black curtains, in front of Rupert, were drawn aside, and he saw that he was before Morecombe's chamber.

A terrible cry left Rupert's lips as he saw Reuben stretched at full length upon the low table, and Morecombe standing over him, a long dagger upraised, and ready to be plunged into his victim's heart!

"Heaven aid me in this direful extremity!" muttered Rupert, as great drops of perspiration gathered upon his brow.

"Listen, Rupert Redmond!" continued Morecombe. "I will instantly restore your friend to his senses if you do exactly as I say."

"Speak on," replied Rupert.

"First you will take off your arms, enter this chamber and place them upon the floor."

"That I certainly will not do."

"Then the life of this friend of yours will be forfeited. He shall die, and by my hand!"

"Bah! You would not slay my friend because you are well aware that I should slay you."

Morecombe smiled grimly, then he raised his hand and pointed above.

"You observe that globe?" he said. "That is in communication with a rod on which my foot is placed. If you attempt to cross the threshold of this room, I press this rod, the globe above bursts, and the chamber is instantly filled with a noxious vapour, which, while it would do me no injury, would at once render you unconscious."

"I see," replied Rupert, "double-dyed scoundrel that you are! Had I complied with your demand, and entered the chamber to place these weapons upon the floor, you would have set the infernal machine in motion. But you forget that I hold a loaded pistol in my hand."

"I fear it not. While you hesitate your friend is losing his life. The effect of what he has inhaled will be that he will be slowly poisoned. Suppose you fired your pistol, and that you struck me down, your friend would die; for no human power but my own could restore him to consciousness."

"'Tis false!" thundered a voice.

Instantly the doors of the huge cabinet were burst violently open, and a tall figure, clothed from head to foot in black, sprang through.

"'WHO IS YOUR FRIEND? HAVE I EVER SEEN HIM?' ASKED SIR FERDINAND."

With an awful cry of terror More-combe started back.

But he had not taken more than two or three paces before the mysterious personage darted upon him and seized him by the throat.

"It is the Man of Mystery!" gasped Morecombe. "Mercy! mercy!"

The Man of Mystery did not utter a word.

He seized him in his arms, raised him high over his head, and dashed him to the ground.

Then, hurrying to Reuben, he placed his hand upon his heart.

"Reuben Renard," he said, in solemn tones, "I command you—rise!"

These words were no sooner uttered than a terrible noise, as of thunder, was heard ; the room seemed to rock violently, and strange noises, as of human beings in mortal agony, was heard.

Reuben sat up, rubbing his eyes, as if just awakened from a sound sleep.

Rupert, during this wondrous scene, remained rooted to the spot.

But as soon as he saw Reuben start up, he, with a loud, joyous cry, dashed into the chamber, and placing his hand upon the arm of the mysterious being, cried—

"Hold, I entreat! Let me look upon the face of him who has so frequently befriended me."

"Back!" was the stern reply ; "back! Be satisfied with what has been, is, and will be done for you. Besides, what would the sight of my features avail you? Back, I command you—stand back!"

Rupert obeyed.

Reuben was watching him and Morna with astonishment.

"Ha!" gasped Rupert, pointing to the peculiar-shaped cap worn by the Man of Mystery, the front of which glittered and flashed as he moved, "what is this I see—the mystic letters which are upon my weapons!"

The mystic letters were worked upon the cap in diamonds of infinite small-ness.

"What *is* this fearful mystery?" cried Rupert, wildly. "But if you will not let me see your face, at least tell me this—Art thou human?"

"As human as yourself," was the grave reply.

"Art thou in league with Satan, then, that you can appear anywhere with such marvellous rapidity—that you possess powers possessed by no other mortal man?"

"If I were in league with Satan, should I be here to help you? But yonder wretch is in league with Satan. Listen! Away, Rupert Redmond — hasten to London, for there thy services are required."

"Since you seem gifted with the power of knowing what is occurring miles away, tell me, has Miriam——"

The Man of Mystery waited not for him to complete the sentence.

He walked backward to the cabinet, the doors of which opening he disappeared through them with the rapidity of lightning, and they resumed their former position.

"Reuben," cried Rupert, stretching forth his hands and taking his friend's, "we are saved. But willingly would I have sacrificed my life to have saved yours."

"You have, indeed, a noble heart, Rupert. For the future we will be as brothers. Our courage has been sorely tried. This, then," he added, looking towards the cabinet, "was the Man of Mystery?"

"Yes."

"Most wonderful! But you shall tell me all as we proceed. Do you not think there must be something strange about that cabinet? There must be some secret entrance, which hitherto has escaped the notice of the murderer over yonder."

"My curiosity is so far excited," replied Rupert, "that I am determined to look within it."

Thereupon he advanced towards it, Reuben being at his side.

The doors had not locked of themselves, and both easily opened.

"Wonderful!" exclaimed Rupert and Reuben in a breath.

Yes, it *was* wonderful and mysterious in the extreme, for there was no visible outlet.

The cabinet was crammed with all sorts of strange objects, the most prominent being skulls and bones of every portion of the human anatomy.

"Is it to be wondered at that he should be called the Man of Mystery?"

said Rupert. "Truly, the mantle worn by Bowolf has fallen on the shoulders of one whose movements are more marvellous in every way. But let us take his advice, Reuben. Let us at once set out for London When he said that my presence was required in London, he, of course, referred to Miriam. But I may be too late."

"Ay," replied Reuben, "too late to stay the marriage; but not too late to make Miriam a widow; for if they have forced her to marry Richard Melburn, you will have no hesitation in slaying the villain?"

"I will cross swords with him. But now let us see what injuries this inhuman monster has sustained. By heaven, he was hurled to the ground with force sufficient to have killed him!"

Both approached Morecombe, who had not stirred from the spot whereon Morna had hurled him.

"His head is bleeding," said Reuben, "and freely, too; but he is not dead."

"Nay; neither is he unconscious!" cried Rupert, seizing him, and turning him face upward, though he is trying to persuade us that he is unconscious. Get up thou wretched poisoner!" he shouted, shaking Morecombe violently.

But the poisoner made no reply.

"We may be mistaken," said Reuben, significantly, "and he may be really dead. Still, ere we go we will make sure of the wretch, so stand aside while I use this dagger."

And he picked up the weapon dropped by Morecombe.

But the villain soon showed that he was perfectly conscious, for, with a fearful cry, he started up, and in loud tones begged that mercy might be extended to him.

"Ay," answered Rupert, grimly; "you shall have the same mercy that I showed your fiendish servant. Seize him, Reuben, and follow me!"

Only too glad of the chance was Reuben, who seized him by the neck with such a mighty grip, that Morecombe thought he should be choked.

"Listen," he gasped, "I have something to say—something of importance to you. Oh, let me breathe! I choke! I choke!"

"Out with it, then," said Reuben.

"Tell us what it is you have to say, and speedily, for we have no time to lose."

"Tell me, first," whined Morecombe, whose face was ashy pale, the paleness being greatly enhanced by contrast with the jetty black busby beard. "Tell me, what are you about to do with me?"

"You will soon be satisfied as to that," replied Rupert. "But what have you to say?"

"In an upper chamber," said Morecombe, "I have a chest containing money to a large amount. Release me, and every golden piece shall be yours."

"Fool!" replied Rupert, contemptuously. "Are you not now in our power? What is there to prevent our possession of the money, if we felt so disposed, *without* setting you free? And now, I will tell you what we are about to do with you.

"You are about to be placed in the same vault wherein I was confined. In the one which was occupied by my friend here, your miserable factotum has been placed. So you will be near each other."

"Mercy," yelled Morecombe, "I shall be starved to death!"

"So your man said of himself," replied Rupert, drily, "and a fitter punishment for such wretches as you could hardly be found."

Again and again did Morecombe yell for mercy, but he was not listened to.

Between them they dragged him down the stairs, and thrust him screaming into the vault.

The door was then locked upon him.

"What shall you do with the keys?" queried Reuben.

"I will leave them here," replied Rupert, throwing them on the ground beside the door; so if by any chance anyone gains admission to the house and comes down here, the scoundrels may be rescued in time to save their lives. After all we have treated them better than they treated us."

"By heaven, you are indeed right! But now, Rupert, let me urge you to hasten. No time whatever should be lost. I am as anxious as you to foil Master Richard Melburn. There must be some villainous arrangement between that villain and Sir Ferdinand Lockhart. Know you ought of what it is?"

"Nay!" answered Rupert, "though

of course I can guess. Come now, and let us find our way to the stables. But ought we not to pay a visit to the chamber above? Ought we not to get possession of the money he spoke of? There are poor people who would be thankful for a few pieces."

"I would recommend you to leave that until a more covenient opportunity," replied Reuben. "No doubt we shall pass this way one of these days."

So the two then proceeded to the stables.

They soon discovered them, and to their astonishment they found that they were *full* of horses.

Rupert soon found his beautiful steed, and the animal instantly recognised his voice, neighing joyfully as Rupert led him forth.

"You can have your pick, Reuben," said Rupert, "and from what I can see of them, there are some fine horses among this lot; two or three are saddled and bridled, and have pistols in the holsters. Here, too, attached to this saddle, is an excellent blade."

Reuben quickly selected his horse and arms as well.

Both now mounted and, in a few moments, they were speeding along the high road *en route* for London.

CHAPTER VIII.

OF THE ARRIVAL AT CHELSEA PRIORY—OF THE INTERVIEW BETWEEN SIR FERDINAND AND MATTHEW HOPKINS, THE WITCH FINDER—AND OF HOW THE "WEDDINGS" WERE ARRANGED.

RICHARD was wrong.

The coach *was* again stopped, and not far off London, by a band of freebooters, who demanded "toll" in the shape of money before they would allow the coach to pass them.

The amount in the pcssession of Sir Ferdinand and Mistress Melburn the villains did not consider anything like sufficient, but they eventually accepted it, and when this was safely in their possession, the leader made Sir Ferdinand give up a signet-ring he had in his possession.

Sir Ferdinand, not thinking what was intended, at once parted with it.

The leader then made him dismount, and swear that whenever, and by whomsoever the ring should be presented, he would pay the holder the sum of a hundred golden guineas.

The tones of the leader left no doubt in Sir Ferdinand's mind that if he did *not* do as he was told, it was likely that a bullet would cleave a passage through his brain.

He gave the required promise, and he was then allowed to remount and depart.

"May the miscreant present that ring under more favourable circumstances," he muttered, fiercely; "and he shall pay dearly for this! I recognised the wretch. It was Captain Brasblade. Let him wait. Let him wait. I will have my revenge."

In due time Chelsea was reached.

The whole of the interior of the Priory was most beautifully furnished; but, judging from the exterior, which was somewhat gloomy, one would have thought it was not a very desirable residence.

Sir Ferdinand, when in London, frequently entertained his "friends" at this house, which was considered to be his own especial property.

That there was a tragic history attaching to it was very well known.

It was reported that a beautiful young lady, the wife of a certain Walter Dubois, died by her own hand in consequence of the murder of her husband.

The chief of the servants was a man of the name of Kneller, who was of gigantic stature, and stout in proportion.

At Chelsea Priory he occupied a position similar to that occupied by Hawkswell at the Abbey.

To this man was entrusted, among a multitude of other things, the care of a room called the "Treasury."

Sir Ferdinand, after seeing that all was right, called the burly Kneller to his side.

"Lead the way to my apartments," he said ; "I have something of importance to tell you."

"And I have something of importance to tell *you*," replied Kneller, as he led the way to Sir Ferdinand's apartments.

"Well, what is it ? " queried Lockhart.

"A notable character has been here."

"A notable character! Who is he ?"

"Master Hopkins."

"Hopkins!" repeated Sir Ferdinand, opening wide his eyes in astonishment. "What does that wretch require ? "

"He wishes to see you."

"On what matter ? "

"Various matters. He requires information from you."

"Oh, indeed. Nothing else ? "

"I had a long conversation with him, in the course of which," continued Kneller, "I learned that he had been commissioned by the king as a leader of a number of men, who are about to stamp out witchcraft in Pendle Forest."

"Ah !" exclaimed Sir Ferdinand, " he is the very man for that sort of thing. A more atrocious ruffian never breathed."

"Except you," thought Kneller.

Then aloud he asked—

"Is Master Melburn to arrive tonight ? "

"He will be here in the course of a few hours, but I am about to ask your opinion, Kneller, as to the best way of capturing a certain Captain Brasblade."

Kneller started as this name was uttered.

"I can give you no hint as to how he should be captured," he said. "He is a dangerous man — a *highly* dangerous man."

"More dangerous than Master Hopkins ? "

"I think so—at least, I am sure he is in some respects. If I were you, Sir Ferdinand, I should satisfy his demands."

"Never — never ! " thundered Sir Ferdinand. "But do you think he will have the impudence to come here personally ? No, no, he will send one of his followers."

Kneller shook his head.

"I don't think so," he replied. "Captain Brasblade has the impudence of a hundred men put together. It is not so very long ago that he actually forced himself into the king's presence,

and asked his majesty if he would partake of some wine with him."

"And his majesty's reply was ? "

"His majesty was too astonished to make one. It was his grace of Buckingham who replied."

"Ay. What was *his* reply ? "

"He simply took him by the shoulders and bundled him into a ditch which happened to be conveniently handy. I mention this circumstance to show you that it is quite likely that Brasblade, unless engaged on a matter of greater importance, will present himself here."

"Then do you keep a sharp look-out for him, Kneller. If he *does* come, make short work of him. You are quite big enough."

"What should I do with him ? "

"Do ?" asked Sir Ferdinand with a wild laugh. "Do ? Why slay the villain ! Wipe him off the earth as I wipe *this* off the table."

And with a swinging, savage stroke of his whip handle, he swished off a massive glass decanter, smashing it into a hundred pieces.

"I will endeavour to do as you say, Sir Ferdinand," replied Kneller.

"You will endeavour to do it, eh ? It will not be well with you if you do *not* do it. But now about this Hopkins —when will he again make his appearance ? "

"I cannot say. At the present moment he is getting his men together."

"A pretty crew ! " laughed Sir Ferdinand. "I always hated Matthew Hopkins. But now it will be different. If he wants any assistance in finding these imps of the forest, he shall have it."

"Is the one who calls himself the Man of Mystery in command of these witches ? "

"I cannot say that he is in *command* of them."

"But he directs their movements ? "

"Even *that* I cannot answer for. That he is something to do with them, however, there can be no doubt ; but I believe a hag named Frampton is the chief of these wretches. The very sight of the ugly viper and her howling crew is enough to turn one's blood cold. But I am not so much interested in *their* extinction as I am in the finding of the

Man of Mystery, and the strange men— *men* I am not so sure they are, for I saw not the face of a single one——"

"Then you *have* seen them?" interrupted Kneller.

Sir Ferdinand saw that he had made a mistake.

"No matter what I *have,* nor what I have *not* seen," he replied, sharply. "I repeat that I am interested in the ousting of the Man of Mystery."

Then he continued—

"So you don't know when Hopkins will again do me the honour of calling, eh? Well, whenever it may be, I will see him. And now attend to what I say. First, however, take this."

And from off the little finger of his left hand he took a diamond ring.

"I want you," he continued, "to pay a visit to that wretched wine-bibbing parson, Bentley, at Chelsea Walk, and tell him that I desire to see him at once."

Kneller looked up, and stared hard at a massive clock on the mantelpiece.

"Well," queried Sir Ferdinand, "and what are you looking at?"

"At the time. At this hour I fancy I shall find the parson hopelessly drunk, and, therefore, incapable of taking any instructions."

"Visit him and see. But drunk or *not* drunk, I must see him."

"Good!" replied Kneller, who at once departed, and made his way to Chelsea Walk.

The houses on each side were old.

To one of these houses went Kneller.

The whole alley was in darkness, and it was with the greatest difficulty that Kneller avoided the huge pools of river refuse in the centre of the "Walk."

For a moment we will precede him.

Several persons occupied rooms in this ruinous old house—persons having terrible reputations; but, nevertheless, the first floor was occupied by "Parson Bentley," a man who might have done well in the world, and have made a name to be handed down to prosperity.

But the drink had ruined him almost beyond the hope of redemption.

Just half-an-hour before Sir Ferdinand despatched Kneller to this hovel, Parson Bentley received a visitor.

He came to the door, and finding it ajar, pushed it wide open, and mounted the stairs; but he did so carefully and cautiously.

Reaching the door on the first floor, he delivered a thundering rap upon it with his clenched fist.

So effective was the blow, that the door was instantly burst open.

It was evident that the occupier of the "apartment," who was no other than the drunken parson, was near the door at the time, for he received such a stunning blow from the broken handle, that he went flying back several paces, and fell with a crash on the floor.

The visitor burst out into a loud roar of laughter.

He was between forty and fifty, tall and strong, with rough, grizzly beard and moustache, and a pair of cunning-looking grey eyes.

His attire was that of an ordinary working citizen.

Having recovered from his fit of laughter, he assisted the fallen parson to rise.

"Never did mortal eyes behold such a parson," he said. "Why, brother Bentley, you are *always* drunk."

"And you, always violent," growled the parson, as the visitor placed him, puffing and panting, in a rickety old chair, the only one the room afforded; "but this time I am not drunk; for," he added, after a pause, "a very good reason."

"Ah, ah! You had not the money, eh? Well, brother Bentley, fancying that you might be somewhat thirsty, I thought that I would bring a *little* flask —and here it is."

And he produced a flagon from his pocket, and handed it to the parson, who, seizing it with avidity, placed it to his lips and took a long pull.

"Captain Brasblade——," commenced Bentley; but the visitor checked him.

"Not that name," he said, in an undertone. "Though I care nothing for all the crew in the Walk, I don't want it to be known that I am here. It is supposed that I am miles away. I was a few hours ago, but I have come to London in order to claim a large sum, of which I stand greatly in need."

"I stand in need of a *small* sum," was the reply; "but that I can't get. Nothing is stirring now—nothing."

"Well, it shall never be said that I

didn't give you an occasional dole," said Brasblade. "Here are a couple of gold pieces. It's all I have to spare now."

"Ah, you are indeed kind," whined the parson. "I will not ask you how you came possessed of the money; but it is evident you are more successful than I am."

"It is your own fault, Bentley. Why don't you use your right name? Call yourself Bentley Brackstock as of old. Your name would be recognised, and your pockets would be full."

The parson slowly shook his head.

"Too late, Mark!" he said; "too late! I have no heart or inclination for anything now—only drink. I *must* have that, at any cost."

"Well, I'll tell you what. You have heard the stir that is being made with regard to the witches?"

"What witches?"

"The witches all over the country."

"Nay; I hear but little here."

"Do you mean to tell me that you have not heard the king's proclamation?"

"I have not heard it."

"Well, one has been issued; and I was about to say that you might move in the matter. Why not place yourself at the disposal of one side or the other?"

"Who is the leader of the party against the witches?"

"Can't you guess?"

"Is it Matthew Hopkins?"

"It is. The greatest torturer the world ever saw. In my time I have had to kill a few men; but at any rate, it has been in fair fight. I have never shot a man behind his back, and I have never slain nor wounded a defenceless man. But Hopkins has done all this, and more."

"What you say, Mark, with reference to Matthew Hopkins, is correct. So then he has at last come under the notice of the king himself, eh? Then his fortune's made."

"Don't be too sure. *He might meet with a worse death than any he has devised for the witches.* He is a false, treacherous hound, and many a man has been punished through him for crimes he never committed."

"It's the way of the world, Mark. The witch-finder now has more power than the poisoner: but I should have

nothing to do with any of them. I suppose, though, you will?"

"That remains to be seen," replied Captain Brasblade, as we shall continue to call him (though we mention that these two were brothers). "You are well aware that I am, and always was, the foe of Sir Ferdinand Lockhart, and —ha! who is that?"

Captain Brasblade was interrupted by a loud knocking on the door below.

Both listened to ascertain whether any of the other inmates would answer it.

But no one stirred.

Again came the knocking, and this time a gruff voice cried—

"What ho! there, Parson Bentley. Admit me!"

"By heavens," whispered Bentley, "it's Kneller!"

"Kneller? What can he want with you?"

"Can't say with certainty; but I fancy I can guess, having already received certain hints that my services might be wanted."

"With the *book?*"

"Ay, and the *ring!*"

"I must not be seen by this man. You must conceal me."

"Quick, then! Here—in here with you."

Parson Bentley pulled open a cupboard, Captain Brasblade darted in, and the parson then turned the key on him, and placed it in his pocket.

Then, going to the door, he asked—

"Who knocks?"

But the knocking had ceased, and, as the dissipated parson spoke, the noisy visitor was ascending the stairs.

"Why," cried the parson, "it's Kneller, isn't it?"

"Yes," was the surly reply, "you know well enough it is. What do you mean by keeping me down there all this time? And I do believe that you are *sober*. Well, well, times must *indeed* be bad."

"You are correct, Master Kneller, they *are* bad. But enter."

"Are you alone?" queried Kneller, looking round the miserable apartment.

"Quite," was the reply. "I am always alone since all my friends have forsaken me."

"All have not forsaken you, for behold."

"Ah! What is that? A diamond

ring! What— But I have seen that on your master's hand."

"True. That is where it now comes from. You know the meaning of it."

"To be sure," grinned Bentley. "I am to go and see him, and he will exchange this ring for hard cash."

"When what you have to do is completed. You are not to go and see him, however, because in a couple of hours he is coming to see you *here*."

"Why am I not to go and see him at the Priory?"

"Because— But he has his reasons."

"Is the young lady there?"

"She is."

"Well, I will prepare to receive Sir Ferdinand."

"Do so," replied Kneller. "And now I must hasten back to the Priory."

Bentley waited at the top of the stairs until Kneller had descended, and his heavy footsteps had died away up the Walk, then he opened the cupboard.

"A nice scheme appears to be afloat," said Brasblade—"a scheme between Sir Ferdinand, Richard Melburn, and yourself."

"I am but little to do with it. A marriage — a double marriage, as I understand it—is about to take place. I am to perform the ceremony—that is all."

"The young lady, who is she— the same I saw in the coach, I wonder?"

"Sir Ferdinand's adopted daughter."

"And they are going to *force* her into a marriage with Richard Melburn?"

"Exactly."

"The girl, I suppose, loves someone else?"

"She does."

"Who is her lover?"

"A very poor and insignificant youth, I've *heard*."

"But his name?"

"Rupert Redmond."

Captain Brasblade started back with a low, startled cry.

"Ah!" said the parson, "then you know him?"

"I do not; but I knew his father, Randall Redmond. A fine fellow was Randall. I would do him a service if I could; or I would do his son a service. By heaven, brother, it *can* be done!"

"What mean you?"

"Would you do *me* a service if you could?"

"You know I would."

"Then listen, and if you consent to do as I ask you, I will add two more guineas to what I gave you."

"Proceed then."

Brasblade sat himself on the edge of the rickety table, and wove a plot which astonished the parson in no small degree.

"It is risky," he said. "Sir Ferdinand is a powerful man in high quarters, and would have vengeance upon me."

"I will look to that, brother. Will you do it? You know well enough that I can act the part to perfection."

"Well, I suppose I must agree."

"Good! Then I will go and get a little more wine, and we can arrange matters until Sir Ferdinand's arrival."

"Just before which you will depart, I suppose?"

"By no means. I will again be locked up in yonder cupboard."

During the two hours which elapsed ere Sir Ferdinand's arrival, the singular brothers enjoyed themselves, consuming a large quantity of wine, which, while it did not visibly affect the captain, made a very great impression on the parson.

At last a loud knocking was heard below, and at once Captain Brasblade rose and was locked in the cupboard.

The first part of the plot hatched by Brasblade now came into operation.

One of the upstairs occupants descended, lamp in hand, to show Sir Ferdinand up, while the parson, collecting a number of bottles, placed them upon the floor beside the pallet he slept on.

Then he went to the door and whistled softly.

This signal being answered in a similar fashion, he laid down on the pallet.

Another moment an elderly man, attired in rusty black, crept into the room, and taking the parson's wrist, consulted a massive watch—or rather what had once been a watch, for it was now perfectly innocent of any interior mechanism.

It was thus that Sir Ferdinand found them as he stepped into the apartment.

Drawing himself haughtily erect, he asked—

"What is the meaning of all this?"

The man at the bedside gravely looked round.

"Sir," he said, in low and apparently affected tones, "this is a most serious case."

"What mean you?" was the stern reply. "My man was here two hours ago, and the parson was then well enough to partake of a flagon of wine."

"Alas! that is only too true," was the reply, "and if I could discover the persons who gave him the wine, they should answer for it to the law. It was the contents of the flagon which has stretched poor Parson Bentley on this pallet."

Sir Ferdinand bit his lips with vexation.

Stepping to the pallet side, he exclaimed—

"My man told you what I required?"

"He did, and presented me with the ring with which I was to gain admission," replied the parson, in a weak voice.

"Are you a doctor?" queried Sir Ferdinand of the man beside the pallet.

"At your service," was the reply.

"Your services would not be accepted by me at any price. But tell me this— can the parson quit this house to-morrow night?"

"If he does anything of the kind I will not answer for his life," was the grave reply.

"Perdition! What then am I to do?"

"Fear not that your arrangements need come to a standstill because I shall be unable to go to the Priory," said the parson. "If you will accept of his services, my friend Parson White will take my place."

Sir Ferdinand's face brightened considerably.

"Who is your friend?" he asked. "Have I ever seen him?"

"More than likely," replied the parson. "He has often been here with me."

Once more addressing the supposed physician, he asked—

"You are quite certain that Parson Bentley will not be able to leave this house by to-morrow night?"

"As certain as that I am here."

"Then, Parson Bentley, let it be as you say. You will send for this reverend friend of yours, instruct him in all that is necessary, give him the ring, and to-morrow night, at ten of the clock, he will present himself at the back of the Priory —you know the spot. He will be admitted on presentation of the ring. The ceremony over, he will receive fifty guineas; as to its division, that must be arranged between you."

"It shall be as you say," moaned the parson; "he will be there without fail."

"But so that I shall be certain as to that, you must send someone to me with a note in the morning. Perhaps your friend here will do the favour?"

"Readily," replied the supposed doctor.

Sir Ferdinand in another minute had left the house.

He had no sooner gone, than the parson hastily rose.

"Hand me the flask," he chuckled, "for I am as thirsty as a fish. And let out that gentleman in yonder cupboard."

*   *   *   *

Sir Ferdinand let himself into the Priory by a small secret door, used only by himself—a door which could be reached either by land or water, for close to it a narrow flight of stone steps descended to the river.

Making his way to his apartments, he was met by Kneller.

"He is here, sir," said Kneller.

"Who is here?"

"Matthew Hopkins."

"Ha! Where?"

"Well, I showed him into the servants' hall, but he laughed in my face, and made his way into your study, which apartment he walked direct to, just as if he were familiar with the whole house."

"Humph!" growled Sir Ferdinand, "the insolent hound! But I must be civil," he muttered. "His power has increased tenfold now that he is under the king's warrant. Besides, I require him to assist me."

Entering the study, the silver lamps in which had been lit by Hopkins himself, he found himself face to face with the man whose name was now upon everybody's lips.

Matthew Hopkins was of about the middle height, and possessed of a muscular frame—a frame entirely spoilt, so far as appearance went, by a remarkably short neck.

A large, ugly, closely-cropped beard was rendered still more unattractive owing to the mouth being inordinately large, and the eyes just as uncommonly small.

The habitual expression of the face was one of low cunning and gross brutality.

This expression frequently changed, and he was then a perfect fiend in the form of a man.

Born in an obscure country village, possessed of no education, he had made a name by the persistent fashion in which he had hunted down to death those who had been dubbed as witches.

The majority of people being under the impression that no punishment was too severe for witches, or for their male associates, Matthew Hopkins was seldom interfered with in his system of torturing, which was perfectly fiendish in its horrible cruelty.

Eventually Hopkins's persistent hunting of the witches reached the ears of the king, and he was sent for, for James had repeatedly sworn that he would leave no stone unturned to rid the country of "sic vermin," and in the result Matthew Hopkins left the Court a great "hero," with an order for a substantial sum in his pocket, and a promise of a great reward in the future.

This patronage of the King *made many persons in excellent position tremble with fear at the mention of his name.*

"I am pleased to behold you once again, Sir Ferdinand," said Hopkins, in tones which entirely disproved his words.

"What you say may be correct," was the reply, "but I am strongly inclined to doubt it."

"My advice to you, Sir Ferdinand Lockhart, is to let bygones be bygones."

"Your advice!" cried Sir Ferdinand, haughtily drawing himself erect. "Who gave you the right to advise persons of my rank and position?"

"The king!" was the calm reply.

"It is false!"

"Not so. The king has been pleased to bestow his patronage upon me. He will render me any assistance in my profession. All that I shall do will be UNDER THE KING'S ROYAL WARRANT."

"That may be, but the king does not permit you to override his courtiers."

"Ah, ha! say you so? I am not the person I once was. I am of far greater importance than you, for while my word would be believed by the king, yours would not. For instance, suppose I said that Sir Ferdinand Lockhart was a dealer in the black arts, and that I got certain persons to swear that this was a fact, what would follow?"

"I understand what you mean, villain, you would falsely swear."

"Ay!" chuckled Hopkins, "you may well say that. With all your villainy, Sir Ferdinand, I cap you. But though England has heard a deal of me, it will hear more in the future. I say again, Sir Ferdinand, would it not be better that bygones should be bygones? It is to your interest that we should be firm friends."

"What makes you think so?"

"I know more of Pendle Forest than you think it possible, Sir Ferdinand. I know that it swarms with witches—that it is well-known as the 'Home of Mystery.' There are a number of persons there whom you would like to see burned at the stake."

"I admit that you are right."

"Very well!" chuckled Hopkins. "Make me your friend, Sir Ferdinand, and I will sweep your enemies from your path, but make me your enemy, and you will bitterly regret it."

"Well, Matthew Hopkins, since circumstances compel it, we will be friends."

"Good! Then let us crack a bottle between us, and arrange what is to be done. If it is your wish, we can repair to Pendle Forest without delay."

Sir Ferdinand called Kneller, and told him to bring up wines and spirits, and this having been done, Matthew Hopkins and Lockhart proceeded to discuss the hunting down of the occupants of Pendle Forest.

Sir Ferdinand was presently more than ever convinced of the power wielded by the man before him, for Hopkins said—

"The king has placed before me many particulars with which you furnished him by despatch. He also mentioned the name of Rupert Redmond. This is evidently one of your and Richard Melburn's worst enemies."

"You are correct! But there will be no necessity for you to trouble about him. We have caged him securely."

"But are you sure that the cage contains no weak points?"

"Quite," grinned Sir Ferdinand; "now it will be better if you are made acquainted with the whole story—but hark! someone is at the door."

"Master Richard Melburn has just entered the courtyard with his man," said Kneller.

"Conduct him here at once."

Then, as Kneller disappeared, Sir Ferdinand said to Hopkins—

"This is opportune, for Richard can tell you much. You don't know Melburn?"

"I haven't the honour."

"Nor his mother, the beautiful Mistress Melburn?"

"Of Melburn Manor?"

"The same."

"I have seen her in London, once or twice."

"Well, she is about to become my wife."

"No doubt—she is rich!" replied Hopkins, with a significant smile.

Richard Melburn, travel-stained, here strode into the study.

"Well?" queried Sir Ferdinand, eagerly.

"Ay! all is well."

"Is Rupert Redmond dead?"

"No; but he had not recovered consciousness when I left."

"And the other?"

"Refused to answer any questions."

"Well, he and Rupert Redmond are in our power. But allow me to introduce you to Matthew Hopkins, the witch-finder."

Richard returned Hopkins's bow without any remark as to whether he was pleased or otherwise at making his acquaintance.

"I recognised him at once," he said.

"Why, where did you last see me?" asked Hopkins.

"I have never before, to my knowledge, seen you; but it is not so long ago that my attention was drawn to a portrait of you."

Hopkins's heart beat more rapidly as Richard said this.

Was it possible that he had become so great that his portraits were being published.

"May I ask where you saw the portrait?" he asked.

"To be sure," replied Richard. "It was drawn with a piece of chalk on the black board of a tavern. There was a gallows close to it. The sketch was so excellent that I at once recognised you as the original."

"By heaven!" shouted Hopkins, rising in a towering rage. "The name of the tavern?"

"If I gave it, it would be of no use. The landlord was not clever enough to have made the sketch."

"But I again ask you to give me the name of the tavern."

"I forget it; but likely you will pass that way, and see your portrait and the gallows."

"Ay! I will find it out; and I will make the landlord suffer."

"Perdition on the sketch!" growled Sir Ferdinand. "We have other and deeper matters to attend to, so let us arrange how to trap our enemies."

"Let the subject drop. I can guess the object of Master Hopkins's visit. Do you propose to visit Pendle Forest?"

"I do."

"You will have no ordinary witches to deal with. They who haunt the forest are possessed of superhuman powers. Is it not so, Sir Ferdinand?"

"Quite correct," replied Sir Ferdinand; but his reply was delivered in tones which showed him to be uneasy.

He glanced hastily round the superb apartment, as if under the impression that the Man of Mystery might start out of any corner.

"The men under me," said Hopkins, "have been so trained that they would not shrink if the Evil One himself appeared before them. Let us but get to Pendle Forest, and we will render a good account of ourselves."

"Do I understand that my visit to the king is not now necessary?" asked Sir Ferdinand.

"Yes. When giving me instructions, his majesty said that you were about to personally lay the full particulars before him. Indeed, he said that he strongly desired to see you on account of the many rumours which had reached him. But he no sooner mentioned your name than the young Duke of Buckingham took him aside and whispered in his ear

Immediately afterwards his majesty said that after all he need not see you—that, in fact, your interview with me would be more to the purpose."

"By heaven!" exclaimed Richard, "what can the Duke of Buckingham have said?"

"Nothing of me, I should say," replied Sir Ferdinand.

"Still, you would like to know if the duke is plotting against us?"

"Yes."

"I think it was nothing to your advantage, Sir Ferdinand," chuckled Hopkins, "for I saw the king start with astonishment."

"The matter is of no importance," said Sir Ferdinand, impatiently; "everyone knows that the Royal Favourite is in the habit of interfering in matters which do not concern him, and one of these days he will burn his fingers."

"I hope he will," cried Hopkins, "for he looks upon me as one would look upon some ogre. His grace has a number of lovely ladies, who are ready to bestow their all upon him. Several he visits; who knows? *some of them may practice witchcraft!* I will look to it."

"Don't let the game you fly at be too high," hinted Sir Ferdinand, "or you might over-reach yourself. But be seated, Richard, and we will arrange when to start for the Forest. In the meantime, the principal thing to attend to is our marriage."

"And after that the visit to the Heath should command our attention."

"The Heath?" queried Hopkins.

"We will tell you the story," said Sir Ferdinand, who thereupon commenced it.

He was greatly assisted by Richard.

On the conclusion of the story,

Hopkins took out a book, opened it at the letter "M," and carefully ran his eye over the page.

"Morecombe," he said. "As I expected, the name is here: 'Morecombe, of the Round House, Bickley Heath, strongly suspected of being a professor of the black arts.' It was my intention to drop upon that man."

"He is in league with the Evil One," said Richard. "Drop on him, as you say, and you will rue it till the day of your death."

"Ho, ho!" laughed Hopkins. "I shall begin to fancy that *you* are a professor of the black arts. But apart from your acquaintance with this man, he is down in my book, and, therefore, his case must be investigated, and his place searched. Besides, you admit that he is a wizard."

"Yes, and a clever one to boot. But, then, I change what I have said—thus," and Richard took some gold from his pocket and placed it beside Hopkins. "There, now I say that he is *not* a professor of the black arts."

"To be sure," chuckled Hopkins, eagerly pocketing the gold—"and *I* say that he is not; consequently, I scratch his name out."

And this the scoundrel instantly did.

The three now set about their plans, which, before they separated, were thoroughly well arranged.

Owing to what Sir Ferdinand and Richard said, Hopkins decided to take with him no less than fifty of his men, while Sir Ferdinand and Richard agreed to supplement them with as many men as they could spare.

Thus the forest was to be invaded by a small army of witch-finders.

CHAPTER IX.

OF THE STRANGE CIRCUMSTANCES WHICH TOOK PLACE IN THE CHAPEL.

ABOUT half-an-hour after the three villains had separated, and when Sir Ferdinand and Richard had retired for the night, Kneller ascended the stairs, ostensibly to retire.

But this was not his intention.

He had secret work in hand, and after a short time he descended, and was quickly outside the Priory.

In returning to the mansion an hour or so afterwards, and very much the worse for something he had imbibed, he passed Chelsea Walk.

Suddenly a hand descended upon his shoulder, with sufficient force, considering his condition, to nearly send him spinning to the ground.

"Zounds," he growled as he snatched

his blade from its sheath, "who dares to so insult me?"

"Insult you!" laughed a voice. "Ay, that's what I should like to know. Who would dare to insult the mighty Master Kneller?"

"By all the saints!" exclaimed Kneller, "it is Captain Brasblade."

"Right, my worthy Kneller. But how fares it?"

"Fares what?"

"I mean, how do you hit it at the Priory?"

"I make what I can."

"You find it better than the old way? But you don't make old friends very welcome."

"Well, you see, you came so unexpectedly upon me. I thought that someone, taking advantage of my condition, was about to assault and rob me."

"Your condition! Why, I've seen you thoroughly drunk, Kneller; now you are only partially intoxicated. Ha, ha! I've no doubt you could drink a little more. So here we have it."

And he brought out a flask.

"Good, wholesome stuff this," he said. "Drink heartily, Kneller, though not so deeply as to leave none for your once boon companion, Captain Brasblade."

"Your health," said Kneller, and he placed the flask to his lips, while at the same time, he thought: "Just my luck; if I had kept inside the Priory, this would not have happened.

"And yet, perhaps, it is just as well. I will warn him with respect to Sir Ferdinand, and thus be certain that he will not venture within the Priory. It would not do, so far as I am concerned, for he has a knack of opening his mouth just when one don't want him to."

"I thought you were miles away, captain," he added, as he handed back the flask.

"What made you think that? Ah! I understand. Sir Ferdinand has been telling you of how I met him once on the road, eh?"

"He has."

"Then he recognised me?"

"Yes, and I would tell you something serious—I would put you on your guard. Was it your intention to come to the Priory for the money in exchange for the ring?"

"To be sure it was. What am I to be afraid of? You are his principal man. And I well know that you would offer me no harm, in remembrance of old times, eh, Kneller?"

"No. But Sir Ferdinand is determined to give you a warm reception. In fact he authorised me to slay you."

Brasblade's eyes flashed furiously.

"Ha, ha! will you try it now?" he said. "Draw your sword if you dare, Kneller!"

"I have no wish to fight with you, and if you will take my advice, captain, you will keep away."

"I certainly shall not visit the Priory now," replied Brasblade, "but I will meet Sir Ferdinand on the road, and take my revenge."

Having received this assurance, Kneller felt disposed to be communicative, and Brasblade learnt all that was going on at the Priory, including Hopkins's visit and what arrangements had been made between the witch-finder, Sir Ferdinand, and Richard Melburn, all of which Kneller had learned by placing his ear to the keyhole of the door.

Having finished the contents of the flask, the two separated, Kneller proceeding to the Priory, and Brasblade to his brother, the parson.

*   *   *   *

The hour of midnight was fast approaching.

Everything was in readiness for the consummation of the two singular marriages, but "Parson White" had not arrived.

Sir Ferdinand had received the promised note from Bentley, and it was to the effect that his friend would be at the Priory at the appointed hour without fail.

The marriages were to take place in the little chapel adjoining the Priory, and which could be reached by a side door leading from the house.

For some considerable time Sir Ferdinand and Mistress Melburn had been within the chapel, and it struck the latter as being singular that they should be there so long without anyone else appearing.

"Where can Richard be?" asked Mistress Melburn. "Is he aware of the hour?"

"Quite. But there is no doubt that he is looking out for the clergyman."

"I now wish I had not consented to this midnight marriage," said Mistress Melburn.

"Why?" queried Sir Ferdinand, hastily, while at the same time he glanced savagely towards the door.

"Midnight marriages are frequently the commencement of unhappiness, but in our case it seems as if the parson——"

She was interrupted by the sudden opening of a side door, and the appearance of Richard, with Kneller following.

"At last!" exclaimed Richard, whose face showed how agitated he was—"at last has t' villainous parson arrived."

"Richard!" exclaimed Mistress Melburn, indignantly, "how dare you use such a term here, in this sacred edifice?"

"Sacred!" replied Richard, with an ironical laugh. "Well, if it is sacred to you, it is not to me. A strange-looking man is this White, Sir Ferdinand. He presented your ring, but would not part with it. He simply showed it, and then replaced it in his pocket."

At this moment sounds of voices and the shuffling of feet were heard.

In a few seconds Parson White appeared.

He was a very benevolent-looking old man, and yet there was, as Richard had said, something strange about him.

He was clad in the ordinary clerical garb.

His hair was perfectly white, while his cheeks were clean shaven, and his eyes were protected by a pair of dark-coloured glasses.

"Parson White," said Sir Ferdinand, fiercely, "this delay on your part is unpardonable."

"It was unavoidable, sir," replied Parson White, in low, lisping tones. "*If you knew all, I am sure you would be of my opinion.*"

"I do not require to be told the reason of your delay. And now," he added, turning to Kneller, "let Miriam be conducted here."

"Is her maid to accompany her?" asked Kneller.

"Yes, let her be present. She is required as a witness. Let several of the other servants be also present."

Kneller departed, and ascending to Miriam's apartments, knocked upon the door.

Margaret opened it.

"The time has come," said Kneller. "I am requested by Sir Ferdinand to tell you and your mistress that your presence is required in the chapel."

"What if my mistress should refuse to enter the chapel?"

Kneller shrugged his shoulders.

"I should not advise her to refuse," he replied, "because force will be used."

"Ay! and you, villain! would be the first to use it."

"I should be compelled to obey the instructions of my master."

"Your master!" sneered Margaret. "Behold my unfortunate and unhappy mistress—would your master, and his colleague, Richard Melburn force this lady in her present condition into a marriage?"

And drawing aside the curtains, she showed Miriam stretched upon a couch, the victim of grief and despair.

Her appearance was enough to have excited sympathy in the stoniest of hearts, but Kneller was not moved.

"I am not responsible for what Sir Ferdinand orders," he said gruffly. "I have only to see that his commands are obeyed, and therefore I urge you to hasten."

"There is no help for it, Margaret!" said Miriam, rising slowly. "I must go, or force may not only be used towards me, but also towards yourself."

"Let them attempt it if they dare," replied Margaret, fixing her bright eyes upon Kneller's face.

"Patiently have I waited for news from Rupert," said Miriam, the tears now fast falling down her pale cheeks.

"Trouble not yourself about him," said Kneller, "for you will never hear from him again. He is in the safe custody of a man who will see that he is kept under lock and key, until such time as Master Melburn can attend to him in his moments of death."

"Go, go!" cried Margaret. "See you not how your presence distresses my mistress? Go!"

"I am to conduct you to the chapel," replied Kneller.

"Lead the way then," said Miriam in tones which she vainly endeavoured to make firm.

Kneller complied, and the hall being reached, they were joined by a number of servants.

The chapel was quickly reached, and here Kneller drew back, allowing Margaret to conduct her pale and trembling mistress forward.

Richard stepped up to Miriam, fixed a triumphant stare upon her face, bowed ironically, and then offered his arm.

Sir Ferdinand greeted her with a dark, savage scowl.

"The ceremony can now proceed," he said, quickly.

In the meantime, Parson White had taken his place, book in hand.

Being made aware of the fact that all was in readiness, he coughed, slightly adjusted his glasses, and then placed the book immediately before him.

"One moment," he said. "My friend Parson Bentley informed me that fifty guineas was to be paid for this service."

"So it is," replied Sir Ferdinand, sharply, "but the service has not been concluded, and certainly the amount will not be paid in advance."

"If you do not at once proceed," cried Richard, "I will make you suffer for it. We will not allow ourselves to be fooled with."

"Oh, certainly not. But are you sure there will be no other interruption?"

"Ay."

"This young lady," pointing to Miriam, "is not being forced into a marriage with this young man?"

Richard became livid with rage. Sir Ferdinand's black looks, too, showed the state of mind he was in.

"Will you proceed?" thundered Richard.

"To be sure!" answered the parson, with provoking coolness; "but I should first like the young lady herself to answer my question: Is this marriage with or without your consent?"

"Without my consent," answered Miriam, firmly. "I may suffer bitterly for my answer, but I will not tell a falsehood in this sacred place."

"Scoundrel!" hissed Richard, "how dare you attempt to play with persons in our positions? Either proceed with the ceremony or else close the book. We shall then know what to do with you; and you may rely upon it that directly you close the book and retire from that spot we will take our revenge on you."

"To be sure!" grinned Parson White; "but since it seems to me that the young lady is forced to carry out this contract, the opportunity should be given for *someone* to forbid the ceremony proceeding."

"Indeed!" sneered Richard. "To whom should the opportunity be given?"

"*To me!*" shouted a loud voice.

At that instant Parson White moved swiftly aside, and the little desk at which he was standing rolled back as if it had been placed upon a pivot.

A flight of steps were revealed, and before either of the astonished persons present had time to express their astonishment, two figures bounded up, and the next instant the party found themselves faced by Rupert Redmond and Reuben.

Both had their naked blades in their hands, while their pistols were ready for instant use.

Richard was the first to recover himself.

With a terrific yell he bounded forward.

"This can be no delusion!" he screamed, fixing a pair of starting eyes upon Rupert's pale but determined features. "No, it is Rupert Redmond! It is the hell-hound! Did I not say that he was in league with the devil? If he were not, how would he be here? But by—" he shouted, as he snatched a pistol from beneath his doublet, and pointed it full at Rupert's breast, "he shall die where he now stands! Fool to have entered here!"

His finger was upon the trigger, and had he pulled it, and the weapon had gone off, Rupert would most certainly have been shot dead; but he was not allowed to pull that trigger.

Brasblade threw down his volume, and seizing Richard's wrist with one hand, he wrenched the weapon away with the other.

In the tussel it exploded, but without doing more harm than filling the little chapel with a cloud of sulphurous smoke.

Sir Ferdinand caught sight of Brasblade's hand, and he at once noticed that the thumb was missing.

Instantly it dawned upon him that he had been the victim of a plot—a plot unquestionably conceived and carried out by Brasblade, with the assistance of Parson Bentley.

"'WERE I TO WHISTLE AGAIN, YOU WOULD SEE MY MEN SWARMING UP THAT APERTURE!' CRIED BRASBLADE."

At once his blade flashed from its scabbard, and dashing forward, he, with a wild, savage cry, seized Brasblade by the hair.

It at once gave way, and remained in Sir Ferdinand's hands.

At the same moment Brasblade jumped out of his clerical gown.

There he was himself, the redoubtable Captain Brasblade, with his well-known doublet, and his plentiful supply of arms.

"Not yet, not yet, Sir Ferdinand!" he chuckled. "You don't generally catch me asleep! Here am I now, sword in hand. It suits me far better than a book. Beware, Rupert Redmond," he shouted, as he saw several of the men-servants creeping round the chapel, "keep a sharp look out!"

"Never fear," said Rupert, "we are observing their movements."

"Look," said Brasblade, taking the signet ring from his pocket, "I call upon you in the first place, Sir Ferdinand, to redeem this little article. The trifling sum of a hundred golden guineas can never be missed by so great and mighty a man as you."

"Never shall you receive them from me!" roared Sir Ferdinand; "and, moreover, your inpudence has allowed you to overstep the bounds of prudence. For, though you may call upon the two imps beside you to assist you, my servants are in such numbers that resistance will avail you nought."

"Wait but a moment," replied Brasblade, still in the same cool, offhand tones—"wait, and you may have reason to alter your opinion. Let me tell you, in the first place, that it was I who showed Rupert Redmond and his friend the secret entrance to this chapel—an entrance with which you and your servants are entirely unacquainted. It was understood that they should remain inactive until I had been paid the amount due to me. After that, Rupert Redmond will, without your permission, and without the permission of this brave young villain," pointing to Richard, "conduct this young lady from the house, while this young man, Reuben Renard, will do the same with the lady's maid."

"So far," said Sir Ferdinand, "the trick has been successful, but it goes no farther. Attempt to move towards these women, either of you, and my men shall have orders to fire upon you."

Mistress Melburn, who on the appearance of Rupert and Reuben had been rendered speechless with terror, had moved slowly back until, reaching the door, she had vanished through it, and at the risk of breaking her neck— so dark were the many passages—she had made her way into the house.

But Miriam had not moved from the chapel; indeed, the servants took good care that she did not.

The astounding appearance of her lover had such an effect upon her that she, like Mistress Melburn, had become speechless, though not with terror—nay, it was with a joy that is indescribable."

"It is well for you to say that you will give orders for your servants to fire upon us," said Rupert; "but we happen to know that they are not provided with firearms."

"Very true," chuckled Brasblade; "but they have other weapons. Though as to whether they can *use* them or not remains to be seen. I should advise them not to do so, and for this reason —that this house is *surrounded.*"

"Surrounded!" gasped Sir Ferdinand. "By whom?"

"By my men. Did I but blow a blast upon this whistle, you would speedily find it answered by the rush of my brave men."

"Kneller!" roared Sir Ferdinand, turning fiercely to his "confidential servant," "*you* shall answer for this."

The giant was standing against one of the pillars, with a face as white as death.

"I know nothing of this," he replied. "I have nothing to do with this cursed plot. If Brasblade speaks the truth, he will tell you that I had no hand in the matter."

"Nay, you did not," said Brasblade, "for if you had you would soon have spoiled the whole affair."

"Surrounded or not," shouted Richard, "the plot shall not succeed as far as Rupert Redmond is concerned. Think you, Rupert Redmond, that I would surrender Miriam to you? Nay, sooner than I would yield her," he hissed between his clenched teeth, "I would drive this blade deep into her heart!"

And drawing his dagger, he advanced to where Miriam was sitting.

But Margaret was ready for him.

As swift as lightning, she snatched Kneller's sword from its sheath, and with the gleaming blade clutched firmly in her hand, she faced Richard.

"Off!" she cried, raising the sword until its point was on a level with Richard's breast—"off, off! lest I be tempted to drive this blade deep into *thy* heart! Monster, you are foiled at the last moment! Oh, Master Redmond," she added, in passionate tones— "oh, leave us not until we are safe from this house; be brave and save us!"

"Fear not," replied Rupert, "you shall be safely conducted hence."

"Rouse yourselves, fools!" shouted Richard to the servants, "rouse yourselves. Bring firearms and slay these villains!"

"Ay," cried Sir Ferdinand, "we will try conclusions with them. Kneller, away with you and procure arms."

"Stay where you are, Master Kneller," said Brasblade. "It will be far better for you."

Apparently Kneller thought so, for he never moved.

Sir Ferdinand and Richard stormed and raved in vain.

They were completely checkmated.

The men-servants would have attacked the three had they been armed.

Several times Richard's hand wandered to his other pistol, but every time he glanced up he saw that Reuben's sharp eyes were watching his movments.

"I again request you, Sir Ferdinand," said Captain Brasblade, "to hand over the sum agreed upon."

"And again I refuse."

"Very well; I will not ask you again. And now, Master Redmond," he added, fearlessly stepping forward, "you claim this young lady? I advise you to at once conduct her from the chapel and the house."

Rupert and Reuben advanced, but their movement so enraged Richard that, springing forward, he aimed a fearful blow at Rupert with his sword.

Round his head Rupert whirled his mysterious weapon — another moment and Richard's blade was dashed from his hand, and fell cleft in twain upon the chapel flags.

"I have neither the time nor the inclination to deal with you at present, Richard Melburn," he said, "but by-and-by I will have a reckoning with you. No doubt you and Sir Ferdinand Lockhart would like to know how we contrived to escape from the den in which you had us confined. But you will not know from me. Ascertain for yourselves. By all the saints, you will be astonished. Miriam, my love," he added, "let me conduct you from this house that should be yours."

At these words Sir Ferdinand staggered back, as if from a severe blow.

But quickly recovering himself when he saw Richard's eyes fixed enquiringly upon him, he said in hoarse tones—

"Explain your meaning."

"*At a future time*, Sir Ferdinand Lockhart," replied Rupert, "I will! Beware what you do in the future! Your every movement will be watched."

Richard stepped up to Sir Ferdinand, and whispered—

"Know you not what he means? He means that your movements will be watched by the mysterious brotherhood of Pendle Forest."

"Ay, he must mean that; but let him go, and let him take Miriam with him. Since the house is surrounded we cannot hel pourselves. Depend upon it that Rupert Redmond will return to Whalley and his associates. Shortly Hopkins and his men and our own forces will make a sudden and unexpected attack on the forest, and then we shall capture Rupert Redmond among the number. What would be a greater revenge than to let Hopkins practise his torture upon him?"

Richard's eyes glittered at these words.

"I think you are correct," he said, "and therefore we will let them go."

Rupert had raised Miriam, and supporting her by passing his arm about her waist, led her, not towards the door, but towards the secret staircase by which he had entered.

On the other side of Miriam—the sword still clutched in her hand, the look of defiance still upon her pretty face— walked Margaret, while Reuben, ready to strike down the first who dared to bar their progress, followed, and Brasblade, who took the precaution to walk backwards, brought up the rear.

At the edge of the steps Brasblade cried a halt.

"Sir Ferdinand Lockhart," he said, "your looks have no terrors for me. I am ready for any emergency."

He placed the whistle to his lips and blew a shrill blast.

At once it was answered, the answer appearing to proceed from a long distance.

A moment Brasblade paused, then again he whistled.

This time the answer was certainly much nearer.

"Twice," grinned Brasblade. "Were I to whistle again, you would see my men swarming up that aperture. But I see you will give me no occasion to whistle again. Descend, Rupert Redmond."

One after the other they descended the steps, Sir Ferdinand and Richard looking on with savage scowls, afraid to move lest Brasblade should discharge the pistols he held in his hands.

Reuben having descended, Brasblade did the same: but it was backwards.

His head was no sooner on a level with the ground, than Richard, raising his pistol, fired.

Too late!

For, as the report rang out, down went the trap, and all within the chapel heard distinctly enough a sound as of ponderous bolts being shot.

"Kneller," said Sir Ferdinand, "do you tell me that you knew not of the existence of this secret passage?"

"That I certainly do. I had no more knowledge of its existence than the dead."

"The first thing to be done, then, is to prize that trap open."

"Ho, ho! What? Have the birds flown?" asked a loud, gruff voice.

"Hopkins!" cried Sir Ferdinand.

"Ay; Hopkins it is," replied that worthy. "I hope I shall not be considered an intruder; but the fact of it is, I am punctual to my time. I should have stayed above, only one of the servants was pleased to inform me that some disaster had occurred below. And by the fiend," he added, looking about him on all sides, "I should think there has, for I can smell powder. Yet I see no dead men. Ha! here is a broken blade—here a crumpled book! What! have you slain the parson?"

"Nay; I would I had," answered Richard, in surly tones.

"The birds have *not* flown," said Sir Ferdinand, who considered that it would be of no earthly use for him to resent this man's persistent familiarity. "We allowed them to go."

"Compelled to allow them to go, eh? Well, certainly that *is* a wondrous thing."

"I did not say compelled. But listen, and we will tell you what has occurred, and for this reason: that we shall count upon your assistance."

"You have but to command me," replied Hopkins, with a low bow.

"And pay you well, eh?"

"To be sure. We must all live."

"You do not think so."

"What mean you?"

"You say 'we must all live;' whereas you make it a rule to slay as many as you can."

"Ha, ha! Excellent."

Sir Ferdinand now made Hopkins acquainted with what had transpired.

Matthew was unquestionably startled to hear of the extraordinary appearance of Rupert and Reuben; but he was much more startled to hear of how they were assisted by Captain Brasblade.

"I have owed that man a grudge for years," he said. "I have met him on more than one occasion in the country, and he has always interfered with me. If, as you think, we should meet him in the neighbourhood of Pendle Forest, we will make short work of him."

"What will you propose to do with him? Lodge him in Lancaster Castle?"

"Certainly not. Why should I give my men unnecessary trouble, when I have full license from the king to do as I think proper with prisoners?"

"Captain Brasblade, then, would come under the heading of——"

"Professor of the black arts," grinned Hopkins; "and I trust you will assist me in his punishment."

"Do not fear. Most happy shall we be to do so," replied Sir Ferdinand.

"Ay; but far more happy should we be in the capture, and the punishment of Rupert Redmond," said Richard.

"Let us at once make arrangements for setting out," said Sir Ferdinand. "How many men have you altogether, Hopkins?"

"Fifty."

"Good. And Richard and I will be able to swell the number to at least a hundred. So we shall have a small army of thoroughly well-armed men."

"And if we do not root out of Pendle Forest every witch and every member of this mysterious brotherhood, as it is called—but by no means so mysterious as some people think, I'll warrant—then it will not be the fault of Matthew Hopkins."

CHAPTER X.

WHEREIN MIRIAM AND HER MAID ARE PLACED IN THE CHARGE OF THE DUKE OF BUCKINGHAM, AND RUPERT AND REUBEN SET OUT FOR PENDLE FOREST.

THE reader is, no doubt, curious to know how it was that Rupert Redmond and Reuben managed to make the acquaintance of Captain Brasblade.

It was at an hostelry close beside the river, and not far from the Priory.

Rupert and Reuben, tired and weary with their journey, and wishing to rest their horses, which had behaved splendidly on the road, had arranged with the host to take charge of their animals until they should be called for.

They then ordered some refreshment, and it was while partaking of this that they became aware of the fact that they were not the only persons in the room.

Hearing a yawn, as of a person first waking up, they turned, and as they did so Brasblade got from off a long form, whereon he had been asleep.

"I hope we have not disturbed you," said Reuben, eyeing Brasblade with some curiosity.

"Nay, gentlemen," was the reply, "I was awake just as you entered, which was fortunate."

"Fortunate! How?"

"Because I can do you a good turn."

"Indeed! In what way?" asked Rupert, suspiciously

"I will tell you. I heard you mention Chelsea Priory, and you also let fall a name or two with which I am acquainted. Let me tell you my name. I am called Captain Brasblade."

Reuben started visibly, and the start escaped not the notice of Brasblade.

"You have heard of me before?" he laughed.

"I have," replied Reuben.

"Ever seen me before?"

"Not to my knowledge."

"Ah, if you had you would not recognise me, and for this reason—that my black bushy beard, in which I have ever taken great pride, has this very night been sacrificed."

"What a pity!" cried Reuben, sarcastically.

"You are correct, my young friend, it *is* a pity. But it will grow again, that is one comfort. But now that I have told you my name, let me tell you yours, gentlemen. One is Rupert Redmond, and the other is Reuben. I may have mixed you up," he laughed, "but that you are the owners of the names I have given I am certain."

"Certainly you are either a wizard or you have had our descriptions," replied Rupert.

"Be careful what you say, young man," whispered Brasblade. "Don't call anyone a wizard, lest you be overheard by Matthew Hopkins or his bloodhounds. But now let me tell you how I got to know who you were."

He then gave them particulars of all he had heard, and the part he had to perform.

"And now let us depart, my young friends," he concluded. "I have got to collect my men, and there will be a sufficient number of them to prevent any accident occurring."

*   *   *   *

When the descent was made from the chapel, Rupert found two of Brasblade's men awaiting, their lamps in hand; and we may add, pistols also, for they had been expecting to hear the third blast from the whistle.

Going forward, these men led the way.

The end of the passage being reached, Brasblade said—

"We part here; but it will, perhaps, be but for a short time. Something tells me that ere long we shall meet near the place you came from."

"May it be our lot to render you as great a service as you have rendered us," replied Rupert. "If this lady was in a fit condition to understand the great service you have rendered her, she would most warmly thank you."

"I *do* understand," murmured Miriam, "and from the bottom of my heart I thank him. Had he not have shown you this passage your assistance might have come too late."

"Indeed it would," replied Brasblade, "for he would have had the greatest difficulty in getting into the house. And then he would have had to find the chapel; but my advice to you, Master Redmond, is to take the ladies to a place of safety. Take them where Sir Ferdinand's spies will be unable to track them. But above all things, let them remain in London; for, as I have hinted, Sir Ferdinand and Richard Melburn will be off to Pendle Forest with Matthew Hopkins. It is their firm intention to hunt down every occupant of that place."

"I will do as you suggest," replied Rupert.

Captain Brasblade now called his men together, and once more bidding Rupert and the others adieu, set off.

Reuben conducted the party to the hostelry, when the horses were at once brought out.

After some difficulty a sedan-chair was hired, and into this got mistress and maid.

"Whither, sir?" asked the bearers.

"To the residence of his Grace the Duke of Buckingham," answered Rupert.

Then turning to Reuben, he said—

"You did not ask me where I proposed to take them, Reuben?"

"Nay," was the reply; "but I fully expected that that would be your destination. Every reliance can be placed in his grace."

"Ay; of that I am assured," replied Rupert warmly, "and I trust to him to obtain for me an audience of the king. Then will I lay before his Majesty the full particulars as to Sir Ferdinand's villainy."

"Including the awful story you heard?"

"Yes; even including that,"

"Mistress," whispered Margaret, as the chair moved on, "did you not hear what Master Rupert said? He has ordered the chair to be taken to the residence of his Grace of Buckingham."

"I heard him, Margaret," replied Miriam; "but I refrained from questioning him—to him I must entirely trust. I have no other friend in the world except you, Margaret."

"And you could not place your affairs in better hands than Rupert Redmond's. Oh, that I may be spared to see you come together! It will be the happiest day of my life. But he must first seek his fortune, mistress."

St. James's was soon reached, as was also the residence of the king's favourite.

It was now nearly two o'clock in the morning, and the house was in darkness.

The porter, however, was quickly roused.

"Your business?" he asked.

"Is with his Grace of Buckingham," replied Rupert.

"His grace happens to be here, but he retired an hour ago," replied the porter, looking in astonishment at the party.

"Tell him that Reuben Renard and Rupert Redmond are here," said Reuben.

The porter at once recognised the name of Reuben Renard, and telling them to remain where they were, he passed through the great hall and ascended the stairs.

On his return he said that the duke would be with them in a few minutes.

His grace only waited to throw a few articles of clothing about him.

When he appeared he carried in his hand what looked like a letter.

"I am right glad to see you, Master Redmond," he said, shaking Rupert heartily by the hand, "and also you, Reuben. But why this delay? Have you only just succeeded in your object?"

"But a short time ago, your grace," replied Rupert, "and I ventured to bring Miriam and her maid here. I know that I have taken a great liberty, but I appeal to you, your grace, to take compassion upon her, and allow her and her maid to stay within this house for a short time."

"My young friend, you have taken no liberty. I shall be only too glad to be of service to you. The favour you ask is but a trifling one. Mistress Miriam and her maid shall be accommodated here, and they shall remain as long as they think proper. I will place them in charge of the housekeeper, Mistress Monkhouse, and they will be happy enough with her. Longville," he added to the porter, "arouse Mistress Monkhouse. Say that I require her at once."

Then, as the porter once more ascended the stairs, the duke, lowering his voice, said—

"Master Redmond, it is most fortunate that you thought of coming here. Had you not I should have made search for you."

"Indeed! How did your grace learn that I was in London?"

"I will tell you. This evening at about ten of the clock I was in company with a lady on the terrace at Whitehall. The lady left me for a few moments, and while looking over the parapet into the river, a black object rose before me—it seemed as if it had certainly arisen out of the river. I was so thunderstricken that I could neither move nor speak. Then it suddenly occurred to me that assassination was intended, and I at once snatched my sword from its sheath. Still on came the object, and presently it stood on the parapet, a living black mass.

"It was remarkably short, though straight, and in a few seconds I found that it was a man, for in a deep voice he said—

"'Put up your blade, your grace, for you will not find it necessary to use it on me.'

"He then continued—

"'Your grace, Rupert Redmond, who saved your life, is in London. You will be pleased to find him out, and hand him this letter.'"

And the duke handed Rupert the document he held in his hand.

"Marvellous!" exclaimed Rupert; "but pray proceed, your grace."

"I told him that I would certainly endeavour to find you. I asked him whether he knew aught of your attempt to recover this unfortunate young lady. He answered that he knew more than he had any authority for saying. I was about to question him as to his name, and so on, but he disappeared in a much

more rapid manner than he came. Such an extraordinary adventure I never had in all my life."

"It was Fendyke," muttered Rupert.

Hastily he broke the seal and read these lines—

"RUPERT REDMOND,—Once more you hear from me. You will not have forgotten the assistance you have received from me. In return for this I ask that you repair with all speed to Pendle Forest. If the friend whose acquaintance you made in London, offers to accompany you, let him do so. It is your known bravery which causes me to ask you to repair without delay to the forest. As soon as this missive is placed in your hands, set off.   MORNA."

"I am summoned to my native place," said Rupert hastily.

"Summoned to Whalley—the home of the Black Witches?" cried the duke.

"Yes, your grace."

"In a very mysterious fashion, too. That there is something remarkable about you and your associations, there can be no doubt, Rupert. But I will not seek information from you. You can depart with the full assurance that Miriam and her maid will be well cared for. 'Summoned to Whalley.' Well, there will be bloodshed in that neighbourhood soon, I fancy. Are you aware that Matthew Hopkins, the Witchfinder, has been commissioned by the king to make an especial visit to that locality?"

"I am, your grace."

"And that he has received full license to do almost as he may think proper?"

"Yes."

"Well, he will be assisted by Sir Ferdinand Lockhart and Richard Melburn. Thus will three of the biggest rogues be working hand in hand. Bear in mind that they hate you, Rupert, and that Matthew Hopkins is a man of blood. If, therefore, you have any relatives at Whalley, warn them to fly for their lives."

"I have no relatives, your grace."

"You are not, perhaps, familiar with the history of Matthew Hopkins? Let me tell you that he wields a terrible power. More than once he has denounced an enemy of his as a witch or wizard, and has awarded that enemy punishments which have ended in death. So beware of him!"

"I do not fear him, your grace," replied Rupert.

"Personally, no; but because of the power he possesses, I tell you he is a man much to be feared. He is a brutal, heartless ruffian! But now, you say that you have no relatives at Whalley. May I ask whence comes the summons?"

"From Pendle Forest."

"Ha! Beware, Rupert Redmond, or death may quickly be your portion!— a terrible death, too! The mysterious beings of Pendle Forest have some sort of influence over you."

"I trust your grace does not think that I am in any way associated with the witches?"

"No, I do not."

"I am certain he is not," said Reuben. "And if he will let me I will readily accompany him."

"I thank you, Reuben," said Rupert quietly, as he shook him warmly by the hand. "With you at my side, I shall fear nothing. I would refuse to go, but I cannot forget the services which have been rendered me by the one who summons me."

"The service rendered *us* you should say," said Reuben; "for without the assistance of the man who summons you you, we might at this moment have been dead."

"Say you so?" cried the duke. "Well, I am most anxious to hear your story. But here is Mistress Monkhouse, and we have been so wrapped up in our conversation, that we have almost forgotten Mistress Miriam. Mistress Monkhouse, I wish you to take charge of two ladies."

Mistress Monkhouse bowed.

As Miriam entered, leaning on Margaret's arm, Rupert advanced, took her hand, conducted her to the duke, who was much stricken with her singular beauty.

"I am truly pleased to make your acquaintance, Mistress Miriam," he said, and I cannot tell you how happy I am that you have escaped from the clutches of Sir Ferdinand Lockhart.

"Your lover, Rupert Redmond, rendered me a service, for which I must ever be grateful. In fact, he saved my life. Let me assure you, that here you and your maid will be in perfect safety, and in charge of my housekeeper, Mistress Monkhouse."

Miriam could only murmur her thanks, and as for Margaret, she could not take her eyes from off the duke.

"But I must leave you for a time, Miriam," said our hero.

"Leave me, Rupert?" cried Miriam. "Oh, surely you will not!"

"I am compelled to, Miriam. I am commanded by him who has rendered me such great services on so many occasions, to repair to Pendle Forest at once."

"Oh, Rupert! what can this mystery be? Why is it that this strange man takes so great an interest in you? Think over it, Rupert," she said in pleading tones; "think that I shall be alone in London, and——"

"And safe, madam," interrupted the duke. "I pledge my honour that you shall be safe."

"No fear have I as to that, your grace," replied Miriam. "Yes, I feel that I shall be quite safe here. But I fear that if Rupert repairs to Pendle Forest, something terrible may happen to him. Both Sir Ferdinand and Richard Melburn have sworn to be terribly avenged."

"Have no fear for Rupert Redmond. He is well able to take care of himself."

"You must remember, your grace, that *traps* are laid for the strong."

"You are correct, my dear Miriam," said Rupert; "but I promise I will keep my eyes open. I will not willingly run into danger."

"But have you no idea why you are required to go to Pendle Forest?"

"At present I have not."

"Rupert," whispered Miriam, "as you know, I never had any fears respecting the mysterious brotherhood. But then I never actually learned the object they have in view. Oh, let me caution you, Rupert, to make no rash promises; enter into no compact; be guarded in every word. You promise this?"

"Faithfully. And I shall not be alone, Miriam. Reuben Renard, this brave young fellow, to whom I owe so much, will accompany me."

"And I shall soon hear from you?"

"Yes."

At last the time came for parting between Rupert and Miriam.

He managed to tear himself away, and quickly mounted his horse, Reuben following him.

Eager and tearful eyes watched them until the darkness shut them out of sight.

CHAPTER XI.

WHEREIN WE GET AN IDEA AS TO THE BRUTALITY OF MATTHEW HOPKINS—AND LEARN HOW AMOS ARLINGTON MEETS WITH A FEARFUL DEATH.

IT was marvellous how the news that Hopkins had been patronised by the king, and was about to visit all parts of England, spread from town to village all over the kingdom.

At the time of our story there was not a village in England which did not contain its foretellers of the future.

These were people who could not be called witches, but it was well known that Hopkins was not a man given to long investigations, and just as well known was it that his punishments were swift and terrible.

"Be just and merciful" was not written in the "Black Book" of Master Hopkins.

It was the night after the proceedings at Chelsea, and Hopkins with his men were well on the road.

Only one man was mounted, and that was Hopkins himself.

He bestrode an enormous and powerful grey horse, carried pistols in his holsters and in his belt, and a sword and dagger at his side.

His men, with one exception, were each armed with two pistols and a sword, while several of them had links thrust into their belts.

A more horrible-looking set of scoundrels never marched through the green lanes of England.

Neither Sir Ferdinand nor Richard was with them. They had gone in advance to the Abbey, in order to raise the required number of men.

Matthew Hopkins was a most vindictive man, and he had not forgotten about the sketch Richard had said he had seen.

Among his "bloodhounds"—which was certainly a most appropriate title for his men—there was a man who was different from all the rest,

His name was Ebenezer Watson.

In height he was about six feet, and remarkably thin.

He was attired in a long black habit, black silk hose, and an enormous and peculiar-looking Spanish hat.

Instead of pistols, he carried an inkpot and pens, and beneath his arm two or three books, one of which was the precious "Black Book."

Ebenezer Watson was an attorney, but having for some offence been thrown into prison, Hopkins, by some means, procured his release in consideration of "services to be rendered."

Watson found his new occupation suited him exactly.

Naturally brutal and merciless, he was just the man Hopkins wanted.

He had the law of his country at his "fingers' ends."

Watson went on in advance, and entered every hostelry on the road, but, nevertheless, by some means or other, everybody knew that the witchfinders were not far behind.

At last the identical tavern with the sketch of Hopkins and the gallows was discovered.

It was late in the evening that Watson entered.

The tavern contained a number of customers, and the host and his wife were, as it seemed, looking over some accounts.

After a loud, preliminary cough, Watson walked up to a door, on which was the sketch Richard had seen.

It was a marvellous likeness of Hopkins!

That the man and the gallows had been drawn by a clever hand Watson quickly saw.

The host, hostess and guests turned wonderingly towards him.

Who on earth could this scarecrow of a fellow be?

Having had a good stare at the chalk representation of what the artist foretold for his "master," Watson turned, pompously marched up to the counter, and placing his books thereon, demanded the name of the house and the name of host and hostess.

"Who are you, thou ugly imp of Satan?" asked the indignant hostess. "Who are you who thus demand our names?"

"My name is Ebenezer Watson," smirked the villain.

"What of it?" asked the host, who had his hand on the neck of a heavy leathern bottle.

"What of it? Have you never before heard the name of Ebenezer Watson? But you decline to give the names? Good."

So saying, Watson gathered up his books, and after another stare at the chalk sketch, marched off amid the loud laughter of all present.

Little did the host dream that this was no laughing matter.

"Who can he be?" asked the plump hostess.

"Some eccentric who has taken a fancy to that sketch, I'll warrant, and wants to find the artist, perhaps," replied the host.

About half-an-hour after this, a number of customers came rushing pell-mell into the house.

"Have you heard that the witch-finders are close here?" asked one.

"Nay," laughed the host; "and what if they are? The ruffian Hopkins will find nothing about here on which he—but, by heaven!" he suddenly added, as he looked at the sketch, "we had forgotten that. Quick, wife! Quick! Wipe it off!"

The hostess seized a wet rag, and rushed round her counter.

She had no sooner reached the other side, than a firm hand was laid upon her arm, and she was thrust aside.

"Away!" growled a voice. "Away, I tell ye! We'll see who has the laugh *now!*"

Turning she found herself once more before Watson, who laughed spitefully at her surprise, and before she could open her lips, loud voices were heard without, and the next moment in marched Hopkins.

Host, hostess and customers shrank back from the notorious ruffian, who marched straight to Watson.

With arms akimbo, with scowling brows, and with eyes blazing with savage ferocity, Hopkins stood for a few moments surveying the "picture."

And while he looked, a dead silence fell upon all present.

Not a word or whisper was uttered; not a rustle was made.

Having finished his examination, he turned and faced the host and hostess.

"Your name, sirrah?" he asked the host, in hoarse tones; but it was with the greatest difficulty that he could speak, so enraged was he at that moment.

"My name, sir," replied the host, "is John Gillet."

"John Gillet! Watson—your book!" thundered Hopkins. "John Gillet! Down with it! And now, John Gillet, the name of the wretch who drew that sketch!"

"I am unable to furnish you with it," replied the trembling host.

"Unable!" shouted Hopkins, as he brought his heavy riding whip, with a thundering crash, upon the counter. "Furnish me with the name instantly."

By this time nearly every customer had slunk off, and as they did so, Hopkins's men crowded in until the interior of the hostelry became full of them, and many a look of satisfaction was cast upon the numerous bottles, casks, and the little piles of money on the desk at the back.

"I repeat," replied the host, "that it is out of my power to furnish you with the name."

"Do you tell me that you don't know it?"

"I say that I am unable to furnish it."

"That means," said Watson, "that he knows, but that he will see you hanged before he gives you the name."

"Look you," said Hopkins, "if you do not at once give me the name, my men shall strip you, and on the village green, in the presence of all who like the sight, you shall be thrashed within an inch of your life!"

"John! John!" pleaded the wife, "give up the name. Do give it up."

"Oh!" cried Hopkins, "so *you* know

the name, eh ? Well, tell me, or you shall be treated in the same way as your husband ! "

"Treated in the same way—monster ! You *dare* not offer me such an indignity."

"Dare not ? By heaven, madam, you shall see that I *do* dare to do anything I may think proper. The name ! Quick ! "

"I shall not give it," answered the host. "I will not betray a true friend ! I will suffer death first ! "

"But, John—John ! " cried the wife, "I am sure that when he knows the danger we stood in he will forgive you ! "

Seeing that her husband was determined not to give the name, she added—

"The name of the gentleman who did that sketch is Amos Arlington, the well-known artist. He has but lately come to reside in this neighbourhood; and when he was in here one day, we were speaking of the witchfinder——"

"You were speaking of me," interrupted Hopkins. There is only one witchfinder, and that is Matthew Hopkins. And this gentleman, as you call him, drew that to show you what would eventually happen to me. By all the saints ! that is what may happen to him. Now, then, where does this man reside ? "

"I cannot tell you more."

"There is no necessity, madam. He resides in the neighbourhood, you said, and therefore I am pretty sure to find him out."

"Find him out ! but what do you intend to do with him ? "

That is my business, madam. Now, then," he shouted, once more facing the terrified host, "now, then, John Gillet, you shall know what it is to allow a villainous customer to draw a sketch of me. You shall have a lesson which you will do well to take to heart. Seize him ! "

At once half-a-dozen hands were roughly laid upon the landlord.

The wife sprang forward, a large decanter in her hand.

She would no doubt have used it on the men who had thus laid violent hands on her husband.

But she was not allowed to, for Hopkins, raising his whip dealt her such a slashing blow across her cheek with the butt end, that, bathed in blood, the unfortunate woman fell with a bitter cry of agony to the floor.

Seeing what had happened to his poor wife, the host essayed to free himself from the grasp of the ruffians.

But he was powerless.

His arms were seized, pulled behind his back, and securely fastened.

"Now," said Hopkins, "it appears that there is no lack of anything here, therefore, help yourselves, my men ; but be moderate, for there is work to do. And look you, Watson, see that yonder money is handed over to me. If I do not take care of it for this man, the men will pocket it."

"Oh ! I'll see that it is duly and formally handed over to you," replied Watson

"Perdition on your formalities. Hand over the money."

The host—down whose cheeks bitter tears were flowing, his emotion being caused, not by the idea of what might be in store for himself, but by his wife's dreadful appearance—turned to Hopkins and said—

"Listen to me. There are many pounds behind my counter, and I have more above stairs. Let me go to attend my wife, and every fraction I possess shall be yours.

"Not by any means," replied Hopkins fiercely. "You have allowed me to be grossly insulted, and you and your wife have also insulted me. Do you think I'm going to stand it ? I ! Matthew Hopkins ! Never ! Sharp at it, my men ! "

But the men required no second telling.

Watson by this time had swept all the money he could see into his huge Spanish hat, while the others, with wild yells, broke the necks off the bottles, and proceeded to drink the contents.

Not satisfied with what they got from the bottles, they stove in the heads of numerous casks and dipped in whatever measures they could find.

The havoc they made in a few moments was tremendous.

Having drunk what they thought proper, they deliberately smashed everything within their reach, much to the diversion of Hopkins, who laughed heartily.

The terrific row made by the men was heard far away, and crowds of villagers collected.

Among these people were dozens who had the greatest horror of the doings of witches, and who considered that it would be a magnificent thing to have the whole of them stamped out; but not until this moment had they known what sort of men Hopkins and his crew really were.

These were the ruffians commissioned by the king to rid the land of all who practised witchcraft.

Many would have interfered, but for the knowledge that it would have been useless.

The house swarmed with Hopkins's men.

"Out with him!" shouted Hopkins, making his voice heard above the din; "out with John Gillet to the village green!"

Once more the host was seized upon and dragged outside the house.

His appearance was hailed with a murmur of indignation; but no one was bold enough to protest against this inhuman treatment.

But Hopkins, fearful lest he should be interrupted—perhaps, by any magistrate residing in the vicinity, and who would have the right to call upon him to produce his warrant for acting as he was—arranged his men so that Gillet was in the centre of the howling crew.

Then, half-a-dozen links having been lit, the whole party proceeded to the village green, which was but a short distance off.

Hopkins, now remounted, called a halt beside a clump of trees.

"Now," he said, fiercely, "I will teach you what it is to insult Matthew Hopkins. D'ye hear it, ye dogs?" he asked the villagers, as he suddenly turned his face to them. "Ay," he chuckled, "I see by your faces that some of you would interfere if you dared. So much as raise a finger any of you, and I will order my men to fire into the whole lot of you! Why, fools, I am patronised by the king himself! Now, then, my men, strip him!"

"Strip him!" repeated the villagers, in low, horror-stricken tones. "What can he be about to do with the poor man? Surely he does not intend to murder him?"

Poor Gillet's cries were most pitiful; but they were entirely unheeded.

In a few seconds he was stripped of almost every particle of clothing, and then tied to one of the trees.

Hopkins now called out to one of his men—a tall, powerful, brutal-looking ruffian, named Kemp, to take his whip and use it on Gillet's bare back until he should order him to stop.

Then, by Hopkins's orders, the men formed upon each side (those with the lighted links being nearest the tree), so that the villagers could see all that was going forward.

The first stroke was delivered, and it was, indeed, a terrible one, the sound of the blow being heard a long distance off.

Again and again did the lash descend on the bare back. Again and again did Gillet's shrieks of agony ring out.

Suddenly a great cry arose among the villagers.

The crowd opened, and the hostess rushed through.

That she had not entirely recovered from the effects of Hopkins's brutal blow, was evident from the way she staggered, rather than walked, towards the trees—that she had received no attention from anyone was equally evident from the fact that her face and dress were covered with blood.

Behind her came an elderly man—a member of the family.

"Seize that woman!" shouted Hopkins. "Seize her! Back with her! Go back, woman, or by all the powers of darkness, I'll serve you the same! Hold a moment, Kemp—wait."

"I protest! I protest!" cried the old man. "I protest against this inhuman treatment of a man against whom no offence has been proved."

"Oh," sneered Hopkins. "In whose name do *you* protest?"

"In the name of justice, in the name of all that's right."

"Silence, you white-headed old fool, or I'll kill you!" yelled Hopkins, snatching a pistol from his holster. "I know what I am doing; and what I am doing is under the royal warrant."

"Here is my lawyer. Now, if you want to talk about protesting, talk to him."

And placing his hand on the collar of

Watson's coat, he pushed him towards the old man, saying—

"If he wants law, Watson, give him extracts from the Black Book; but mind that you don't let him go. I shall want him in a moment."

Now riding up to the tree, he examined Gillet.

The poor man's back was in a sadly mutilated state, and he had fainted.

Hopkins drew his sword, and severing the cord which bound Gillet's hands to the tree, allowed him to fall to the ground.

In the meantime the wife, alternately begging and praying to be allowed to go to her husband, and denouncing Hopkins with all the power she could command, had been kept back by the men, while the old man had been detained by Watson.

Hopkins once more made up to him.

"Look you, old man," he said, "I want you to tell me which is the residence of a certain Amos Arlington."

"Thou murderous hound, in the guise of a witchfinder," replied the old man, fiercely, "I will tell thee naught!"

"If you do not tell me, I will wring it out of you against yonder tree."

"No, no, no!" exclaimed a young woman with a babe at her breast, as she rushed from out the crowd. "Oh, injure not my poor old father. I will tell thee. He lives at Marsden Rise, yonder—there beyond the wood."

"You're sure of that?"

"Yes! His residence is well known to all here."

"So then he is a person of some importance?" muttered Hopkins. "The hostess said 'the well-known artist,' but on my soul, I can't call his name to mind. It seems, however, evident to me that the fellow must be well acquainted with my appearance. If he were not, how would he be able to sketch me like he did?"

"On a gallows," he almost hissed through his set teeth—"on a gallows! Matthew Hopkins on a gallows! By all the incarnate fiends! When I think of it, it is like anyone driving knives into my heart. But I must avenge myself. And why? Well, that is easy enough to answer. Master Melburn laughed and chuckled over the idea, but when he knows how I avenged myself on the man who permitted the sketch to be drawn, and the man who actually did the sketch, he will treat me with more respect."

These thoughts flashed like lightning through Hopkins's brain.

"Well," he said aloud, "since you are certain that that is the residence of Amos Arlington, my good wench, I'll let your father go; but let him beware how he interferes in the future. Remember that Matthew Hopkins has no respect for grey hairs or anything else. Let the old man go; and you can let the woman go to her husband now. Sharp about it, my men," he thundered, riding up and down like a madman—"sharp about it! Marsden Rise next! Marsden Rise, Watson!"

"Ay, ay!" replied that worthy, who was making an entry in one of the books by the light of a link held by one of the men.

"Ever heard of it before?"

"Never," was the calm reply.

This was a deliberate falsehood.

Watson had heard of it many a time, and he recognised the name of Amos Arlington as soon as the hostess had uttered it.

But he expressed no surprise.

He was not going to tell Hopkins whether Arlington was or was not a person of importance.

"Never heard of it, eh? Neither have I; but I think it must be a good house, Watson. Look over yonder—there are its towers rising beyond that dark wood."

"In which there may be many witches," said Watson.

"Yes, very likely; but we are not going to stay to see. We have already wasted too much time. Now, my men, form."

The men formed, and a very neat formation it was.

The links were not extinguished.

The four men having them placed themselves at the head, and the others followed, Hopkins and Watson bringing up the rear.

The word being given, away they went.

And now the feelings of the crowd found vent in howls of execration.

Bitter imprecations rained thick and fast on Hopkins's head, but the only notice he took of them was to laugh loudly.

"Mind this, Watson," he said, "a report of this might reach the king's ears. Mind you have your report ready. What shall you say the host was?"

"A man having a number of witches concealed on and about his property, and declining to give any information respecting them."

"Good! And, remember, attach a dozen or so of villagers' signatures to the document."

"Do not fear, I shall not forget; but I fancy that no report will be made, the villagers being fearful of a return visit."

"Ah!" chuckled Hopkins, "I think I made a good impression on them But this is a dark, desolate spot. Hold!" he shouted. "Are we going right, Kemp?"

"How am I to know?" growled Kemp, who more than once had narrowly escaped falling headlong into a ditch, and who, in consequence, had lit a link himself.

"Have you never been this road before? Perdition! have none of you been this way before?"

"Nay," replied Kemp; "none of us. The paths through this wood are so narrow, that we shall have to walk in single file. As to you—well, you will not get your horse through."

"Won't I?" replied Hopkins. "I'll tell you what it is, Kemp, I am determined to get my horse through; and if I could do it no other way, I'd have a path cleared by cutting down the trees."

"That would be all very well if you had the time."

"Throw the lights forward; and you, Watson—ha! What is it now?"

This sudden exclamation was caused by the men in front uttering a loud shout; and on Hopkins riding forward, he found that they had suddenly pounced upon an old man, who at that moment had been coming from the wood.

Several men had pounced upon him, and the glitter of weapons and the flashing of the links so dazed, terrified, and confused the old man that he turned as pale as death, and trembled so violently that he appeared incapable of saying anything.

He could only look vacantly from one to the other.

Hopkins surveyed him from top to bottom over and over again.

"Who are you?" he demanded.

"Nobody," was the reply.

"You look it," laughed Hopkins; "but you had better put a little life into him, my men. Now if he does not answer my questions, shake him like a rat! Listen! Where is the principal path in this wood? We want to reach—quickly—Marsden Rise."

"The residence of Amos Arlington?" faltered the old man.

"The same. So you well know it, eh? Good. All our difficulties are now removed. Hands off him. Now, my man, turn and lead us."

"Pardon, sir; pardon, gentlemen, I—I—am on an important errand. I am about to go to the village to summon medical aid."

"For whom?" asked Watson, eagerly.

"For—for my poor old wife."

"Let her wait!" exclaimed Hopkins, brutally. "I've no doubt she's able to do so for a few hours. At any rate, it is a matter of no importance to us whether she can or cannot wait. Turn and show the way, or take the consequences."

The old man, promising to lead the party, turned and moved slowly off, Kemp being close at his heels.

The principal path—a broad, fine thoroughfare, lined on each side with enormous and handsome chestnut trees —was soon reached, though a stranger would have had some difficulty in finding it, and Hopkins enjoining silence, the whole party traversed it.

They made no noise beyond that caused by the rustling of the leaves beneath their feet.

A most extraordinary sight they presented.

Anyone would have taken them for a party of robbers bent upon some desperate expedition.

As the old man proceeded, he quickened his pace.

The centre of the wood was reached, and the party had arrived at a spot where the trees and undergrowth were more dense than ever, when suddenly the old man started to the left, and, in the twinkling of an eye, disappeared.

Kemp rushed towards the spot with the intention of dragging him back; but he received such a tremendous blow with a heavy stick, that, with a loud cry, he fell back, and the link, falling from his hands, fired the brushwood.

It was with the greatest difficulty that it was extinguished; and in the meantime the old man had got clean away.

Terrible was the vow Hopkins made as to what he would do with him if he were fortunate enough to behold him again.

"However," he said, "you are not much injured, Kemp. No doubt you will find plenty of things to heal your wound at Marsden Rise. Oh, oh! we are on the right road. So let us hasten. If we follow this path no doubt we shall be right."

The old man, whose name was Wanstead, was in the service of Amos Arlington, the owner of Marsden Rise, and the errand upon which he was bound was to summon Master Arlington's physician, Mistress Arlington having for some considerable period been grievously ill.

Indeed, it was for this reason that Master Arlington had taken up his residence at Marsden Rise at this period of the year.

Wanstead had said that he was about to summon medical aid to his wife, because he thought that if allowed to go, he could at once return by another route and warn his master.

But, failing this, and determined to warn Arlington, he had made his escape from the party on the first opportunity.

Of course, from what had been said on the way, he easily recognised what the party was, and by whom it was led, though he could not understand what object Hopkins could have in a visit to his Master, who was well-known as a man who entirely set his face against witchcraft and the like.

Familiar with every path the wood contained, Wanstead made his way at a rapid pace along one, which was a narrow cut to his master's residence, whither we will precede him.

Marsden Rise was a fine old building, constructed principally of grey stone.

The present owner, Amos Arlington was a man of at least seventy years of age, and his wife, once the lovely Court beauty, Alice Grey, was a lady of about sixty-five.

They loved each other passionately; but there was one great drawback to their supreme happiness, and that was the continuous illness of the wife.

Married some thirty-four years previous to the opening of our romance, one child only was the result of their union—a son, Amos, and now in London.

Master Arlington kept several women, but only two male servants; for, though well able to afford many more, two were quite enough for the humble wants of himself and his wife.

When Wanstead entered the house his wild looks told the servants that something unusual had taken place.

"Where is the physician?" asked one.

"He has not had time to get there and back," said another. "Depend upon it he has been frightened by witches. Look at his scared face! Look at his hair and his eyes!"

"No, no!" gasped Wanstead, endeavouring to get his breath. "Not witches—no; but go, Martha, and tell master to come to me at once. Something is about to happen! Something dreadful, I'm afraid!"

"I must not disturb master," replied Martha, who, like the others, had turned pale at Wanstead's startling announcement. "He is now with mistress, who, alas! is very bad. But tell us what it is which has so alarmed you. Tell us all!"

"No, no; there must be no delay. Go!"

"What is it? What is it?" asked a calm voice.

The servants immediately drew back, and allowed the speaker—the master of the house, himself—to come forward.

A fine old man was Amos; tall, erect, considering his age, with a massive head and long flowing hair and beard—in fact, the *picture* of an artist.

"Oh, master, master," cried Wanstead, "I entreat of you to conceal yourself! Matthew Hopkins with a large troop of his bloodhounds are on the way here!"

"Here? To this house? You must be mistaken."

"No, no; they are on the road here, master. They made me show them the way through the wood. The ruffians are nearly drunk, and what they will do when they get here, heaven only knows."

"THE FIRST TO REACH AMOS FELL PIERCED THROUGH THE HEART."

And Wanstead groaned aloud.

"There must be some mistake about this," thought Arlington. "He can have no business with me; for though he knows my appearance he cannot know my name? No; he can have no —but, ha! By heavens, I had forgotten! That sketch!"

As the thought of the sketch he had laughingly made, flashed through his mind, his face turned pale, and that sudden pallor was noticed by the servants.

"Do not alarm yourselves," said Arlington, turning to them and assuming a calmness which he now most certainly did not feel. "If it is Hopkins's intention, on some pretence to come here, he will find that there is no admission for such villains as himself and the vile crew he commands. Where is Nelson?" he added, looking over the heads of the now thoroughly alarmed servants.

"Wanstead, I place the care of the house in your hands. Get Nelson—ah, here he is," he said, as the other manservant, a young and powerful one, came forward. "You and Nelson see that all the doors and windows are securely fastened. If Hopkins come here I will speak to him from from the window."

"But, master, I tell you that if Hopkins is determined to obtain admission, resistance will be useless."

"How so?"

"There are at least fifty men, determined, well-armed ruffians, who will, I feel sure, stop at nothing. Now, is it possible that we can defend the house against any attack they might make? God knows I am ready and willing to sacrifice my life in your defence."

"Ay, and so am I," said Nelson; "and if the house is about to be attacked, as you think, why, let us not talk, but close up the place, arm ourselves with whatever weapons the house affords, and hold out to the last."

"I have heard that Hopkins is now under the king's patronage," said Arlington, "but his majesty will not permit his loyal subjects to be outraged, and if the villain does attack this house, he will quickly find his position wrested from his grasp. Now, you women, ascend to your rooms, and leave us three in charge of the house. I would my brave son Amos were here! His advice in a matter like this would be of the greatest assistance."

Hurrying to his study, on the walls of which he kept a number of weapons of all kinds, more for ornament than use, however, he, with Nelson's aid, took a number down.

Nelson had considerable experience with firearms, and he quickly selected several horse-pistols he thought would be useful.

Powder and shot were next sought for and found, certainly; but there were only a very few rounds.

Master Arlington told Wanstead and Nelson to take the pistols, while he armed himself with a sword and dagger only.

The two men then proceeded to lock and bar up all doors and windows, and to put out unnecessary lights.

In the meantime, the women, from the windows above, had been vainly looking for the links of the advancing party.

Nothing was seen of them, but this was not strange, because of the density of the wood.

But Master Arlington ascended to the tower, and peered forth.

He made out several tiny lights in the distance, lights which flickered hither and thither like Will-o'-the-wisps.

Watching them for a few seconds, he made out that they were advancing slowly towards the house.

No doubt had he but that this was the party.

Nearer and nearer came the lights, until at last, the end of the wood being reached, the party emerged, and he could make out a black mass behind the links.

In a few seconds he saw a large number of men with a horseman behind them.

Descending, he entered his wife's bedchamber.

Two of the servants stood beside the bed, their faces as white as the poor lady's on whom they waited, and on whose features rested an expression of the greatest uneasiness.

"Amos," said Mistress Arlington, as she partially succeeded in raising herself, "what is this unusual commotion?

what secret are these women withholding from me? Oh, tell me not that aught has happened to my dear boy!"

"No, no, Alice; nothing has occurred to our dear boy, thank heaven. There is absolutely nothing for you to alarm yourself about. We simply anticipate a disturbance from—from someone, that is all."

"Disturbance? But, ha! you are armed, Amos. Oh, husband! what is it? Tell me, I implore you! What is it?"

"Do you remember Matthew Hopkins?"

"The witchfinder?"

"The same."

"Yes; I remember him in Gloucestershire—at least, I remember that the name of the man, who called himself a witchfinder, was Hopkins—a brutal ruffian—the man from whom you, on many occasions, rescued those who were unlucky enough to get into his clutches, and who had not the slightest connection with witches."

"The same. The same man is now in this neighbourhood—in fact, is almost at our doors."

"Whom does he seek?"

"Me."

"You? Gracious heaven! what does he want of you?"

"You remember the conversation I told you I had with John Gillet respecting the rooting out of all these dealers in the Black Arts? And perhaps you remember that I laughed at the idea of Hopkins being the man to be the 'king's witchfinder,' as people said he, one day, would be? Perhaps, too, you may remember that I made a rough sketch of the man in the tavern?"

Mistress Arlington uttered a startled cry.

"I *do* remember, Amos," she said, in low tones. "You represented Hopkins hanging from a gallows."

"I did. It was a foolish thing to do, no doubt. But then I had no idea it would remain for any length of time."

"Amos, it is Hopkins's intention to make you answer for that sketch. Oh, my dear husband, what will he do? You well know what a vindictive man was the wretch you dealt with in Gloucestershire?"

"Yes; but hark!" he suddenly exclaimed, as loud voices fell upon his ears. "I believe the villain has arrived. Do not alarm yourself, Alice. Remain calm. No harm will happen to you; but take the precaution to lock the door. I shall return directly."

Hastening downstairs, he entered the principal reception-room, which contained three long windows, secured by heavy oaken shutters; but there was no balcony, and the distance from the ground was about ten feet.

"You are in darkness, Nelson," said Master Arlington.

"Yes, sir," was the reply. "We thought it better to extinguish the lamp, for they can hardly make marks of us in the dark."

At this moment there came a thundering upon the door, accompanied by loud cries.

Master Arlington stepped to one of the windows, and opened the shutters.

Fearlessly he advanced to the front, and the glare of the torches, now greatly increased in number, made his figure perfectly distinguishable.

He was astounded when he looked down and beheld the great crowd of brawny, travel-stained and partially intoxicated ruffians, who surrounded the door.

But the principal object which attracted his attention, was the figure of Matthew Hopkins.

Hopkins surveyed the noble form above him for some few seconds, and in those few seconds his mind travelled backwards at a prodigious pace.

He thought of every place at which he had been, and at last his thoughts came to a sudden check, and he muttered—

"By heaven, I've hit it! Gloucestershire! That is the very man who got the magistrates to interfere with me so many times. Ah!" he growled, "*the* man above all others who, in the past, was a stumbling block to my advancement. Oh, oh! No wonder he was able to draw such a sketch; but my time has come now! Here, right away from witnesses, am I and my men! I'll have a mighty revenge on this man!"

"Matthew Hopkins," said Amos calmly, "what is your errand here? You see, I well know who you are."

"Ay, that you do," replied Hopkins;

"that you do, you hoary-headed old villain! And I know *you*, now—that is, I know your *name*, now—Amos Arlington."

"Ay; that is my name. And now, what seek you?"

Hopkins burst into a loud roar of derisive laughter.

"What do I seek?" he said. "You well know that I want something to say to you. I want a reckoning with you. And that you have been warned that we were on the road hither, is evident from the fact that every door and window is barred and bolted. But you shall see that that fact will not prevent us from gaining admission to this house."

"Master," whispered Nelson, "I have now a most excellent opportunity. Let me fire at him."

"No, no; let us not offer violence at at present. Let us act on the defensive, if necessary; but not on the offensive."

Again addressing himself to Hopkins, he said—

"Whatever reckoning you may have with me must be left for a future time. My wife is lying dangerously ill."

"Dolt!" shouted Hopkins, "what care I for that? Listen to what *I* say. Let your servants open this door. If they do not, I will order my men to open it. Hark ye, my men, d'ye think ye can open this massive door?"

A loud yell in the affirmative was the reply.

"I refuse you admission," said Master Arlington; "and before you can attempt to force an entrance, you must produce a warrant from the presiding magistrate of the county."

"Fool! what I do is under the *royal* warrant! I denounce you as a wizard, Amos Arlington; and it is well known, too, that you are a dealer in the *Black Arts*. Watson, read the proclamation."

"Heaven forgive you for such a monstrous falsehood!" said Amos Arlington. "This, then, is what you do to those against whom you entertain feelings of animosity?"

His last words were lost amid the loud cry which broke from the men as Watson slowly took a huge sheet of parchment from one of the books, and read the "King's Proclamation."

But we may add, that this was Hopkins's Special Proclamation, and contained passages never even dreamed of by the king or any of his too numerous advisers.

"That proclamation affects me not," said Arlington. "I emphatically deny that I have any connection with those who deal in the Black Arts."

"I don't care what you deny!" replied Hopkins, furiously. "I have denounced you, and it is my intention to search this house from top to bottom. Therefore, open this door."

"Never!"

"Then we will burst it open and enter!"

"And with the help of heaven, we will do our best to keep you and your ruffianly crew at bay."

"Hear that, my men!" yelled Hopkins. "Hear how the white-headed old scarecrow of a gallows sketcher insults you? Those with the axes come forward!"

This order was quickly obeyed.

Kemp and several other men were armed with axes.

With these they commenced upon the door; and so ponderous and fierce were the blows they delivered upon it, that the house seemed to shake beneath them, and the sound of the blows were sullenly echoed by the wood.

Above the din was heard Hopkins's voice, urging the men to keep at it, and not to leave off until they had battered down the door.

But the men required little urging.

The strong drink they had imbibed at the hostelry had now got hold of them, and they were in a fit state for any kind of villainy, especially when they were sure that plunder was to be obtained, and plunder they thought they should have in plenty from the house.

The women servants were above, but what should they do towards defending their kind master and mistress, and themselves?

One of them—a girl about seventeen—named Pauline, proposed that she should enter their master's study, and bring the arms, so that in the event of their mistress being attacked, they could at least, endeavour to defend her with their own lives.

The girl's proposition met with approval, and down the stairs she went; and while her master and the two men-servants were in the reception room, she carried up an armful of weapons, which were eagerly seized upon by the women.

After a short consultation it was decided that they should all go into a chamber which adjoined and led into their mistress's bedroom ; and it was this brave girl of seventeen who led them into the room and saw the door securely fastened on the inside, the whole being done in semi-darkness.

The delight of the scarecrow attorney, Watson, knew no bounds.

Though he possessed no strength worth speaking of himself, and could not have wielded any weapon with effect, he delighted to see destruction wrought by others. Moreover, he was delighted because he thought he might come across some valuable jewels which he could secrete about his person.

One *principal* object had this rascally attorney, and it was this—

The desire to scrape and scrape, and save every fraction that he could get, so that one day he might be able to get out of Hopkins's clutches.

Then, he considered, he would pay him for the insults he hourly heaped upon him.

Scoundrels work together, but at the same time they scheme as to the taking of each other's lives.

The men found that the door was indeed a massive affair.

Though their blows sent splinters flying in every direction, it took them a long time to cut a hole.

At last Kemp, who was really the most powerful man of the lot—save Hopkins himself—made a hole half a foot wide.

This fact he proclaimed with a loud exclamation of joy.

"Bravo!" cried Hopkins. "Now put your hand in one of you and draw the bolts."

One of the men at once inserted his hand.

No sooner had he done so than a piercing yell of agony rang out.

The next moment the man reeled, and fell flat on his back, Kemp never offering to break his fall.

Links were held over him, and a mighty yell arose.

And well might the men cry out.

The man's hand had been completely severed from his arm.

Ay; and that mighty blow had been dealt by Nelson.

A heavy cavalry sword he held, and with one blow had stricken the hand off.

"Revenge, my men!" shouted Hopkins. "You shall have revenge. Don't fear it. Stand away, Watson," he added, as he leaped from his saddle.

Approaching the aperture, he levelled his pistol and fired into it.

But no cry answered the report.

"On again with the axes!" he thundered. "On again, while I cover the hole with my pistol; and do you," he added to the other men, "keep watch all round. As soon as ever you see a human head, be it man or woman, fire! Perdition! we will make it warm for them directly."

Again the axes were brought to bear upon the door ; but the first blow had scarcely been struck when a pistol was fired from the inside.

And with deadly effect too, for the ball, passing between the men with the axes, struck down a ruffian close beside Watson, causing the latter to utter a loud, terrified exclamation.

Clean through the breast the man was struck, and he never stirred from where he dropped.

The men would have left off, for they now considered that they were only presenting their bodies as marks for those within ; but Hopkins, with bitter oaths, called upon them to continue.

Then he placed a dozen men in position, and ordered them in succession to fire into the aperture, and by that means prevent anyone within from again taking aim.

This proved effective, for no more shots were fired from there.

But presently two more were fired from the window above, and two more ruffians were stricken down.

In the meantime the men had redoubled their efforts, and the axes made tremendous havoc on the ponderous door.

They had literally to cut away the woodwork, for the locks and bolts stoutly resisted all onslaughts made upon them.

Suddenly what remained of the door flew open, and those within the house were made aware of the fact by the tremendous cheer the ruffians gave.

Links were raised on high, as Hopkins, his drawn sword in one hand and a loaded pistol in the other, rushed into the hall, the whole of his scoundrels following close behind his heels, and yelling as the hounds yell at the huntsman when he raises aloft the trophy of the chase.

The men with the links kept close up, while Watson, now that all danger was passed, elbowed his way through the throng, and ranged himself beside his master.

The hall in which they now were was a splendid specimen of a clever architect's most fanciful conception.

At the end of the hall Hopkins paused.

There at the foot of the stairs stood Amos Arlington, his magnificent and striking figure drawn to its fullest height.

His sword was in his hand, and the expression on his face was one of stern determination.

He stood there as much as to say—

"You pass not except over my dead body."

Hopkins looked very closely at him, and then he burst out into a loud, coarse howl of laughter.

"Well," he said, "you must be in possession of the impudence of the Evil One himself thus to defy me and the men behind me! Why, you fool, are you under the impression you can beat us off with that sword?"

"State your reasons for this gross outrage," replied Amos, calmly.

"Gross outrage, eh?" sneered Hopkins. "Well, what do you call the slaying of one or two of my men? Is that outrage or murder?"

"Neither the one nor the other. Every man has the right to defend his own house."

"Not against me. Not against Matthew Hopkins when he demands admission. But a word with you—you who had the audacity to sketch me in a tavern."

"On a gallows," added Watson.

"Ay; on a gallows! By heaven, every time I think of it I feel my blood boiling in my veins! Now, you white-headed old wizard, what did you mean by it?"

"It was done in a spirit of mirth."

"In a spirit of mirth. "Oh, oh!

Well, *you* don't look like a humorous man. Does he, Watson?"

"No; assuredly not," replied Watson. "He looks more like a sexton."

"Or more like a man who will soon need the services of a sexton, eh? Mark it, Amos Arlington, you, the artist with the touch of humour, I have denounced you as a wizard, and you will be punished as such. I call upon you to put down that weapon and surrender yourself."

"You may just as well call upon the stars to fall," was the firm reply.

Hopkins turned, whispered in Watson's ear, received a reply in a like manner, and then again addressed himself to the courageous old man.

"How many men have you within this house?" he asked.

"That is my business!" was the reply.

"Watson, you see that this man, though we have proved him to be a wizard, offers us a stout resistance."

"He is a desperate man," smirked Watson.

"Remember, my man, that you can swear to having heard his confession as to his being in league with Satan, and that in his house we found all the paraphernalia used by professors of the black arts!"

"Infamous scoundrel!" cried Amos. "If I am spared, your conduct shall be reported to the king, for I myself will tell him all."

"Hear that?" whispered Hopkins in Watson's ear. "He'll himself tell the king. Think that is likely? Do you think that he could get the king's ear?"

"It has just struck me as very possible, and for this reason—he is an artist. His majesty, as you know, has taken a great interest in artistic matters."

"No, I *don't* know, and don't *want* to know! But you think that he can get the king's ear? Good. Then I will not spare him."

Again turning to Amos, he said—

"Once more, and for the last time, I call upon you to surrender."

"I refuse, and I warn you against continuing this monstrous outrage!"

Hopkins, sword in hand, advanced threateningly towards Amos, who, moving back a couple of paces, placed himself on the defensive.

Hopkins attacked him furiously, though, of course, not scientifically; indeed he used his blade more after the fashion that a butcher uses his chopper.

And he found his match; ay, more than a match, for the old man was a splendid swordsman. And he no sooner realised this than, drawing back, he commanded his men to dash forward.

This they instantly did; for they were impatient to proceed to the rooms above.

The first to reach Amos fell, pierced through the heart.

The second received a ball in the head from Nelson's pistol.

But the next moment Amos received a fearful blow on the side of the head from one of the axes, and he fell at the foot of the stairs.

With wild yells the men swarmed up the stairs, Hopkins being at their head.

"Fly," whispered Nelson to Wanstead. "Fly! further resistance is useless. Fly! and leave me to try and recover our poor master. He is not dead, I hope. Fly, I tell you, as you value your life!"

"But the women—the women?"

"They will not injure the women."

"Ha, you know them not."

"Escape, man, escape! Go to the back; for if they get hold of you, they will recognise you, and slay you at once."

Wanstead turned, and darted across the landing, while Nelson, concealing himself beside a large statue, waited.

Hopkins had stopped to speak to Watson, and while he waited, the men swarmed on.

The first of them reached the spot whereon Nelson stood.

Out rushed the courageous young fellow, and raising his ponderous cavalry sword, he swept it round his head.

Down went the first, a mutilated, writhing mass of humanity.

The second would have met a like fate had he not dropped upon his knees.

Again was the blade swung round; but the sweeping blow was not delivered, for Hopkins, snatching his pistol from his belt, fired, and the brave fellow, Nelson, fell, to be at once almost hacked in pieces by the now infuriated men.

"All in darkness," said Hopkins, with an oath, "so be careful, my men. We know not how many men there may be here. But," he added, raising his voice so that it could be heard all over the place, "if any more shots are fired, we will surround the house and fire it. Now, up you go; but hold! here are the first rooms. What are these, I wonder? This one is open. It is a study."

"Yes," said Watson.

"But these other doors are locked. Ha, I see the glimmer of a light in one. What ho!" he shouted, as he brought his ponderous fist, with a crash, on the door. "Open here, and delay at your peril!"

There was no answer; but Hopkins did not again knock.

Kemp came forward, and with one blow of his axe, burst the door open.

Almost at the same instant the door of the chamber, *within* this apartment, was opened, and the women servants, with Pauline at their head, rushed into the bedchamber, and made towards the door.

Pauline carried a musket, which, having no powder, she held by the barrel in order to use the butt.

Fearlessly she made towards the ruffians, and her fellow-servants, goaded almost to madness at the sight of their mistress, who knelt upon the bed in the act of prayer, followed her closely.

Hopkins and his men were astounded.

What should they do? Disarm them?

Hopkins very quickly gave his orders.

"Treat them as *men!*" he roared. "Sex should be ignored when deadly arms are taken in hand."

"Ay," shrieked Watson. "That is the advice on page eighty-four of the Black Book."

"Hold!" cried Pauline. "Look, villains! Look at that bed! Can you see nothing which will cause you to depart from this room?"

And she pointed to her mistress.

"See?" sneered Hopkins. "Fool, what is there to see? We see sights like that every day. Down with your arms! Down with them, or we will show you not one spark of mercy!"

"Dare to cross this threshold!" replied Pauline, as, ignoring a pistol, pointed full at her breast, she raised the musket over her head, "and I'll kill the first!"

"Desist, Pauline!" murmured the

poor old mistress of the house. "Desist, child! Resistance will be useless."

But this advice came too late, for one of the men, pushing forward, Pauline brought down the musket fair on his head.

No doubt the men had thought that she would not dare to use the weapon.

"Upon them!" cried Pauline, and her fellow-servants at once responded to her cry.

But of what use was their attempt at resistance?

Of no use whatever.

Hopkins sprang upon Pauline, seized her throat with his big, muscular, horny hand, and flung her brutally backwards.

At the same moment the savage ruffians swarmed into the chamber, and seizing upon the other servants, quickly disarmed them.

"Now," said Hopkins to Mistress Arlington—"now, then, woman, tell us where is the money kept? We are not robbers, mark you; but we must bury those comrades of ours who have been killed by your husband or his servants."

"I know nothing of where the money is," replied Mistress Arlington, wringing her hands. "Tell me—what of my dear husband?"

"Your husband is dead, for what I know. I say, what of the money? Where is it kept? She pays little heed to me, Watson; so go close to her, and bawl as loud as you can in her ear."

Watson did as he was told, and shouted into the poor lady's ear with all the power of his lungs—

"The money, woman—the money!"

Mistress Arlington slowly shook her grey head, while bitter, scalding tears chased each other down her wasted cheeks.

"My husband always had charge of money matters," she faltered. "I never trouble myself about such affairs."

This reply so enraged Hopkins, that, suddenly rushing forward, he caught Mistress Arlington by the arm, and savagely pulled her from the bed.

The unfortunate lady had no strength; she could not clutch at anything, and the result was that she fell upon the floor.

"Where is the money, I say?" again the brutal "witchfinder" roared. "Tell me, or by all the incarnate fiends, I'll send you straightway to your death!"

"Amos," murmured Mistress Arlington, now in tones little above a whisper. "Amos! where are you, husband? Oh, come to me quickly. I am dying! The light fades. Yes, I go—I go! Amos, we have been so happy for many years. Hold me—hold me, husband! Tell my son that I blessed him! Amos——"

"I am here," cried a broken voice, and Amos Arlington—a fearful sight, for he was completely saturated with blood—staggered into the room.

The men, hardly knowing what to do, cleared a passage for him.

But he no sooner reached Hopkins, than the ruffian seized him by the collar.

"Hold!" he growled, as he fiercely knitted his beetle brows. "Hold! Stay where you are!"

"Let me go to her; but for a moment, and then you can do whatever you like. Oh! one word—one "

"No, no!" shouted Hopkins, hurling him backward among the men; "I'll see you in Hades first. I'd have my way even if the Evil One stood before me. I swore to have my revenge, Amos Arlington, and I'll *have* it."

"You *have* had it, monster."

"Oh, you're changing your tone now, eh? It is more like you. You shall not go near her. I say so; what is the use of your struggling? Why, you are no more in my hands than a rat would be," he added, shaking the poor old man violently backwards and forwards,

"My God!" cried poor Arlington, "let my servants raise her and place her upon the bed. Ah! she moves not—her eyes are closed; she is dead, dead! Amos, my son, would that you could see your loved mother now."

"Ay! she is dead enough," said one of the men, as he stooped over and examined Mistress Arlington.

"And a good thing too," replied Hopkins; "but," he added, once more raising his voice, "no more fooling here. Where do you keep your money?"

"Ah!" replied Arlington, "robbery, after all, is the real motive of this outrage."

"I never said so," shouted Hopkins.

"A terrible punishment shall be yours, Matthew Hopkins.

"Will it! Look you, you will not

live to tell the king anything. Not that it would be of any use if you did so, because the king would believe me before you."

"Never!"

"No! Let me tell you this. In this book, which is my Black Book, more lies are entered than even you would bargain for. That's plain enough, isn't it? Well, all those lies I read to the king himself, and every word he believes. He thinks that Matthew Hopkins is a pious man, and therefore incapable of telling falsehoods. And so he is; ho, ho!"

"Time flies," whispered Watson, "and it would be far better if we get away from the neighbourhood as fast as possible."

"Again I ask you, Amos Arlington," said Hopkins, "where do you keep your money? It is wanted to bury those who either by your hand or orders fell."

"Thank heaven, you will get none of my money, thou depraved monster! All of it is in the hands of my bankers."

"Indeed!" replied Hopkins, fiercely, "that will not do for us. We must search for it. So spread yourselves over the house, my men, and look into every nook and corner. But first look at yonder cabinet, through which that girl was lucky enough to fall. Ha, ha! Fetch out what it contains."

"No, no," cried Amos, "search wherever you like, but touch not this. All that it contains is my private papers, and little presents treasured by my poor wife."

Kemp, who had gone towards the cabinet, heeded him not.

Lifting his hand he pushed him violently aside.

Driven to despair by what the ruffians had already done—by the fearful agony he was suffering, Amos lost all control of himself, and with a loud, passionate cry he suddenly threw himself upon Kemp.

An instant's fierce struggle, and then with a mighty cry of death, Kemp reeled back, and fell almost at Hopkins's feet, a dagger plunged to the hilt in his heart.

The blow required the exertion of all the strength Amos had left.

It left him powerless. He dropped upon his knees.

But Hopkins's vengeance was swift and horrible.

He snatched an axe from the hands of a man standing beside him, rushed forward, thrust the servants aside, and dealt Master Arlington a fearful blow on his head, killing him instantly.

The sight was too much for the servants.

Several dropped fainting upon the floor, while the remainder rushed away into the other apartment, and barricaded themselves in.

They thought they should all be murdered, and they had good reason to think so.

The cabinet was now searched, everything in it being pulled out, and scattered about in every direction.

Nothing which could be turned into money was found, and so the villains left the apartment, allowing the bodies of Arlington and his wife to remain as they were, but the body of Kemp was removed, and placed with the others, downstairs.

Every room this magnificent residence contained was ransacked, and every article of jewellery was confiscated, Watson secretly pocketing two or three valuable ornaments.

Even the boxes belonging to the servants were broken open, the contents examined, and articles of the slightest value were taken.

But Hopkins was not content.

No money had been discovered.

This fact infuriated him beyond measure.

"Well, we can't make the old man answer for it now, Watson," he said, grimly; "but there's the son, who is now the proprietor of this property. We'll make *him* suffer."

Thus resolved, he ordered his men to take all they could find.

Like wild beasts, they ran from chamber to chamber.

The room in which lay the body of the master and the mistress, as well as that wherein the servants had locked themselves, was not again entered.

The study was used by Hopkins and Watson, to write particulars of what had taken place (or rather what had *not* taken place) in their Black Book.

The lies thought of and written by Watson, would have put a modern outside reporter to the blush.

The next thing attended to was the burial of the slain on Hopkins's side.

After some consideration it was decided to bury them in the wood.

Those that were wounded received what attention their comrades could give them.

The man with the severed hand was found to be in such a serious condition that Hopkins decided that he should be left at the next village.

Silence having prevailed for some time, one of the servants ventured to peer from the window, and found that they had taken their departure.

Wanstead had concealed himself some distance away from the house.

Fortunate circumstance.

For if Hopkins had laid hands on him, it is certain that he would have slain him; whereas now, he could take charge of the house, and shortly could lay the true particulars of all that had taken place before the son.

CHAPTER XII.

OF THE VISIT OF MATTHEW HOPKINS TO THE ROUND HOUSE—AND OF WHAT TRANSPIRED THERE.

THE burial of the fallen men having taken place, the whole party moved off to the next village.

Though their advance was performed with extinguished links, and the alarm was given with the least possible noise, yet dozens of people turned out to view the arrival.

Hopkins singled out half-a-dozen of the best houses, and in the king's name he billeted his men within them.

Not the slightest authority had he for so doing; but if anyone attempted to remonstrate, he ordered Watson to open one of the books, and read some doggerel extract, the effect of which generally was to send the listeners into a state of nervousness as to what they would be liable for if they did not comply with Hopkins's demand.

So, after some delay, and amid tremendous excitement, the wretches were provided with apartments.

For what length of time, Hopkins did not say.

But the next evening, to the great joy of the villagers, a general turn-out was ordered, and away once more went the whole party *en route* for the "Round House," for Hopkins pretended that he was desirous of forming the acquaintance of the man who, among others, was patronised by Sir Ferdinand Lockhart and Richard Melburn.

But it must not be supposed that he passed by every village without making inquiries respecting those concerned in witchcraft.

No; at the commencement of each village or hamlet a halt was called, and Watson, standing beside Hopkins, read aloud the "Proclamation," and then inquiries were made as to whether this or that person had had any cattle maimed of late; whether the milk was in the habit of suddenly turning sour; whether ricks had been fired, and whether any member of a family was suffering from any mysterious malady.

The proceedings of the men at every opportunity were atrocious in the extreme, and were always unchecked by Matthew Hopkins.

The commonest outrage among the men was to insult every female they met.

Maid, wife, or widow, they cared not.

They knew well enough that they were too powerful to be interfered with.

It was close upon midnight when the Round House was reached.

"By thunder!" exclaimed Hopkins, as he drew rein some distance from the gloomy-looking building, "the whole place is in darkness; but I have told you all about the extraordinary circumstances which took place at the chapel—of the startling appearance of Rupert Redmond and his comrade."

"But you did not tell me how they effected their escape," returned Watson.

"I know not."

"They are in league with Satan, I should say."

"I don't think there is much doubt about it. But then Richard Melburn said that Morecombe was in league with Satan—that he had sold himself body and soul to the fiend."

"Ha!" replied Watson, "then we have an excellent subject."

"Fool! Have I not said that I accepted a certain sum to overlook this house?"

"Ah! to be sure—to *overlook* instead of *looking* over. A great difference, since it leaves the owner in peace. But how do you imagine that those young fellows managed to get from this stronghold?"

"I am going to find out."

"Do you think it is likely that Sir Ferdinand and Richard Melburn have called here on the road?"

"No. Business of the utmost importance commands their attention at Whalley. They will leave their reckoning with Morecombe for a future time."

"Their reckoning would hardly be so swift and so sure as yours is."

"Right, right, thou scarecrow limb of the law," cried Hopkins, giving Watson a clap on the shoulder. "Right you are. But now, Watson, let me whisper in your ear—quick, for the men are becoming restless. We will enter the house alone. Do you understand? It is my opinion that there is something in that mysterious house worth having. Keep a still tongue in your head, in the event of our getting anything, and you shall receive a fair share."

"Agreed, agreed!" replied Watson, an eager, greedy glitter in his eyes.

"Among yonder trees the men may rest," continued Hopkins, "until our return."

Hopkins now gave orders that the men were to rest among the trees, but they were to be ready at a moment's notice to answer to his call.

Leaving his horse in charge of the men, Hopkins, with Watson, proceeded to the house.

They examined the front, but could see no light in any one of the windows.

They listened intently, but no sound fell upon their ears.

So they proceeded to the back.

There also were darkness and silence.

"Suppose we knock?" said Watson.

"Nay," replied Hopkins, "that would not do. There is—but hush! hush!" he suddenly exclaimed, as he caught sight of the faint glimmer of a light in an outhouse. "Hush! Keep silent! I see the figure of a man."

He was correct.

The figure he saw was the scoundrel Macrone.

Apparently he was either searching for, or hiding something.

Hopkins and Watson, drawing back in the shadow of the building, narrowly watched his proceedings.

Backwards and forwards from the house to the shed or outhouse he went; but neither could see anything in his hands.

At last Hopkins's impatience got the upper hand of him, and, creeping forward, he suddenly laid his hand on Macrone's shoulder.

With a loud, startled cry, Macrone started back, nearly dropping the lantern he carried.

"Don't look at me like that," growled Hopkins, as he fixed a fierce stare on Macrone's face—a face distorted with terror. "I am not the Evil One, nor am I one of his imps. So don't be alarmed. Who are you, sirrah?"

No answer did Macrone return.

Watson, by this time, had reached his master's side, and had taken the lantern from Macrone's hands, and its rays now fell full upon Hopkins's face and formidable figure.

"Now, man," continued Hopkins, as he shook Macrone as a dog would shake a rat. "Who are you? Are you a servant here?—a thief, or what?"

"I am my master's servant," was the hoarse, quivering reply.

"Of course, you are. But who is your master? Is Morecombe your master?"

"He is."

"Well, where is he?"

"In his house. Where else should he be?"

"Oh," chuckled Hopkins, "as to that, if you ask where else he should be, I should say dangling from the nearest gallows."

"Oh."

"You may cry 'Oh,' but that is a fact, and you know it."

"So it is evident that Rupert Redmond did not slay them," said Watson.

As he uttered the name of Rupert Redmond, Macrone, with another cry, glanced up at him.

"Don't alarm yourself," said Hopkins; "we are not friends of Rupert Redmond. Very far from that. Now I will tell you who I am. I am Matthew Hopkins. Why, fool, you look more alarmed than ever!"

"And no wonder," grinned Watson.

"Nay, as you say," said Hopkins, "no wonder. For this man knows well enough what his master's proceedings are. But you say that your master is within the building? Awake, of course? For all the servants of the Evil One are awake at night."

"Yes," replied Macrone, "he certainly is awake."

"How is it we see no lights?"

"Because——"

"What part of the building is he in?" interrupted Hopkins.

"In yonder room," replied Macrone, pointing to a long, narrow window on the first floor.

"Then how is it we see no light? For I suppose that Morecombe, clever as he is supposed to be, can't see in the dark?"

"The windows are painted black, and then they are covered with heavy black curtains."

"Now I understand. So he is within that room? And now tell me, how did Rupert Redmond and his daring companion manage to escape?"

"They were assisted by the Man of Mystery."

Hopkins and Watson exchanged rapid significant glances.

"I see how it is," groaned Macrone, "you have come to arrest Master Morecombe? But I assure you that I have had no hand in his affairs."

"Pay attention to what I say, and then you may get off scot free. What is your master doing at this present moment?"

"He is conversing," replied Macrone, slowly, and after considerable hesitation.

"Conversing! With whom? With Satan, his master?"

"Nay, with his friends."

"Male or female friends?"

"Male."

"What are these friends?"

"I cannot tell you."

"You mean that you *will not* tell me?"

"I say that I am unable to."

"But why? Have you never seen them before?"

"I have admitted them to the house many's the time; but I know not what they do. They are careful to keep their movements concealed from me."

"But what are your ideas in reference to them?"

"I have so many of my own affairs to attend to," was Macrone's evasive reply, "that I have not even considered what they may be or for what purpose they meet."

"My impression of this man," said Watson, "is that he is deceiving us."

"Ay," growled Hopkins, "I also have arrived at that conclusion. But let me tell him that if he does not answer my questions truthfully and at once, his life will not be worth a snap of the fingers. Now, I want to know what these people are with whom your master is conversing."

"Members of a secret society."

"Who is the chief?"

"Master Morecombe."

"Good! Now we have got at it. And I'll be sworn that these men are poisoners—are they not?"

"Something of the sort."

"Good! How many are there?"

"Five."

"Now let me know this. Did Rupert Redmond and his friend attempt to have revenge upon your master?"

"I fancy that they *had* it. They slew some of Morecombe's men, and placed me and Morecombe in the places in which they had been confined."

"Then how did you get out?"

"A visitor to Master Morecombe made his way into the house, found the keys, and released us."

"After how long?"

"Forty hours."

"Well, now, attend to this, the most important matter of all. Under the king's recent proclamation your master can be put to death. Do you know that?"

"No."

"You know that he is a professor of the Black Arts. It is known to me that he has sold his soul to Satan. Now you as his servant, are entitled to suffer the same penalty."

"No, no," gasped Macrone, "I swear that I am innocent."

"I am willing to let you go scot free," continued Hopkins, "if you will tell us where your master keeps his gold."

The expression on Macrone's face instantly changed from terror to astonishment.

After a pause of a few seconds he slowly shook his head.

"Ah! you may deny that you know where he keeps it," said Hopkins, "to suit your ends; but it will not pass with us. Now tell us where he keeps it, and you shall not only be free, but you shall, if you like, join us."

Macrone considered.

He had not the least doubt that Morecombe's life would be forfeited, and he soon arrived at the conclusion that so also would his life be forfeited if he did not agree to share the booty, for that was what Hopkins meant.

"Well, well," he said, "I certainly am tired of this place, and was, in fact, getting ready to go."

"Indeed!" exclaimed Hopkins, as his restless eyes suddenly fell upon a large piece of dirty canvas placed in a corner, evidently for the purpose of concealing something. "And what were you getting ready to go with you?"

And he stepped towards the canvas.

Macrone made a movement as if to obstruct him, but Hopkins, catching him by the collar, hurled him aside.

"Stand back!" he hissed. "I will see what is beneath this canvas, or my name is not Matthew Hopkins."

With this he seized upon the canvas, and threw it aside.

A huge pile of silver plate, and other costly articles were disclosed.

These things had evidently been brought there from time to time.

Hopkins seemed struck with amazement.

As for the scarecrow attorney, his eyes appeared as if about to start from his head.

Never had he beheld such a valuable collection.

Could those articles have spoken, what terrible stories of crime and bloodshed would they have told!

Many an unfortunate wretch, trusting to Morecombe's skill as a physician had been slowly but surely poisoned, and the property confiscated by Morecombe.

Wealth in the eyes of the poisoner,

was sufficient reason for the signing of a death-warrant, and the death-warrant was certainly signed and executed—that is, of course, if Morecombe was certain he should not be detected.

The whole of these articles had, from time to time, been secreted in a loft at the top of this most mysterious residence.

The poisoner had tried to keep many of his secrets from Macrone.

The majority of those secrets Macrone did not care for.

But the secret as to the money, or that which would produce money, was a matter of the greatest importance to him.

The loft was reached by a trap in the ceiling in Morecombe's experimenting room.

But there was another way, known to Macrone to the loft, which he paid secret visits to.

It had not been until after considerable search that he had discovered a small door which, on being opened was found to lead to the very loft of which he was in quest, and here Macrone had found human skeletons.

Whether they were the remains of persons who had been murdered he could not say.

Probably they had been murdered.

Macrone had to be very cautious in the removal of the articles he desired to "put away," until such time as he wished to dispose of them.

A goodly pile, on my soul," said Hopkins.

"A little mountain of wealth!" said Watson.

"It is all mine," whined Macrone.

"All yours! What? Suppose your master missed it?"

"It would be impossible unless he examined his treasures."

Has he so much, then?"

"He has."

"Well, do you agree to my proposition?"

"Listen to me," whispered Watson. "Since it is evident that Morecombe has so much, would it not be worth while to let this man go with his booty, first making him take an oath as to silence?"

"What then?"

"Then," leered Watson, "then bury Morecombe beneath one of his vaults, take his property—at least, what can easily be turned into money—and bury that in some spot whence we may take it at our convenience."

"This, Watson, is of course *legal* advice, eh? But it is advice that I don't think I shall act upon. I took money to look over the fact that Morecombe was a person to whom I should devote my attention on account of his practices; and besides, I have no wish to offend either Richard Melburn or Sir Ferdinand Lockhart."

"But what would be easier than to lay the blame of the murder on the shoulders of Rupert Redmond and his comrade? Then it would not be necessary to bury him."

"That is feasible; it is, in fact, excellent legal advice, ho, ho! But no; if we can get some of the treasure without slaying Morecombe, well and good."

"But you don't mean to let this man have all this goodly pile?" asked Watson in amazement.

"Look into my face," replied Hopkins, "and then tell me if you think I should be such a fool."

"I do not; I thought such a thing was out of the question."

Then turning to Macrone, Hopkins said—

"You agree?"

"I do."

"Then lead the way. But beware! Attempt to play us false, and by all the saints I will send a ball into your heart!"

"I will not play you false if you will stand by what you have said. But I have no desire to join your party."

"Why?"

"My reasons are numerous."

"I will not ask them. Go on."

"I had better take the lantern, because it will be necessary to occasionally shut off the rays."

Creeping cautiously forth, he led the way to the wood cellar.

He was closely followed by Hopkins and Watson, the former carrying a loaded pistol in his hand.

The wood cellar being reached, Macrone said—

"It would be safer if we took off our shoes here, because the flooring sounds so."

"Oh," replied Hopkins, "I am quite willing to take off my shoes. Off with yours, Watson."

Shoes having been taken off, Macrone was the first to crawl through a little doorway.

Hopkins and Watson kept close to his heels.

A passage of considerable length was cautiously traversed.

After some few moments, Hopkins laid his hand on Macrone's shoulder.

"Hist!" he whispered. "What is that I hear? Voices?"

"Yes," replied Macrone; "we are now beside the chamber in which Morecombe is conversing with his friends."

"Is there a hole or anything about here? I should like to see Morecombe and his friends."

"Do you know Morecombe by sight?"

"Not yet; but is there a hole or window that I can look through?"

"I will show you a small hole; but whatever you do, do not pass your hand across the wainscotting. He might hear it, and all his friends are well armed."

"Indeed," sneered Hopkins. "You may depend upon it the fact of his friends being armed will not make me quake with fear. Now the hole."

Macrone took him to a certain portion of the woodwork, then bade him kneel, and Hopkins having complied, he pointed out a tiny hole.

Looking through it, Hopkins saw six men seated at a table, and from the description furnished by Macrone as he looked, made out Morecombe.

Who the others were, of course he had no way of telling, since Macrone persisted in declaring that he did not know them.

They were each clad in black costumes, and as Macrone had said, were well armed, not only with swords, but with pistols.

That they were discussing a matter of the greatest importance was certain.

When Hopkins looked through, Morecombe was gravely addressing them, but in so low a tone that, though the witch-finder pressed his ear right against the hole, he failed to hear more than a word or two.

But suddenly a scraping of feet was heard.

Hopkins placed his eye to the hole again, and saw that the men had risen.

"They are going," he whispered· "Watson, something must be done at once! If they pass by the trees they will see the men; and they would return to Morecombe and inform him. Do you return—quickly with Macrone, and tell Cooper, who will take the lead, to seize the men if they should pass that way."

It was certain that neither Watson nor Macrone liked the idea, but they dared not refuse to obey, and so they returned.

Macrone took the lantern with him, and thus Hopkins was in darkness.

But pushing along, he at last reached a trap, which led directly into the loft.

Macrone had furnished him with the way the door was opened, which was by means of a spring of the most simple construction, and Hopkins had his hand upon the knob when his attention was called to what he thought was a noise within the loft itself.

He listened intently and looked, with the object of ascertaining whether a light was within it.

Nothing of the sort did he see.

Yet the sound within the loft was repeated.

But presently it ceased, and as several minutes passed, and Hopkins did not again hear it, he determined to enter.

He considered that he would be just as safe within the loft as without.

And now, for a moment we will descend to Master Morecombe.

The "friends" with whom he had been conversing were certainly members of a secret society, but Morecombe was not their chief, nor was he a "member" of their body.

The fact was that the five men were gentlemen holding high positions, and Morecombe was a tool of theirs—bought and paid for, and sworn to do whatever they might ask him.

Had Hopkins overheard their conversation, he might have gathered sufficient to have put a sudden check upon a tremendous design, and have reaped a rich harvest from no less a personage than King James himself, for it was against the life of that monarch that the secret society was plotting.

"So that is now all settled," chuckled Morecombe, rubbing his hands together with great satisfaction. "Of this I am certain—that King James will lose his life, or else a dozen gentlemen high in the land will know what the rope is. The poison I shall supply will be certain."

"They agree that it should be administered at a certain banquet," he mused, opening one of his drawers and taking out a small phial closely sealed and labelled. "Well, we will say that James drinks the poison placed in his cup at the hour of nine. The poison will take eight hours to accomplish its work, so that the king will be found dead in his bed. Excellent! And now to get the required money, which must, of course, be in gold."

Lighting a lantern, he brought from the corner of the chamber a ladder, and this he placed against the trap in the ceiling.

Then taking the lantern he ascended.

The trap was reached, and the flap raised and thrown back.

Still higher went Morecombe, and, the top being reached, he placed his lantern on the floor of the vault

He was about to hoist himself up, when he chanced to raise his eyes, and encountered the fierce, terrible-looking face of Matthew Hopkins.

Morecombe uttered no cry.

No word of any kind passed his lips for a few seconds.

But finding his tongue, he yelled—

"Who art thou—man or fiend?"

"Fiend!" sneered Hopkins. "Why you know well enough that your master comes not until summoned. I am a *man*—and what am I here for? To send you down to your grave!"

So saying, Hopkins caught up a huge vase of tremendous weight, and dealt Morecombe a blow full upon the top of his head.

It was a fearful blow, and it was an effective one, for it smashed Morecombe's skull completely in, and sent him to the bottom of the ladder, devoid of life.

Even as Hopkins knelt over the trap, the better to look at his handiwork, Macrone, with Watson behind him, entered.

Advancing to the trap, both saw what had taken place, for the lantern still burned at the edge, while the lamp below was also alight, and threw a strange red glow on the ghastly corpse.

"WHO SENT YOU HITHER TO ENACT THE PART OF SPY?' CRIED RICHARD."

MATTHEW HOPKINS, THE WITCH-FINDER.

In the year 1645 the atrocious witch-finder, Matthew Hopkins, hanged no less than sixty witches in his native county of Surrey alone, and received twenty shillings a head for every witch he could discover. Butler in his note thus alludes to him:

Has not the present Parliament
Mat Hopkins to the devil sent,
Fully empowered to treat about
Finding revolted witches out?
And has not he within a year
Hanged threescore of them in one shire?

Neither Macrone nor Watson were horror-stricken, though the latter was considerably surprised that Hopkins, after what he had said, had taken the poisoner's life.

As for Macrone, he, after the first few moments, breathed a sigh of relief.

"He is dead!" he thought; "and therefore my right to the property I have from time to time stolen will be undisputed."

Foolish man!

He knew not the real character of Matthew Hopkins.

It never struck him that, though not an actual witness, he, nevertheless, knew who was the murderer, and that consequently this man of blood, Matthew Hopkins, would put him out of the power of ever betraying him.

No, this never struck him for a moment; almost all his thoughts were concentrated upon the treasure lying in the shed—that treasure for which he most assuredly, had repeatedly risked his life.

"That's an end of Morecombe!" grinned Watson, opening one of his books. "I'll just make an entry."

"No entry just now!" interrupted Hopkins, snatching the book from his hand, and dealing him a tremendous blow on the head with it.

"Is Morecombe quite dead?" ventured Macrone.

"Dead? I should think so. He bears a striking resemblance to a dead man, doesn't he? Yes; he is dead, and his master, Satan, never came to his aid. Now, then, let us select the articles of the most value. Hold the light, Watson —high up. Soh! Now we can see what we are about. Zounds! what mighty treasures are here. Look at yonder gold casket. Is it gold, Macrone?"

"Yes; solid gold."

"Get it down. Here, stand on this box, and reach it down to me."

Macrone got upon the box as desired, and he was reaching out his hands to take the box from the shelf whereon it was placed, when Hopkins suddenly sprang forward.

Watson had not the slightest idea what his intention was.

But it was soon apparent.

The bright blade of a long dagger flashed in the rays of the lantern; another second, and it was buried in Macrone's back.

The cry Macrone uttered was dreadful to hear.

As he staggered backwards from the box, Hopkins seized him by the collar, and pushed him headlong down the trap.

Even the hard-hearted scarecrow attorney shuddered.

More than ever was he beginning to understand the man whom he had sworn to serve.

Hopkins, noticing the look on his face, suddenly asked him—

"What! Do you think *your* turn has come. No, no, Watson, I have need of your services. But you want to know why I have thus acted, and without a hint or a warning of any description? I will tell you. Below in that room I saw a bunch of keys; those keys, beyond doubt, are the keys of this house. Very well; it occurred to me that if both these men were dead, we could dispose of their bodies in the vaults, and then, after bringing the articles from the shed, and placing them within the house, they could remain until a convenient opportunity arrived for removing them. It is a far better plan than taking the trouble to dig a hole and bury the treasure. What think you?"

"You have acted very well."

"I have acted as you would have advised, eh?"

"As I should have advised, yes."

"What I have done is perfectly legal, Watson, eh?"

Watson laughed outright, and his laugh was echoed by Hopkins.

"After all," he said, "I have but slain two imps. But, of course, their deaths can be laid at Rupert Redmond's door —that is, if such were necessary. But now let us hasten. The shed first. Let us take the things in the house, throw them anywhere, then take these two bodies below. But," and here for a moment Hopkins paused and stared cunningly into Watson's face—"but as I am not acquainted with this house, and as there may be a few dangerous traps here and there, do you show the way."

Watson's face turned ashy pale.

What he had already seen of this mysterious house showed him plainly enough that it was quite probable there were scores of dangerous traps in it.

But could he refuse ?

Certainly not.

Under his arm he tucked his books, and holding aloft the lantern with a trembling hand, he prepared to lead the way.

The task occupied but little time, for the property was thrown into a corner in a confused heap.

Beautiful gold and silver ornaments were by this means smashed ; but Hopkins reflected that he did not require the ornaments, but the precious metal of which they were composed.

The bodies of the master and the man were then dragged below.

The murdered men were thrown one on the top of the other in one of the open vaults, there to remain for the present.

Hopkins had secured the keys, and without waiting to make the least examination of the room in which he found them, he locked up the place.

Then the pair returned to the men, who by this time were not only impatient, but fast becoming enraged.

The five "gentlemen" whom Hopkins, through Watson, had ordered them to seize, were safe in their custody.

They had been disarmed, and their hands were fastened behind their backs.

Loud and furious were they at the outrage offered them.

"Light a link or two," said Hopkins, "and let us have a look at these persons."

The glare of half-a-dozen links soon lit up the scene.

Hopkins took one and flashed it in the face of the first prisoner—a tall, slender, elderly man, with a stern and haughty expression.

"Your name, sirrah?" asked Hopkins.

"That is my business," was the furious reply. "And perhaps if I ask *your* name you will return a reply similar to the one I have given *you*."

"Oh, oh!" chuckled Hopkins, "so the men have not given my name, eh? Why, thou long-jawed, hungry-looking villain, I am the redoubtable Matthew Hopkins!"

The gentleman started, but made no observation.

Hopkins saw that his name was recognised, not only by the prisoner he was addressing, but by all of them, a fact which gave him much satisfaction, since this was evidence that his name was becoming known to everyone.

"Your name, I say?" repeated Hopkins, in threatening tones.

"I refuse to give it," was the haughty reply.

"Well," replied Hopkins, "you are not the first by many who has refused to give me his name, nor would you be the first by many whom I compelled to speak. By heaven! if you don't give your name when next I ask you, I'll have you torn limb from limb."

"Vulgar scoundrel!" was the scornful reply, "you are beneath my contempt."

"What?" yelled Hopkins; "what? I—What are *you* staring and grinning at?" he asked, as he suddenly turned to Watson, whose eyes were fixed upon the face of the prisoner Hopkins was addressing.

"I recognise him,' replied Watson. "I *thought* I knew him, but was not quite sure. There seemed to be some alteration in him. That alteration I can now trace to the fact that he wears a beard."

"Well, who is he?"

"Master Prior, once a client of mine."

Master Prior's countenance at once changed, by which means Hopkins considered that Watson was right.

"And who is Master Prior? I mean, what position does he hold?"

"He is a gentleman of fortune."

"In that case I am *fortunate* to have him in my custody. Hark ye, Master Prior. Perhaps you will explain to my satisfaction, the reason you were in secret consultation with Morecombe, a well-known professor of the black arts."

"I shall do nothing of the sort."

"Very well. Wait a moment."

The others were asked their names, but each refused to give his.

Hopkins, thereupon, consulted with Watson for some moments.

Presently he turned to the men.

"Search them!" he cried.

Thereupon the voices of the prisoners were united in loud protestations.

But they were unheeded.

The whole of the men pounced upon them, and turned their pockets inside out.

The contents of those pockets were of a miscellaneous character, so far as four of them were concerned.

Master Prior's pockets contained a great deal of money in cash and goldsmiths' notes, but the principal thing upon which Hopkins pounced was a packet of documents secured with a silken cord and inscribed with secret characters.

This he handed to Watson, warning him not to lose it on peril of his life.

"No doubt," he said, "that will give the particulars of their relationship with Morecombe. It might be a fortune in our pockets."

"Most true," replied Watson.

Master Prior's haughtiness had entirely disappeared.

He now fairly shook with terror.

"Restore my packet," he gasped, "and whatever sum you ask shall be yours."

"No," replied Hopkins, "I will do nothing of the sort—at least, I will not at present. On a future occasion I might be inclined to make terms. But, first of all, I intend to go through those papers.

"It may pay me better to make terms with someone else. And now," he added, "you will each see what it is to decline to give Matthew Hopkins information. Still, I will give you another chance. Your names—quick!"

There was no reply, though there might have been had Hopkins not got possession of those papers.

Getting no answer, Hopkins flew into a fearful rage.

"Look you, Cooper," he said to the ruffian who had taken the place of Kemp, the man who, as our readers will remember, met a well-deserved doom at the hands of the unfortunate Master Arlington, "yonder is a stream of some kind; that I can tell by the mill, on which the moon shines. Take these men there."

Again rough hands were laid upon the five gentlemen, and they were hurried towards the stream, which was known as the "Silver Streak."

It was a pretty piece of swift running water, but exceedingly dangerous at all times.

The side of the water being reached, Hopkins shouted—

"Hold! Let them have another minute."

The men accordingly paused, though still retaining a firm hold of their victims.

"I protest against this most monstrous outrage!" cried Master Prior, "and depend upon it, you shall suffer."

"Oh, you threaten, eh? Well, your threats have no more effect upon me than a straw would have in turning the current of that stream. The whole five of you I denounce, in the presence of these witnesses, as participators in unlawful proceedings."

"*What* unlawful proceedings?"

"Witchcraft."

"It is false! And in the presence of *what* witnesses?"

"These—my men," chuckled Hopkins, "who are ready to swear whatever I tell them to. But we will have no further delay. Away with them to the water!" he shouted.

Instantly each man was hurled off his feet, and sent headlong into the water.

So quickly was this done, that, before any one of them could realise what had actually occurred, they were floundering in the stream.

At once every man was for himself.

Their cries and frantic struggles caused Hopkins and his ruffians the greatest amusement.

The stream carried them in the direction of the mill.

The mill-wheel was some two hundred yards off; but neither Hopkins nor his men took the trouble to see how many out of the five had contrived to reach and get a hold of some portion of the woodwork."

Torches were extinguished, the word was given, and away once more went the whole party.

CHAPTER XIII.

OF THE CAPTURE OF THE STRANGE OLD WOMAN—OF THE JOURNEY TO BLACKROCK CASTLE—AND OF WHAT HAPPENED THERE.

IT now becomes necessary to allow one week to elapse.

During that time, however, much that is highly important had occurred.

Sir Ferdinand and Richard had gathered their forces, but they had come to the conclusion that it would be better and safer if they could get a few more.

Well aware of the fact that they could not get them in the neighbourhood, they sent to London for them.

The man who undertook this commission was Hawkswell.

He was perfectly familiar with all parts of London, and as he went provided with plenty of money, he would have no difficulty in getting what he sought.

No attack had been made upon Pendle Forest.

Hopkins, after long persuasion had consented to wait for reinforcements.

But, in the meantime, spies had been sent into the forest—one after the other.

Not one of these men had returned.

So even Hopkins, who had always been in the habit of carrying everything before him, began to comprehend that the inhabitants of Pendle Forest were likely to prove more formidable than the individuals he usually encountered.

On the night of the sixth day after Hopkins's arrival, Hawkswell returned with a large party, all mounted.

Sir Ferdinand, Richard, Hopkins, and Watson now working hand in hand, were, on the night of the seventh day, in Sir Ferdinand's study, discussing the particulars of the intended attack, and being aided by a rough plan, the work of a man with whom our readers are acquainted—Black Braddell.

Suddenly a tremendous commotion was heard; voices were shouting; and arms were clanking, as if something important had occurred.

Such proved to be the case.

Hawkswell and Cooper, followed by a host of men, were proceeding up the corridor, dragging between them a strange-looking old woman.

"What is this?" asked Sir Ferdinand.

"This old woman was found prowling about the Abbey," replied Hawkswell; "and I recognise her as one of Mother Frampton's witch assistants — Martha Burgoyne."

"What!" cried Richard; "*this* old hag Martha Burgoyne? I've heard of the detestable witch. *This*, then is the loathsome assistant to the horrible fiend, Mother Frampton."

"Mother Frampton's assistant, eh?" said Hopkins, seizing the woman, and thrusting his face into hers. "A more fortunate circumstance could not have occurred! By heaven, we *are* lucky! Hark ye, Martha Burgoyne, can your master, the Evil One, get you out of our clutches?"

"I serve not Satan!" replied the old woman.

"You serve not Satan!" mimicked Hopkins. "Know you who *I* am, Martha Burgoyne?"

"I don't."

"No," chuckled Richard; "*she never saw the sketch!*"

Hopkins's eyes flashed furiously at this allusion.

"So you don't know me, eh?" he said to the old woman. "Well, let me enlighten you. I am Matthew Hopkins, the witch-finder—the hunter down of all such as you! But we will examine her, Sir Ferdinand?"

"Ay; that will be the thing. Let her be brought into the study, and we will question her; tie her hands behind her back. Some of these hags have the power to mesmerise men and women."

"Bah!" cried Hopkins. "Let children and not men talk such nonsense! Do *you* possess the power of mesmerism?"

The old woman made no reply, so Hopkins, seizing her by the throat, bawled in her ear; and still receiving no reply, he dealt her a blow on the face with his open, horny hand.

No cry of pain left the old woman's

lips; but, for a moment, a dangerous light shone in her eyes.

Her hands were tied behind her back and secured to her waist by Hawkswell, and with such force that it seemed as if the blood would burst through her veins.

Then she was taken into the study and placed at one end of the long table in the centre.

"Now," said Richard, "no doubt, thou wretched, deformed lump of humanity, you well know that the vaults of this Abbey contain instruments of torture! Bear in mind that we can put you to the most horrible agony. And we *will* do so if you refuse to answer our questions. Understand it?"

"I hear what you say," was the reply.

"How came you to be in the vicinity of this Abbey? Who sent you to enact the part of spy?"

"No one. I lost myself."

Hawkswell and the men, who crowded round the doorway, burst into derisive laughter.

"Oh, you lost yourself!" sneered Richard. "It was fortunate we contrived to find you. Now who sent you hither to enact the part of spy?"

"No one."

"You are Mother Frampton's assistant?"

The old woman smiled disdainfully.

"I *know* Mother Frampton," she said.

"And you can give us much information concerning that infamous old hag?"

"I cannot. Her movements are as much a mystery to me as they are to everyone else. I say that I know little of her."

"Hear that?" whispered Hopkins, with a chuckle. "Can't you *see* anything?"

"No," replied Richard.

"Nor can I?" added Sir Ferdinand.

"Ah!" said Hopkins; "you have not had the experience I have with these people, or you would see that the hag is *jealous.*"

"Jealous! Of whom?" asked Richard.

"Of Mother Frampton. Such a thing is of frequent occurrence."

"Hark ye, woman!" said Richard. "Have you heard that an attack is to be made upon Pendle Forest by order of the king?"

"I have."

"You could give us information if you thought proper, no doubt. Well, listen to this: If you will answer my questions, one hundred guineas shall be given you."

The hideous face of the old woman beamed with satisfaction.

"I will give you what information I can," she said.

"First about Pendle Forest?"

"Nay; of the forest I know little, and nothing which would be of service to you."

"But you know about Mother Frampton?"

"I do; and I would, if I could, bring her to the stake! For she has wronged me thrice even within the last week."

"Ah!" chuckled Hopkins, "here we have it."

"Continue," said Richard; "fear not—the reward shall be yours. We have ascertained that as soon as our intentions were known, Mother Frampton and the horrible troupe with which she is surrounded quitted their huts. But we have sought in vain for her present abode. You can furnish us with it?"

"I can."

And again the old woman's face glowed with satisfaction.

"Proceed," said Richard.

"Mother Frampton," was the reply, "with her body-guard——"

"Her *what?*" interrupted Hopkins.

"Body-guard, consisting of sixty women, are at this moment occupying Blackrock Castle."

"Ha!" ejaculated Sir Ferdinand. "Has she ever occupied it before?"

"For years she has frequented it, but, of course, not permanently. She travels from place to place."

"Under whose orders is she?"

"I don't understand you."

"Is she acting under the instructions of the Man of Mystery?"

"Not that I am aware of. His secrets are not known to Mother Frampton."

"Although her secrets are known to him?"

"So I believe."

"There is no doubt of it. Ah! through Mother Frampton we can strike the first blow."

"Look you!" said Hopkins, rising in a state of intense excitement; "you can lead us to this castle?"

"I can—but the reward ? "

"Will you, if the reward is first of all placed in your hands ? "

"I will," replied the old woman,.

"Can you lead us in such a way that our movements will be unobserved by anyone ? "

"Yes."

"Then, Sir Ferdinand," said Hopkins, "rely upon it that Mother Frampton shall be in my hands in a very short space of time. By all the fiends, what punishment shall be *her* portion ? "

"The stake ! " said Richard; "but not until we are present."

"You do not intend to accompany him, then ? " asked Sir Ferdinand.

"I do not; but wait ! Let me think. Yes; I *will* accompany him. You must remain here, though."

"Ay, I will remain here," replied Sir Ferdinand, eagerly. "The Abbey must remain in charge of one of us."

Only too thankful was Sir Ferdinand to remain at the Abbey.

The word was passed, and at once the call to arms was given by Hopkins.

Sir Ferdinand counted out the sum agreed upon, and handed it to Richard, who placed it in his pocket.

"You see," he said, " that I have the money all ready for you. But we have been so often deceived that it is necessary we should proceed with the utmost caution. You can lead the way just as well with your arms tied behind your back as with them free."

"I do not object."

"Rely upon it that we will take care Mother Frampton knows not who our informant was. Now, my men, hurry— hurry ! By heaven, there is work before you ! "

"There will be but little *work*, I fancy," grinned Hopkins. "The hag will be taken unawares. How I long to get her into my clutches. Depend upon it, she can give important information respecting the Man of Mystery, and the so-called secret brotherhood. We will promise her anything—freedom and money—to reveal what she knows, and then when she has supplied us with every information, we will subject her to every torture with which I am acquainted, and, finally, we will burn her alive.' "

"Ay," said Richard; "and the crew found with her."

After some discussion, it was agreed that fifty unmounted men would be quite sufficient for the expedition.

Hopkins and Richard were mounted.

All being in readiness, the whole party set out, the old woman walking with her arms tied behind her back.

Blackrock Castle was, many generations before the period of our romance, in the occupation of a family of the name of Greenaway, the head being Lacy Greenaway, who was executed for treason, and his property confiscated to the Crown, and the castle allowed to go to ruin; and in time it was said to be haunted by the spirit of the executed man.

By some this was ridiculed, but the majority of people believed it to be true ; and many had sworn that, in the dead of the night, they had seen the spirit of Lacy Greenaway slowly and solemnly pacing the battlements.

The castle was still a magnificent old building, but was now, in many places, falling to pieces in consequence of neglect.

Mother Frampton and her mysterious crew had been, from time to time, the occupiers of this old place.

But not a soul was ever seen to enter or leave by any of its many doorways, gateways, or windows.

No lights had ever been seen within it; nor did anyone ever see smoke ascending from its roof.

The castle stood on the south side, at the edge of Pendle Forest, amid the wildest of vegetation, and surrounded by enormous rocks.

The old woman led them slowly, but without hesitation, to the forest which, for some distance, was skirted.

The only light they obtained was from the moon, the rays of which, however, but dimly penetrated the dense masses of foliage beneath which they passed.

Richard, becoming impatient with the slowness at which they proceeded, directed Hopkins to order two or three links to be lit.

"No, no," was the reply. "What ! show a light and frighten the quarry. That will never do."

"The quarry would not be alarmed," replied Richard, " for we are too far away."

"But there may be someone about who would quickly convey the warning to the witches. Hold! Let us pause a moment. Now, Martha Burgoyne, how long do we follow this path?"

"But a few moments more," was the reply.

"Then we come to the subterranean passage of which you spoke?"

"Exactly."

"How long is it?"

"Eight hundred yards I have been told."

"And it leads whither?" asked Richard.

"It leads directly under the great reception-room."

"Where Mother Frampton holds her councils?"

"Yes."

"You think it is likely that she is there at this moment?"

"I do, for this is the hour at which she holds her councils?"

Again the party proceeded, and, in a few moments, the entrance to the subterranean passage was reached, and here Hopkins and Richard left their horses.

It now became absolutely necessary for the production of light, consequently, a single link was lit.

It afforded just sufficient light to enable them to proceed with caution.

The passage was a broad one, but the roof was remarkably low, and, like the sides, was dangerous, on account of the jagged nature of the rock of which it was composed.

The ground, unlike the sides, was *of soft earth*, and perfectly level.

Being soft it emitted no sound of footsteps.

Little did that party imagine that they were traversing the top of a huge burial ground, but such was the case.

With every yard traversed the face of the old woman became more agitated; her eyes glittered like diamonds, and more than once a low chuckle of intense satisfaction escaped her lips.

Her agitation, however, was not observed by Hopkins or his party.

Presently the old woman slightly increased her pace.

Another moment and a strange rustling fell upon the ears of the party.

The man with the link held it higher, and just as he did so, *two white owls* fluttered round it and sped away like the wind.

"What was that?" asked Hopkins. "What birds were they?"

"Two white owls," replied one of the men.

"By heaven!" exclaimed Hopkins. "that is proof that we are nearing the abode of witchcraft."

"Ay," said Richard, "owls and witches are closely connected. But it would be something to know how they contrived to get here."

"By the same way as we entered, I'll warrant."

The owls that had just taken flight had been *nestling in the dress of the old woman.* They came forth at her command.

Very shortly now the end of the subterranean passage was reached.

"Hold!" whispered Hopkins. "Pass the word—every man ready with his arms!"

Each man drew his blade and a pistol, and eager was everyone for the rush.

"Stay!" said Richard, "there is a stone door. Look you, old woman, how are we to pass this door?"

"You see this hole? One of you must crawl through it, then turn to the left. That will bring you on the other side of the stone. Beside it is an iron ring; if that is pulled the stone revolves."

"Ay, ay," said Hopkins, impatiently; "but who is to crawl through that hole? I question whether there is a man among us who is small enough to do so."

"Quick!" said Richard; "let us try."

One by one the men were brought forward; but try how they would, not one of them could get his shoulders through.

"Well," said Hopkins, "there's no other way—the woman must go through. But mark this well, Martha Burgoyne. If you attempt to play us false I will tear you to pieces! Now, untie her hands, and let her get through."

Her hands being unfastened, the old woman got upon her knees, and was quickly through the hole.

Dead silence now fell upon the party.

Each was anxiously awaiting the revolving of the stone.

Presently were heard the clanking of chains, and sounds as of iron rods being drawn aside.

Suddenly the man holding the link muttered a sharp exclamation, and at the same instant the link, with a hiss, went out.

The whole party were plunged into darkness.

"Fool!" growled Hopkins, "why didn't you pay attention?"

"Someone snatched the link from my hand," whispered the man.

"Bah!" replied Hopkins. "Do you fancy that I am a fool? By heaven, what a time the hag is pulling the ring as she said! But, ha! here we have it! I feel it moving! Ready, my men—ready!"

Richard, now trembling with suppressed excitement, stood, sword and pistol in hand, ready to dash through the aperture as soon as it was made.

Slowly, the stone—a huge mass of masonry—revolved, and then was heard the voice of the old woman—

"Enter! Cautiously—cautiously!"

Without making much noise, the whole party passed through, and the stone resumed its previous position.

"Light another link," whispered Hopkins.

"It is not necessary," replied the old woman, "for there is light enough. Behold!"

Instantaneously the place was brilliantly illuminated, though by what means it is impossible to tell.

Certain it is that no links, lamps, nor anything else was seen.

Hopkins and his men were astonished.

They found themselves in a chamber of tremendous length and width, the high-vaulted roof being supported by pillars of massive thickness.

"Betrayed!" shrieked Hopkins.

"Ay," shouted the old woman; "find the aperture by which you entered if you can. Richard Melburn, villain and fool, behold your guide!"

The old woman ran backwards a few paces, then abruptly stopped.

As she did so the rags she was wearing fell to the ground, and there was revealed the unmistakable figure and the fearfully ugly face of FENDYKE!

Richard, with a bitter cry, aimed his pistol at him, and fired.

As the shot rang out the brilliant light vanished, and the place was once more in total darkness.

"Links!" yelled Hopkins. "Links, men! If this is a trap, we'll soon get out of it. What are you muttering at, you craven-hearted curs. Why, I hear your teeth chattering. What! afraid of a parcel of old women? But hish! What is that?"

Again came a light, but it did not flood the place like the first.

It shone in one straight stream from the stone flooring.

With hearts beating wildly, the men watched it.

It slowly increased in volume until a light of extraordinary brilliance was burning.

Hopkins was about to rush towards it, when a deep voice cried—

"Hold, Matthew Hopkins, murderer! Hold!"

"Who utters my name?" shouted Hopkins.

"I," was the reply.

"And I," said another voice.

"And I," shrieked a third; and then were heard another and another, until the whole vault rang with the cries.

The brilliant light gradually faded, and gave place to a strange blueish vapour, which quickly filled the vault.

Again and again did Hopkins and Richard command the men to follow them.

But they refused to move.

They seemed absolutely fascinated by the strange events happening before their eyes.

The vapour increased in density, until the pillars, the roof, and the walls became hidden from view.

In the meantime the cries had increased, until it seemed as if the names of Matthew Hopkins and Richard Melburn were being uttered by a thousand voices.

Suddenly the vapour vanished, and Hopkins and his startled men saw, at some little distance from them, a host of old women, and a more hideous, fiendish crew they had never beheld.

They had formed a huge ring by joining hands.

In the centre of that ring was a huge caldron, suspended from the vaulted roof by means of a powerful chain and hook,

Beneath it burned a number of faggots.

Beside the caldron stood Mother Frampton.

She, like the hags by whom she was surrounded, was only partially attired.

What they had wrapped about their attenuated forms was nothing but a mass of rags.

Their dishevelled grey locks flew about their shoulders in wild disorder, while their sunken eyes glittered furiously.

"By the powers!" said Hopkins, "we have caught them in the very act of witchcraft."

"Silence, Matthew Hopkins!" cried Mother Frampton, in harsh, grating, peculiar tones, "and list to what I tell you. Listen to the warning, thou murderer. List to it, thou murderer of the innocent. You have been led here to learn the nature of the fate in store for thee."

"Blasphemous hag!" hissed Hopkins. "Foul worshipper of the Prince of Darkness! Let me tell you what is in store for *you* and the hags with you. Ay, you may jabber and shriek, but it will have no effect on me. We are here to arrest you, Mother Frampton, so surrender yourself, or by heaven we'll slay you without showing you the least mercy. Surrender!"

And sword in hand, he advanced a pace or two.

Instantly the old women, giving utterance to an ear-piercing shriek, commenced to go round and round.

Gradually their pace increased, until they flew round the caldron with marvellous speed, all the while uttering an incantation, in which the names of Hopkins, Richard Melburn, and Sir Ferdinand were mingled.

Mother Frampton took from her bosom a number of small phials, together with what seemed to be various herbs, and one after the other she hurled them into the caldron.

The flames within increased as each article was added, until a mighty column of flame, in which all the colours of the rainbow were blended, ascended until it licked the roof.

The scene now presented was truly appalling.

The fearful shrieks, cries, and bursts of wild laughter, the speed with which the women whirled round and round,

dazed, bewildered, and terrified the men to such a degree, that they would have fled had the opportunity presented itself.

One of them secretly endeavoured to find the ring in the door the old woman, or rather Fendyke, had spoken of.

But though he again and again passed his hands over the spot where he considered they had entered, he felt no ring; nor, indeed, anything which would indicate the existence of a secret entrance.

All power seemed to have deserted Richard.

With his sword still grasped in his hand he stood, his eyes fixed upon the caldron.

Suddenly the weird gallop stopped, the flames in the caldron died down, and in their place rose a column of white vapour.

"Behold, Matthew Hopkins!" shrieked Mother Frampton. "Behold your doom!"

And she pointed to the white vapour, which now appeared full of strange figures.

Hopkins fixed his eyes upon it, so did his men, and so did Richard.

The confused mass took shape.

Clear and distinct there was the representation of a huge building.

Before it was a pile of flaming faggots, and in the midst of those faggots stood the life-like representation of Matthew Hopkins.

Giving utterance to a cry of rage, Hopkins dashed forward.

But he had not taken half-a-dozen strides before once more the place was in darkness, and Hopkins received such a stunning blow in the face that he was stretched bleeding upon the stone flooring.

But he was quickly upon his feet again.

"A link!" he thundered. "A link!"

Lights were hastily produced, and a couple of links lit.

Hopkins seized one and Richard the other.

They flashed them about, but nothing was to be seen.

Not even a trace of ashes showed the spot whereon the caldron had stood.

"Here indeed is mystery," said Richard.

"Ay, mystery if you like," growled Hopkins; "but I'll find these fiendish hags, or, by heaven, I'll raze the castle to the ground! What! defy me thus? Am I to be made the laughing stock of hideous witches?"

"Take my advice," said Richard, "let us first of all find the way out of this hole. The men will thus regain courage, and we shall be able to do more with them. See, here is what looks like a door. Maybe we can get it open."

And he pushed it with his hand.

To Richard's great joy it yielded and rolled back.

"Ho, ho!" chuckled Hopkins. "They have evidently forgotten to secure this on the other side. But whither does it lead?"

"That we must find out. Are you willing to lead the way?"

"Yes. Now forward, my men, forward! If we get hold of these hags, I promise you some amusement. We will not leave one of them alive, except Mother Frampton."

By this time the men had recovered a little of their courage, and they swarmed after their leaders.

They now found themselves in a stone passage of great length.

From its appearance it seemed that it communicated with the castle.

Hopkins had no doubt that it did.

"Keep your pistols ready," he shouted, "and if you see a figure of any kind, fire upon it."

The result of this order was a tremendous waste of powder and shot, for the men, more than once fancying they saw a figure, fired again and again.

After each shot a halt was made to listen.

But no sound greeted their ears.

Silence the most profound now reigned.

In a few moments a narrow flight of stone steps was reached.

Round they wound like a corkscrew, but it was evident from the moss and lichen growing in the crevices that they were seldom used.

Without hesitation, Hopkins and Richard commenced the ascent, and they were eagerly followed by the men, who considered that they were safely on the road out of the trap they had been so neatly and cleverly led into."

Another minute or two, and to their astonishment they found themselves in a courtyard.

It was, in fact, the courtyard of the castle.

The men breathed a sigh of relief.

Free! they considered, free!

But what was before them, or on either side of them, they were unable to distinguish, in consequence of the darkness, for though the moon shone brilliantly, its rays were completely shut out by the foliage of the enormous trees with which the whole of the ground was studded.

"Not a soul to be seen," cried Matthew Hopkins.

"It is false!" cried a voice—a voice which made Richard's heart palpitate violently.

From out of the surrounding darkness emerged a number of figures.

The first, in a moment, stood within the dull glare of the links, and Richard instantly recognised that figure as belonging to *Rupert Redmond*.

So astonished was he that for a few seconds he stood rooted to the spot.

"Rupert Redmond!" he gasped.

"Rupert Redmond," repeated Hopkins. "Then it is certain that he is in league with the Evil One. But pause not, Richard Melburn; down with them! On to them, my men; cut them down—cut them down! Spare not!"

So saying, he rushed forward, his blade raised high over his head.

Rupert's sword gleamed before the witch-finder's eyes like the rapid flashing of lightning.

Hopkins heard the clash of the steel as the weapons met, but at the same instant a series of violent pains shot through his arm, and with a howl of terror he let the blade fall from his hand.

In the meantime Richard became engaged with the man who had stood exactly behind Rupert, and he quickly recognised him as Reuben.

Hopkins's men had dashed forward, and they quickly found themselves engaged in a hand-to-hand encounter with a number of strange-looking men, attired from head to foot in black, and masked.

Tall, active men they were, and that they were thoroughly used to the weapons they wielded was soon evident, for in a very few moments half-a-dozen of Hopkins's followers were lying dead upon the courtyard flags.

Repeatedly did Hopkins's men fire their pistols, but they saw no man fall.

Their hearts were beginning to fail them when they saw that the mysterious men in black were rapidly falling back, and evidently making for an open door on the right.

Taking this as an indication that they were backing out of the fight, they responded to the cries of Cooper, who was a brave but brutal and savage man, and hurled themselves upon them.

They heard Hopkins's voice shouting to them, but the loud clashing of the steel and the shouts and cries of the men prevented them from hearing what he said.

However, they thought that his shouts were to urge them on.

But such was not the case, for Hopkins, as soon as he noticed the men in black retreating, came to the conclusion that a snare was laid for his party.

In a few moments he saw that he was correct, and he was only just in time to prevent Richard from following the men, for Melburn had been frantic in his endeavours to pass Reuben and confront Rupert.

And when at last Reuben suddenly, and in the most mysterious manner, disappeared from before his eyes, he, as we have said, attempted to follow the men, who, like a lot of howling wild beasts crowded through the doorway.

Hopkins's hand descended upon Richard's shoulder.

He seized his collar and pulled him back.

"Hold!" he said, in hoarse tones; "hold, Richard! Come back, or you will lose your life. We are in another and a worse trap than ever."

"What mean you?"

"They are leading them into the castle, where they will kill them or detain them as prisoners."

"But can we not try to recall the men?"

"I cannot get them to hear! I will, however, make one more attempt. Follow me!"

Both rushed once more to the doorway, but they had no sooner reached it than it was violently slammed in their faces.

"Let us delay not another moment," cried Hopkins. "We must endeavour to make good our escape, return to the Abbey, and gather together the whole of the men. Then we will return here. And——"

"But," interrupted Richard, "of what use will that be? In the interval the men may all be slain."

"Ay," replied Hopkins with a ghastly grin, "but there are hundreds more men to be had for the paying."

The pair turned and walked swiftly across the courtyard, the only light to guide them being the remnant of a link held by Richard.

Their swords were ready in their hands, and both inwardly swore that nothing should stop them in their attempt to escape.

They were not obstructed.

But half-a-dozen or more dead bodies of Hopkins's men showed the ruffians which had been the victorious party.

They looked closely, but they saw not one body of those mysterious men in black.

These individuals, they had no doubt, were members of the Secret Brotherhood, all of whom were under the sway of MORNA, THE MAN OF MYSTERY, and, as it now appeared, under the command of Rupert Redmond, whose chief assistant was Reuben Renard.

The wall of the courtyard was reached; but for some moments they searched in vain for a means of getting over the barrier.

At last, however, they found an old and somewhat rotten ladder.

Reaching the top safely, Richard steadied it while Hopkins ascended, and handed him what remained of the link.

Then, with Richard's assistance, Hopkins managed to reach the top of the wall, which was so broad that three or four men abreast could have walked along it.

But now a greater difficulty presented itself.

Beneath them was a broad moat, the stagnant water in which was only partially concealed by the leaves in it, the accumulation of years and years.

The two stood and stared blankly at it.

"What is to be done?" asked Richard, in hoarse tones.

"I know not," replied Hopkins, "we are certainly caught."

"While we wait here," growled Richard, savagely, "we make our bodies marks for Rupert Redmond and his crew!"

"I see nothing of any of them," said Hopkins, turning and looking at the castle; the whole place is in total darkness, and I do not hear the slightest sound. Do you?"

"No; all this is a profound mystery."

"Perhaps it is; but I will yet solve it. It has struck me that Rupert Redmond is the leader of the secret brotherhood, and will keep those men as hostages. If Sir Ferdinand makes an advance into the forest the men now in the castle will be slain."

"Perhaps that may be so."

"But if the Evil One and all his angels went hand in hand to try to keep *me* out," said Hopkins, gnashing his teeth, "I would still make the attempt; but since there is no help for it we must jump."

"Into the moat?"

"Yes. How are we to get away without?"

"We shall be drowned."

"If what Amos Arlington said about my being hanged," muttered Hopkins, is correct, then it's certain I shan't be drowned. But then, Mother Frampton has prophesied that I shall be burnt alive! Let me but get hold of the ugly old bag, and she herself shall perish at the stake!"

"Now," said Richard, "are you ready?"

"I am."

"Jump, then."

They jumped together.

The distance from the top of the wall to the moat was about twenty feet.

They sank into the moat right up to their shoulders, and it was some moments before they could make any movement towards the shore.

"Do you go first," said Hopkins. "You are light. No doubt, you will see a long branch, or, maybe, a young tree. Then, if I can get hold of it, you can assist me out."

Despite every endeavour, it took Richard some time to reach the bank.

Then he was some time in finding a branch long enough.

But at last he secured one, and Hopkins was finally drawn to the bank.

Exhausted and thoroughly sick at heart, the pair sat down on the bank.

They had scarcely been seated, before the loud clattering of horse's hoofs fell upon their ears.

Was it *one* horse?

No, that rapid thundering was not caused by four hoofs.

Both rose and looked in the direction of the sound.

Nearer and nearer came the beating of the hoofs, then, suddenly a series of unearthly cries arose.

Shrieks, yells, wild bursts of laughter, together with the hooting as of a thousand owls rang out.

The two hurried to and stood upon a sort of mound, the better to ascertain what all this could mean.

They soon saw.

In the space between the castle and the forest—an avenue overhung with dense foliage—appeared first, the figure of a man mounted on a black horse, and riding almost with the fleetness of the wind.

Behind him came at least two score more horses, each ridden by a *woman*.

The air was thick with owls, bats, and birds of all kinds, which not only kept pace with these strange riders, but also added to their cries by hoots and shrieks.

Presently they dashed across an open space, and, by aid of the moon, both Hopkins and Richard recognised Fendyke as the first rider, and Mother Frampton as the second.

Away they went, dashing madly through the trees, now partly hidden by the brushwood, and now by the foliage overhead, until at last they disappeared.

But for some moments after the crew had vanished, their hoots and yells were heard by the two thoroughly astounded men.

CHAPTER XIV.

OF HOW SIR FERDINAND WAS VISITED BY A MONK—OF WHAT PASSED BETWEEN THEM—AND OF THE DREADFUL DEED SIR FERDINAND WAS LED TO COMMIT.

WE will now return to the castle.

The reader, as a matter of course, has had no difficulty in arriving at a conclusion as to how and why Rupert Redmond came to be at the castle, for he has not forgotten who the Man of Mystery really was; but though for the past week Rupert had been associated with Morna, he had never seen his face, neither had he recognised his voice.

As soon as the door had been closed the fight came to an abrupt termination, for the simple reason that a door was thrust suddenly across the passage and separated the combatants.

Hopkins's men found themselves alone, with but one lantern, and no visible means of egress.

True there was a window on the right —or, rather, an aperture—but that was heavily barred.

Once more terror seized upon them.

What if they should be left there to starve?

Or, perhaps, they considered they should be suffocated.

There were a hundred ways they thought of being put to death, and they would be unable to offer the least resistance.

Again and again they threw themselves against the door.

But it never even moved.

Then they began to revile Hopkins, and Richard Melburn, to call them cowards, and to vow vengeance upon them if they should get free.

In the meantime, Rupert Redmond and Reuben had withdrawn to a small chamber in the left wing of the castle, while the members of the Secret Brotherhood remained in an apartment adjoining.

Rupert had barely seated himself before Mother Frampton appeared.

"What do you require?" asked Rupert, sternly.

"I am here, young master, to thank you for your timely assistance. But for your arrival, we might all have been taken, despite the way Fendyke led them into the trap. You see, with all we did, we could not frighten Hopkins."

"No doubt. He has had too much experience with women of your description. But what caused you to decoy him and his men here?"

"To slay them all. And they would all have been dead at this moment had the machinery connected with the subterranean passage acted."

"I don't understand."

"No," chuckled Mother Frampton; "but let me explain to you that near the end of the passage is fixed some machinery. Had it properly acted, a tremendous stream of water would have filled the passage."

"I see; but even then some might have escaped."

"No!" replied Mother Frampton, firmly; "no! And for this reason, that the water is impregnated with a deadly poison. The whole would have been killed, and we should have buried them beneath the flooring of the passage, which already holds the remains of many who have dared to interfere with us."

"We did not come to your assistance because we hold with you," said Rupert. "Do not imagine that. But it appears you have on many occasions rendered valuable assistance to the Secret Brotherhood, and so, when I was told to make all haste here, I obeyed."

"Hopkins has gone."

"I know it."

"And Richard Melburn has gone with him."

"True."

"I wonder you did not slay both of them. They are your deadly enemies."

"So I believe. But their time is yet to come."

"Ay," muttered the hideous old woman, "the vision I showed Hopkins will come true."

"Mother Frampton," said Rupert, "your reign is, I fancy, drawing to a close. The king has sworn to stop witchcraft, and he will do so at any cost."

"Ay, and he will also unravel the secrets of the Mystic Brotherhood!" said Mother Frampton, fiercely.

"Of that I cannot say."

"You are not one of them, nor is your friend here, Reuben Renard—why, then, are you suddenly appointed their leader?"

"Seek answer to your question at the hands of the Man of Mystery," replied Rupert. "I am here to aid him, because he has aided me in the past. But now let me tell you this. Take the advice I shall give you, Mother Frampton, and quit this castle never to return."

"And why should I do so?"

"Ask me not, but accept my advice. Take what articles you require and begone."

"I have nothing here of any importance."

"Then you will have no difficulty in departing at once."

"But off and on this has been our home for years. I love the old place. 'Tis here that I have trained my owls, my toads, my lizards—'tis within these walls that I have initiated new members into my secrets."

"All that is a matter of no importance to me," replied Rupert abruptly. "Again I say go! If you stay but a few hours more I cannot say what may happen to you."

"You are about to do some desperate deed, Rupert Redmond."

"Probably."

"I am certain of it. But I appreciate your coolness," she said, admiringly. "Sir Ferdinand Lockhart, Richard Melburn, and Matthew Hopkins are, as you well know, your deadly enemies. Destroy them, Rupert Redmond," she hissed, "destroy them! If you do not, you will never know a moment's peace. 'Twas not so long ago, when consulting the stars, that——"

"I pray you, cease," interrupted Rupert. "We have important matters to discuss. Go, therefore, and take your companions with you. Where is Fendyke?"

"Here!" cried a voice, and a narrow panel on the right sprang open, and Fendyke entered the chamber.

Rupert looked hard into his strange face, and he noticed that a significant glance was exchanged between him and Mother Frampton.

He well knew the story that Fendyke was supposed to be the son of this woman.

Now that he looked at them as they stood so close to each other, he saw that there was a resemblance between them.

"I have warned Mother Frampton to depart," said Rupert.

"Is that so?" was Fendyke's reply. "I recommend her not to hesitate, but go at once."

"You, then are in the secret," said Mother Frampton.

"What secret?"

"As to what is about to be done here?"

"I know nothing of Rupert Redmond's plans or intentions."

"You obey his orders, though."

"Assuredly, as I am directed. But hesitate not. Come, you know the stables are well stocked. Hey for the midnight ride! Ho, for the wild chase!"

Mother Frampton's features relaxed, a grin of joy o'erspread her countenance, and in wild, exultant tones, she echoed Fendyke's cry—

"Come, come! The midnight ride! Hey, for the wild chase!"

Then she dashed from the chamber, followed by Fendyke.

In a few moments the whole of the horses were led out, no saddles being placed upon them, and the women with loud cries, swarmed round them.

"Hop-o'-the-wind! Hop-o'-the-wind!" they screamed. "He will lead, and we will follow."

Hop-o'-the-wind was Fendyke.

"And now," said Rupert, "let us arrange our plans."

For some half-hour they sat discussing a project Rupert and the Man of Mystery had already conceived.

It was a desperate and dangerous plan, as the reader will see.

Rising, Rupert produced a small key.

"The Man of Mystery told me," he said, "that this key will unlock the door of the room marked 'Sixteen,' which is on the fifth staircase, so I will take the lantern, ascend, and select what costume I can see best suited to my purpose. Do you, Reuben, proceed to the brothers. Tell them that I require their services no longer at present, and that they must at once return whence they came. Let them convey to the Man of Mystery the intelligence that all has, so far been successful."

"WITH THE EXPLOSION, BOTH LEAPT TO THEIR FEET."

"Good! I will join you directly," replied Reuben, "when we will proceed to the vaults. Do you think it likely that Hopkins and Richard have got away from the castle by this time?"

"Probably. As I told you, they must cross the moat to do so, but how they are to manage that, I neither know nor care."

"And the men, Rupert—it is not your intention to supply them with anything?"

"No, Reuben, *no!* Such wretches as they are deserve a terrible death, and by heaven, they shall meet with their deserts; But not at our hands, if our plan succeeds!"

"I only regret that Hopkins and Richard are not there with the men," replied Reuben.

So saying he left the apartment, and Rupert soon followed.

The members of the secret brotherhood, we may mention, left the castle by the subterranean passage.

Rupert ascended and opened the door of the chamber marked "Sixteen."

It was a small apartment, and had at one time been used as a bedchamber.

That was apparent at a glance.

The dark oaken walls were hung with costumes of many descriptions.

That they had never been disturbed for many years was certain, for the dust had accumulated in many instances so thickly as to hide the colours of the costumes.

Raising the lamp aloft, he carefully examined them.

Presently she stopped before one, and reaching it down, shook off the dust.

It was a monk's costume, and perfect in every detail.

He then proceeded to one of the corners of the room.

A lofty cabinet stood there, and Rupert easily pulled open its doors.

He found what he wanted directly.

It was a small wooden box with various compartments, containing paints, together with brushes of various sizes.

It was, in fact, a painter's pocket-box of those days.

Having selected all he required, he descended, and found Rupert awaiting him.

"Have you found what you wanted?" asked Reuben.

"I have. Behold them! Now, Reuben, you are clever with the brush."

"I know a little of painting, but I am far from being clever."

"No doubt you will be clever enough to transform my features to the extent required. So now to it at once, for if we delay, Hopkins and Richard may reach the Abbey before me."

"I happen to know that such would be utterly impossible."

"Indeed. How do you know?"

"Chancing to look from one of the windows above, I saw both of the scoundrels on the top of the wall, and was just in time to see them leap into the moat."

"Ah, and what occurred after that?"

"There they stuck."

"They did not sink?"

"No; but they did not move."

"Is it likely they will be drowned?"

"Nay; for from what I could see, the moat is filled with leaves—choked up in fact. They will get out in time, no doubt; but, certainly, they will not reach the Abbey for a long time to come. Do you hear the men?"

"Ay; but let them hammer; their hammering will not break down the door, nor will their cries have any effect upon me. The vile scoundrels! The passage in which they stand will be their tomb."

"And now you have discovered the articles you require. Is this a complete costume?"

"Yes; everything, sandals and all."

Reuben assisted Rupert to don the costume, which was found to suit.

Reuben proved himself to be remarkably clever with the brush, for, with a few touches of the various paints in the box, he wrought an extraordinary transformation in Rupert's countenance.

Presently all was ready, and Rupert was, for the time being, a monk, and so remarkably well was the painting done, that no one would have had the slightest suspicion that he was other than he looked.

Rupert's own clothes were now rolled up into as small a compass as was possible, and of them Reuben took charge.

"Having ascertained that no one is left within the castle but Hopkins's men," said Rupert, "we will depart. On the

Blackburn road, as agreed, you will await me."

"I would far rather be nearer to you," replied Reuben.

"Nay; wait fearlessly, Reuben. I feel certain of success. So far as appearances go, I am perfection, and, as you know, I can change my voice that not even you would recognise it as mine. And now let us go. We will leave the castle by the subterranean passage. But first we have to visit the magazine, *and see that the train is well and truly laid.*"

"The villains deserve their fate."

"Have you the links, Reuben?"

"I have—here they are. Also the cotton."

"Follow me, then."

And Rupert left the apartment, followed closely by Reuben.

The shouts of the imprisoned men had by no means diminished; indeed, if anything, they had increased.

They shouted, they howled in a fearful manner.

With the butts of their pistols, the pommels of their swords, and with the toes and heels of their boots they hammered upon the door, thereby causing a din which was perfectly deafening.

Descending a long, narrow flight of stone stairs, and guided entirely by a description furnished him, Rupert traversed several corridors, and at last stood before a low-vaulted door, having upon it the letter "M," which stood for "magazine."

It was secured by a large screw, which being turned round came out, and the door was opened.

Lantern in hand, Rupert entered.

"Behold!" he said. "Exactly as the Man of Mystery has said."

"He has evidently been a frequent visitor here," observed Reuben.

"On the contrary," replied Rupert, "he told me that he had never crossed the threshold."

"Marvellous!"

"It is very marvellous. But I have no reason to doubt his word. Look around at the barrels of powder here."

"There are many; but do you think it possible that Mother Frampton is aware of what this vault contains?"

"I am unable to say. Now hold the lantern, Reuben."

Rupert took down four or five of the barrels, the heads of which he smashed in with a large stone.

The powder was perfectly dry, and fit for instant use.

"All is now ready," said Rupert. "Sir Ferdinand will fall headlong into the trap. But now there must be no further delay."

On went the pair, and the end of the subterranean passage being reached, Rupert pressed forward, while Reuben went towards the Blackburn Road.

*   *   *   *

Two hours had passed, but no tidings of Hopkins had reached the castle.

But Sir Ferdinand did not consider this as being at all strange.

True, he had expected that a messenger would have been despatched by Richard to say that the black witches had been captured.

As no one came, he began to consider that probably some of them had escaped, and pursuit was being given.

In the meantime, Sir Ferdinand, remembering that hard work was before the men, gave permission for those within the Abbey, with the exception of the usual sentries, to retire.

So, at the expiration of three hours, the Abbey was buried in silence.

The sentry posted at the small gate on the eastern side of the building, had heard no sound of any description during the past two hours; and taking it for granted that no danger was to be apprehended, he seated himself on a stone beside the gate.

It was such a lovely night, the air was so still, that repose was invited.

But suddenly a rustling sound fell upon his ear.

He was on his feet in an instant, and holding firmly his halbert, and cocking his pistol, he levelled it in the direction of the sound.

"Who comes?" he queried.

"A friend!" was the reply.

A dark figure emerged from the gloom of the trees, and stood before him.

It was the figure of a monk, otherwise Rupert Redmond.

At once the pistol was lowered.

This man, like his fellows, belonged to no religious sect, but to some extent they treated the monks with a certain amount of respect — a respect, however, which vanished immediately if the said monks attempted to interfere with them.

"Well, holy father," growled the man, "and what want you? You are not here to tell me that you have come to administer the rites of your Church to Sir Ferdinand."

"No, my son," was the grave reply; "but I am here on a most urgent matter."

"You wish to see Sir Ferdinand?"

"I do, at once."

"It's impossible, father."

"Why? Sir Ferdinand has not retired?"

"True."

"Well, my son, stand aside, and I will go to him. I well know my way to his study."

"I tell you that it is impossible. I dare not allow you or anyone else to pass me."

"My son, am I a man of peace or of war?"

"I neither know nor care. It is more than I dare do to allow you to pass me."

"Is the gate open?"

"It is, but——"

"Listen! I again say that I have news of the utmost importance for Sir Ferdinand. You had better summon Hawkswell."

"I must not leave this spot," replied the man, stoutly.

"Then how is Sir Ferdinand to know that I am here?"

"I don't know. It is certain that Sir Ferdinand did not expect you, or the sentries would have had notice."

"That is true. No, Sir Ferdinand certainly did not expect me."

"But, look you," said the sentry, after a moment's consideration, "if you can give me some proof that your business is with Sir Ferdinand, I will risk it and let you pass."

Rupert had found two or three papers in an inside pocket of the gown.

They were papers of no importance, but they were filled with writing.

Rupert, knowing well that it was more than likely that this man—like the majority of those of his class—could not read a single word, resolved to risk it, and so, producing the papers, he said—

"Read that, my son—that is a private letter from Sir Ferdinand."

"Then, as the man took the papers, Rupert thought—

"If the fellow can read he will discover my attempt to impose upon him, but ere he can raise an alarm I will strike him down."

But it was as Rupert had surmised.

The man knew not even the letter A, but he did not wish the monk to know that.

Handing back the papers, he said—

"I see that it is indeed Sir Ferdinand's handwriting; but you see, reverend father, we have to be very careful."

"To be sure, my son—to be sure."

The sentry pushed open the gate, saying—

"Pass on, father. You say you know the way to the study?"

"Right well," replied Rupert, quickly passing on.

"So many wolves are about now disguised in sheep's clothing," said the sentry.

"True—most true."

"And men disguise themselves in monk's clothing just as much as they do any other," continued the man.

"Alas! yes," replied Rupert, gravely. "But I thank you, my son. Presently Sir Ferdinand will personally assure you that you acted quite right in allowing me to pass."

Without staying to say anything further, Rupert proceeded up the low-roofed, gloomy-looking passage.

Ascending the first flight of steps he came to, he found himself in a corridor.

One lamp only was burning, but it shed sufficient light for him to proceed.

At present he had not seen anyone.

His sandalled feet made not the least noise as he traversed the stone flooring.

Presently he reached the partially open door of a small room, within which a taper was burning.

Rupert's gaze was upon the figure of a man at the table.

It was the scarecrow attorney, Ebenezer Watson.

He was fast asleep, his head resting upon one of his arms, which was placed upon the table.

From the fact that his arms were resting upon a number of documents, Rupert considered that while in the act of perusing them he had fallen asleep.

Such was the case,

"Heaven only knows," thought Rupert, "they may be of the greatest importance to Miriam."

Cautiously he entered the chamber, leaned over, and read something of the contents of the papers.

What he read astounded him.

"Gracious powers!" he thought, "I must and will have those papers. From what I see of them the king's life trembles in the balance. But how shall I get them?"

Ay, that was the question.

Ebenezer's arms rested upon the documents, and he could not possibly pull them away without disturbing him.

While considering what he was to do, he suddenly remembered that, by Reuben's advice, he had transferred from the pockets of his own clothes to the garb he now wore a phial containing a drug, compounded by Bowolf and given him by Fendyke.

Taking it out he cautiously uncorked it, and placed the mouth beneath Ebenezer's nose.

Ebenezer inhaled it, but for some few seconds it made no perceptible alteration in his face.

It was the very first time Rupert had used the contents of the phial, and he watched the effect.

Suddenly Ebenezer's face turned ashy pale, and his lantern jaws dropped.

Rupert placed his hand upon the documents and gently pulled them.

Ebenezer moved not.

Again Rupert jerked them, and then he pulled them out.

Quickly he rolled them up, and fastened them with the silken cord which lay beside them.

He had just placed them in the folds of his mantle, when he heard the slow, measured sound of spurred boots advancing towards the room.

Another moment and Hawkswell, sword in hand, confronted him.

Much astonished was Hawkswell at the totally unexpected encounter.

Quickly recovering himself, however, he asked—

"Who are you?"

"My name is Father Knowles, and I—"

"But where did you spring from? How did you get here?"

"I passed the sentry at the eastern gate."

"Oh!" scowled Hawkswell, "so then he was asleep, eh? He shall suffer for it."

"Nay, he was wide awake. But recognising me as one of the fathers of St. Joseph's, and knowing me well—"

"Hold! Enough!" roared Hawkswell. "I want to know what you want here? What is your business? Know you not that you are risking death thus to enter this abbey without Sir Ferdinand's authority?"

"Oh, I have come to see Sir Ferdinand, and I should be with him at this moment but for the fact that I have lost myself. I have wandered from corridor to corridor in the hopes of meeting with someone. But I feared to shout lest I might cause alarm."

"You have walked from corridor to corridor, eh? Well, if that is so, it is strange I have not met you. However, you wish to see Sir Ferdinand? Come, then, give your explanations to him," he chuckled, "and see what the result will be. Sir Ferdinand is no lover of monks."

"Nor are you, my son."

"No, that's true enough. I should get so little out of them. Now follow."

The study was soon reached.

Sir Ferdinand was found pacing the floor in the greatest agitation.

Hawkswell no sooner knocked, than he sprang to the door.

No doubt he expected that news had come from Hopkins at last.

"What news?" he asked, in breathless tones.

"None from Hopkins," replied Hawkswell; "no messenger has yet arrived."

"Sir Ferdinand," said Rupert, in grave tones, "*I am the messenger!*"

"*You!*" cried Hawkswell, starting back.

"*You?*" echoed Sir Ferdinand. "Hawkswell, who is this?"

"A monk."

"Or some traitor in the disguise of a monk?"

"Nay," said Rupert, in firm but reproachful tones. "I am Father Knowles, of St. Joseph's, and I am a messenger from Master Hopkins."

"Your pardon, reverend father, but it seems so utterly impossible that you can be a messenger from him."

"I must admit that it does. But I will quickly give you the particulars as to how and why I became for the time being Hopkins's messenger."

So saying, Rupert glanced at Hawkswell, and then looked significantly at Sir Ferdinand.

The baronet understood him.

"Retire, Hawkswell," he said. "I will call if I require you."

Then, as he ushered the monk into the study and closed the door, he said, in agitated tones—

"Quick, quick! Tell me, what of Hopkins?"

"All is well! The greater part of the witches have been captured; but Mother Frampton and a few others managed to get away to the forest. Thither she is being pursued by Hopkins and Richard Melburn."

Sir Ferdinand uttered a cry of joy.

"'Tis as I expected," he said. "The hags are hunted from their nest."

"Ay, indeed," replied Rupert; "but others have taken their place."

"What! Others have taken their place? What others?"

"Listen to my story, Sir Ferdinand. First, as to how I became Hopkins's messenger. I was passing through the forest, and using a path which until to-night I had considered was never used by anyone but myself. Suddenly I heard shouts and cries; then hoots and unearthly howls fell upon my ears. I drew aside from the path, and between a couple of oaks waited. The cries increased. Then I saw the glare of links. Nearer and nearer came the cries. Then, with a sudden rush, a number of those dreadful beings, who for years have been the scourge of the forest" (and here Rupert cleverly forced himself into a state of excitement), "rushed past me. At that instant there rang out a number of shots, and three or four of the women lay at my feet.

"Though scarcely able to contain myself, I kept perfectly still.

"Another few minutes, and Hopkins and Richard Melburn rode up, followed by a large number of men. Just as they seized upon the bodies of the fallen hags, I came forth. Truly it was a wonder I had not been shot dead!"

"Of a truth," replied Sir Ferdinand, "it was indeed a wonder, for Hopkins's men might easily have mistaken your monkish garb for the garments of a witch."

"Exactly. But to continue. A halt was called, Hopkins dismounted and questioned me. I quickly convinced him and Richard Melburn that I was what I represented myself to be. They saw how deadly embittered I am against this dangerous class of women, and after a brief consultation they begged of me to convey a message to you. I promised, and I believe that I have faithfully fulfilled my promise."

"By the saints! you have, holy father, and if any gold pieces——"

"Nay, nay! I require not gold. But now, Sir Ferdinand, I will tell you the other part of my story. But first, what would you say to this— what if, when Hopkins and Richard Melburn return triumphant with what they have done, you could tell them that you had been far more successful than they?"

"I crave your pardon, holy father," answered Sir Ferdinand, with suppressed excitement, "but I fail to understand you."

"Listen. On my way hither I passed the very castle from which these witches had been so cleverly ejected by Hopkins."

"Ah! Blackrock Castle."

"The same."

"Well, did you see anything?"

"I did. I saw two or three dozen men attired in black, and wearing masks."

Sir Ferdinand changed colour the very instant this description was given.

"The Secret Brotherhood!" he muttered.

"You are right. I know their appearance well. I have said, Sir Ferdinand, that the Black Witches are a dangerous set of women—that they have been a terror for years, but they are not one quarter so much to be feared as the strange beings who have as their chief this Man of Mystery—Morna."

"By heavens!" cried Sir Ferdinand, "you are right. They are a thousand—nay, ten thousand—times more dangerous than the witches, and I would that I could slay them all."

"Sir Ferdinand Lockhart, it is in your power to exterminate the whole lot of them. I watched them as they filed into the dark castle, and when the last had entered, I passed down a long subterranean passage into the vaults—

with an object. I know it is a wrong thing for a man of my cloth to think about, but I remembered how dangerous to society were these beings. I reflected that it would be no more than justice if a terrible and a sudden death overtook them.

"I well know the vaults of this castle, and after some little conversation, I struck a light, and proceeded to the magazine."

"Magazine! What, is it possible that Blackrock Castle contains a magazine?" asked Sir Ferdinand.

"It is! Moreover, that magazine is full of powder."

"Gracious powers! Proceed!"

"I examined the powder, and found that it was in a fit condition for instant use. So I took down and opened one of the barrels, and strewed half the contents all over the place. Then I took the barrel in my arms, and laid a train from the vault to the passage. I was in the act of doing this when I heard voices, and after listening for a few moments, I ascertained that these voices proceeded from the chamber overhead.

"Ascending a few steps, I listened. I heard a voice ask—

"'For what length of time shall we remain?'

"A deep voice replied, 'That is uncertain, but, at any rate, until we arrive at some conclusion with reference *to the property of the daughter of Walter Dubois*, and that will take a few hours.'"

Sir Ferdinand started back, as from before the fangs of some poisonous reptile.

"They said that?" he gasped.

"Yes," returned Rupert, calmly.

"Then," replied Sir Ferdinand, in hoarse tones, "it is certain that they are there now, and that they will be there for some time to come."

"I think there can be no doubt as to that. But let me continue. I laid the train from the vaults to the centre of the subterranean passage, and there communicated it with a link. So you see, Sir Ferdinand, I have placed in your hands the means of destroying with one blow the men whose destruction you and others have been so long planning."

Sir Ferdinand rushed forward, and clasping the hands of the supposed monk, pressed them warmly.

"You have indeed rendered me a service for which it is impossible I can ever repay you!" he exclaimed. "This Man of Mystery—a man whom I believe is in league with the Evil One—a man possessing strange and supernatural powers—this man, I say, holds a secret of mine. It is a secret, father, which, if it should reach the ears of the king, would deprive me of all I possess."

"I understand."

"Look," continued Sir Ferdinand, advancing, and taking from a drawer a small leathern case. "Behold! Did'st ever see such a glorious specimen of workmanship as this?"

And opening the lid there was displayed a most beautiful tiara of diamonds.

No sooner did Rupert behold this, than he recognised it.

Of this beautiful article Miriam had given him a most minute description.

She had told him that it was worn by her mother at her wedding.

"It is indeed beautiful," replied Rupert.

"'Tis thine!" said Sir Ferdinand. "Well have you earned it."

"I thank you," replied Rupert, his hand closing upon the precious article. "And now, Sir Ferdinand," he continued, "let us at once set out."

"You will accompany me, then?"

"I will, indeed."

"Good! I had thought of taking a few men with me."

"They will not be required. Take a lantern with you. With the flame of that you will light the link I spoke of. In a few seconds the cotton with which I have connected it will ignite, and the next instant the Secret Brotherhood will be no more."

"Oh, that I were sure the Man of Mystery himself is among them."

"I feel that he is. At any rate you can be assured that, even if he were not there, by destroying his associates you break his power."

"That is true. Let us go, then."

"And let us leave the Abbey by the eastern gate. I wish you to assure the man on duty that he did right in admitting me."

Sir Ferdinand took up and lit a lantern. Then off he strode, Rupert at his side.

Not once had he doubted the truth of what the supposed monk had said.

Yet, had he calmly thought the matter over, he must have arrived at no other conclusion than that there was something peculiar about this man's statements.

Quickly they reached the eastern gate.

"Guard," said Sir Ferdinand, "you did right in allowing this reverend father to pass."

The man bowed, and the pair passed rapidly onwards.

But little was said on the journey to the subterranean passage, which was entered by Sir Ferdinand for the first time.

"Marvellous!" he said, "that none of my men have ever spoken of this place."

"Depend upon it, none of them knew of its existence. You see the mouth is nearly hidden by the foliage. And now let us enter. But first, it will be as well to light the lantern."

Accordingly Sir Ferdinand proceeded to kindle a light.

"Now," said Rupert, going forward, "I will show the way. But let us preserve silence, for these passages are so apt to carry sound."

The centre of the passage being reached, Rupert paused and pointed to the link.

"As I said, Sir Ferdinand," he remarked.

"Ay," replied the other, "it is exactly as you have said. Reverend father, you should have been a man of arms, for you are cunning and clever. And now, what is the distance from here to the castle?"

"Four hundred yards."

"How long will it be before the flames of the link communicates with the cotton?"

"About ten minutes."

"Good! We shall have time to retreat. So now, accursed crew," he cried, "thus do I exterminate thee!"

So saying, he lit the link.

"Now, let us hasten to the other end," said Rupert, at once striding off.

Sir Ferdinand only waited to see that the flame burned steadily, when he followed.

The other end being reached, the lantern was extinguished, and the two waited — waited for the tremendous result.

Others were watching for what was to follow.

Far away in the depths of the forest, the Man of Mystery was watching for that mighty signal—the signal of what he himself had commissioned Rupert to carry out, if he could get the men into the castle, and the Man of Mystery was surrounded by the Secret Brotherhood.

Five minutes passed.

Sir Ferdinand was now in a fearful state.

Presently the darkness of the subterranean passage was most brilliantly illuminated, then there burst high into the star-studded sky, a mighty sheet of flame, of a brilliancy dazzling to behold.

It was followed by a mighty roar— the simultaneous discharge of a hundred heavy cannon could not have equalled the report.

The ground trembled as if the bowels of the earth had been violently agitated by an earthquake, and huge fragments of stone fell in all directions, many close against where Rupert and Sir Ferdinand stood.

Darkness followed — profound darkness and silence.

No word was uttered until the thick, sulphurous smoke, which was wafted in every direction by the light breeze had cleared away. Then Sir Ferdinand turned his face, now distorted with savage fury, to Rupert.

"Reverend father," he cried, a terrific blow has been struck, even if the Man of Mystery was not there."

Rupert drew back a pace.

Then, with the swiftness of the tiger, he dashed upon Sir Ferdinand, seized him by the throat, and bore him backwards to the ground.

"Fool!" he roared, "accursed fool! The Man of Mystery was *not* there, nor were any of his cherished friends. 'Twas your own villains within the walls of that castle—all, with the exception of Hopkins and Melburn—your hand has destroyed!"

"What!" gasped Sir Ferdinand, "what is this? You, then, are no monk. Who are you?"

Rupert threw back his cowl, and resumed his natural voice,

"Who am I," he replied. "Can'st thou not see? Can you not now recognise the voice of Rupert Redmond?"

"Rupert Redmond!" cried Sir Ferdinand.

Then he thought—

"I am doomed! He will most certainly slay me, I am powerless in his his hands."

"Sir Ferdinand Lockhart," said Rupert, "you are aware that I have you at my mercy. Well aware that I could take your life. Unprincipled scoundrel, you deserve death at my hands.

"Ah! villain, you would like to know where Miriam is. She is in safe hands, Sir Ferdinand—very safe hands. Presently a day of reckoning will come, and you shall restore to Miriam that which is lawfully hers."

"Sir Ferdinand Lockhart, beware! In the Man of Mystery, you have a terrible enemy!

"Take the advice I now give you— close the Abbey, and quit this part of the country, and advise Hopkins and Richard Melburn to do the same. For years you have been a man of blood.

"Rise, thou monster—rise and depart."

Sir Ferdinand rose, and, without a word, turned and staggered off.

In that short space of time a most extraordinary transformation had taken place in his countenance.

He looked the picture of the most bitter misery as he tottered on.

Rupert's last words had made a great impression upon his mind.

What secret did he hold?

So many secrets had Sir Ferdinand of a terrible character—secrets that dissipated sleep and caused him to pace his bed-chamber at all hours of the night.

CHAPTER XV.

OF THE RETURN OF HOPKINS, RICHARD AND SIR FERDINAND, AND OF THE VOW OF VENGEANCE.

RICHARD MELBURN and Hopkins were frequently compelled to stop. They were not certain that they were in the right direction for the Abbey.

Most earnestly did both hope that they would meet with someone who would direct their footsteps.

But not a soul did the two encounter until they had been tramping for a length of time.

Then they came upon a pedler.

This individual put them right as to their direction.

He informed them that they were two miles from Blackrock Castle, and, at least, a mile from the Abbey.

In answer to further questions, he produced from his wallet a leathern flask, which was filled with a cheap kind of wine.

Richard had no hesitation in purchasing it for a goodly sum.

The pair drank of the vile stuff until not a drain remained.

It went down their parched throats like the veriest nectar, and feeling somewhat refreshed and invigorated, they again proceeded on their way.

They reached what was known as the Red Stone—part of an old landmark— and what had been mentioned by the pedler, and here they halted to rest.

Scarcely had they seated themselves, when a report of an appalling character fell upon their ears.

For an instant it seemed as if the whole of the surrounding country was enveloped in a vast sheet of dazzling flame.

Then all was still.

With the explosion both had leaped to their feet.

For some few seconds neither spoke.

At last Richard whispered—

"In the name of all the saints, what can that be? Is Satan himself at work within the forest?"

"Unless I am much mistaken," replied Hopkins, "that report came from the direction of the castle. Ah, by heaven! Powder! I smell it plainly enough. Look at the vast clouds of smoke."

"Ay," replied Richard, "powder has been fired sure enough. But witches do not store gunpowder,"

" But it might have been in one of the rooms of the castle ? "

" Nay ; generations have passed since it was occupied by anyone who would require powder. No. I will not believe that the report was in the direction of the castle. Besides, since it has been proved that we wandered far from the correct paths, we are not now certain *which* is the direction."

" There is some truth in that," replied Hopkins. " However, we are in no fit condition to go towards the spot whence the report came. Let us go on to the Abbey as fast as we can. Depend upon it we shall hear all about it there."

In about half-an-hour they reached the Abbey.

It was no longer in silence and darkness.

Every man had risen from his couch.

The battlements were lined with eager faces.

In the highest tower the men had perched themselves, and were staring towards the forest.

It seemed as if they were expecting another explosion.

In front of the principal gate—a drawn blade in one hand and a pistol in the other—stood Hawkswell, surrounded by a group of men armed like himself.

The glare of a score of flaming links lit up the anxious but savage faces of the men.

The principal question was—Where had Sir Ferdinand gone ?

The man on duty at the eastern gate had simply said that Sir Ferdinand had spoken to him, and then vanished with the monk in the darkness.

As soon as Hopkins and Richard made their appearance, they were hailed with loud cries; for the men thought that reinforcements had arrived, and they could resist any attack if it was the intention of anyone to assail them.

But they quickly noted the forlorn appearance of the two leaders, and they just as quickly saw, by the expression on their faces, that something out of the common had occurred.

" You may well stare," growled Hopkins. " The Prince of Darkness has been out to-night, and has foiled us."

" Where are the men, Master Hopkins ? " queried Hawkswell.

" Boxed up in that accursed Blackrock Castle."

" What ! " roared Hawkswell. " That is where the explosion occurred."

" Bah ! Let us go to Sir Ferdinand. And do you, Hawkeswell, get the whole of the men ready. We must advance upon the castle and rescue our companions."

" Sir Ferdinand is not here," replied Hawkswell.

" Where is he ? "

" That is what I should like to know. He went away with a monk."

" Let us enter," interrupted Richard, " and while we are changing our clothes you can tell us what has occurred here."

Fresh clothing was at once brought for the pair.

While they changed, Hawkswell told them of his sudden and unexpected meeting with the monk, and of how Sir Ferdinand had left the Abbey with him.

Both Richard and Hopkins were mystified.

The monk's object in that visit was a mystery to them, for they well knew Sir Ferdinand's strong aversion to monastics.

" It is a mystery which only Sir Ferdinand himself can explain," said Hopkins. " But now bestir yourselves. To the castle at once ! And, by all the fiends ! when we have released the men, we will at once march into the forest. Not one hour's further delay shall there be. Where is Watson ? "

" In the chamber next the study, fast asleep."

" Asleep ! " cried Hopkins. " Do you tell me that that thundering report never woke him up ? "

" Nay, it did not wake him. He is the only one that it did not wake."

" I will quickly arouse him," replied Hopkins.

So saying he strode off, followed by Richard.

The chamber was in darkness, but Hopkins having got a lantern from the passage, threw its rays upon Watson's figure.

His face had fallen on his arms upon the table, and he was breathing heavily, as if he had the greatest difficulty in fetching his breath.

" What ho, here ! What ho ! thou snoring limb of the law. Wake, wake ! "

And raising his clenched fist, Hopkins dealt Watson a blow on the shoulder.

It was sufficient to have awakened a giant.

But Watson never moved.

"Something strange here," said Richard.

"Ay, strange enough by the look. The papers have vanished—papers of the greatest value."

"Do not needlessly alarm yourself," replied Richard. "Here, let us look at him."

He raised Watson's head.

His face was ghastly white, his lips were blue, and this was also the colour of his hands.

A sudden thought struck Hopkins.

He shook him fiercely.

A thick, greenish fluid oozed from his mouth.

"I thought so!" yelled Hopkins. "He has been drugged! Can you not see that a vile trick has been played? The monk did it, and it was the thieving hands of the pretended monk that took those papers! They have disappeared forever. And they might have brought me fortune and fame."

"Brought you fame!" sneered Richard.

"Bring the sentry who was at the eastern gate here!" thundered Hopkins. "Bring him hither that I may question him. But—what is that? Listen!"

Loud shouts were heard, and Hawkswell cried out that Sir Ferdinand had returned.

Both instantly rushed to meet him.

Before they could open their lips, Sir Ferdinand asked, in faint, trembling tones—

"What are the men waiting for?"

"The word to advance," replied Hopkins.

"Whither?"

"To the castle."

Sir Ferdinand raised his hands.

"Too late!" he gasped; "too late! The castle, with the men within it, has been blown to atoms! Moreover, mine was the hand which fired the powder!"

Not one man among the whole band uttered a single sentence.

They shrank back appalled—thunderstricken.

Hopkins was the first to recover himself.

"The castle blown to atoms?" he gasped; "and *you* fired the train?

You sent your own men headlong into eternity? You must be mad!"

"Not so, although it is true that this right hand fired the train, which communicated with the powder. But quick—tell me this—whom did you see at the castle?"

"Rupert Redmond!"

"And it was Rupert Redmond who, in the disguise of a monk, entered this castle——"

Sir Ferdinand was here interrupted; for the first time, a tremendous yell left the men's lips.

The whole mystery was cleared up.

The hand of Rupert Redmond was visible in both instances.

"Let us enter the reception-room," said Sir Ferdinand, in hoarse tones. "Let all the men accompany us; for all should know the way we have been beaten by Rupert Redmond. But I will have a terrible vengeance. No further rest will I take until I have him in my clutches!"

"Nor will I!" growled Hopkins. "The events of the night have not chased all the courage out of me. No, no. For a long time past have I been feared, and when not feared, respected, and I'll maintain the reputation I have earned at the risk of my life."

"Hawkswell," said Sir Ferdinand, who noticed that some of the men regarded him with a savage scowl, "let refreshments be at once brought up. Bring up and broach three or four barrels of the best, and forget not the wine."

While Hawkswell and a few of the men went off to attend to this order, the party proceeded to the reception-room, where Hopkins and Richard told their story.

By the time the narratives were given, the ale, wine, and tankards were produced, and the latter filled to the brim.

Hopkins, taking his tankard in his hand, stood upon a chair.

"*Now*, companions!" he cried. "Here is to the destruction of the Black Witches, and to that of the Man of Mystery, Rupert Redmond and their associates. We swear that we will know no rest until we have hunted the whole of them down."

"We swear we will fight to the death!" cried the men.

"Listen to me, men," said Sir Ferdinand. "Your exertions will not go unrewarded. Let me tell you that the secret haunts of the Man of Mystery, and his followers, contain untold wealth. I now know that Bowolf, who for years was known as the Man of Mystery, died suddenly; but knowing that his death was close at hand, he appointed someone to take his place.

"Who that person is, is a mystery. But, whoever he is, there is no longer any doubt but that Rupert Redmond and his friend are hand in hand with him."

"Yes," added Hopkins; "young Redmond may not be a party to his mysterious proceedings, but he would join him if only to be avenged on you and Richard."

"True!" said Richard, gnashing his teeth; "but I may yet meet him in the forest, and force him to tell me who has charge of Miriam!"

"Your marriage and mine," said Sir Ferdinand, "shall yet be consummated —ha! what is it, Hawkswell?" he added as he heard a stir without the door, and observed his henchman pushing his way through.

"Sir Ferdinand, Black Braddell has arrived with most important news."

"Let him be at once admitted."

Way was made, and Black Braddell stumbled into the room.

CHAPTER XVI.

IS OF THE STRANGE CIRCUMSTANCES WHICH TRANSPIRED AT THE "BULL INN"— OF HOW BLACK BRADDELL MET HIS DEATH—AND AS TO WHO WAS CAPTURED.

BLACK BRADDELL was thoroughly exhausted by running.

The perspiration poured down his bronzed face, and as he fell into a chair, he fairly gasped for breath.

It was some few moments ere he recovered himself sufficiently to speak.

A flask of wine was offered him, of which he partook freely.

"Now for your news," said Sir Ferdinand, impatiently.

"Blackrock Castle has been blown down—people say by the witches."

"Well?"

"I have been on the spot."

"Ah! And what did you see?"

"Nothing but a mass of blackened stone and wood, iron, and trees scattered about in every direction. Then I saw fragments of human beings—here a leg —there a head."

"No matter for that. Proceed with your *news*."

"I am coming to it. People say the castle was blown down by the witches. But I know that Rupert Redmond and his friend, whose name is Reuben Renard, some sort of distant relation to the Duke of Buckingham, are to do with it."

"Some sort of relation to the Duke of Buckingham?" exclaimed Richard.

"Whoever put that idea into your head is a fool."

"But that is not your news," said Sir Ferdinand. "How did you know that Rupert Redmond had a hand in the blowing up of the castle?"

"I saw him, in the garb of a monk, join his friend on the Blackburn Road. I was behind a hedge, and heard a little of their conversation."

"Proceed."

"Knowing well your anxiety to get him in your power, I followed the pair, although Rupert had treated me kindly."

"You followed them?"

"Yes, I followed them to the 'Bull Inn,' which, as you know, is in the occupation of Master Trentham. They entered by the front."

"But how came the inn to be open at such an hour?"

"The explosion it seemed had shaken the whole place, and alarmed the occupants of the inn. Rupert Redmond and his friend marched boldly through the group."

"In the garb of a monk, eh?"

"Nay. He had taken that off on the way."

"Well, go on. And you followed them into the inn?"

"No, no! They went in by the front,

and entered the public room, while I stole round to the back. The window was open, and so I heard what transpired. The host at once recognised Rupert Redmond, whose father, Randall, was at one time a friend of his, and he consented to find him and his companion accommodation for a few hours. I heard the host say that he had a double-bedded room which he would place at their disposal. I well know the room—it is called the Red Chamber."

Sir Ferdinand turned his face to Richard.

"We have them!" he said—"we have them! Master Trentham, the host of the 'Bull Inn,' *is entirely in my power.* He is bound to do my bidding. Now listen, Black Braddell. You shall, if you like, earn the sum of a hundred golden guineas."

"How?" exclaimed Braddell, whose black heart was palpitating violently at the idea of becoming the possessor of such a sum.

"You say," continued Sir Ferdinand, "that you know the chamber allotted to these two?"

"I do right well. I am thoroughly acquainted with all parts of the house."

"Good! Then you shall be the leader."

"I will be the leader," said Hopkins.

"Nay," cried Richard, who now took it for granted that the capture of Rupert Redmond was the easiest matter in the world; "nay, I will be the leader."

"Hopkins and you may lead the men," said Sir Ferdinand, "but since Black Braddell is so well acquainted with the premises, he must be the leader of you all. He will convey a letter from me to the host—a letter which Master Thomas Trentham will be bound to pay attention to. Now get ready."

"I will take my men," cried Hopkins. "See that your arms are in fit condition."

"We shall capture them easily," chuckled Richard.

Sir Ferdinand went to his study and wrote this letter—

"*To Master Thomas Trentham.*

"It has come to my knowledge that Rupert Redmond and a companion are about to occupy the 'Red Chamber' within your hostelry. I am desirous of securing Rupert Redmond. Presently

Matthew Hopkins, the Witchfinder, and Richard Melburn, of Melburn Manor, at the head of a number of determined men, will arrive at your place. You will conduct the former to the room you have allotted Rupert Redmond and his friend. But you must do this carefully, and without noise. If you refuse, I will have you arrested, and the information, relative to your former connection with the *Whalley Smugglers,* will bring you to the gallows. Fail not, at your peril!

"FERDINAND LOCKHART."

By the time he had written this document, Richard and the men were ready.

*   *   *   *

All that Black Braddell had stated in reference to the arrival of Rupert and Reuben at the hostelry was correct.

But he had *not* overheard all the conversation; and when he said that he knew all the house, he told a falsehood; for there was one room in that hostelry that he had never entered.

"And now, Master Redmond," said the host, after a long conversation, "I will conduct you to your chamber."

"We will accompany you directly we have perused these papers," replied Rupert.

"Don't disturb yourself," replied the host. "I am by no means in a hurry, for that explosion has completely upset me, and dissipated all desire for sleep, as, indeed, it has my wife and daughter, for I can hear them moving about. In a quarter of an hour I will enter again."

So saying, the host withdrew.

He went to the front of his house, but he had scarcely reached it before a man stood before him.

For a moment the host was considerably startled, but he quickly recognised the individual.

"What!" he said, "is that you, Black Braddell?"

"Yes," replied Braddell, "and I have a letter for you."

"Who is it from?"

"Sir Ferdinand Lockhart."

The face of the host turned very pale as Braddell made this reply.

"From Sir Ferdinand Lockhart?" he muttered, turning the missive over and over in his hand. "What on earth can he want?"

Aloud he said—

"Enter Braddell, and I will read the contents. I suppose you are to await an answer? No doubt the letter is something to do with the explosion."

Braddell made no reply as he followed.

The host quickly made himself acquainted with the contents of the letter.

He felt inclined to tear the missive into fragments, and in that condition return it to the writer.

But then he remembered that Sir Ferdinand's threats were no idle ones.

He knew well enough that he certainly *did* hold documents which could prove a lot against him.

"I am to place the son of my old friend where he can be arrested," he thought. "Great heavens! what a terrible thing to do. How am I to get out of this? He threatens not only me, but my wife and daughter. The scoundrel! I will say 'Very well,' but when they come they will find the birds have flown. Black Braddell," he said aloud, "what do *you* know of this?"

"I know nothing. I am simply to obey orders given me."

"By Sir Ferdinand?"

"Yes, or by Richard Melburn or Matthew Hopkins."

"What! Is it possible you have sold yourself to them?"

"Nay, I have not. What I am doing is simply for a certain reward."

"I understand you perfectly. You are a two-faced wretch, Braddell."

"Thank you, host."

"It is my belief that you must have been handy when Rupert Redmond entered this inn, and that you it was who conveyed the news to Sir Ferdinand. But I am compelled to do as he asks, so return and say that all shall be as the letter directs."

Instantly Braddell hastened off.

"The hundred is now certain," he considered.

Now he had no sooner disappeared than round the opposite bend in the road emerged another figure.

The host, catching sight of it, waited at his door, letter in hand.

Presently the figure stopped before him.

The host saw a man, muffled in a long dark cloak—the collar of which was placed high up — with his broad-brimmed Spanish hat, in which waved a long sable plume, pulled low down over his brows.

Before addressing the host, the stranger gave a careful survey around.

Being apparently satisfied that no one was about, he said—

"Well, master host, have you any doubts as to my being real flesh and blood? Why, man alive you look thoroughly scared. But have no fear. I am a traveller in search of a quiet spot to stretch my limbs for a few hours. Have you any visitors?"

"One or two only."

"Do I know them?"

The host felt inclined to smile at this artful question.

"How should I know?" he replied.

"Well, don't you see, if you give me their names——"

"Sir," interrupted the host, "I never give the names of those who favour me with their custom."

The stranger delivered an approving tap on the host's shoulder.

"You are a man after my own heart," he said, "and you are just the man I should select for my host. Now, can you give me accommodation?"

A startling thought at once flashed through the active brain of the host.

"I can," he instantly replied.

"Good. Look you, my friend, I can pay you well for what I have; but it is necessary that I should neither be seen nor heard by your guests."

"Then if you will follow me, I will at once conduct you to a room. No one will know that you are in the house."

"Lead the way then."

Master Trentham led the way through the passage.

The host took a taper at the end of the corridor, and conducted the man upstairs to a small and prettily-furnished chamber.

No one, to look at this comfortable apartment, would have thought for one moment that it was fitted with a cunningly-contrived secret door.

But such was the case.

It was a common thing in the days of which we are writing.

"Here are bolts and a lock if you wish to use them," said the host.

"Use them! What for? You don't wish me to understand that this is a house of call for footpads?"

"Oh, dear, no."

"Well, then, I shall not want to use either bolts or lock. Now, master host, just a small bottle of Hollands, that is all I require."

"No eatables?"

"None. Be as sharp as you can, for a little sleep is of the greatest importance to me."

The host nodded, and descended the stairs.

He had placed the stranger in the "Red Chamber."

Hastily procuring the bottle of Hollands, he returned to the guest with it.

Next he repaired to Rupert and Reuben.

He found them awaiting him.

"Master Redmond," he said, "I will at once show you and your good friend to your room. But before I do so let me ask you this: Do you know that Matthew Hopkins, the Witchfinder, is marching this way?"

"No," replied Rupert.

"There must be some mistake about that," said Reuben.

"No mistake whatever," replied the host. "Matthew Hopkins and Richard Melburn are on the road. They may stop here."

"For refreshments?" queried Reuben, calmly.

"Ay; and to search the premises. This Matthew Hopkins has the impudence of the Evil One himself. Under some pretence he may order his men to search the house."

"In that case," said Rupert, "do not show them to the room we occupy. You are aware that Richard Melburn is an enemy of mine?"

"Most assuredly am I! Show them to the room you occupy? Never! But you have heard your father speak of the 'Dean's Room' in this hostelry?"

"Many a time."

"He spoke of it as a curiosity?"

"He did."

"Follow me at once. It is to that room I am about to show you."

Both followed the host through one or two passages, and a short flight of narrow wooden stairs being ascended, the apartment was reached, and the three entered.

Now this was an apartment of about twice the size of the "Red Chamber."

The object which at once attracted Rupert's and Reuben's attention was the bedstead.

It was a most massive affair, with well-executed carvings placed at the four corners.

The construction of this bedstead and the flooring upon which it stood was a masterpiece of mechanical skill.

There was a mysterious appearance about it.

"I see that you are looking at the bedstead," said the host.

"Yes; it is a strange looking one," returned Rupert.

"Right, and there are only two men who know the secrets of that bedstead, and they are your father and myself. You see this ring?"

He moved the pillow, and showed them a heavy brass ring attached to the woodwork.

"We do," replied Rupert.

"Very well. Should danger threaten —should that villain Hopkins persist in searching every room in the house, you have simply to pull this ring."

"And what will follow?"

"You will see if you have to pull the ring," replied the host. "You must keep tight hold of it, remember. Something startling will occur, but if you continue to hold the ring both of you will be safe. So be not alarmed at anything which happens."

"And in case of danger you will warn us?"

"It may be impossible. But if Hopkins and Richard Melburn search the house, be assured that the room below this shall be searched first. You will hear them—but I leave the rest to your judgment."

The honest fellow longed to tell Rupert all, but dared not.

When the host had retired, Rupert said—

"Reuben, we will not lock or bolt the door. Let us leave it as it is. It will be as well to be prepared, so I propose that we do not undress."

"Ay; we may have to fight for our lives."

*　　*　　*　　*

"'RASCAL!' YELLED RICHARD TO BRASBLADE, 'WHO DID THIS?'"

An hour passed, but Hopkins and his party had not arrived.

The host had retired to his chamber.

He was beginning to fancy that the baronet had reconsidered the matter, when he caught the sound of the steady tramping of feet.

He cautiously rose and peered from the window, thinking to see a lighted link or two.

But he saw nothing of the sort.

Ahead all was darkness.

But not silence. Only too distinct was that sound of heavy tramping.

Nearer and nearer it came, and then he made out a moving black mass.

Next, he made out two horsemen riding together, and these he had no doubt were Matthew Hopkins and Richard Melburn.

He closed the window, and putting on a few of his clothes descended the stairs.

He reached the door just as the party arrived.

Not a word was uttered by anyone; thus it was evident that the men had had strict orders to preserve silence.

Black Braddell knocked softly upon the door, which the host cautiously opened.

Hopkins and Richard, both chuckling at the easy way they were to take Rupert and Reuben, dismounted.

"They are here," whispered Braddell.

"Ay," replied the host, "any fool could see that. Well, sirs, and does Sir Ferdinand still hold to the contents of the letter to me?"

"To be sure he does," answered Richard, in angry tones.

"You will not delay," said Hopkins, "for I am not in the humour to stand it. You will show us—that is, myself, Matthew Hopkins the Witchfinder, under the immediate patronage and protection of the king, under whose directions I am acting——"

"At *this* moment?"

"Always! Hang your impudence, *always*. I repeat, you will show myself, Richard Melburn and this man, Black Braddell, to the — what is the name of the apartment?"

"The Red Chamber," replied Braddell.

"Ay, the Red Chamber. Now, Coulston," he added to a man beside him, "do you see that the house is entirely surrounded. Let every man have his arms ready, and if you see anyone attempt to leave the house, fire! Understand?"

"Quite well."

"And now, host, lead the way," said Richard, in peremptory tones.

"Wait a bit," said Hopkins. "No doubt the room door is locked. But Braddell knows a secret entrance."

The host was more than ever convinced that all that had occurred was entirely owing to the two-faced villain Braddell.

But yet how he became possessed of the knowledge that the Red Chamber contained a secret panel he had not the slightest idea.

"Yes," said Braddell, "I know the way to the secret panel; and, moreover, I know the way it can be opened."

"Very well, Master Braddell," thought the host, "when I get the opportunity, I will thrash you until there's scarcely a sound bone in the whole of your dastardly carcase."

Aloud he said—

"Since Black Braddell is so familiar with the secrets of my house, I suppose you can dispense with my services?"

"No," answered Richard, sternly, "you will also go on in advance of us, or you may feel inclined to change your mind and warn the pair."

By Hopkins's direction the host held the taper while Braddell walked in front of him.

Black Braddell did not hesitate.

Opening a door close against the "bar," he entered, crossed a cellar, ascended a flight of stairs, and stood in a narrow corridor.

The host was behind him, while Hopkins and Richard were immediately in the rear, swords and pistols in hand.

*   *   *   *

The stranger who occupied the Red Chamber seemed to be somewhat of an eccentric customer.

For instance, when the host had retired, he burst into a fit of laughter— it was not loud, but long.

He was evidently much amused at what was passing in his mind.

When he had swallowed the first glass of the liquor brought him, he stretched out his legs, and thus ruminated—

"Well, it is about the strangest thing

I ever heard of in my chequered career. Fancy being compelled to dismount and yield up my horse at the bidding of a little scarecrow of a fellow, who had the audacity to stop me. Ha, ha! I can't get rid of his words—'Dismount, sirrah, or I'll blow your brains out!' Oh, oh! And then when I was about to blow *his* brains out for his audacity, lo! I suddenly remembered that my pistols were unloaded!

"I never made such a mistake before in all my life! I offered the villain money; but no, he must have a horse. He was not a footpad, he said. He was a gentleman who had important business in another part of the country. Well, hang me, if he was not a footpad, I should like to know what he *was*. However, he had the horse, and a good one, too! and he rode off and left me to perform my journey on foot.

"Yet, if I *do* happen to come across him, I'll pay him for getting across my horse. It is lucky I stumbled upon this inn. I can rest here in safety for a few hours, and heaven knows I want rest, and then off again.

"So here's to my good health," he added, as he poured out the third or fourth glass of Hollands. Here's to my good health and good luck! And now for bed. But I will not take all my things off. I will sleep with my weapons at my side."

Thereupon the stranger took off his boots, and then, laying his sword and a pistol, which he ascertained was loaded, by his side, he blew out the candle, and very soon was fast asleep.

For what length of time he had slept he could not tell. It was not for long, because the daylight streamed not through the shutters, but he was awakened by a sound as of the cautious tread of footsteps, and then he heard a noise as of hands being passed along the wall.

He was wide awake, and in possession of all his faculties in an instant.

He was evidently a man who was continually in danger, and consequently, always on the alert.

But though his hand closed upon the hilt of his naked blade, he did not move his body.

Very quickly he discovered that it was not the door which was being tampered with, but a secret panel.

"Robbery is intended," he muttered. "Robbery, and perhaps, murder! And, no doubt, that shrewd host is at the bottom of it. By heaven! they will find that they have no fool to play with!"

He watched the panel at the foot of the bed, and presently it was cautiously opened, and a light appeared.

By its aid he saw four men—the first, Black Braddell, he failed to recognise; but he knew the others.

"Matthew Hopkins, and Richard Melburn, as I'm a living sinner!" he muttered. "Then how the deuce did they get to know that I was here? Ah, I'll lay my life that this scarecrow-looking fellow must have identified me. Well, it's a fight for life; for if they take me I am doomed!"

"There," whispered Braddell "are your men. Now, Master Melburn, the hundred will be mine."

"Rascal!" thundered the stranger, leaping from the bed. "So you are the informant? Villain, take what you deserve!"

Braddell darted back with a wild cry; but he was too late; the stranger's sword had passed clean through his throat, and was instantly withdrawn and again raised.

Braddell did not fall.

Giving utterance to an unearthly shriek, he dashed to the window, and rushed upon the balcony.

He had no sooner reached it, than a volley of shots rang out, and Braddell fell, pierced to the heart by a dozen bullets!

The men had obeyed their leaders' instructions, which were *to fire at the first figure which appeared*.

In the meantime the stranger had raised his pistol to fire at Melburn, but Hopkins, rushing forward, threw all his weight upon him, and bore him with a crash to the ground, where, with Richard's assistance, he was pinned.

"By all the fiends," shouted Hopkins, "whom have we here? This is not Rupert Redmond!"

"No!" yelled Richard, "*it is Captain Brasblade.*"

CHAPTER XVII.

OF WHAT OCCURRED IN THE ABBEY VAULT, AND OF THE JOURNEY TO THE FOREST.

" Ay," said Hopkins, as he wrenched the weapons from Brasblade's grasp, " Brasblade it is ! The traitor host has deceived us ! Host ! " he roared; " host, come hither, thou scoundrel ! "

But the host had vanished.

" We will make him suffer for this ! " said Richard, savagely.

Brasblade at once saw through the trick which had been played.

He saw that the host, who, of course, had no idea who he was, had placed him in that room instead of Rupert Redmond.

" Had I been unknown to them," thought Brasblade, " of course, I should not be injured. Well, I forgive the host the trick for Redmond's sake. But those shots ! The house is surrounded by Hopkins's men, and to attempt to break away would be useless. Lord, here's a pickle to be in, and my own men not ten miles away."

In a few seconds his hands were firmly tied behind his back, and three or four of the men were summoned to keep guard over him, while Hopkins and Richard searched the house.

In the meantime the noise had awakened our two young friends from a sound sleep.

They listened, and they not only heard, but recognised the voices of Hopkins and Richard.

What was the reason for the tremendous noise, or the cause of the shots being fired, they could not form any idea.

Presently the noise increased, and it became evident that the house was being searched from top to bottom.

No longer was either in doubt as to the reason of this.

" By some means we have been traced here," said Rupert. " The house must be swarming with men. Ha ! listen ; they are below."

Yes, this was plain enough.

They heard Hopkins shouting—

" Search all the bottom part first."

Presently the door of the lower apartment closed with a bang.

Then Rupert seized the ring, pulled, and retained tight hold of it.

The effect was instantaneous and wonderful.

The massive structure rocked violently for a moment, and then, without any noise, commenced to descend.

The flooring in the centre beneath the bed had fallen.

They could feel themselves slowly descending, but by what remarkable means they knew not.

Suddenly they stopped with a jerk, the flooring above closed together and fastened itself.

Then something occurred which they did not see.

In the bedroom above, at the left hand of the bedstead, a huge cabinet had stood.

As the flaps closed, this piece of furniture, by some wondrous mechanical means, swung itself right round, and stood where the bed had been standing.

A few seconds only had elapsed ere Hopkins, sword in hand, and looking the very picture of a fiend, burst the door of the room open and entered, followed by a number of his men.

" No," he said, " this is not a bedchamber, but we will search it. Open that cabinet. Quick ! "

The doors were soon wrenched open, and the contents shown.

There was nothing but rows of mouldy books.

Still Hopkins was not content.

In furious tones he ordered his men to drag out the contents.

They did so, but nothing was discovered.

Baffled completely, Hopkins bade his men follow him.

He met Richard on the landing.

" You have not found them ? " asked Hopkins.

" Nay. Have you ? "

" Not a trace of them. Yet Black Braddell could not have been mistaken. That traitor host has defied Sir Ferdinand, and given them timely warning. And now we'll make him pay for it."

*　　*　　*　　*

To return to Rupert and Reuben.

As soon as the bedstead stopped, both jumped from it, to find themselves on firm ground.

Rupert was about to observe that they would have to stop where they were until it was convenient for the host to wait upon them, when suddenly a door immediately before them quickly opened, and a young girl carrying a taper appeared.

It was Ruth, the host's daughter. Her hand trembled, so that it was with difficulty she could hold the taper.

"Gentlemen," she whispered, "follow me, and I will lead you to a place of safety. But my father told me to say that, if you would be so disposed, I was to lead you to the stables. There are several horses there, and you could be quickly mounted and perhaps escape."

"My good girl," replied Rupert, "we thank you. But have you not been risking your own life or liberty in coming hither ?"

"I always do as my father directs me, without considering the danger, sir."

"But, for what your father has done, I am afraid that he will get into serious trouble."

"You would be sure of it if you knew all, sir," replied the girl; "I am certain something serious will, indeed, happen to him. At present he is hiding himself."

"Tell us what has occurred."

The girl did so, as far as she knew.

"And so Black Braddell, it seems, saw us, and gave information, eh ? And he has met with his death ! It serves him right ! But as to the stranger who was captured, I suppose you know not his name ?"

"Oh, yes, I heard them shouting his name. It is Captain Brasblade."

"Can it be possible ? " exclaimed both Rupert and Reuben.

"Yes, that is his name," said the girl, "and they have tied his hands behind his back. Several men are standing over him with loaded pistols, and orders to put a bullet through his heart if he dares to stir. I heard the one named Hopkins—a brutal ruffian—swear that to-morrow night they would *burn him alive!* "

"The scoundrel ! My good girl, how many men think you are with Hopkins ?"

"I cannot tell you, sir : but the house swarms with them. There is a very large number, and all of them such brutal-looking wretches ! Pray heaven they do not lay hands on me ! "

"Amen !" said Reuben.

"If you are friends of the man taken," continued the girl, "and think that an attempt may be made to rescue him, let me dissuade you. You would stand not the slightest chance."

"You are correct," replied Rupert, sadly. "Burnt alive ? Never ! Oh, that a message could be conveyed from us to him. But he heard our names mentioned ?"

"Yes. Many times."

"Good. Then he will be certain that we will not desert him. And now, my good girl, show us the way to the stables. We would be mounted, for we shall at once plunge into the forest."

Through a series of passages the young girl led them, and, at last, the stables, which were at some considerable distance from the house at the back, were reached.

Two horses were quickly saddled and bridled, and led forth.

The shrubs at the back effectually screened them.

But none of the scoundrels were in this direction.

Having been unsuccessful in finding the two they had set out in search of, they were now very successful in smashing in the heads of casks, breaking the necks of bottles, and so on.

Having cautioned the girl to hide herself until Hopkins and his men had departed, and receiving a promise from her that she would, our friends mounted and rode away.

Their destination was the mysterious home of the Man of Mystery.

The host had not been found.

What had become of him no one ventured to form the least idea.

"It is evident enough that this house, like many more, has secret traps and doors," said Hopkins, fiercely, "and it is likely that the host has unwittingly caged himself. May such be the case. May he die. But Sir Ferdinand spoke of a daughter. Yet we cannot find a trace of her."

"We have found the mother," chuckled Richard.

"True," growled Hopkins; "and of what use have we found her?"

The fact is that when they ascended to the room in which the hostess was, they found the poor woman speechless with terror.

Most bitterly did Hopkins revile her; brutally did he thrash her more than once with his whip, but it was of no use—the woman was simply powerless to utter a single sentence.

After the men had regaled themselves with whatsoever they fancied, orders were issued to once more search the house.

This was done, but with no success.

Neither the landlord nor the daughter was discovered.

So the order was given to return to the Abbey, and Brasblade was dragged forth.

His hands were secured behind his back with double cords, while about his neck was placed a halter, this being held by Hopkins himself, and every now and then violently jerked.

In this way, in the centre of the ruffians, was Brasblade conducted to the Abbey.

Sir Ferdinand, with Watson—now recovered from the effects of the drug he had inhaled—at his side, was eagerly awaiting them.

Sir Ferdinand no sooner heard what had occurred than his face, which had glowed with demoniacal triumph, changed to gloomy dismay.

His fears as to what Rupert would eventually do seized him again.

But when he knew who had been captured, his spirits rose considerably.

Captain Brasblade was at last in his power.

Hopkins and Richard between them very quickly made him acquainted with all that had occurred.

Then pointing to Brasblade, Richard said—

"See the wretch who was the means of foiling us at Chelsea. Behold the mock parson."

As he said this, Richard seized Hopkins's riding-whip, and dealt Captain Brasblade a tremendous slash across the face.

But it wrung no cry of pain from his lips.

"Wait!" thought Brasblade. "Wait! To Rupert Redmond I look for deliverance, and then my revenge shall come."

"Villain!" cried Sir Ferdinand, eyeing Brasblade with a savage scowl. "Master Hopkins will settle as to how you shall be punished."

"Don't fear," replied Hopkins. "That conclusion has already been arrived at. We will burn him to-morrow night in the forest."

"As a wizard? I understand."

"If we could only place Mother Frampton, Rupert Redmond, or the Man of Mystery beside him," said Richard, "what a glorious feast we should have. But now, my men, get ready. Let him be placed below in the strongest vault, and do not forget the irons."

"Leave that to me," said Hawkswell. "I will place such irons on him that not even the files from Satan's own workshop will cut through."

"May the Lord help you if he should happen to slip them," growled Hopkins.

Sir Ferdinand remembered the marvellous manner in which Randall and Rupert Redmond had slipped their chains and got away.

He remembered that days had been devoted to searching the vaults, in order to discover by what extraordinary means they managed to escape, and without the slightest success.

What if he had three or four of his bloodhounds placed in the vault with the prisoner?

A bloodhound, if asleep, would be awakened by the faintest noise.

"What say you if I put two or three bloodhounds in with him, Richard?" he said.

"Ha!" replied Richard; "a very good idea. What say you, Hopkins?"

"Yes, the idea is a good one, if you can depend upon the hounds."

"I can depend upon them."

Brasblade heard these arrangements, and his heart sank.

To be fettered—heavily fettered—was bad enough; but to have the company of two or three savage bloodhounds, which were likely to turn upon him at any moment, and tear him to pieces, was fearful.

As he thought of it, a shudder ran throughout his frame.

A strong party, with Hawkswell at their head, was formed, and Brasblade, in the centre of them, was conducted below, Richard and Hopkins bringing up the rear, while Sir Ferdinand went off to select the hounds.

In the strongest vault Brasblade was placed, and as Hopkins did not consider the chains and band within it strong enough, another set in addition was procured, and in a few moments the captain was doubly chained.

So tremendous was the weight placed about his body, that he found it impossible to stand.

He was compelled to sit beside the wall.

"And my own men only ten miles away," he thought. "By the Holy Virgin, it is enough to drive a man mad! But Rupert Redmond will not desert me. No, no; he will know who has been captured. But how is it possible that he could procure my liberation from a place like this? The only chance of rescuing me will be when I am taken into the forest to be burned alive. But then," and a cold shudder ran through him as he thought of this, "they might change their minds and burn me alive *here;* or they might set the hounds upon me. Well, well, I have been in many troubles in my time; but I fancy this is the very worst. If I could only send my men a message!" and his head drooped in deep thought.

"If you get out of those chains, Captain Brasblade," chuckled Hopkins, "you *deserve* to be free."

Another few moments and Sir Ferdinand entered, and followed by three men, each of whom had a fully grown bloodhound.

Three horrible and dangerous-looking creatures were they — animals which make a man shudder, and cause many to loathe even the sound of the word "dog."

But these were the hounds Sir Ferdinand delighted in; these were the creatures on whom he bestowed a large amount of his attention, and the best food from his own table.

"It is not your intention to chain them up?" asked Richard.

"Most certainly not," replied Sir Ferdinand. "They must be entirely unshackled, and then they will give a good account of the prisoner if he attempts to escape."

"Or if Fendyke or such like wretches

should in some marvellous manner gain an entrance here," said Richard.

Hopkins looked round the gloomy vault in astonishment.

"*Where* could anyone gain admittance?" he asked.

And walking round the walls he sounded them with an iron hammer.

No echo was returned; they appeared to be perfectly sound.

He did the same to the stone flooring. This also appeared sound.

"I have had considerable experience in such matters," grinned Hopkins, "and if there is any secret door in this vault, or any secret trap, my name isn't Hopkins."

"But still," said Richard, "we will post double sentries round the Abbey. We cannot be too careful. Now listen, hound," he roared as he strode in front of Brasblade, who was wise enough to have said nothing since he came into the vault.

"Attempt to tamper with those chains, and these bloodhounds will tear you in pieces. Mark you, they are trained to act as I say; and forget not that tomorrow night you will be taken into the forest and burned alive."

Brasblade looked up at the villain, but said nothing.

"Have you no communication which you would like conveyed to your friends?" sneered Sir Ferdinand.

Brasblade's eyes flashed.

He was thinking of his men.

He shook his head.

"His courage has deserted him, you see," said Hopkins. "Ho, ho!"

The whole party now withdrew, Hawkswell locking and barring the door.

Two men, each armed, were placed without.

*   *   *   *

Hours passed away, and in that time the "chiefs" in the Abbey had rested.

So also had the men, in turns, and the sentries at the door had been several times changed.

But for some few hours great preparations were being made for the invasion of the forest.

At Hopkins's suggestion another messenger had been despatched, this time to Manchester—thirty-two miles distant from Whalley—for more men

That messenger conveyed a letter from Sir Ferdinand to a man of the name of Kemble, who could raise a number of men if provided with the means.

The means, in the shape of money, were despatched, and Kemble quickly raised the men required.

He presented each with a certain sum in cash, and gave them a highly-coloured account of what they should find in the "secret caves" of Pendle Forest. So glowing was his description that the men were ready to at once depart.

* * * *

And what of the truly unlucky Captain Brasblade?

How had he fared?

The atmosphere of the vault was impregnated with the horrid breath of the three bloodhounds, and he was in total darkness, and loaded with chains, every movement of which elicited a low, threatening growl from the savage beasts crouching upon the flags.

Once only had his door been opened.

But not to give him food and drink?

No! Not a drop of water was offered him, nor a bit to eat.

Three large bowls of milk and water, together with three trays, containing some excellent venison, were brought in by Hawkswell and his men, and were set before the hounds, who devoured their meal ravenously.

While they ate, Hawkswell taunted Brasblade in the most brutal fashion.

But Brasblade made no reply.

The fact was, that he was now thoroughly crestfallen.

He had lost all heart.

Though, of course, he could not guess what time had elapsed, he knew that many hours must have passed since his capture.

Yet it was evident from what Hawkswell had said, that they had got no inkling as to whether a rescue would be attempted.

"If Rupert Redmond does not arrive and attempt to rescue me," thought Brasblade, "I shall think that he has got into some danger, and that it is impossible he can make any such attempt."

With all his faults, Captain Brasblade was the possessor of a generous heart.

The hounds finished their meal, Hawkswell and his men withdrew, and silence and darkness again prevailed.

Hours had Brasblade been awake; but at last his head fell forward upon his breast, and he slept.

He had been asleep an hour, when suddenly a dull thud was heard, and it sounded in the very centre of the vault.

The noise was as if someone had dropped something rather heavy, soft, and wet on the flags.

The hounds uttered a low, threatening growl.

Again came the sound, and again the threatening growls.

But the latter ceased as quickly as they commenced, and now could be heard a sound, as if the hounds were devouring something, and something which suited their palates.

This noise presently ceased, and all was still for a few moments.

Brasblade still slept on, though his sleep was a troubled one.

Presently one of the hounds, with a deep groan, dropped on the stones.

He was quickly followed by another.

Their low groans continued for a few seconds, and again all was still.

The third hound knew that something was wrong.

He stood keenly watching and sniffing, and ready for a spring.

And now a portion of that apparently solid wall suddenly opened, and a man's figure appeared.

The third hound, without so much as a growl, gave one mighty spring, and was upon that figure—a figure clad in black tight-fitting velvet, and wearing a mask of the same material—the figure of Rupert Redmond.

It was quite evident what Rupert had done. He had poisoned the two hounds.

Two only, he thought, were within that vault.

But he was ready.

As the hound dashed upon him, he stretched forth his powerful hands, caught it by the throat, and instantly exerting all his strength, he bore it to the ground.

The noise made was sufficient to awaken Brasblade. He started, rubbed his eyes, and looked at the wondrous scene before him.

He was able to see, for just within

the aperture, stood another figure—a strange-looking figure—also clad in black.

That was Reuben.

He held a lamp in his hand.

In his intense excitement, Brasblade would have cried out, but Reuben raised his hand in warning.

With the utmost fury the dog struggled to release itself, dashing its head from side to side, and gasping for breath.

Not for long was the struggle continued.

The brute became weaker and weaker with the passing of every moment, and at last Rupert, seeing that his opportunity had come, suddenly released one of his hands, snatched forth his dagger, and plunged it to the hilt in the hound's broad chest.

The stones were instantly deluged with a stream of blood.

"Thank heaven!" whispered Brasblade. "It is Rupert Redmond—brave Rupert, and his equally brave friend Reuben."

"'Tis even so," replied Reuben, also in a whisper.

"Thank heaven for your help!"

"But do not deceive yourself," continued Rupert; "we are not here to release you at present."

"No, no, that would be impossible," groaned Brasblade, "for see how they have fettered me. And yet you possess the power of passing through stone walls."

"I am acquainted with their secrets. And I am also acquainted with the secrets of the fetters about your body, for I could at once cause them to drop from you to the stones."

Brasblade was alarmed—so much so that he cautiously looked Rupert up and down.

Then he said—

"If you do really possess such power, in the name of high heaven, why don't you release me?"

"I am coming to that. You proved yourself a friend, and a friend will I be to you, Captain Brasblade. Whatever you may be, or may have been, you rendered me a service for which I and Miriam must ever be deeply grateful. Now, Captain Brasblade, let me tell you that the time for taking you into the forest is rapidly approaching. You can learn nothing here, but we know all that is going on in the Abbey."

"Wonderful!"

"No, it is not so very wonderful, for I have a spy there, in the person of a page—a youth named Stockholm. It was he who brought me the information with reference to these hounds, but he made a mistake, for he said there were two, whereas there were three. Still, that is of little moment. All preparations for what is to transpire in the forest have been completed, and the details have been carried out with fiendish delight by Hopkins.

"At the edge of the forest there are men cutting down logs to be used in making the piles to burn you alive. Now, attention. Did I release you, the journey to the forest would probably not be undertaken at all. Whereas, now we know the exact spot where the faggots are to be placed.

"If you will consent to remain a prisoner here, and to be taken to the forest, I can make arrangements to surround the men, and probably Hopkins as well. But if you do not feel inclined to risk this, then I will release you."

"No, no, let me remain. I shall no longer be fearful of the consequences."

"But are you ready to risk what will follow when the bodies of these animals are seen?"

"I am. You are certain that arrangements have been made to burn me alive in the forest, consequently little harm will happen to me here."

"You are right. Nothing whatever would alter Sir Ferdinand's, Richard's, and Hopkins's determination to take you into the forest to burn you alive! And now we will depart."

"My thanks are due to both of you," faltered Brasblade, "for I had already given up all hopes. But stay," he added, "I have not told you that my men are not such a great distance away."

"Your men?" whispered Rupert, joyfully. "Where are they?"

"Do you know the village of Creek?"

"Right well."

"Then my men, thoroughly well armed and ready for anything, are there at a hostelry called the 'Hunter's Rest.' Poor fellows, they will be nearly crazy at my prolonged absence. If you could convey them the intelligence——"

"I will go to them," said Rupert. "Ten miles is soon covered."

"Unfasten my shirt-collar," said Brasblade, "and you will find a locket and chain about my neck. Produce that, and the men will do what you ask."

The chain was taken from his neck by Reuben, who placed it in his pocket.

Then with a pressure of the hands, Rupert and Reuben departed.

And well was it that they did so, for at that moment the loud tramping of feet was indistinctly heard.

Another few minutes and the door was thrown open, and Hawkswell, at the head of a score of armed men, entered.

The scoundrel leader carried a flaming link in his hand.

The light of this instantly revealed what had happened to the bloodhounds.

Hawkswell and the rest started back.

Was it possible? Could they believe their own eyes?"

The three bloodhounds lying dead on the stone flags!

The cry was—"The prisoner has escaped!"

Within a few minutes Sir Ferdinand, Richard, and Hopkins were rushing to the vaults, followed by numbers of the men.

The dark corridors were illuminated with links and lanterns.

Swords in hand, the three chiefs rushed to the vault.

A cry of joy was uttered by all three when they saw that the prisoner was safe.

"Stand up," cried Hopkins, dealing Brasblade a brutal cut across the face with his whip. "Stand up—or I'll drive this blade through you!—why, what ails the hounds?"

"Dead!" answered Sir Ferdinand, hoarsely, as he took a link and leaned over the bodies of the once powerful animals. "All three are dead! By what marvellous means did this come about?"

Hopkins looked at the walls, then at the vaulted roof, and finally his eyes sought the ground.

Nothing being visible which would indicate that the vault had been entered by other means than the door, he gave vent to a fierce exclamation,

"Satan's work!" he said. "It is plain enough!"

"Rascal!" yelled Richard to Brasblade, "who did this?"

And he pointed to the hounds.

Brasblade shook his head.

"You don't know?" said Richard. "Do you say that you saw no person within this vault?"

"Nay; not a soul. I was fast asleep and heard no noise at all. I did not know that anything had happened to the hounds until the man came in with the links. I am just as much astonished as you are."

Brasblade spoke with difficulty, for so severe had been the slash dealt him by the brutal wretch, Hopkins, that he felt it with every movement.

"Bring the sentries," shouted Sir Ferdinand.

The two men, terrified beyond measure at what had occurred, and what was most likely in store for them, were brought forward.

"What were you doing that you heard no noise within this vault?" asked Sir Ferdinand.

"We were playing cards outside the door for a long time."

"And you heard no sound?"

"Nay; not a movement of any kind."

"Not the rattle of the prisoner's chains?"

"No."

"What say you, Richard?" asked Sir Ferdinand.

"What say I? I say—let them be disarmed, and placed under arrest! We will deal with them by-and-by."

"No!" cried Hopkins, "they are my men, and I believe them. Satan makes no noise with his work, and this *is* his work, I'll swear! No; they shall not be placed under arrest. Besides, we want all the men we can get."

This was true enough. So neither Sir Ferdinand nor Richard persisted.

"One of these hounds has been overpowered," said Sir Ferdinand, "and stabbed in the chest. Now *one* man did that. By all the fiends, I would give everything I possess could I find out this mystery! All the vaults seem the same. And yet no one, except those from the forest, was ever known to pass through the walls or the flooring. Every vault has been searched from roof to floor."

"But it is now evident that they are *not* sound," said Hopkins, "though Satan or his imps can pass clean through stone walls."

"Have *you* ever seen them do such a thing?" sneered Richard.

"Nay," replied Hopkins, turning suddenly round, "have *you?* For you would be the more likely to see Satan or his imps than myself."

"Let us not fool away the time," interposed Sir Ferdinand. "Get ready for the journey to the forest. This fellow shall be burnt at the stake—ha! what is that noise?"

A great cheer was heard.

Soon three or four men came racing towards the party.

"Kemble, with eighty horsemen, has arrived," they cried.

"Bravo!" shouted Hopkins; "now we will to action. Let the prisoner's arms be strongly bound behind his back."

Accordingly preparations were at once eagerly pushed forward, and in less than an hour the whole party were ready.

A huge party it was, horse and foot.

Ay, and a formidable party, Kemble's men, especially, being powerful and determined looking.

Every man was thoroughly well armed.

They carried pistols, daggers, and swords.

In the midst of the party Brasblade was placed.

A horse and small cart had been procured, and in that cart Brasblade was tied in a sitting posture.

The night was just the sort for this kind of fiendish work.

There was no moon, neither was a single star to be seen.

Hopkins, who had now come to the conclusion that, as the Man of Mystery beyond all doubt had spies in every direction, they might just as well light links as not, ordered a score to be set fire to and distributed at intervals along the line.

Thus they reached the outskirts of the forest, where they found the men who had been sent to cut and place the faggots awaiting them.

"Have you seen ought of the witches?" asked Richard.

"Nothing," was the reply.

"Nor any of this so-called Secret Brotherhood? nor of Rupert Redmond?" asked Sir Ferdinand.

"Nay, we have not observed a soul."

"You are quite certain that while you were busy cutting the faggots," said Hopkins, "this demon in the shape of a man—I mean Fendyke—did not fly past you with a hundred mounted hags behind him?"

"*Quite* certain," was the reply.

"Lead on to the tree," said Richard, "for, by all that is unholy, I am anxious to see the flames dancing about this mock parson."

"And so am I," cried Sir Ferdinand. "I only wish I had the *real* parson here. By heaven! he should burn beside Brasblade."

The spot which had been fixed upon as the place where the "execution" should be carried out was some distance from the edge of the forest.

Here was a sort of hollow, known as "The Sponge."

It derived this singular name from the fact that the ground was of a most peculiar character, and instantly absorbed whatever moisture descended upon it.

But little earth was to be seen.

It was covered with a very thick growth of moss.

In the rainy, wintry season, this place was dangerous.

But in the dry weather it was soft, springy, and beautiful to walk upon.

While the party, which had been cutting down, and placing the faggots, had been so actively engaged, others had been equally industrious.

Dark mysterious figures flitted hither and thither like Will-o'-the-Wisps.

Their movements were swift, silent, and remarkable.

The leader of these figures was Fendyke. The overlooker of all was Rupert Redmond.

The tree which had been selected as the place where Brasblade should die, was a gigantic oak.

Around this oak was piled an enormous quantity of faggots, together with bunches of twigs.

Around the trunk had been placed a heavy chain, together with an iron hoop for encircling the waist of their victim.

Two or three hundred yards distant stood a number of dark figures—with two exceptions, all on foot. Those exceptions were Rupert Redmond and Reuben Renard, who, mounted on beautiful black horses, stood some dozen paces in advance of the others.

All were as motionless as statues.

Even the horses stood as if turned to stone.

Every man was closely masked.

But to return to Hopkins and his crew.

The cart conveying Brasblade was brought up to the tree, and the captain was brutally dragged out.

Bravely had he kept himself up, but now his strength was fast failing him.

He could scarcely walk.

This Hopkins, and in fact everyone else, took for terror, and with loud cries they dragged him to the fatal tree.

"What think ye of this?" bawled Richard, dealing Brasblade a brutal kick. "What think you of this for a funeral-pile?"

Brasblade made no reply.

"Could you wish for a better death, Captain Brasblade?" cried Richard, jeeringly.

And as he spoke he again kicked the hapless prisoner.

So severe was the kick that Brasblade uttered a cry of agony.

"Seize upon him!" cried Hopkins.

At once Brasblade was seized upon by several men and forced against the tree, to which he was quickly chained.

Then the faggots were placed completely round him, touching his body.

"And now," said Sir Ferdinand, "with regard to the disposition of the men. I will tell you what must be done, and I think, Hopkins that you will approve of my arrangements——"

"Your *arrangements?*"

"Well, my suggestion."

"Sir Ferdinand, I am the leader of this party, and it is for *me* to make arrangements. But I'm ready to listen to your suggestion."

Sir Ferdinand bit his lips in his rage.

"This is what I suggest," he said. "We well know that Rupert is on the watch, so also are others within the forest, and it is not likely that they could mistake the position of the flames which will presently burst forth. Now I propose that a number of men sur-round the tree at a short distance, and that the others take up a position some two or three hundred yards farther, and in the form of a circle. By that means we can effectually check any attack."

"I had such an idea myself," replied Hopkins.

"And so had I," said Richard, who, as a matter of fact, had no such idea, nor anything like it.

"But," said Hopkins, "who will have command of those in the outer circle?"

"Let *me* take the command?" cried Kemble.

"I will share it," said Sir Ferdinand.

"Be it so, then," replied Hopkins; "and Richard and I will be in the inner circle. For I would not miss a close view of the burning of Captain Brasblade."

"Neither would I," replied Richard.

Quickly the men were arranged.

Those under command of Hopkins and Richard formed only a small circle, there being but forty, excluding those who had to attend to the faggots.

There were half-a-dozen for this task, and each was armed with a long iron rod, with which to stir the flames.

Presently all was ready, and Hopkins was only awaiting Sir Ferdinand's signal.

This was some time coming, for Sir Ferdinand and Kemble had not yet arranged the men to their satisfaction.

In the meantime the six men stood beside the pile, two of them having the flaming links, ready to apply them.

And now a dead silence reigned.

So profound was it that the low hissing of the burning links could most distinctly be heard.

It was an awful moment for Captain Brasblade.

That Rupert Redmond would come to his rescue he had no doubt; but—would he be too late?

It was this which caused his bloodshot eyes to roll to the right and the left.

It was this which made his heart palpitate violently.

"If Rupert Redmond appears directly *after* the links are applied," he thought, "how is it possible that he can rescue me? Great heavens! chained to this tree by a ponderous chain—how can I be saved?"

Presently arose the piercing blast of a horn.

It was Sir Ferdinand's signal.

Simultaneously a loud cry burst from Hopkins' and Richard's lips.

"*Now!*" they yelled. "Now!'

At once the links were thrust among the twigs.

Like lightning they ignited, and a thick cloud of smoke for a few moments enveloped the gigantic oak.

A tremendous cheer arose from the first circle, and it was echoed by the outer.

Another cheer arose; but it was suddenly checked.

The vast clouds of smoke had suddenly been dissipated.

At once the men rushed forward, and now a startling cry left their lips.

And no wonder!

The prisoner, chains and all, had vanished!

Instantly Hopkins and Richard galloped forward, followed by the men.

"Perdition!" yelled Hopkins, "he has disappeared! *Now*, what of Satan's work?"

No answer did he get from Richard.

That young villain sat upon his horse completely spellbound.

"Who can possess the power of opening the very earth?" cried Hopkins. "Ha, see the fire is *not* out!"

Even as Hopkins pointed to it, several long bright tongues of flame shot upward, and licked the trunk of the noble tree, but strangely enough the flames did not seem to have the slightest effect on the bark.

"The chain may have slipped," suggested one of the men, "and the prisoner, after all, may not be far away."

"Spread yourselves out," cried Hopkins. "Spread yourselves all — ha! what is that?"

Several of the men had uttered loud cries of terror.

They pointed to the ground at a distance of several feet from them.

Hopkins and Richard saw a *circle of flame* advancing steadily towards them.

It burnt with a bright red glow, and, in height, it was at least five feet.

"Holy Virgin!" cried Hopkins, "*the ground is on fire!*"

"Let us dash through it!" shouted Richard. "Quick, quick, our lives depend upon it!"

So saying, and without waiting to see how his men fared, he plunged his spurs into his horse's flanks, and dashed ahead.

Hopkins quickly followed.

It was, however, some few seconds before they could persuade the horses, now neighing and trembling with terror, to plunge through the flames.

But whip and spur combined urged them to dash through.

Not one instant too soon.

In the meantime the men had been rushing round the fiery circle to find an outlet.

But there was none.

Maddened at the idea of the certain fate which awaited them, they threw down their arms, and placing their hands over their faces, made a rush through the flames.

Many were successful, but they only escaped the flames to meet quite as certain a death.

They had no sooner got through the fire than they beheld a large number of men drawn up round the circle.

As they appeared, a loud, commanding voice was heard to shout—

"Fire!"

And instantly a volley of shots ran round the circle.

Every man was shot down.

Not one was left alive to tell the tale.

We have said that while the men were cutting down and placing the faggots, a number of dark figures were flitting hither and thither.

These figures were Fendyke, and many members of the Secret Brotherhood, and they were emptying on the moss small barrels of a highly imflammable compound.

The moss became thoroughly impregnated with this

Sir Ferdinand, Kemble and Hawkswell, with their men, were greatly astonished when that fiery circle suddenly appeared.

Astonishment changed to dismay when Hopkins and Richard dashed madly towards them.

The consternation into which they were thrown prevented them from seeing the rapid advance of the men in black.

But when the shots rang out they knew only too well who was at work.

"Every man will be lost!" groaned

Hopkins. "But let us have our revenge. Let us fight to the bitter end!"

"No, no," cried Sir Ferdinand; "it would be useless. Let us away at once, or we shall be surrounded, and treated like the others. Let us away!"

He did not stop for Hopkins's reply.

Neither did Richard.

Both turned, shouted to the men to follow, and dashed madly on.

The only man who did not seem at all terrified at what had occurred, and what was still occurring, was Kemble.

He and Hopkins roared out to the men to "Hold firm!"

But it was of no use.

The fellows hesitated a moment, and then they turned and dashed away as if the Prince of Darkness and all his imps were at their heels.

It was a desperate rush for life.

There was no help for it—Kemble and Hopkins had to follow them.

No stoppage was made until the Abbey was reached, and then the men looked back.

They expected to see that the centre of the forest was a mass of flames.

They saw nothing of the sort.

The forest was as black as pitch.

CHAPTER XVIII.

OF THE REMARKABLE MANNER IN WHICH EBENEZER WATSON MEETS HIS DEATH.

THE gigantic oak, to which Brasblade had been chained, contained a hollow.

Nature had formed it, and the ingenuity of man had remodelled it so that it would deceive the closest observer.

The hollow had been covered over with bark stretched upon iron, which formed a door, in which were ventilators.

The bark had been placed upon the iron by Fendyke, and it had then been treated with a chemical so that it would resist the action of fire.

This was the idea of the mysterious Bowolt, who always had a dread that one day the forest would be burned down by his enemies.

But before this was done, the earth about the roots was carefully taken away to a depth of several feet, then a stone cavity was made, so that it communicated with the hollow, and the earth was then restored.

Thus, within that tree, there was a safe hiding-place, screened from the eyes of man, and which would defy the action of fire.

Fendyke was within that hollow when Brasblade was placed against the tree, and, as soon as the smoke arose and hid his movements, he commenced operations.

As he opened the door, which moved inwards, the chain, of course, became loosened, and dropped from the prisoner's body.

This had no sooner occurred than Brasblade found himself seized, and dragged inwards.

What afterwards passed he had no idea, for he became insensible.

When he recovered he found himself in bed in a large vaulted chamber.

Beside him stood a tall, finely-formed man, clad from head to foot in black.

There was such a commanding, mysterious air about this individual, that Brasblade looked upon him with awe.

It struck him that this strange being must be no other than the dreaded Man of Mystery

On his left stood Rupert and Reuben; while at the foot of the bed was a short, grave-looking, elderly man, whom Brasblade rightly took to be a physician.

"Thank heaven," said Rupert, as he took Brasblade's hand within his own, "the critical moment has passed! You are saved!"

"Saved?" replied Brasblade. "Was I then in danger of my life?"

"You have been in danger of your life for a long time past," replied Rupert, gravely.

"A long time?" repeated Brasblade, slowly. "I am beginning to remember all. Was it not last night that I was chained to the tree?"

Rupert smiled.

"It no doubt appears so to you," he said, "because you have been wandering in your mind. But the terrible ordeal through which you passed *occurred a month ago.*"

"Gracious powers! A month ago?"

"Yes," said the Man of Mystery, for he it was, standing beside Brasblade; "it is just a month ago."

"And what has occurred in the meantime?"

"Matters of the greatest importance. But nothing has occurred within the forest."

"What are Sir Ferdinand and Hopkins doing, Rupert?"

"They have been making preparations for another attack upon us. But though they have done nothing *within* the forest during the past month, Hopkins has been busy on the outskirts. He has been merciless in running down the unhappy wretches who, for so long, have used the forest to practise witchcraft. Many have been taken—some subjected to torture in the vaults of the Abbey—some have been drowned, and others have beeen burned alive! Hopkins and some of his men are now on the track of Mother Frampton."

"What of my comrades?"

"They are close handy."

"Did they join you in time on that terrible night?"

"They did."

"No doubt they will be of great service to you. I hope I shall soon be able to get about. If I can be of any aid to you in hunting down those savage brutes," he added, fiercely, "command me. I offer you my services, and the services of my men freely, and I trust that you will accept of them."

"We shall," replied the deep voice of the Man of Mystery. "They will no doubt be of the greatest assistance to us. And you and they shall be rewarded.

"And now, Rupert," the Man of Mystery continued, "and you, Reuben, be seated. Captain Brasblade is a good hand at scheming. His advice on the matter which is now prominently before us, will therefore be of the utmost importance. A bottle of wine, captain, will not hurt you, I fancy. Is that the case, doctor?"

The physician nodded.

"It will not hurt him now," he replied. "Indeed, taken moderately, it will be of great assistance to him."

"He shall drink the best we have."

The plan to be discussed was in reference to Mother Frampton.

"I have no sympathy with the woman nor with her associates," said the Man of Mystery. "Though I may say that, though she has practised some fiendish tricks—for she is certainly a wonderful magician—I must not forget that she is the mother of Fendyke."

"Ha!" muttered Rupert, "I thought so."

"Fendyke," continued Morna, "has served not only me, but my predecessor, Bowolf, faithfully and well.

"He has had charge of many most important missions, not only here, but in London and other parts. Not once have I known him to fail. It is for his sake that I will do what I can towards keeping his mother from Hopkins's clutches. Unless something is done, and done speedily, Mother Frampton must fall into the villain's hands.

"The wretch has sworn to burn her alive on the top of Coldwater Hill; and when I say that Hopkins has offered five hundred guineas for Mother Frampton delivered to him alive, you may guess how anxious this witchfinder is to get hold of her."

"I shall be glad to hear the particulars," said Brasblade.

"Then Rupert will tell you, and if you can give any advice, do so."

What passed between them it is not necessary to say, as we shall see how the plans Hopkins had in view were carried out, and with what result.

*   *   *   *

During the month which had elapsed, a very great deal had been accomplished by Sir Ferdinand and those about him.

More men were required, and Kemble offered to provide a hundred if the necessary sum was handed over to him.

Both Hopkins and Richard looked to Sir Ferdinand to provide the money.

He refused point blank.

But he offered to provide one-third of the sum.

Richard offered a like amount, and expected Hopkins to find the balance.

But though the witchfinder had vast quantities of stolen property, which would have realised an enormous amount of capital, he laughed to scorn the idea of *his* contributing towards the necessary expenses.

"SUDDENLY TWO BLACK MOUNTED FIGURES APPEARED BESIDE HIM."

So, after some discussion, it was resolved to send a messenger to the Court in London.

The letter was sent by Sir Ferdinand, and Watson wrote one on behalf of Hopkins, which was enclosed.

The messenger (one of Kemble's men), duly arrived, and the letter was placed in the hands of the Duke of Buckingham by the king himself.

"Read it, Steenie," said the king, "and tell us what it's aw aboot."

No sooner did his majesty know than he replied—

"Naw, naw, not a bawbee, Steenie—not a bawbee shall be provided, nor a mon sent until Sir Ferdinand and Hopkins have satisfied us aboot the rumours that have reached our ears. Murder and rapine—that's what we're told has been committed, and I must have these matters explained to my satisfaction."

The duke soundly denounced Sir Ferdinand, Hopkins, and all their associates, and advised the king to issue a warrant ordering Hopkins to return and give an account of himself, and another warrant for the arrest of Sir Ferdinand Lockhart and Richard Melburn.

To this, however, the king would not listen.

As a matter of fact, not one-tenth part of the excesses committed by the witchfinder and his men had reached his majesty's ears.

The people generally were afraid of laying the information.

They credited Hopkins with greater powers than he actually possessed.

So the messenger returned, not with a written reply, but a verbal one.

It was given to him by the duke himself, and these were the words—

"Say that the king refuses to pay any attention whatsoever to the documents you have brought."

Sir Ferdinand understood the actual meaning of that message, and so did Richard.

But such was not the case with Hopkins.

When Sir Ferdinand told him that the reason of the king's refusal to attend to the message was that he was so satiated with State affairs, he fully believed it.

He consulted with Watson, and, acting on his advice, he offered to advance Sir Ferdinand a sum of money on proper security.

After consulting with Richard, and both coming to the conclusion that most likely Hopkins would be killed in some affair, and that, consequently, the money advanced would not have to be repaid, Sir Ferdinand accepted a loan of five thousand guineas.

So, with part of this sum, Kemble, with Watson for a companion, went to Manchester, and the requisite number of men were quickly forthcoming.

It was on the evening when the conversation was taking place between Brasblade and his friends, that Sir Ferdinand, Hopkins, Richard, and Watson were in the study at the Abbey.

Before them was an assortment of wines and spirits, as well as a pile of papers.

The four were gloomy in the extreme; for they could get no information respecting Rupert Redmond or the Man of Mystery.

They were now discussing a most important matter—the capture of Mother Frampton.

"You see," said Richard, "it is from this hag that we shall be able to obtain all the information we want respecting the secret places in the possession of the Man of Mystery."

"It is from her that I expect to get the information as to who the Man of Mystery really *is!*" said Sir Ferdinand; "*that*, above all things, puzzles me."

"Hawkswell says that she has sought refuge in the 'White Cave,'" observed Hopkins.

"That is doubtful," said Richard, shaking his head; "for the White Cave has been for years in the occupation of the man known as the 'White Monk.' You have seen this man, Hopkins?"

"Yes," growled the witchfinder; "but I must say that I saw nothing *white* about him. On the contrary, I noticed that what he wore was particularly *black*. You saw him, Ebenezer, and questioned him?"

"I did as you told me," replied Watson with a scowl. "I asked him his name, for I was about to write it down. I had the book open in my hand for that purpose. No sooner did I ask him for his name than he snatched the book from my hand, and dealt me a sounding blow on the face with it."

"And what did *you* do?" asked Richard.

"I picked up the book and walked off."

"That shows how wise even lawyers are, sometimes," sneered Richard.

"Let us have Hawkswell here," said Sir Ferdinand.

Hawkswell was accordingly called.

"Tell us the particulars of your visit to the cave once more," said Sir Ferdinand.

"Acting on your instructions," returned Hawkswell, "I donned the disguise of a farm labourer. I sauntered by the White Cave, and when opposite the entrance, I sat down just as if I had no idea there was such a place, and began to count some money.

"It had the desired effect. The White Monk heard the jingling of the coin, and came cautiously forth. He at once commenced a conversation, and finally invited me into the cave.

"I told him the story I had already prepared, to the effect that I had lost myself, and that in my wanderings I had come across a bag of money.

"I saw his eyes sparkle as he looked at it. As I said I was hungry he set some refreshments before me. Presently I began to express surprise at the cave, and he offered to show me the place if I would divide my finding. I consented, and he took me over his abode; but it was only a *part*, for I know that there are caves below those which he showed me. Chancing to look down a sort of well, I saw a number of witches seated around a huge log."

"And among them you saw Mother Frampton?" asked Hopkins, eagerly.

"I am almost positive that it was she."

"Did the White Monk think that you saw these women?" asked Richard.

"I am certain that he did not. My disguise as a farm labourer was so perfect—my language was so simple that he was completely deceived, and he must have thought that had I seen the women I should have asked questions respecting them."

"Yes, yes," said Hopkins, "you acted well and cleverly. But yet we must proceed with the greatest caution. It would never do to make a sudden attack on the place, because there's no doubt these underground caves have outlets, and ere we could reach them, the hags would be far away."

"For what we know," said Watson, "these underground caves may contain —like the vaults in that accursed castle —barrels of gunpowder."

"That is true," replied Hopkins; "but now we will see what can be done."

"Bring hither the page, Stockholm. He is a cunning youth," said Sir Ferdinand.

"What scheme have you in your mind?" asked Richard.

"Wait but a few moments and you will see."

The page was soon brought into the study.

He was a tall, slender, rather effeminate-looking lad of about seventeen.

His figure was singularly graceful and his countenance pleasing to look upon.

"Stockholm," said Sir Ferdinand, "we have a task for you to perform."

The page bowed.

"You will undertake it?"

"Certainly," was the reply.

"Even if it is very dangerous?"

"Yes."

"Then," said Sir Ferdinand, turning to his fellow-plotters, "I propose that Stockholm attires himself as a female. Miriam's costumes will fit him to perfection. He will present himself to the White Monk, and saying that he is fleeing from the Abbey to escape the odious attentions of Richard Melburn——"

"What?" thundered Richard, rising angrily.

"Well, well, if you are dissatisfied with that, let him say the attentions of Sir Ferdinand Lockhart—to escape my attentions, and beg the old man to give him protection. He must have with him some valuable jewel to present to the monk, and then he will be protected for a time."

"Proceed," said Hopkins.

"He will then persuade the old man to accompany him some distance. We can then pounce upon the monk, and the rest will be easy."

"The idea is worthy of myself," chuckled Hopkins, "and I think the plan is likely to be an effective one if this youth carries out the part he undertakes, with care."

"You can rely upon that," said Sir Ferdinand. "I have every confidence in him."

"Let preparations be instantly made," said Richard, "or before Stockholm can get to the cave, the hags will perhaps have migrated to some other spot."

Stockholm ascended to the apartments which had once been Miriam's, and attired himself in her clothes.

He took little pains to conceal his identity so far as his features were concerned.

So that when he reappeared below, Hopkins questioned whether he had done enough.

Stockholm replied that the old man had never seen him, and, therefore, it was impossible that he could penetrate the disguise.

He had to make but little effort in the disguising of his voice, which was naturally soft and sweet.

"You certainly make a sweet girl," chuckled Hopkins, "and it is to be hoped that you are not stopped by a man, mistaken for a girl, and carried off."

"Whoever attempted to carry me off would quickly know that I not only possess a dagger, but that I can use it with good effect," replied Stockholm, proudly.

"Bravo! I feel certain that you will bring your mission to a successful termination."

"And now," said Sir Ferdinand, "as to the article, which it will be necessary to present to the old man, I am afraid I have parted with all I possess."

"Take this," said Richard, removing a fine diamond ring from his finger. "Place it upon your own finger, Stockholm, so that you don't lose it."

Final instructions were now given the page, and he set out upon his journey.

Slowly he proceeded until he reached the wood.

Then, plunging into a dense mass of brushwood, he pursued his way as if well used to the place he was traversing.

Presently he reached a huge tree, whose wide spreading limbs and dense foliage formed a splendid canopy.

Here Stockholm paused, stooped, and pulling aside some of the undergrowth, took hold of a large wire handle.

He pulled this, and brought to the surface a large cage.

In this were two great white owls, whose large, brilliant eyes glowed in the semi-darkness like stars.

The page took one of the birds in each hand, and raised them over his head.

At once the owls rose high into the heavens, whirled round and round the magnificent tree, and then went across the forest with wonderful speed.

Stockholm must have been waiting for some twenty minutes, when a rustling fell upon his ears.

The next moment the bushes before him were pushed aside, and a little black figure appeared.

It was Fendyke.

He uttered no word, but holding aside the bushes, allowed another dark figure to emerge.

This was Rupert Redmond.

"Brave Stockholm," said Rupert, clasping the young page's hands; "and so thou art come hither once again?"

"Yes, Master Rupert. You well know how anxiously I wish to serve you?"

"I do. And you forgot not the spot where the white messengers were concealed?"

"Nay. Both safely arrived?"

"Yes."

"You do not express any surprise at seeing me in this garb."

"I do not. I have already guessed that you are bound upon some errand for Sir Ferdinand, and as that errand is a secret one, your identity must be concealed. But I fancy that I can guess something of your mission."

"Indeed!" said the page.

"Are you not about to visit the White Monk?"

The page started in astonishment.

"I am," he replied; "but how, in the name of heaven, do you know this?"

"Because I have already received intelligence that the White Monk has been visited by Hawkswell."

"Ha! then his disguise was penetrated?"

"It was. Though he little thought it, his disguise as a farm labourer, though good, was instantly seen through. This was a very fortunate circumstance, for it has put us on our guard."

"Listen now to the instructions I have received," said Stockholm.

Thereupon he told Rupert all that had passed, and added—

"So certain are they that Mother Frampton will be captured to-night, that they are about to despatch Watson to the magistrate—the man who has already issued so many warrants with respect to the witches—and get him to issue the formal document, authorising her immediate punishment, and that is, as you may guess, burning at the stake."

"By heaven!" ejaculated Rupert, "that is what I expected."

"You know Watson?" said Stockholm.

"By sight, well. Now listen attentively to what I shall tell you, Stockholm, and, if all goes well, Hopkins will once again fall into a trap. You are well aware that this same Watson is a rascal of the very worst description?"

"I am. He has urged Hopkins to the commission of many horrible crimes."

"Of that I have no doubt, though Hopkins requires little urging. It was from Watson that I took the documents, I believe."

"Yes."

"Then wait, Stockholm, and see what plans we have formed. I think you will easily understand them."

He then informed the page of what had passed at the home of mystery.

Having placed him in possession of these facts, Rupert continued—and his tones were now earnest and grave—

"You must be well aware that I can have no sympathy with these witches. I think it is desirable that they should be completely stamped out. But the Man of Mystery, as I have before told you, has a sort of claim upon me. At first, I was strongly inclined to believe what was said of him—that was, that he had sold his soul to Satan in return for certain miraculous powers.

"I have discovered that this mysterious man, who certainly wields so many strange powers, has an object in view, something at which he is ever toiling. But in the meantime, Stockholm, be assured that the man with whom I am at present associated, is not in league with the powers of darkness."

"My dear Rupert," replied Stockholm, warmly, "I swear to you that I never had any doubts of you or your movements, mysterious as they have undoubtedly been,"

"Thanks, thanks! You see we are, as it were, compelled to protect this Mother Frampton"—and here Rupert looked round, but Fendyke had vanished—"who is the mother of the strange man Fendyke, because she is in possession of many secrets concerning the brotherhood.

"It is for this reason that Sir Ferdinand is so anxious to get hold of her. Yet, even if he did, I believe that no torture would ever wring from the breast of that withered old woman one word of confession. I am certain that she fears not death in any form. But you have seen this Mother Frampton?"

"Twice."

"Plainly?"

"Yes."

"Then compare her and Watson."

"Ah!" cried Stockholm, with a sudden start. "They are marvellously alike."

"And now what think you of the plans?"

"Excellent! But what a death!"

"He will deserve it, Stockholm."

"Yes, that he certainly will."

"He was as guilty of the murder of poor Master Arlington as was Hopkins and his men."

"Most true."

"Of that horrible crime, I suppose, Sir Ferdinand and Richard are well aware?"

"I know not, for I have not heard them mention the matter. I should not have known had you not told me."

"Well, now pursue your way, and quickly, for already a long time has been lost. You said it was likely that Watson would set out for Hollymount, the magistrate's residence, in about an hour?"

"Yes."

"Good! There will be just time."

Warmly clasping hands, the page went on his way to the White Cave, while Rupert, placing a horn to his lips, blew a loud blast upon it.

It was quickly replied to by Fendyke.

Pushing aside the bushes, he came forward, stretched forth his hand, and took Rupert's.

Another instant and both were rushing through the dark forest with incredible speed.

Every obstacle was surmounted with

as much certainty as if their path were brilliantly illuminated.

* * * *

The page was right.

Watson *did* set off in an hour, although at the last moment it appeared as if someone else would have been selected for the task, Watson's services with the " Black Book " being required.

Still, Hopkins latterly did not trouble himself much about the " Black Book " or Ebenezer.

He had not forgotten the papers—those precious documents which he considered would have brought him fame or fortune.

Watson knew more of the contents of those papers than did Hopkins.

Had the documents been still in the possession of the witchfinder, Sir Ferdinand Lockhart would have been entirely in his power. Watson had discovered that Sir Ferdinand was actually one of the conspirators in the gunpowder plot to destroy the king.

After some discussion it was decided that Ebenezer Watson should set out for the residence of Ivan Hall, the magistrate of Hollymount, one of the Great Unpaid — a scoundrel of the deepest dye, an individual who laughed JUSTICE to scorn, and returned judgments for those with MIGHT, and not of RIGHT.

His residence was Hollymount, but by some people it was significantly called " Gallow's Hill."

It was distant some two miles from the Abbey, where it was reached partly by the high road, and partly across a piece of marshy land called " Wastewater," a dreary place, on which nothing but rushes and all sorts of water weeds ever grew.

Moreover, at certain periods of the year it was exceedingly dangerous.

Ebenezer was provided with a horse. It was a miserable creature.

Attired in his customary broadbrimmed hat, and carrying the " Black Book " under his arm, he set out on his journey.

All went well enough until he reached the marshes.

Here he had to pause for some little time in order to select the path which he had previously traversed.

But he had had a guide then, and now that he was alone, he found the greatest difficulty in proceeding.

He feared to dismount lest he should not again be able to get into the saddle unassisted.

A most important thing he had forgotten. That was a link.

If he had that, he thought, he was certain not to fall into danger.

Some distance ahead of him Will-o'-the-Wisps disported themselves, spreading a curious weird glow over the marshy ground.

He was wise enough to know that to approach them was to cast himself into a danger from which it would, perhaps, be impossible to extricate himself.

After many groans he went on, determined to trust to his horse as much as to his own judgment.

He was not far wrong in that, for the horse was a most careful creature, and proceeded with the utmost caution.

At last a black mass loomed before him, and Ebenezer recognised it as the small park which surrounded the magistrate's house.

With a grunt of satisfaction Ebenezer pushed on.

He reached a clump of trees, and was about to dismount, when suddenly two black, mounted figures appeared beside him.

So terrified was Ebenezer, that he found himself quite unable to utter a cry of any kind.

Those two black figures were Rupert Redmond and Reuben Renard.

Reuben seized Ebenezer by the collar, while Rupert, snatching the book from him, said—

" Now mark you, Ebenezer Watson, if you utter a single cry for help, your life will pay the forfeit."

" Who — who are you ? " gasped Ebenezer.

" Who we are I shall not say now. Put your hands behind your back."

" Oh, I beg ! I entreat——"

" Silence," interrupted Rupert, sternly. " Your entreaties fall on deaf ears. Put your hands behind your back. It is our intention to bind them, and also to gag you."

" Just Providence ! what have I done that I should be subjected to this gross outrage ? "

"Ask your own conscience, thou rascal!" said Reuben; "but take the advice given you, and preserve silence, or a sudden death will be your portion."

By this time Ebenezer's face had turned as white as the face of a corpse; his eyes rolled wildly, while his hair seemed to be actually standing on end.

He did not have to reflect what he had to do.

He felt certain that he had fallen into the hands of two of the terrible Brotherhood; and felt that meek obedience to their orders was the only way to escape a severe punishment.

Therefore he placed his hands behind his back, but at the same time his dilated eyes wandered to the outline of the magistrate's house, and a deep groan escaped his lips.

Oh, he thought, that he could have made the servants overhear him.

There were many men-servants there, and they might have rescued him.

In quick time his hands were tied behind his back, and he was gagged.

Then Rupert dismounted, seized him by the waist, and, with remarkable ease, raised him from his saddle, placed him behind Reuben, and passed a strap round the two.

Then turning Ebenezer's horse in the contrary direction, he dealt him a blow on the haunches.

The startled animal pricked up his ears, snorted loudly, and dashed off as fast as he could possibly go.

The party now proceeded slowly at first; but when the marsh had been crossed, they went along at a tremendous pace—a pace that filled the soul of Ebenezer Watson with terror, and caused him to shut his eyes.

Thus he saw not the direction in which he was being taken.

This was in a direction quite contrary to the way he came.

When, on the pace becoming slower, he ventured to open his eyes, he found that they were in the intricate paths of the forest.

"They cannot be about to slay me," he thought, "or they would have done so long ago. I suppose they will question me. Well, well, I am ready to confess all, everything, anything, so that they spare my life. I will betray Hopkins! Ha! if he were *slain*, and I contrived to get *free*, the whole of that wealth would be mine!"

He kept his eyes wide open now in order to see whether he could recognise any of the paths through which he was taken.

But he recognised not *one*.

Presently they descended a short, steep hill, at the bottom of which was a door, though it was almost concealed by the mass of ivy which grew about it.

On Rupert uttering a few words, the door was opened by unseen hands, both horses entered, and the door was again noiselessly closed.

No longer were they in *semi*-darkness.

No, the darkness was now *profound*, so that nothing whatever could be seen.

Yet the horses proceeded as if they were being led by guides.

Ebenezer noticed particularly that their hoofs caused not the faintest noise.

It was quite evident to him that they were traversing a subterranean passage.

That it was a passage of great length he could tell from the time occupied.

As a matter of fact they were passing through a series of caves, and those caves were beneath that known as the White Cave.

Presently the faint glimmer of a light ahead was seen.

In a few moments a small chamber—a chamber formed by Nature—was reached, and this was illuminated, though faintly, by a link thrust in a bracket in the wall.

Of furniture it was destitute.

A piece of solid rock in the centre did duty for a table, while several smaller pieces surrounding it answered the purpose of chairs.

On the centre piece of rock were several bottles and tankards.

Not a sign of a human being was to be seen.

Rupert dismounted, and lifted Ebenezer down, and then Reuben also dismounted.

Taking the horses by the bridle, he led them back through the dark passage, but for what distance Ebenezer could form no idea, nor did he know whether they were or were not taken in charge by anyone in waiting.

Rupert now took out his dagger, cut Ebenezer's bonds, and took the gag from his mouth.

The rascal breathed a great sigh of relief.

"Ebenezer Watson," said Rupert, "you have reached the end of your journey."

Ebenezer glanced eagerly towards the bottles.

Even a cup of water would have been welcome.

After a pause, he said—

"For the love of the Virgin relieve my mind. Tell me who and what you are, and why I am brought to this spot."

Rupert shook his head.

"Well," continued Ebenezer, "at least tell me where I am?"

"Nay, that is impossible," replied Rupert. "I am simply obeying orders, and they were to tell you nothing. But here," he added, pouring from a bottle into a tankard what looked like red wine; "drink this."

Ebenezer took it with a trembling hand, but he was suspicious.

Rupert saw that he hesitated, and so, taking another tankard, he poured a quantity of wine from the *same* bottle and raised to his own lips.

Of course Ebenezer thought it was the same wine as that given to him.

It was not.

The bottle was *divided in the centre*, and all the way down, and each compartment held a different liquid.

On this occasion one was drugged, the other was not.

Ebenezer had the drugged wine.

"You will not remove your masks, so that I may see your faces?" asked Ebenezer.

"No; our masks remain on."

"Answer me this, then, gentlemen, I beg. Tell me whether my suspicions are correct. I am brought here to be questioned—to confess?"

"You are."

"Good!" cried Ebenezer, as if a tremendous weight had been lifted from his mind. "I am ready to confess. I will betray all of them at the Abbey—all, I will, indeed, if you will but let me go."

"Drink, man, drink," replied Rupert, placing his own wine to his lips, "and we will talk of that afterwards."

Ebenezer was parched.

He raised the wine to his lips, and consumed the whole.

Rupert slowly drank his, poured more out, and handed it to Reuben, who drank it.

Scarcely had Reuben placed his tankard on the stone table before Ebenezer, with a wild, gasping cry, started up.

"Oh!" he cried, "fearful pains are shooting through me. Tell me—assure me that you have not poisoned me!"

"I assure you that I have not!" replied Rupert, sternly, as he drew himself erect. "A far more dreadful fate is in store for you, Ebenezer Watson."

A wild, fearful scream left Watson's lips as Rupert uttered these words.

He was about to speak, but he found himself unable.

The drug was taking rapid effect. Ebenezer rocked violently backwards and forwards, staggered hither and thither, and finally fell in a heap at Rupert's feet.

"You did not tell me the effect of that drug, Rupert," said Reuben.

"Did I not? Well, it was an omission which I will at once rectify. That drug will render him totally unconscious, as he now is, for some considerable time—at least, an hour. At the expiration of that time, he will recover possession of consciousness, but he will be *deprived of the power of speech* for a long time after that."

"I understand. But think you that he will recover in time to make himself understood?"

"So as to be saved? Nay, 'tis impossible. He will not recover the power of speech until he is subjected to great bodily pain."

"His punishment will, indeed, be a terrible one. But he deserves it. And, besides, his fate should be a fearful warning to the others."

"You are correct. And now let us commence."

So saying, Rupert placed his horn to his lips, and blew a blast upon it.

It was at once answered.

A huge piece of the naturally-formed wall rolled aside, and there entered the chamber the page, Stockholm, and the White Monk, a tall, handsome, old man, of at least eighty, who was attired in a white robe, fastened at the waist with a black sash.

This singular being had occupied these caves for many years; but Sir Ferdinand never thought that there was the least suspicion attaching to the old man.

He looked upon him merely as an eccentric with an intense love of money.

Beneath his arms he carried a huge bundle of women's old clothes and a box.

"Let no time be lost," said Rupert; "but commence at once."

"Ay," replied the White Monk, bending low and looking closely into Ebenezer's face. "No time must be lost. By all the saints, so far as the formation of the face is concerned, this man bears a most striking resemblance to Mother Frampton."

"I so informed you," replied Rupert.

"You did. But I had no idea that the resemblance was so wonderful. Now, first we must dye his face."

The whole party set to work with a will, and in the first place Ebenezer was divested of almost every article of clothing.

Concealed in various places were jewels of enormous value, together with money and other articles, the whole of which were handed to the White Monk.

In a short time Ebenezer was attired in the discarded clothes of Mother Frampton, and so altered that he resembled her in every way.

It was impossible that Hopkins, Sir Ferdinand or Richard, or indeed anyone else, could detect the trick which was being played.

An old mattress was now procured and laid in a corner, and Ebenezer was stretched upon it.

Then against his hand were placed several bottles, one or two of which were upset, the liquor being spilled all around.

"And now," said Rupert, "what of Mother Frampton and her women?"

"At last they have taken the good advice given them, and have gone."

"Whither?"

"That I cannot say."

"And that beautiful young woman, who used to rise from the hollow?"

"Alas! she is dead. She was escaping from some of Hopkins's hounds, and she rushed across the Twin Rocks, which spot, as you have been told, was the hiding-place of the traitor, Black Braddell. The locality was strange to her, and she fell headlong into the well which is situated between the two rocks.

The distance to the bottom is fully a hundred feet.

"The men descended by command of Hopkins, and they brought up the young woman's body. In getting the body the men found one or two articles of value. This roused Hopkins's suspicions, and he directed the men to search.

"The result was that a large amount of booty, in the shape of valuable articles and money, was discovered. All this had, of course, been placed there by Black Braddell."

"Whom I always thought to be poor," said Rupert.

"I have had my suspicions of him for many years," said the White Monk. "But now, Master Page, are you ready?"

"Yes," said Stockholm, "quite."

"I trust they will do you no injury," said Rupert.

"Nay," replied the White Monk. "I shall, of course, offer only just sufficient resistance to throw them off their guard. So for the time adieu to thee, Rupert Redmond, and the same to thy friend."

"Adieu!" replied both Rupert and Reuben, who now re-entered the subterranean passage.

*　　*　　*　　*

At the appointed spot Hopkins, Richard, Sir Ferdinand and the greater part of the men were in waiting.

Concealed amid a dense mass of brushwood, they were ready at the word of command to spring forward.

But they had to wait where they were much longer than they expected.

"By all the fiends," hissed Hopkins, at last breaking a silence of considerable duration, "this is strange! What can have befallen that withered attorney?"

"Most likely his horse has pitched him into a morass," replied Richard with a chuckle, "and in that case, away goes the precious 'Black Book,' as well as the lawyer."

"Hush!" whispered Sir Ferdinand. "He, no doubt, has been detained at the magistrate's house, for it is likely that Master Hall was in bed. Fear not. He will be here directly. As to Stockholm, I would wager he has the greatest difficulty to get the old man to accompany him any distance, as we arranged. Let us be patient."

"But can't you hear the men muttering?" asked Hopkins. "Can't you tell that they are becoming impatient?"

"What of it? They are paid for their time, whether it be passed in waiting or in action."

Presently a man, who had been placed some distance in advance, came hurriedly up.

"They come," he whispered. "They are close here!"

He was right.

So close were they that they could not only see Stockholm and the old man, but they could hear what was said.

"You see how completely Stockholm has deceived the old man!" chuckled Sir Ferdinand.

So it appeared.

"So now," the White Monk was saying, "I shall soon place you on the right road, and if you pursue it according to my directions, Sir Ferdinand Lockhart will not again molest you with his intentions. 'Tis dark hereabouts, and dangerous; but anon I'll——"

"*Now*," said Hopkins, impatiently.

Instantly four men sprang forth, and laid violent hands on the old man.

"Holy Virgin!" he cried in well-simulated astonishment and terror, "what is this? What have I done? Unhand me—unhand me! I choke! I choke!"

"Hurt him not," said Sir Ferdinand. "Simply hold him so that he does not get away."

"Oh, it is *you*, Sir Ferdinand Lockhart," gasped the White Monk. "*You*, from whose clutches I was endeavouring to shield this poor young lady. What are you about to do with me? Beware!"

"Now listen to me," replied Sir Ferdinand. "For years I have taken you to be a harmless old man. But it has come to my knowledge that you have afforded protection to numbers of forest hags, and among them that accursed wretch, Mother Frampton, the doer of all sorts of evil things! Speak, and tell me, is she hereabout? Beware how you answer, for if you tell me a falsehood, you shall pay for it with your life! Is mother Frampton within your caves?"

The White Monk hesitated for a moment or two, and then replied—

"I am sorry to say she is."

"And the other witches?" asked Sir Ferdinand,

"There are no others."

"But there *were*."

"Yes, there were; but they have gone—whither, I know not. Mother Frampton brought with her a number of bottles of vile spirits, and of these she has been continually partaking."

Hopkins and his men burst into a loud roar of derisive laughter.

"My men," said Sir Ferdinand, in exultant tones; "at last this defiant hag is within our grasp. As soon as ever we take her, we will drag her to the top of Coldwater Hill, and there we will burn her alive. If she is *not* a witch, the flames will not touch her body; but if she is one of Satan's own, then the flames will consume her. So now let us forward. Let the White Monk walk behind, and Stockholm—where is Stockholm?"

"He was here a moment ago," replied one of the men.

"Oh, well, he is close handy. Now, let us on."

"One moment," said Hopkins. "The faggots are not ready."

"Tar barrels, I know, have been already placed there, but we must have faggots. Now those with axes go forward, and, Hawkswell, do you take command of them."

"Ay, ay," was Hawkswell's reply, as he proceeded to get together the men with the axes.

This was soon done, and he led them towards the hill.

Before starting, Sir Ferdinand made another enquiry for Stockholm.

But he was not to be seen, and so Sir Ferdinand considered it likely that he had departed to the Abbey in order to get rid of his disguise.

A very great mistake indeed, as Stockholm was already deep in the wild paths of the forest.

All being in readiness, the whole party advanced as fast as it was possible.

The White Cave being reached, Sir Ferdinand, Richard, Hopkins, and a number of men dismounted.

The three leaders each took a link, and thus they entered the cave.

They found the steps leading to the caves below, and with loud shouts they rushed into the chamber where lay Ebenezer.

The deception which had been prac-

tised was completely successful, for
Ebenezer was instantly recognised as
Mother Frampton.

The lurid glare of the links fell upon
the repulsive face—a face apparently
distorted by drink.

The whole place smelt most horribly
of the disgusting compounds which had
escaped from the bottles.

The fearful noise of the jingling spurs,
the crash of arms, and the yells of the
men did not cause the supposed mother
of witches to move one inch.

Hopkins, blinded by rage, had
snatched forth his dagger, and was about
to rush forward when Sir Ferdinand
held him back.

"Hold!" he said. "Slay her as she
lies, and see what a vast amount of
genuine pleasure will be dissipated."

"You are right," replied Hopkins;
"but on my soul I can scarce keep my
hands off the hag. Pah! she is about
the most horrible-looking wretch I ever
beheld. What ho, there! Drag her
up."

Several men pushed forward, and
Ebenezer was seized and dragged up.

But he was quite unable to stand.

"Drag her out!" shouted Hopkins.
"Let there be no ceremony about it.
Drag her out, and tie her to the back of
one of the horses. Quick! let no time
be lost."

Thereupon two men took hold of
Ebenezer and dragged him from the
cave.

Several strong straps were procured,
and with these he was strapped to the
back of one of the horses.

This being done, Richard asked—

"And now what is to be done with the
White Monk?"

"Let us burn him with her," shouted
Hopkins, with a brutal laugh. "A hag
like this should have company."

"Nay," said Sir Ferdinand, "I should
like to question him, and therefore I
propose that he is kept a prisoner and
conveyed to the Abbey."

"But he had better be a witness to
Mother Frampton's execution," suggested
Richard.

"To be sure," answered Sir Ferdinand;
"he shall see her burn. Thus he will
be the better prepared to answer my
questions."

There was now so much confusion and
excitement, that no one noticed the face
of the White Monk.

It had turned deathly pale.

It had never struck him that he would
be *detained* a prisoner.

He had thought—and so, indeed, had
Rupert—that as soon as Mother Frampton, in the shape of Ebenezer, was captured, he would be allowed to go.

"I will not allow the circumstance to
alarm me," he thought, "for Rupert
Redmond or Fendyke, or one of the
brotherhood, will quickly get to know
that I am a prisoner, and I shall be
rescued, although I fear it will cost many
lives."

All being in readiness the party proceeded, the same road being taken as
that pursued by Hawkswell and the
faggot cutters.

Half-a-dozen mounted men, each
carrying a flaming link in one hand,
and a pistol in the other, led the way.

Next came a large number of men,
mounted and on foot, thoroughly well
armed, and ready to fire at the word of
command.

Then came the horse carrying the
supposed Mother Frampton.

This was surrounded with a dozen
men, carrying links and pistols like the
leaders. Behind them, riding abreast,
Hopkins being in the centre, were the
three chiefs, and the rear was brought
up by the White Monk, about whose
waist a rope had been placed, which was
held by one of the men, and then the
remainder of the party.

As the men proceeded, they shouted
these lines, the effect being singularly
weird—

"An imp of darkness here we bring;
Hail, soldiers, let your voices ring!
Hail fire, consumer of a race,
With human forms, but Satan's face!
Oh, let the glow from faggots rise,
And angels see it from the skies!
Oh, let the king's dire vengeance fall
On the cursed wretches, great and small!
Oh, soldiers, let your shouts resound,
For Satan's chief at last is found!"

Little did Ebenezer, when he wrote
those blasphemous lines, dream that
they would be howled while he himself
was on the road to a horrible death.

Coldwater Hill was reached.

The summit looked down upon the
dark forest.

On the top was an enormous stone
column.

On the left, stacked up in one vast pile, were tar barrels, which Hopkins's men had placed there.

All around the column the faggots had been piled.

The chains which had been provided, and which were carried by Hopkins, were now produced and fastened about the column.

Then Ebenezer was unstrapped and pulled from the horse to the ground.

It was at this very moment that he opened his eyes.

But he had to close them again, and instantly, for the glare of the links, several of which were held over him, was too powerful.

In another instant or two, though, he reopened them.

He looked round him in a bewildered fashion, failing to comprehend what was passing before his eyes.

"Ha! thou imp of Darkness! Ha! thou worshipper of Bacchus as well as Satan," yelled Hopkins, dismounting and dealing the supposed witch a fearful kick. "Thou hast recovered, eh? 'Tis well—you will be able to see the preparations for your death. Thou wilt see the column which has long been waiting for thy foul carcase!"

That voice!

It instantly recalled Ebenezer to his senses.

He sat up, he stared around him, he looked at the tattered garments which had been placed about his person, and then his lips opened to give utterance to the fearful scream which rose to them.

It was never uttered.

He was *speechless*.

He had fully recovered consciousness, but his tongue totally refused to perform its proper functions.

"See! the hag has recovered consciousness!" cried Richard, as he dealt the supposed witch a slash across the face with his whip; "see, the drunken hag has recovered! Behold how she stares frantically around her. Observe the look of terror in her eyes now that she sees she is indeed in the hands of those who for so long have hated her! Ay, you may plead, vile, besotted hag! Look yonder! See you not the column on Coldwater Hill? That hill on which you and your crew have practised many an unholy rite. There where many a

witches' Sabbath has been kept, Mother Frampton — there shall you perish! Look at the tar barrels, look at the little mountains of faggots!"

The look upon Ebenezer's disguised face was now awful.

He saw it all.

He now remembered how he had been captured and taken to the secret cave.

Yes, he saw it all plainly enough.

He had been made to resemble Mother Frampton.

And for that old woman his own friends now took him.

Oh, that he could get his hands free!

Then could he tear off his disguise, and prove to them that he was not what he seemed.

Again he tried to use his tongue.

It was of no use. He could not get it to form a single word.

Frantically he endeavoured to free his hands.

Vain endeavour.

Too firmly were they secured behind his back.

Then he commenced to make motions with his eyes and mouth.

"Look!" yelled Hopkins; "can you not see what the hag is trying to do? Can't you see that she is trying to bewitch you, Richard?"

Richard started back with a loud cry—

"Is she?" he said. "Then let me teach her what it is to attempt to bewitch me. Take *that*, you hag!"

And down again with awful force came that whip on the dyed, distorted face.

It left a long, narrow cut—a cut as cleanly made as if it had been inflicted with a knife.

Ebenezer writhed in agony.

The whip was again raised, but it never descended, because Sir Ferdinand, becoming impatient, interposed.

Had it again descended, Ebenezer would have recovered the use of his tongue.

"Now to the column!" thundered Hopkins. "Away with her!"

Again was Ebenezer seized and hurried to the column.

In less than two minutes he was securely chained in a standing position.

Then the men were ordered to take up their positions half-way down the hill.

They did so in the form of a half circle, and in front of them—again mounted—were Sir Ferdinand, Richard, and Hopkins.

And now the faggots and barrels were placed, the former in front, and the latter behind, though only about one-fourth of the number of barrels were used.

Presently all was in readiness.

For the space of a few moments a death-like silence fell upon all.

But soon the men began to chuckle audibly, for the frantic struggles of Ebenezer amused them.

Suddenly Hopkins shouted—

"Links!"

At once half-a-dozen flaming links were plunged into the faggots.

A pause ensued, then small clouds of smoke arose.

This was followed by little tongues of flame, which hissed and crackled, and finally burst into one gigantic blaze.

In a short space of time the barrels behind caught fire, and flamed with tremendous fury.

So well tarred were they that the boiling liquid began to run in streams about the hill, and to fill every little hole.

Presently the whole pile was a mass of roaring, raging flame, and the heat was so great that the men could feel it where they stood.

But every now and then a current of wind blew the flames gently aside, and the doomed prisoner was seen.

Suddenly a great cry rent the air.

The prisoner had recovered the power of speech.

The cry was clear and distinct.

"Oh, Holy Virgin! oh, save me! Have mercy on me! I'm not Mother Frampton! I'm Ebenezer Watson!"

The voice was instantly recognised.

At once tremendous cries arose.

They saw at once the trick which had been played upon them.

So paralysed were the three leaders that they could only sit upon their horses, and stare vacantly at the prisoner being fast consumed by the relentless flames.

To attempt to have liberated him would have been impossible.

Another few minutes, and the prisoner's cries died out—his blistered head fell upon his breast.

He was dead.

Still higher and higher rose the body of flame, hissing and shrieking as if each vivid tongue struggled with the others to be the first to reach the now partly consumed body.

Hopkins was the first to find his tongue.

"Vengeance?" he yelled, "vengeance! The White Monk has had a hand in this! By heaven, we will hurl him into the flames."

"Ay," replied both Richard and Sir Ferdinand, as they turned with Hopkins, "we will at once hurl him into the flames."

They dashed to the spot where the White Monk, guarded by two of the men, had been placed.

This was beside a large tree, and only about twenty yards from where the body of men had been standing.

He had vanished!

No secret doors or trees had been used on this occasion.

Nay, he had been rescued in the most daring and open manner.

Both of his guards lay stretched upon the ground—and quite dead, their hands clutching the weapons they had been allowed no time to use.

The manner of their death was evident at a single glance.

No examination was necessary.

A dagger had been plunged into their hearts.

In the body of one the dagger remained.

Their comrades crowded round them, lost in astonishment that no cry for help had reached their ears.

"Again we are foiled!" said Richard. "It is evident that the whole place swarms with the accursed brotherhood."

"Take the dagger out, one of you," said Sir Ferdinand, in hollow tones, "and let me look at it. I fancy I recognise the handle."

Accordingly the dagger was drawn out and handed to the baronet.

"I thought so!" he said. "*This dagger belonged to the page, Stockholm!*"

CHAPTER XIX.

OF THE CAPTURE OF THE WITCHFINDER—OF THE DEATH OF RICHARD MELBURN —AND OF THE BREAKING UP OF THE WHOLE PARTY.

"ONLY too plain is it," said Richard, bitterly, "that this page has, for some time past, been in league with Rupert Redmond."

"It is, indeed, plain enough now," replied Sir Ferdinand, "everything and everyone are going dead against me."

"If I could but get hold of that page," hissed Hopkins, "I would make short work of him."

"What is now to be done?" said Richard.

"You shall see," replied Hopkins.

He wheeled his horse towards the men, and thus addressed them—

"What say you, my men—shall we return to the Abbey completely baffled and beaten, as we have been before, or shall we continue the search for this accursed Man of Mystery?"

There was no hesitation about the reply.

That reply was, "Let us continue the search."

The men were now enraged, not only at the way they had been baffled, but at the death of their two comrades.

Waving their arms on high, they shouted to Hopkins to lead them.

Scarcely had their cries ceased before a sound, as of a number of men shouting out some chorus, fell upon their ears.

Nearer and nearer it came, and Hopkins, standing in his stirrups, saw the glare of a number of links, and then made out that a large party of men were advancing towards them.

"Reinforcements have arrived!" cried Richard; "it is Kemble."

It *was* Kemble, and the majority of his men were mounted.

Hopkins ordered his followers to shout, so as to let Kemble know their position.

Their shouts were answered again and again, and in less than another quarter of an hour the whole force were together.

And a very formidable force it looked.

Sir Ferdinand, Richard, Hopkins, Kemble, and Hawkswell now withdrew a certain distance so as to form their plans.

It was decided that the force should be divided into three.

Of one lot Hawkswell and Kemble were to have command.

Sir Ferdinand and Richard were to have command of another lot; while Hopkins was to have complete control of the third and largest party.

The witchfinder swore that he would not proceed unless it was thus arranged.

The next thing, and the most difficult to de decided was—*how* were they to proceed?

Hardly one of the men among that large number knew anything of the forest.

It was arranged that one party should proceed in a westerly, another in an easterly, and the third in a southerly direction, and that they should signal each other by means of hunting-horns with which each leader was provided.

"All these horns," said Sir Ferdinand, "are of the same tone, so that there cannot be the least mistake about them. Remember this: if a horn is blown three times, it is a signal that aid is required. The answering signal will be three blasts, and then the one giving the signal in the first place, will continue to blow, so as to lead the on-coming party."

This was considered a very satisfactory arrangement, and in a short time the three parties moved off.

Their orders were to take no prisoners (except Rupert Redmond, Reuben, and other principals), but to slay right and left.

They had no sooner taken their departure than a little black figure scrambled down from the branches of the tree against which they had been standing.

It was Fendyke.

He had overheard all, but he had paid particular attention to the arrangement as to the horns.

Approaching the fatal column, around which the embers were still smouldering, he looked for a few moments at a mass of calcined, shapeless bones chained to it—the remains of Ebenezer—then turning towards the north he sped away like the wind.

His running powers were absolutely marvellous.

*   *   *   *

We are approaching another terrible episode in this romance; and we shall now return to the secret haunts of the Man of Mystery.

Those secret haunts were marvellous instances of the freaks of nature, and of the ingenuity and remarkable patience of man.

Centuries before our romance opens, and when Pendle Forest was scarcely touched by the foot of man—when, in fact, it abounded with wild beasts—there occurred a great earthquake.

That earthquake had been recorded and retained in the local histories, and there was also a tablet in Whalley Church containing a record of it.

There was also a wild legend connected with it, and that legend was to the effect that on a certain night, in the midst of a most terrible storm, Satan had visited the forest.

That, immediately his unholy feet had touched the ground, the earth was thrown into a series of terrible convulsions, which did not terminate until the whole aspect of the forest had been changed.

Mighty chasms had been formed, rocks weighing tons had been torn from the positions they had occupied for centuries, and had been hurled into those black chasms.

However wild the legend, a vast portion of the forest which had been level and solid ground, was suddenly transformed into caves.

Then after the earthquake came a mighty wind—a wind which swept everything before it, a wild wind, which up rooted enormous trees.

The trees, the rocks and the earth formed a sort of roof, or a series of roofs, over the chasms already made, and Father Time finished these wonders, and cemented the whole together by his slow but sure hand.

The forest became crammed with trees and wild brushwood again, and the strangely-formed caves were forgotten until they were taken possession of by Bowolf.

This mysterious man, and the equally mysterious individuals who from time to time joined him, made improvements in the bowels of the earth.

They burrowed and burrowed, and opened up communication with chasm after chasm, until the long, subterranean passages, which from time to time we have introduced, were formed.

One of the naturally-formed chambers which was yards below the earth's surface, had been used, and was still used, by the Man of Mystery as a lion's den.

It was a mighty chamber, the flooring, roof and sides being of solid rock, jagged and uneven everywhere.

The animals placed within that chamber could not have been equalled for savageness.

There were twenty male and female animals, fully grown and of enormous strength.

And now to return to our hero.

Brasblade had not yet been able to rise.

None of his men, nor indeed, any of the members of the Mystic Brotherhood, had left the place.

It had not been necessary, for Rupert, Reuben and Fendyke had done all that there was to be done, and as we have seen, they had brought the plans formed between them, to a successful termination.

Once again then, we are within the chamber in which lies Brasblade.

The Man of Mystery was there, as also were Rupert and Reuben, and also the White Monk and Stockholm, who had discarded his feminine attire.

Suddenly their conversation was interrupted by the entrance of Fendyke.

As we know, he had been a witness to all that had taken place on the hill, and had also overheard the arrangements of the leaders.

Rapidly he told all.

"And now," said Rupert, "it is evident that they will leave no stone unturned to discover this retreat. As regards their numbers, they must be double ours."

"That is a matter of no importance," replied Morna, in his low, deep tones; "for this reason, that they are divided into three parties. And now. By means of their own arrangements shall they fall into the trap we will set for them."

So saying he left the chamber.

"A WILD YELL OF EXECRATION GREETED HOPKINS' APPEARANCE."

He returned in a few moments, carrying in his hand several hunting horns.

"Look at these," he said. "They are not only like those carried by these leaders, but they are of the same tone."

"Ay, ay!" chuckled Fendyke, "that is indeed true."

"There is no necessity to ask what is passing in your mind," said Rupert. "I can guess it."

"Ay, ay," cried Reuben, excitedly; "and so, indeed, can I."

"Let us then at once hasten," said Morna, in tones which showed that he, too, was somewhat excited. "Let all the men be called to arms. Rupert Redmond, *for the last time*, I ask you to take the lead."

"You say the *last* time!" replied Rupert. "What makes you say so?"

"Because I believe that failure now will totally discourage Sir Ferdinand. And something tells me that if we all proceed with caution, and yet with the utmost determination, this murderous witchfinder will himself fall into our hands. Caution your men, Rupert. Be careful of that. Caution them not to slay the man if they happen to capture him. In the same way as he has put to death many human beings—with whom, however, as I have frequently told you, I never had any sympathy—he shall die!"

"By fire?"

"Ay; by fire!"

"May I be able to be present if that comes to pass!" exclaimed Brasblade.

"But, Rupert Redmond," continued Morna, his fine eyes now blazing furiously, "if you should come face to face with Richard Melburn, spare him not. Give him a chance to fight for his life, if you will; but show him not one spark of mercy!"

"Nay, nay," replied Rupert; "let me but come face to face with him. Mercy? I show him mercy? Never!"

"Bravo!" chuckled Brasblade, as he gleefully rubbed his hands. "Bravo! You are, indeed, after my own heart!"

And now were preparations at once made, the first thing Rupert did being to secure one of the horns at his belt—the belt in which glittered the two magnificent pistols—and from which hung that mysterious sword.

The latter he drew from its sheath, and affectionately gazed upon its glittering blade.

Then his glance fell upon the hilt, and upon the mystic words—words which had already been deciphered for him by the Man of Mystery.

The words were—

"*I trust in thy power.*"

The beautiful handle was hollow, and was filled with a marvellous liquid, the effect of which was that when shaken it operated upon the steel of the blade and caused currents—like electricity—to pass along it.

The pistols also possessed wondrous powers, though they were of a different character to those of the sword.

Within five minutes after being called to arms, the men were ready.

Never had Brasblade's followers been so eager to fight as they now were.

Already they had learned to respect Rupert—ay, and to fear him as being in the possession of supernatural powers.

They felt that whithersoever he or Reuben led them, they must follow.

The same sort of respect and admiration had they for the members of the Secret Brotherhood—not one of whose faces they had yet beheld.

To return to Hopkins.

This wretch, though he shuddered at the fearful manner of his death, did not in any way regret Ebenezer's decease.

No; it was not Ebenezer's death which affected him, it was the fact that at every turn he was being foiled.

Certain was he that the men did not look up to him as they had been wont to do.

But now he resolved to do something which would again raise him to the highest pinnacle of popularity.

But he knew that he would have to trust to chance.

However, he led his men to the spot, which, again and again, had been pointed out to him as being the home of the Man of Mystery.

Everywhere darkness reigned.

Suddenly one of the men, who, on foot, had gone on a little distance in advance, hastily approached Hopkins, and laid his hand on his horse's bridle.

Hopkins asked the man what he had discovered.

"A large rock," replied the man, in excited tones. "It blocks the way to the left. Being curious, I clambered up, and looked over. I saw a clear path of great length, and sloping. I am certain that it is a secret path."

"Hish!" whispered Hopkins. "Pass the word for complete silence. Dismount!"

He made as close an examination as was possible, and came to the conclusion that the stone could be removed.

So the men set to work.

But twenty or thirty were necessary before the stone would move.

At last a space was made sufficient to allow a horse and man to pass singly.

The last man of the party had scarcely got through, when the sound, as of the clashing of swords, and the ringing of shots, fell upon their ears.

And then was heard the call of a horn.

Three times it sounded; was replied to by Hopkins, and the horn continued to sound as had been arranged, while, at the same time, the clashing of swords, and the ringing of shots, continued.

"At last!" yelled Hopkins; "at last! Forward, my men, and mind—no mercy. Cut down all who stand before you!"

On, down the slope with a mighty rush went the men, Hopkins bringing up the rear.

The farther the men went the more sloping became the hill, until at last they went down with such tremendous velocity that there was not the slightest chance of stopping their animals.

To say the least, Hopkins must have been mad to allow the men to go forward with such a rush down an unknown hill.

Suddenly what appeared to be a stone wall loomed before them.

It seemed as if they would here come together with a mighty crash.

But suddenly a flood of light burst upon the scene, and it was instantly followed by screams, which left the lips of Hopkins's doomed men, for doomed they were, unless mercy was extended to them.

Away they went, as if swept by a giant *into the lion's den*.

The wall closed suddenly.

Hopkins turned with a fearful scream, but he was not allowed to escape.

Strong hands seized the bridle of his horse, and he was dragged from the saddle, yelling for mercy.

In the meantime, the lions, maddened by this sudden interruption to their rough gambols, sprang upon the men.

Some of the latter, managing to extricate themselves from their saddles, drew their pistols and swords, and prepared to defend themselves.

In the midst of this most terrible scene the wall again rolled aside, and a loud, commanding voice rang out.

Instantly the lions slunk back, yet growling savagely.

The men looked up and saw a tall black figure.

It was the Man of Mystery.

"Throw down your arms and come forth," he said.

At once the men hurled their weapons to the ground, and frantically rushed forward, imploring for their wretched lives.

The Man of Mystery aided man and horse out of the den.

Six men had lost their lives.

Their bodies were taken out by the Man of Mystery himself.

He walked calmly among the lions, who, as he advanced, retreated.

Their whole attitude showed how terribly afraid of this man they were.

As the men left the den they were taken charge of by those in waiting for them, under the command of Rupert and Reuben, and were conveyed to a large chamber.

There they were left in doubt as to the fate in store for them.

Hopkins was conveyed to a small circular stone apartment, ironed, and left to meditate over his terrible crimes, and to wonder what was in store for him.

The door of his cell had no sooner closed than the vision conjured up by Mother Frampton rose before him.

Was that really to be his fate?

Rupert's men were again collected; and with Rupert and Reuben leading them they advanced up the hill.

There, in silence and darkness, they remained for some little time.

At last Rupert placed the horn to his lips, and blew it thrice.

It was at once answered, and presently sounds of a body of men rapidly advancing fell upon their ears.

Soon Sir Ferdinand and Richard, followed closely by their men, rushed forward.

At once Rupert's blade flashed from its scabbard.

Rising high in his stirrups, he shouted—

" Forward! forward! Hew them down! and show them as much mercy as they would show us! "

No shouts left the lips of the members of the Secret Brotherhood.

With whirlwind speed they rushed forward, and a murderous fight at once commenced.

Sir Ferdinand and Richard were quick to see that they had once again fallen into a trap, and both recognised Rupert's voice.

"Do you get to Sir Ferdinand, Reuben," said Rupert, "while I deal with Richard."

But Richard, despite all his boasting, made frantic efforts to escape, and he succeeded in getting as far as the centre of the men.

A fearful slaughter was in progress.

Rupert Redmond, standing upright in his stirrups, dealt death on all sides.

The startling flashes, like fire, which emanated from his sword, filled the men with terror.

Many turned to fly, only to find their retreat entirely cut off, for they were surrounded.

Richard at last managed to work his way through the crowd of struggling, fighting men, and, turning his horse, he plunged his spurs deep in its steaming haunches.

The terrified animal plunged madly forward, and carried its rider clear.

A cry of joy rose to Richard's lips, as bending forward to escape any chance shots, he forged ahead.

Away, away sped the frightened animal, its dilated nostrils and starting eyes giving unmistakable evidence of the terror which had seized upon it.

Richard knew not the paths along which the maddened animal was carrying him; neither did he care.

For at least five minutes the horse continued his mad career.

But at last Richard found himself in a somewhat broad path, the ground of which was hard.

It led to the high road to Blackburn.

That reached, he could soon make his way to the Abbey, or his own place, and thus he would evade all pursuit.

But just as he was congratulating himself, a thundering of horses' hoofs fell upon his ears.

He looked back, and through the gloom he made out the dark figures of a horse and rider galloping onward with marvellous speed.

"Pursued!" he gasped. "Pursued! I shall be lost! But I will not give up hope! No, no. My horse is a good one. Away! Away!" he cried, as once again he dug the cruel spurs into the poor animal's sides. "Away! Away!"

The pursuing steed soon, however, reached him, and a loud, commanding voice called out—

"Hold, Richard Melburn! Stop, coward, and defend yourself! I am alone! *Alone*, I say. Stop coward!"

"Rupert Redmond," gasped Richard, "I will not cross swords with you now."

Once more did he plunge his spurs into his steed, and once again did the noble animal respond to his urging.

But a few seconds more, a couple of shots rang out clear and distinct.

Richard's horse plunged, reared high into the air for an instant, and then fell dead.

Richard disengaged himself as the horse fell, at the very edge of the Mystic Hollow.

Scarcely had he got away from the animal ere Rupert came up.

At once dismounting he strode forward.

"At last, Richard Melburn," said Rupert, "at last we are face to face, man to man! I saw you, coward-like, edging your way to escape. The bloodhound Hopkins and all his men are safely trapped. I intend to give you a chance of your life. Richard Melburn, tyrant, you shall reckon with me on this spot."

"Will you *force* me to fight?" asked Richard, in low, hollow tones.

"Force you?" repeated Rupert, scornfully. "Surely the valiant Richard Melburn—the one who for years has boasted that the greatest dangers have no terrors for him—requires not to be *forced* to fight?"

Richard hesitated no longer.

A sudden thought had struck him—a

thought which filled his black soul with joy.

It was this. His horn hung at his side, and was it not likely that Hawkswell and Kemble were within hearing distance?

If he found the fight going against himself he could give the signal.

He never thought it was likely to be answered by the Secret Brotherhood, as it had been only but a short time before.

"Defend yourself!" cried Rupert, advancing upon him.

The swords met, and as the clash rang out it was echoed by a peal of wild, mocking laughter—it was a laugh which made Richard's blood run cold.

Rupert gave him no time to think who had uttered that laugh or whence it had proceeded.

In but a few seconds Richard saw he had no earthly chance.

In three places he was already wounded.

Finding that, at the hands of Rupert Redmond, he would get no mercy, Richard snatched the horn from his girdle, and blew upon it a piercing blast.

That signal, strange to say, was instantly answered, and it was evident that Hawkswell and Kemble, with their party, were close handy.

A cry of joy left Richard's lips, and he continued the fight with renewed energy.

But Rupert suddenly plunged forward, dashed the blade from Richard's hand, and then plunged his own through his breast.

With an appalling scream, Richard fell backwards.

At the same moment a tattered figure started up before Rupert.

It was Mother Frampton.

A terrible sight she presented.

Her hoary locks were covered with blood, as also was her face.

"Well done, Rupert Redmond!" she shrieked. "Well done! But haste thee away, for yonder comes another troop of men. See!" she yelled, snatching aside a portion of her tattered garments, "see! See the dagger plunged into me by one of these bloodhounds! But I care not! My time has come! But I warn thee, Rupert Redmond— away, for your life!"

"Help!" gasped Richard, frantically endeavouring to raise himself. "Save me! Save me!"

"He is not dead!" cried Mother Frampton. "And Hawkswell will take him hence—no, no! Die he shall!"

So saying, she seized Richard round the body, and raised him completely over her head.

Just as she did so, Hawkswell and Kemble, followed by their ruffians, dashed to the spot.

They heard Richard's cries and Hawkswell pushed forward.

But before he could reach her, Mother Frampton, giving utterance to one of her wild derisive bursts of laughter, sprang forward, and with Richard still in her arms, plunged headlong into the waters of the Mystic Hollow.

Instantly she and Richard vanished from sight.

Hawkswell was about to give orders for the men to dismount and search, when he caught sight of Rupert's horse.

Our hero had not yet remounted.

But as Hawkswell shouted to the men to seize the horse, he vaulted on to its back and turned it.

"Forward!" thundered Hawkswell and Kemble in a breath, "Forward! this is one of the cursed brotherhood!"

Both leaders sped after Rupert.

But not far.

They had not proceeded fifty yards before Rupert wheeled suddenly.

A brilliant flash lit up the surrounding semi-darkness, and Hawkswell rolled from his saddle, dead.

Kemble paused, and snatched a pistol from his holster.

But he never had time to pull the trigger.

Again a brilliant flash was seen, and Kemble started wildly up in his saddle, threw up his arms, and then fell with a crash to the ground.

The horses of both leaders had stopped, and thus the path was blocked.

But had it not been so, the men would not have followed.

Some of them dismounted and bent over Kemble.

He was not dead, but his shoulder was dislocated.

"Pick me up," he groaned; "pick me up, and try and put me in the saddle again. At once we will leave this accursed forest, and return to Manchester."

"But what of our comrades in various parts of the forest?" asked one of the men.

"Let them look to themselves," replied Kemble. " I tell you that we had better go. If we don't we shall all be dead men in quick time."

After some little difficulty he was again placed in the saddle.

"Is Hawkswell dead?" he asked.

"He is," was the reply. "He never uttered so much as a cry. He was shot fair in the heart."

"So much the better. I borrowed a fair sum of him, and now it will not have to be repaid. Has that hag come to the surface?" "No."

"Then depend upon it she has gone straight to Satan, her master."

"If so," observed another of the men, "Richard Melburn has gone with her, for I know it was his voice."

"Ay," replied Kemble, between his groans of pain, "I always thought Satan would suddenly lay violent hands on him. But let us no longer delay."

The whole party turned, and proceeded to search for the quickest way out of the forest.

As for Rupert, he was well on the road back to the home of the Man of Mystery.

CHAPTER XX.

OF THE STARTLING REVELATION—OF THE TERRIBLE DEATH OF THE WITCH-FINDER, AND OF THE JOURNEY TO LONDON.

IN that tremendous fight no less than twenty-five men were slain.

Reuben performed prodigies of valour.

But Sir Ferdinand had contrived to escape.

This was a great blow to Rupert, and so it was to the Man of Mystery.

Without the least delay the bodies of the fallen men, which included many of Brasblade's comrades, and three or four of the members of the Secret Brotherhood, were interred where they had died, arms and all being placed with them.

In the morning Rupert and Reuben were summoned to the chapel—that chapel we have already described.

There they found the Man of Mystery awaiting them, together with Brasblade and many others.

Matthew Hopkins, on whom sentence of a terrible death had already been passed, was imprisoned within a chamber from which it was impossible he could escape, and was at this moment like a raving maniac.

No daylight ever penetrated that strange place of worship.

When it was used, tapers were burned.

"Rupert," said the Man of Mystery, in grave and solemn tones, "you and everyone here are in a strange sanctuary, wherein lie many great men who toiled in the interests of

SCIENCE!

And when the grim hand of death stopped their labours, and stilled their noble hearts forever, they were laid here. Yonder is the grave of one of the greatest men who ever lived—Otto Trevalian—for many generations known as Bowolf, and called ' one of the chiefs of the Prince of Darkness.' I succeeded that great man—I, Rupert Redmond—I, *your own father!*"

So saying, he threw the cowl from off his face.

With the last words, too, he resumed his natural voice—that beloved voice—and Rupert instantly recognised it.

A passionate cry of wonder and joy left the lips of our brave young hero as he was thus made aware of this startling fact.

Randall Redmond, for we will now, once again, call him by his rightful name, stretched forth his arms, and Rupert was folded in them.

The loving greeting over, Rupert was about to ask his father a score of questions without a pause.

It was only natural, but Randall anticipated him.

"I am here for the purpose of telling you *all*," he said. "And all here will hear me. I need not commence with our marvellous escape from the Abbey. It will be sufficient for me to say that that escape was effected in so complete a manner, owing to the fact that Bowolf was familiar with many secret places Sir Ferdinand Lockhart knew absolutely nothing of, and he also wielded a power which is marvellous even to think of.

"He suddenly appeared before me, and offered me and you, my son, our liberty when we were near torture and death, on certain conditions. He produced a book, and in that book I had to sign my name with my own blood. Still, so great was my suspicions of this man, that had it not have been for you, Rupert, I should not have signed.

"By marvellous means Bowolf got to know when he was to die. No doubt it was by dreams, and by the experiments he was continually performing. Certain it is that he died as he had said. When I took his place I first of all examined the vast number of books I found. I need not tell you what the contents of those books were, but this I will at once say. Bowolf was *no* servant of the Prince of Darkness, but the conductor of vast experiments, in which he was assisted by those called the Secret Brotherhood, many of whom you see around you. His principal task was the discovery of an 'Elixir of Life.'

"This study he had pursued, but with only slight success. He did not experiment upon human beings, but *on lions*, as, being about the most powerful of beasts, they were more calculated to resist the action of the various compounds he used. Many would have abandoned what looked like a fruitless search ; but Bowolf was heart and soul in it, and, besides, he was a man of vast wealth, for in his explorations of this forest he had discovered enormous treasures.

"Some few days after his death I examined the book in which I had placed my signature. I then saw, to my great joy, that if the experiments I was continuing should come to nothing *within a certain time*, I could, if I thought proper, abandon them."

A murmur in the affirmative ran round the chapel—a murmur proceeding from the lips of the members of the Secret Brotherhood.

Randall continued—

"We have resolved to leave Pendle Forest. I have said that Bowolf was a man of vast wealth. We have found the whole of it, and I decided to divide it equally among the men, who, for so long, had been Bowolf's assistants. Before I set out," and here Randall's voice was firm, "it is my intention to raze the Abbey to the ground. Before it I will burn the witchfinder, Matthew Hopkins. The scoundrel will meet a well-deserved end.

"Here lie the remains of Walter Dubois, Miriam's unfortunate father, murdered by Sir Ferdinand Lockhart. Miriam shall at once take possession of her estates. And now, my friends," he added, to the Secret Brethren, who still stood without removing the coverings from their faces, "the time has come to bid you farewell ?"

"Will not their services be required for the execution of Matthew Hopkins ?" asked Rupert.

"Nay; Captain Brasblade's men will be sufficient. No doubt he will let them remain and carry out whatever I may require, as well as be an escort to London. Captain Brasblade will be well repaid."

"Remain ?" replied Brasblade. "They will be only too happy to carry out any orders you may favour them with. As to the payment— well, I can't very well refuse what you might think proper to give me for the purpose of division, because we are all but poor men."

The leave-taking now commenced, the Secret Brethren passing along the aisle one by one, and shaking hands with all.

"Remember that you will meet me at the 'Bell Sauvage,'" said Randall, "in fourteen days' time, when the money will be divided."

Another five minutes, and the last had gone.

"I should have liked to have seen their faces," said Rupert.

"They are very ordinary mortals," replied Randall; "that is, so far as appearance is concerned. They are scientific enthusiasts, and are learned, and, like their associates in London, possessed of many marvellous powers. Their agreement was that they were never to show their faces to any but those associated with them, and most zealously have they carried out that undertaking. And now, Rupert, let us arrange for our departure. In the meantime, the wealth, books and papers must be collected ready for immediate removal."

"I trust, my dear father," said Rupert, "that you will leave all arrangements of these matters entirely in the hands of Captain Brasblade, Reuben, and myself."

The whole party now followed Randall from the chapel.

They passed through a narrow door, traversed a passage, descended a flight of steps, and then ascended a slope.

Suddenly Reuben cried—

"Look! A number of mounted men are ascending a hill directly in front of us."

"Describe them," said Randall.

Reuben did so as well as he was able.

"Be not alarmed," smiled Randall; "you are, at least, satisfied, for you have seen the faces of the Secret Brotherhood. They have now discarded the attire they have been accustomed to wear for so many years, and are now, to all appearance, ordinary travellers. But come, let us no longer delay."

The lions' den was quickly reached. A link was lit, and Randall, by pressing a spring, soon had the wall open.

No sooner was the glare of the link observed by the lions, than with loud, savage growls—growls which awoke the echoes of the mysterious places surrounding them—stood as if expecting another such surprise as that so recently given them, the remains of which enormous feast still lay all over the den.

But as soon as Randall stood before them their growls subsided into low mutterings, and they slunk as far back as they could.

Rupert stood at the threshold, and held the link on high.

Randall now took a phial from his breast, and advancing to the first lion, a really superb beast, he uttered a few words in a low tone.

The effect was instantaneous and curious.

The lion fell upon his haunches and opened wide his ponderous jaws.

Randall raised the phial, and dropped into its mouth a small portion of the liquid contained in the phial.

All the others in rapid succession he served in the same way.

In less than five minutes the effects of the compound given the lions was seen.

One by one they stretched themselves on the floor of the den as if in sleep.

Presently Randall spoke.

"All are dead," he said; "they died without the least pain. And now we will leave this place. Rely upon it that the foot of man will not again traverse these passages and chambers."

Randall, resuming his disguise, took his way to the dungeon occupied by Matthew Hopkins.

Matthew Hopkins now presented the appearance of a maniac.

For hours no human footfall had caught his ears. Silence the most profound had reigned, a fact which alone was sufficient to drive him mad.

He was beginning to fancy that he would be left where he was to starve to death.

Presently a portion of the wall rolled inwards, and at the same time a brilliant white light flooded the chamber, and the dark, grim-looking figure of the Man of Mystery stood before the wretched witchfinder.

"Villain," said Randall, "a few hours' incarceration has completely changed you. No longer are you the loud-mouthed, pompous ruffian! You are now the cringer, but let me assure you how vain it would be to sue for mercy! Not one spark of mercy will I show you. Remember, Matthew Hopkins, what mercy you showed to others—those unfortunate wretches who chanced to fall into your clutches.

"I am acquainted with all the particulars of the terrible murder of Amos Arlington. What punishment ever devised by mortal man would be great enough for you? Loathsome murderer! —hypocrite and impostor!—the punishment selected for you is the same as that which befell your factotum, Ebenezer Watson—and that is the flames!"

Hopkins gave utterance to a terrible yell, raised his hands in supplication, and fell upon his knees.

"Oh!" he gasped, "do not subject me to such a death! Think of the fearful agony I should endure!"

"Think of the agony endured by the scores of those who have been your victims!" thundered Randall.

"What injury have I ever done you?" groaned Hopkins.

"What injury have you ever done

my——. But no matter for that. The sentence has been passed on you, Matthew Hopkins, and in a few hours it will be carried into effect. So make good use of the short time left you!"

"Grant me but a week to prepare myself for this awful death."

"Not *half* a week! Not——"

"Grant me but one day—a single day!" screamed Hopkins.

"Nay; not even a day! You have a few hours left. That is more than you ever granted to one of your victims."

"The king will avenge my death! Yes, yes; he will indeed cause a——"

Again Randall interrupted him.

"Do not deceive yourself!" he said. "In my possession is your infamous Black Book, and that, according to my thinking, contains more than even *you* are aware of. There is a tremendous mass of truth in it—facts written by Ebenezer Watson, whose handwriting will be sworn to by those well acquainted with it. And most prominent of all is an account of the death of Morecombe —a man who unquestionably had sold his soul to Satan! He was a villain, and his death at the hands of a villain greater than himself was deserved! And now prepare to meet your doom, Matthew Hopkins."

Again did a wild scream leave Hopkins's lips—again did he frantically appeal for mercy.

But this time he was unheard, for the light and the Man of Mystery had vanished.

*   *   *   *

Fendyke had suddenly become a changed man.

The death of his hideous mother had affected him to an astonishing degree, and he now moved about slowly, like a person in a dream.

The only thing he could console himself about was the fact that his mother's murderers had themselves been slain.

He had searched for and discovered the body of Mother Frampton, and after great difficulty he succeeded in recovering it.

And in recovering her body, he had also recovered Richard's, for the old woman held him so firmly clasped, that he had to use all his strength to pull Richard's body away.

His mother he buried deep in the earth beside the hollow, while Richard's body he again dropped into the dark water.

His mind was made up as to what he would do, and that was to quit the country, for which purpose Randall had promised him a goodly sum, on condition that he aided him in Hopkins's execution.

But he required no reward for *this*.

Only too glad was he to render aid in such a matter.

He procured an ordinary costume, and repaired to the village inn.

Fendyke made known his business to the host, who, while he watched his movements with suspicion, was yet compelled to listen to what he said, and that was the particulars of what was to happen at midnight before the Abbey.

This report the host gave to some of his customers, and it spread through the village.

At first it was not credited, although, of course, the people knew who had got the worst of the many encounters in the forest.

But when evening came on they saw the first signs that something was to happen.

In the first place a number of prisoners, escorted by masked and mounted men, passed through the village and were conducted some miles distant.

Those were the prisoners captured by the Man of Mystery and Rupert.

An hour or two after this, news to the effect that something was occurring at the Abbey was circulated, and the result was that an enormous crowd collected and watched a number of men at work.

These men were erecting the ponderous trunk of a tree—placing it deeply and firmly in the ground, while others were bringing forward tar-barrels and bundles of faggots.

As darkness came on, these ominous proceedings were illuminated by flaming links which were brought by the villagers.

Comparative silence had existed among them for a long time, but presently low mutterings were heard.

These increased, until at last loud cries of vengeance on the man who had made so many happy homes desolate were raised, and the greatest impatience to behold the doomed witchfinder was manifested.

But through all this Captain Brasblade and his men—all of them masked—continued their preparations calmly.

"Now for the prisoner!"

Rupert and Randall entered Hopkins's chamber, which now fairly rang with the prisoner's wild screams of terror.

The chain was not removed from his waist. That was required elsewhere.

The villain was blindfolded, and partly led, and partly carried out of the chamber.

Then Randall took Rupert's hand, and, holding a link aloft, led him along many passages.

Presently a small circular chamber was reached, and here Randall paused.

Placing his foot on a secret spring, he pointed above.

Rupert looked, and beheld a portion of the jagged roof slowly ascend until the star-studded sky was visible.

"Hold the link, Rupert," said Randall, "while I place this ladder in position."

So saying, he approached the wall and took up a long wooden ladder of frail construction.

This he placed so that both could ascend and leave by the aperture in the roof.

The entrance to the circular chamber having been "sealed," Rupert ascended, and then Randall reached from the wall a chain of great length.

One end of this he held, and ascended the ladder.

Rupert was watching these curious proceedings attentively.

Randall smiled, as he said—

"Your curiosity will now be gratified, Rupert. Behold!"

Randall pulled the chain—once, twice, thrice. At the third pull a low, ominous thundering was heard.

This was followed by a noise as of the falling of a number of huge stones.

Another tug, and then was heard a low, strange hissing, which appeared to proceed from a great distance.

But it advanced with wondrous rapidity until, in a few seconds, it resembled the roar of a mighty waterfall.

Another tug, and one half the chamber with a tremendous roar fell inwards—smashed to atoms before a mighty torrent of water, which rushed through with awful velocity.

In a few seconds the water had risen nearly on a level with the roof.

Then it suddenly stopped.

"It has reached its own level," said Randall. "And now let us close this—the last aperture. This, as you see, is also of rock. I shall close it, and cover it with earth, and sow these seeds."

As he spoke he took a small packet from his pocket and handed it to Rupert.

"Those seeds," continued Randall, "are of the weeds and grasses of the forest. Quickly they will grow, and shut out this piece of rock from mortal eyes—perhaps for ever."

Reaching the Abbey, they found a waggon containing the treasures of the cave zealously guarded by Reuben and three or four armed men.

But the spectacle in front of the Abbey!

Never did Rupert or Reuben forget the scene spread out before them.

It was a somewhat dark night.

But many links were burning.

As far as the eye could reach, nothing but eager human faces were to be seen.

When Rupert reached the spot, the prisoner had not arrived.

"Rupert," said Randall, "everything without I leave in your and Reuben's charge. Brasblade and I are going into the Abbey. Now, Brasblade," he added, in low tones, "did you do as I said?"

"Search the Abbey? Ay, that I did; but, of course, there was no trace of the villainous baronet."

"There can be no doubt as to where he is," said Randall; "he is in London."

"It so," said Reuben, who, at this moment, joined the group, "we shall know of his movements as soon as we arrive, for, by Rupert's directions, I despatched Stockholm to the residence of the Duke of Buckingham. No doubt his grace will make all necessary inquiries at Chelsea."

"Yes, no doubt; but what has become of the White Monk?"

"Despite the advice given him, he persisted in returning to his caves."

"Well, well. No doubt what few years remain to him will be passed in peace. At any rate, Sir Ferdinand Lockhart will never disturb him. And now, Brasblade, follow me."

" ᵃ blade accordingly followed, and

startled, indeed, was he at the way Randall led him from room to room, down one staircase after another, and finally into the vaults.

"I think I can tell where you are going," said Brasblade, "and that is, to the armoury."

"You are right. Unless I am mistaken, we shall there find that which I seek—namely, gunpowder."

"Ay; that you will. I saw several kegs there."

The armoury was reached; but it was found that nearly all the arms with which it had been stocked had been taken away, no doubt to supply the numerous reinforcements which had been brought up.

But there were several kegs full of powder.

"Let us not delay," said Randall. "We will convey the powder to the study."

Brasblade and Randall proceeded to carry the kegs away.

All were placed in the study.

The head of one of the kegs was then smashed in, and the contents were scattered over furniture and paper.

Then, beside the door, in an upright position, the link was placed.

When that burned to the end, the paper would ignite, and the powder destroy the place.

Then they quitted the building and reached the front of the Abbey just as Hopkins was brought up.

A wild yell of execration greeted his appearance.

In a few seconds he was fastened to the fatal tree.

Force had to be used to get him against it, and his screams were fearful; but they were drowned in the wild cries which came from the enraged populace.

Suddenly, and just as Hopkins was securely chained, a stir in the crowd was observed, and a horseman rode up to the spot.

He was at once recognised as Hall, the magistrate who had issued so many writs at the instigation of Sir Ferdinand Lockhart.

Hopkins recognised him, and hopes were at once kindled within his breast.

But they were doomed to be quickly dispelled.

With extraordinary assurance and pomposity, the magistrate came forward, and addressed himself to Rupert.

"Sir," he said, "what is this I see?"

"*Sir*," answered Rupert, "you are able to see what it is, and what it means without the aid of anyone."

"This insolence will not deter me from inquiring into the matter," replied Hall, turning very red. "I am a magistrate, and, as such, I, in the king's name, forbid these proceedings to go on."

These words were received with a most derisive roar from the excited populace.

Fendyke had got among the crowd, and, watching his opportunity, he yelled—

"Pull him down! Tear the hypocrite to pieces!"

This was all that was wanted—someone to start such a cry.

The effect was instantaneous.

A hundred men dashed forward.

Some of them seized the animal, while others pulled the magistrate off his horse.

He was kicked, and otherwise so illtreated, that Rupert had to interfere.

As it was, he was hustled from one to the other, until he had run the gauntlet of the whole multitude.

Again did the wild cries of Matthew Hopkins fill the air.

And again was he mocked and jeered at.

Suddenly a loud voice cried—

"Midnight!"

At once the silence of the grave fell upon all.

The sweet sound of a distant church clock stole softly and solemnly over the hills, and, with the last stroke, the fatal command was given, and a flaming link thrust into the faggots.

To describe the condition of the murderer, Hopkins, would be impossible.

As the smoke arose, and shut out from his gaze the flaming links and the sea of faces, he was, for an instant silent.

But when bright tongues of flame shot through the clouds of smoke, and spread a lurid glow over the whole terrible scene, a wild, unearthly scream left his lips, and frantically did he struggle to tear himself from the tree to which he was chained.

Then his supplications for mercy gave way to curses of an appalling nature.

High rose the flames—higher and higher.

The tar barrels burned with extraordinary fury.

At last the shrieks died out, and Hopkins's head was seen to drop upon his breast.

His end had come.

The flames began to die down, but suddenly amid the silence was heard a loud noise, as of the firing of a number of huge cannon.

Then again arose a loud shout, and hands were pointed to the Abbey, from the windows, doors, and roof of which enormous tongues of flame were shooting with resistless fury.

"Rupert," whispered Randall, "now let us take our departure."

"Ay; I will at once give orders," replied Rupert.

Brasblade gathered his men together, and the whole party proceeded to leave the dreadful scene.

CHAPTER XXI.

OF THE ARRIVAL IN LONDON—OF WHAT OCCURRED AT THE DUKE'S RESIDENCE AND AT CHELSEA PRIORY.

THE sending of the lad, Stockholm, to London had been a very wise step, because it prepared Miriam, Margaret, and the duke for the reception of our friends.

London was reached on the night of the third day after the last tragic act had been performed at Whalley.

The journey was, of course, very slow, owing to the fact that the roads were in such a terrible state of unevenness, that the horses attached to the cumbersome waggon had the greatest difficulty in getting their load along.

But the city was reached without a mishap of any kind, and after a brief pause for necessary refreshment, and for complete changes of costume, so far as Randall, Rupert, and Reuben were concerned, the journey to the duke's house was continued, and the mansion was reached just after the hour of ten had struck.

The Duke of Buckingham had prepared a great surprise for them, and the first thing they noticed was that his magnificent residence was brilliantly illuminated.

The second thing they observed was that the front was lined with coaches and footmen, and that the interior of the mansion was filled by guests, whose costumes showed them to be persons of distinction.

No sooner were the party observed than the news was spread, and crowds of guests thronged to the doors, the windows, and the balconies, all eager to get a glimpse of the Man of Mystery and the participators in the great events which had recently transpired in the mysterious forest.

Plenty of reports had been freely circulated, but Stockholm had been the furnisher of the authentic information, and he had set forth the terrible deeds of Matthew Hopkins, Sir Ferdinand, and Richard, and the bravery and daring of Rupert and Reuben in glowing colours.

Of course, the duke required not to be told of Rupert's bravery, nor of the bravery of his "distant" relative, Reuben.

The crowd in the great hall opened in the centre, and the Duke of Buckingham was seen coming forward, Miriam leaning on his arm.

Her face was very pale; but it was suffused with smiles.

No sooner did Rupert behold her, than he broke from the party, and, in an instant, the lovers were clasped to each other's hearts.

In the meantime, the young duke had fixed his eyes upon Randall's powerful and commanding figure, and he advanced to him.

"Am I right," he asked, "in fancying that you are he who, for so long, has been known as the Man of Mystery?"

"You are, indeed, correct," replied Randall. "And am I right in supposing that you are the Duke of Buckingham?"

"I am."

"Then, your grace, let me at once return you my thanks for the kind way in which you have treated Rupert Redmond, and for the protection you have afforded his betrothed ; and also let me thank you in advance for a few favours I wish to ask you."

"Anything in reason I will grant," replied the duke, warmly.

"Your grace," said Rupert, "how is it possible that I can thank you for all you have done ?"

"My dear young friend," replied the duke, taking Rupert's hand, and warmly pressing it, "you forget what I owe *you !* and I have paved the way for an interview with the king."

"I sincerely thank you, your grace," returned Rupert ; "but I would wish to give way in favour of my father."

"Where, then, is your father ?"

"Here, your grace," replied Rupert, pointing to Randall.

"This—the Man of Mystery—your father ?" cried the duke.

"Yes, indeed it is !" cried Miriam. "I now recognise him."

The party now proceeded up the hall, but Randall contrived to get the duke's ear privately, and he informed him of the waggon, and of Brasblade and his men.

The duke at once offered to place a stable at Randall's disposal.

"There," he said, "you may deposit your treasure with perfect safety."

"I gratefully accept your offer, most noble duke," replied Randall.

After a few moments, he asked—

"Is the king aware of Hopkins's death ?"

"Assuredly he is. The page prepared us for the reception of the news, and that news was brought us by a most unfortunate young man, whose vengeance on the witchfinder you anticipated."

"Indeed ! May I ask his name ?"

"It was young Arlington, the son of the painter whom Hopkins murdered. The news was given him by three or four who had been present, and he brought it to Court."

"Ha ! And what did his majesty say ?"

"His majesty was thunderstricken at first ; but as soon as he was made acquainted with the murder of Amos Arlington, with whom he was on very good terms, for Arlington had painted him an excellent portrait, he vowed that the punishment Hopkins had received was well deserved."

"Then I have nothing to fear. I hesitate no longer. Moreover, I will produce Hopkins's Black Book, at the contents of which the king will be astounded."

The duke no sooner received this assurance, than he retired to his study and wrote, and despatched a letter to the king.

While he was engaged in this, Randall and Brasblade paid attention to the stowing away of the waggon and the comfort of the men.

Within an hour after this King James arrived very quietly, and was conducted by the duke to the principal banqueting room, in which a splendid chair of State had been placed.

He received Randall, who was presented, as were Rupert, Reuben, and Miriam, by the duke, with considerable warmth ; but a very close observer might also have noticed that there was some show of fear with it, and then he begged Randall to proceed.

The Man of Mystery, amid a silence which was profound to a degree, related all that had occurred from the time Sir Ferdinand Lockhart ousted him from his old home.

"Respecting a great many of these marvellous mysteries," said the king, "we shall get you to relate them again at a more convenient opportunity. But now let us add—that Matthew Hopkins has met with his deserts ; for we never heard tell of such a monster in aw our lives, eh, Steenie ?"

"I always told you he was a rank impostor and a monstrous hypocrite !" returned the Duke of Buckingham.

"Ay, so you did. But then it is so weel known, Steenie, that you are awways so headstrang. And so Sir Ferdinand Lockhart has not been captured. Aweel, that's unfortunate ; but how do you know that he is not at Chelsea Priory ? Is not Mistress Melburn there ?"

"No ; nor has she been for some time. The Priory has been entirely deserted, and closed up."

"And you say, Master Randall Redmond," said the king, "that this property, as well as a great deal more, belongs to Miriam — this weel-favoured young lady standing before me."

"That is so, sire."

"Then let her take possession."

"The deeds are within the Priory, your majesty," said Rupert.

"If that is so, they had better at once be found. Sir Ferdinand Lockhart will never again show his face there. And so he was the murderer of this poor laddy's father? Ah, that I had known aw' this before! But if he has not left the country, we shall have him yet, and he shall pay dearly for his crimes!"

"I shall use my best endeavours to get hold of the villain," said the duke.

"My lords," said the king, turning to the noblemen, who surrounded him, "we hope you will do your utmost to capture this man. It is but in the interest of justice that he should be placed upon his trial."

After the king had taken his departure, the duke suggested that the Priory should be entered and searched.

To this course Rupert assented, and so Randall, Rupert, Reuben, Brasblade, and the duke set out.

The Priory, though closed, was not fastened.

Almost every apartment showed unmistakable signs of a hasty exit.

After considerable difficulty, the room known as the " Treasury " was discovered.

It was found almost full of deed boxes, lettered and figured, and well arranged.

On the little square table in the centre was a leathern case.

Beside it stood pens and ink, and these appeared to have been recently used.

Rupert took up the case, and there, just beneath it, lay a letter.

It was addressed to " Miriam," and was in a lady's handwriting.

As it was not sealed he opened it, and read aloud the contents.

It was to this effect—

"I am acquainted with all that has occurred, including the death of my son. His death affects me but little, for his conduct caused me to withdraw from him what love I had. As I write this, Sir Ferdinand Lockhart sits beside me——"

"Ha!" interrupted the duke, "then he *has* been here! Would that I had known it!"

Rupert continued—

"He is sadly altered—in fact, he has suddenly become an old man; but when I learned from him what his greatest fear was—when I learned that it was his hand which had stricken down your father, and that he was afraid that this mysterious Man of Mystery would proclaim his guilt to the world, my pity turned to loathing; but I could not fly from him. This you will presently understand, Miriam. But though I shall be his wife, I can never give him the love that I could have once bestowed upon him. My eyes have been opened too late!

"Sir Ferdinand Lockhart has also confessed to me that he has squandered much of your great wealth. But he could not dispose of your property in houses and lands, the deeds of which you will find in this room. Within another hour we start for the Continent. It is my intention never to return to this country while Sir Ferdinand lives.

"Wishing you every happiness, my child,

"Your unfortunate acquaintance,
        "CATHERINE MELBURN."

"That letter clears up a great deal," said Randall.

"It does," replied the duke; "but nevertheless, an active search shall be made. They may not yet have been able to leave the country.

After securing the door of the room, the party returned and Miriam was handed the letter.

* * * *

After darkness comes the dawn.

Preparations for the wedding of Rupert and Miriam were hastily made.

Chelsea Priory, in the hands of a multitude of workmen, quickly underwent a complete transformation.

The Duke of Buckingham persisted in undertaking the inviting of guests, and the result was that on the wedding day a very large number of persons of distinction attended the ceremony, which took place at the pretty Chelsea Church, and subsequently were present at the wedding breakfast.

Reuben was the best man.

And however strange it may seem, on

that very wedding-day Reuben and Margaret were particularly struck with each other.

The result was that a month after Rupert's wedding, Reuben led Margaret to the altar.

Randall resided with his son, and in that fine old house, Chelsea Priory, he continued to labour with his experiments.

He became eminent in the scientific world, and was the discoverer of many important drugs.

Captain Brasblade received a large sum of money, and, by the influence of the duke, a commission in the army.

Fendyke never claimed his money, and out of forty of the Secret Brotherhood living at Pendle Forest and in London, only five ever claimed the sums due to them.

* * * *

The Black Book was copied by experts, and the whole mass placed before his majesty, who, startled enough at the contents of the infamous book, was astounded at the contents of the packet, which showed how, for a length of time, a plot had been hatching against his life. The principal was found to be Master Prior, and one of his accessories was Sir Ferdinand. There it was plain enough.

Master Prior was at once arrested.

His associates managed to fly the country.

Master Prior was tried for high treason and executed; but previous to the sentence being carried into effect, he made a full confession, from which it appeared that a great portion of Miriam's wealth had actually gone, through Sir Ferdinand's hands, to the conspirators and their agents, one of whom was the murderous scoundrel, Morecombe.

Search was everywhere made for Sir Ferdinand; secret agents were sent abroad, but he was never found.

Four years after Rupert led Miriam to the altar, they were visited by a lady, who turned out to be no other than Catherine Lockhart herself.

A wondrous change had taken place.

In that four years she had become an old woman, bowed and grey.

Not a single day—nay, not a single hour while Sir Ferdinand had been with her—had she known what peace was.

One day, in a fit of desperation, he plunged a dagger into his own heart.

Pressed as to her means, she confessed that Sir Ferdinand had gambled the whole of her wealth away while abroad.

Randall presented her with a sum sufficient to enable her to retire to Melburn Manor. But this estate she quickly sold, as well as what little property remained to her in London, and went into a convent, the portals of which she never again left alive.

* * * *

With the assistance of the Duke of Buckingham, Rupert became one of the gentlemen attending on the king, and being a favourite, was knighted by King James.

His majesty frequently held important conversations with Randall concerning the discoveries he was constantly making, and he was a frequent private visitor to Chelsea Priory.

Yet, though for some time, he would be heart and soul in discussion relative to strange chemicals, his conversation would change to the mysteries of Pendle Forest, Matthew Hopkins, and to the horrible deeds he committed—

"Under the Royal Warrant!"

www.ingramcontent.com/pod-product-compliance
Lightning Source LLC
Chambersburg PA
CBHW080840250626
47161CB00009B/3128